The INNOCENT

ALYSHA KING

To all you rebels out there, especially those fighting their own darkness –
you are the light.

And for the real Carey.
You know who you are.

Other works by the author

The Order of the Rose

The Dragon's Heart

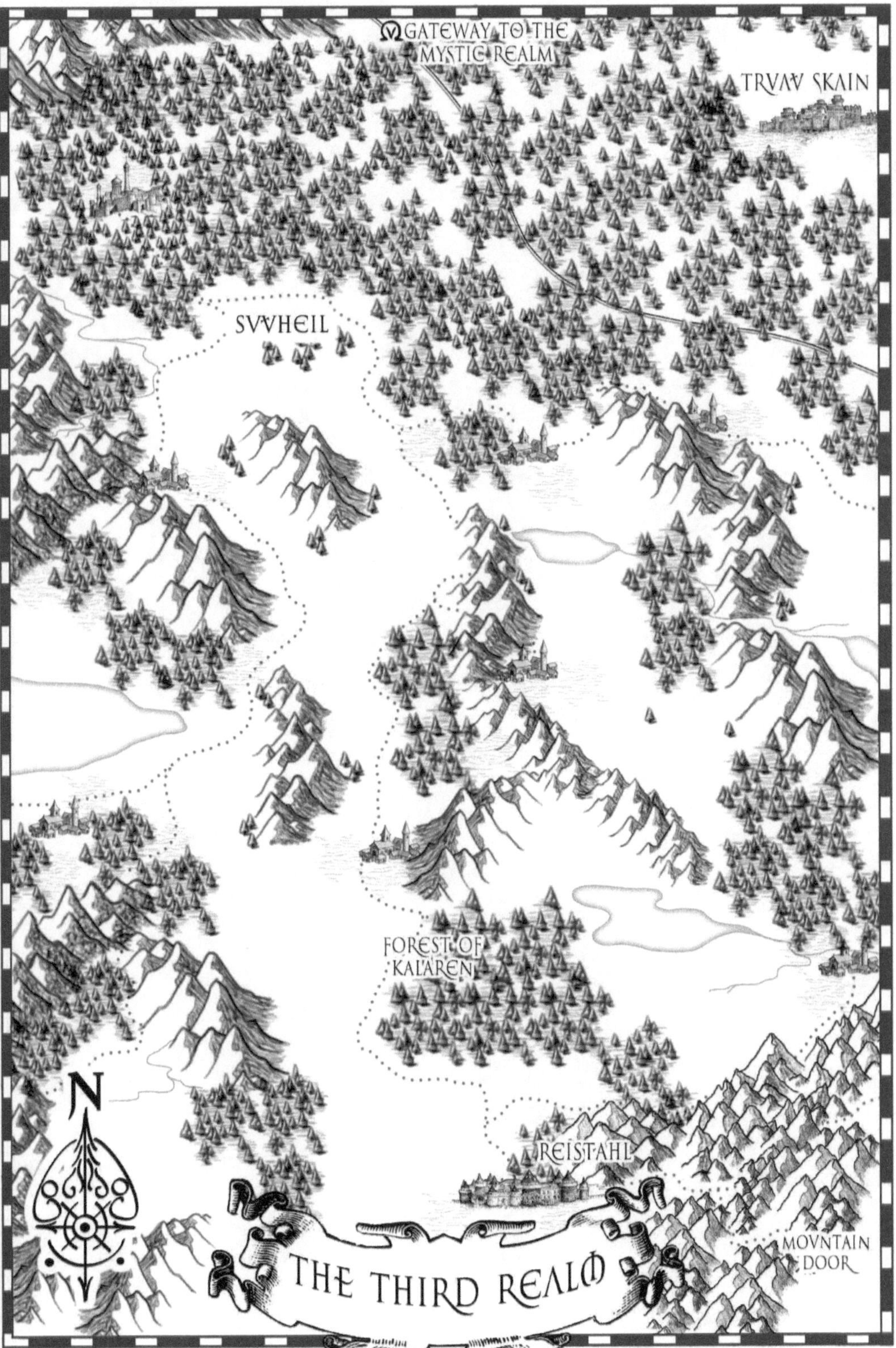

GATEWAY TO THE MYSTIC REALM
TRVAV SKAIN
SVVHEIL
FOREST OF KAL'AREN
REISTAHL
MOVNTAIN DOOR
N
THE THIRD REALM

Prologue

Darkness is creeping at the edges of the world. I can sense it growing. No one speaks of it, but the air is thick with tension, worry… fear. Like a storm brewing on the horizon, it looms threateningly.

What can I do but wait? For what is there to fight when all one can see is shadows?

~Chapter One~

Ultimatum

The tavern by the castle gates rumbled with low voices and laughter. It was late, and Jensen sat at the bar nursing a mug of ale after a long and uneventful guard shift. It was humid inside, the air spiced with the smell of liquor, and Jensen couldn't help his eyelids drooping from exhaustion.

Just for a moment, he promised as he placed his head down on the polished wood.

The sounds of the other patrons swelled around him, a cocoon of warmth enveloping him as his eyes closed *just for a moment.* Laughter, chatter, and the thud of mugs on wood filled his ears. It was oddly relaxing after the hours of absolute silence, and Jensen let it all wash over him.

There was a rush of wind, and at first Jensen thought it was someone coming in from outside, but then everything went quiet. Deathly quiet.

Jensen opened his eyes and cried out in shock.

He was no longer in the tavern.

He stood in the centre of a dark clearing. The edges were blurred by a low-hanging fog and there were no landmarks from which he might discern his location. Shaking his head, Jensen willed himself to wake, for surely this was a dream.

"I wouldn't bother trying to wake up," came a low voice dripping with malice.

Jensen turned to find a familiar face emerging from the fog. He lifted a hand and reached for his magic, aiming at the man's chest.

"Halt, traitor!"

Saar grinned, clearly amused.

"You'll find you have very little control here," he said lazily. "Besides, once you've

heard what I have to say, you'll be falling over yourself to help me."

Jensen narrowed his eyes, unsure of his next move. In any other situation he would have made to subdue the man, but he was acutely aware of his adversary's abilities and knew he did not have equal footing. That being said, he doubted there was anything Saar could say that would convince him to help him.

Saar looked straight at the guard and Jensen's body seized. He made to pull back, but he found himself completely frozen in place. His fear spiked.

Saar advanced on Jensen, pushing the guard's hand aside with his finger as he passed.

Jensen tried to move again, but he could not overcome Saar's magic. He watched as Saar moved to his side, feeling beads of sweat forming on his brow. The traitor considered him, a slow, predatory grin spreading across his face before lifting a hand. The fog swirled as it parted to reveal a scene that made Jensen's eyes pop with terror.

A room appeared before them, a simple bedroom where an ashen-haired man slept soundly on a low bed. Faren. Jensen's gaze flicked manically from the sleeping man to where their two infant wards rested in bassinets by his side. His heart beat painfully as his mind raced with terrifying imaginings.

"What have you done to them?" he asked, his throat dry with fear.

Saar, his eyes on the children, said, "Nothing. At least, nothing yet."

"Please," Jensen said. "Don't hurt them. They haven't done anything."

Saar let out a bark of malicious laughter. It sent a chill down Jensen's spine.

"Their virtue is of no consequence here. It is your actions which concern me." Saar paced slowly around to the guard's other side, drawing himself level with Jensen's line of sight. "Look at me."

Jensen's gaze snapped back to Saar's unblinking eyes.

"You will do as I ask, whenever I ask, or your family here will suffer more than a quick death. Refuse me and I will ensure they do not wake, trapped in an eternal nightmare, only to escape by the slow decay of time and its ravages upon their bodies. What do you say?"

There was barely a moment of hesitation from the paralysed guard.

"I'll do it. Whatever it is you ask of me, I'll do it."

"Good," Saar said, and the scene dissipated. "I will be in touch." He moved away

towards the fog that had gathered once more around them. "Just remember – hesitate but once, attempt to tell him or anyone of this encounter, and I will show no mercy."

Before Jensen could answer, his surrounds vanished and he jerked awake, knocking over the mug of ale he'd been holding. He was drenched in sweat and his heart was racing as he spun around, searching. What was that? A dream?

No. Something told him he'd just experienced a true encounter with the former Council member Lord Acheron – Saar. He knew of the man's ability to travel using his mind, and had Jensen been in the castle, he would've been safe from the man. But Saar had waited for Jensen, singled him out, and the guard's stomach turned over at the thought. He knew what that man was capable of and the idea terrified him. Guilt surged through him as he picked up the mug and apologised to the barman. He'd just promised to help the traitor, to do whatever he asked. Yet, as Jensen left the bar, racing for home through the shadowed streets, Saar's threats echoed back to him. He swallowed his guilt. He had his family to think about, to protect. And to him, that was more important than anything else.

ature # ~Chapter Two~

The Stronghold

Carey watched the battle from the edge of the snow-covered clearing. Snow fell gently, swirling in a graceful dance, its beauty standing in stark contrast to the violence before her. Imperial loyalists surged forwards in small, tight groups, flashes of magic and curses flying at the guards blocking the gateway. They had erected a boundary of wooden spikes facing the loyalists, a boundary that held them at bay yet didn't deter them. Despite the magic that imbued it, it wasn't able to block their attacks completely. The right strike in the right place...

Her gaze drifted to the stone gateway, its carvings thrown into sharp relief in the moonlight. Carey could still see Sirona's body lying there, her blood staining the snow, her murderer standing over her as he opened the gateway.

The guards fought back, holding off the Imperials with their own magic and martial prowess. The attacks were getting worse. In the days following Saar's opening of the gateway, handfuls of Imperials had been drawn to its threshold. They'd seemed jubilant, triumphant in Saar's success. Perhaps they'd known of his plans, or maybe it was something Malevolence had promised. Either way, the news had spread.

Now Imperials were arriving daily and they were becoming more organised. Despite the strength and determination of the City guards, the loyalists would soon prove too strong for the defenders at the gate. Even as she observed, an Imperial slipped by them and passed into the fog churning within the archway.

Oliver Binx's military forces were yet to be deployed to protect the gateway; many were securing other parts of the kingdom still under attack by Imperial loyalists. Carey wished they'd hurry up.

Another group of Imperials passed her in their attempt to make it through the gateway, their breaths rising in clouds in the frigid air. She, on the other hand, felt nothing. This was her projection; she wouldn't feel it unless she wanted to. The enemy around her didn't see her because she willed it. Weeks of practice were finally paying off.

Carey found she could engage with her Twilight Travelling ability far easier than she had before, and as she watched this latest group of Imperials advance on the gateway, she expected Saar had much to do with it. Before he'd left, Carey had struggled with her ability as a Fiorilusa. Now he was gone and she was beyond his influence, Carey felt a mastery she hadn't before. She held out a hand to catch a snowflake and watched as it passed through her. No, she did not feel the cold; what she did feel was rage and an ever-increasing sense of injustice. Within a week there'd be enough loyalists to take the gateway and she would lose her chance to pursue Saar. She would never be allowed to attempt a passing if Imperials took control.

Taking a deep steadying breath, Carey took one last look before closing her eyes and letting go.

She opened her eyes to find herself back in her bedroom. Slowly, Carey pulled herself up into a sitting position, running her hands through her hair as she contemplated her visions. She'd done this every day for the past couple of weeks and each time her frustration grew at her inability to do anything.

The clock on the mantelpiece above the fireplace showed it was almost time for the Council to convene. Shelving her frustration, she got to her feet, pulled on her boots, and slung the sabre Marjen had given her around her hips before setting off towards the chambers.

Carey's footsteps echoed off the walls as she walked purposefully down the hallway, her hand resting almost expectantly on the hilt of her sword. A small cough brought her to a standstill.

"Any news?" she whispered as Rupert appeared from the shadows of a sunken doorway.

His thick, rumpled hair was a midnight blue today, making his pale skin seem almost opaque. A constellation of freckles was mapped out beneath his bright eyes.

"I've heard that they're lookin' ter ask the Vuletians fer help," Rupert said as he fell in beside her. "Apparently, some are comin' ter talk."

She felt his eyes on her, gauging her reaction, and tried not to show the lurch she felt in her stomach.

The last time she'd had contact with the Vuletians was just before she'd lost two of their commanders in a violent storm. Not to mention she was still wracked with guilt over the death of their captain, Marjen Tutari, whom Carey had befriended during her time in their city.

"Did you hear who?" she asked, trying to keep her voice level.

"A lieutenant an' two others. No names," Rupert said. "Sorry."

"Never mind," Carey replied. "I'm on my way to the Council Chambers now. I'm sure I'll learn more there. Thanks for the heads-up."

Rupert winked. "Not a problem."

He headed in the opposite direction, leaving her to consider his news. The Vuletians were easily the superior military force in the region and she would be glad of their aid, should they agree to help. Perhaps with their assistance the Imperial masses would be less inclined to approach the gateway. They could hold them back, giving Carey the opening she needed to get through. The Council guards that stood watch over the gateway were well trained and loyal to her parents, but she'd seen the Vuletians fight. They were ferocious opponents, even without magic, and they did not hold back.

If only Marjen were still here...

"If only..." Carey muttered, thinking quietly of his sacrifice as she so often did.

"If only what?"

She jumped; Carey hadn't noticed Kat's arrival.

"Oh just... nothing," she said, shaking her head. "Don't scare me like that. Can't you see I have a sword?"

Kat snorted. "Yes, but you're so easy to scare. Plus, I have these." She indicated the weapons at her hip – a pair of long, fork-like sai. "I'm always up for a bit of practice."

Kat kept pace with her, her expression hardening, all trace of humour gone. "So, what's the update from the front line? I assume you Travelled there today already?"

Carey quickly relayed what she'd witnessed at the gateway and it was Kat's turn to sigh.

"More loyalists… just what we need," she said as they approached the Council's main chambers.

"I know," said Carey. "It's going to be almost impossible for us to make a go of it without being attacked."

Carey clenched her fists, regretting once more not going after Saar earlier.

"And you're going to tell the Council this," Kat said.

"Of course. And I'll keep telling them until they relent. It's not a matter of *if* but *when* we go through after Saar. I would prefer it be sooner rather than later."

They came to a halt outside the ornate wooden doors of the Council chambers and Carey took a deep breath, reeling in her emotions before pushing them open.

The rest of the Council were already there, talking in low voices. The light from the high windows left them in shadow, lending the room a clandestine atmosphere. Carey's parents sat at the head of the table, with Oliver Binx and his second-in-charge, Sir Barris, and Madame Keller, the court potioneer, opposite. Lord Carron and Lady Marksis were deep in conversation at one side.

Carey took her place by her parents as Kat broke away to join her father, Peter. Everyone fell silent as Carey's father, Robert, stood, signalling the beginning of the meeting.

"As you all know, the situation at the gateway is becoming more troublesome with every day that passes," he said. "It has proved a greater pull for Imperial loyalists than we originally thought, giving rise to the probability that Lord Acheron had people in place to spread the news once he succeeded in activating it. It is therefore a great possibility that his intentions reached far beyond just opening the gateway and these loyalists are heading through to join him in whatever he has planned next."

He turned to Carey.

"What have you seen of the situation there today?"

Carey got to her feet, her gaze flitting from one face to the next. "I've been using my ability to Twilight Travel to observe what's been happening at the gateway, and frankly, it's getting worse. More Imperials arrive daily and more are slipping past our guards. There are just too many for them to handle. What's more, they are starting to strategise and combine their forces. It's really only a matter of time before it goes from them just fighting to get past our guards to overpowering them and claiming the gateway for their own. Give it a few more days and we will lose what little control of the gateway we have."

"If I may, Carey," Oliver Binx said. "We have received similar news from the gateway, and based on this, we have asked the Vuletian army for aid. Their Captain and two of his consorts will be arriving within the next two days to assess the situation before they send for reinforcements. They are more than happy to oblige, and I admit, we could use their expertise."

"What about going after Saar?" Carey said. "Are they going to help us with that?"

She was eager to know if the Council was making plans to hunt down that murderer. Surely calling upon the Vuletians would mean the gateway could be secured enough for a hunting party to go through after him. After all, he was the most wanted man in all the realms.

"Going after Saar?" Sir Barris repeated as though he hadn't quite heard her correctly.

"Yes." She leaned on the table, her palms flat on the polished surface. "Going after Saar. Surely that should be our main priority here. If the Imperials take the gateway, it will make it near impossible to pursue him."

"Sorry to contradict you, Carey," Oliver said, "but stopping any more of his supporters from joining him takes precedence. One man on his own is less of a worry than that one man with an army. We are all very aware of Acheron's abilities, even more so of his compete disregard for life, which is also why we're not taking any risks. We don't know what is waiting on the other side of that gateway. My responsibility is to ensure the safety of my people, and wandering blindly after a man as dangerous as Acheron is not a risk I'm willing to take right now."

Carey looked at Kat, who grimaced as though this answer came as no surprise.

"So, what you're saying is that we're not going after him," Carey said, straightening and gripping the hilt of her sword in an attempt to redirect her anger.

"Not until we can secure the gateway," Oliver replied with a hint of an apology.

Carey bit back a retort. It would do no good to lose her temper in front of the Council. If she was to prove herself capable and be taken seriously, she had to remain civil. When she said no more, Oliver continued with his speech, but Carey heard no more. She was too angry to concentrate; her hand was cramping with the tightness of her grip on her hilt. Besides, if he said anything of note, Kat would tell her – her gaze was flicking between Oliver and Carey, her lips a tight thin line.

As Oliver finished and the other members stood to leave, Carey's mother, Jenny, leant over the table, reaching out a hand.

"Carey, do you mind staying behind? We have something we need to discuss with you," she said.

Kat paused as she walked by, a single eyebrow raised. She gave a small nod to say she'd see Carey in a bit, to which Carey replied with the slightest of smiles.

Her parents waited until the chamber was empty before turning to her. Her mother radiated warmth and undeniable power as she stood within the half shadows, her sandy hair streaked with grey and swept back high on her head. She wore a loose long-sleeved tunic with worn brown slacks tucked neatly in at the waist and her customary leather boots that she often wore on expeditions beyond the city walls. Carey's father stood straight-backed beside Jenny, strong stance and gentle eyes, his formerly black hair a mix of salt and pepper. He similarly wore a loose top and slacks, but his shirt was covered with a dark green vest, and a small dagger hung at his side from a thick brown belt. Their Seeker's pendants peeked from within the folds of their collars, just as Carey's did.

An understanding smile played on Jenny's lips.

"I know what you're thinking, Carey dearest. We know how badly you want to go after Saar, but there is something you need to know first."

"*First?*" Carey's ears pricked at the use of this promising word.

"Yes," Robert said. "We are not going to delude ourselves into thinking we can stop you from going, Carey. We're acutely aware of your connection to Saar and we know you will stop at nothing to get to him."

"There is, however, something we need to talk to you about," Jenny said. "What do you know of Malevolence's magic and what happened to it after you stopped her?"

Carey looked hard at her mother, wondering what this had to do with Saar. "It was enclosed in a Tear Globe. Captured. That's what Kat told me afterwards, in any case."

"And kept here, in the castle, under strict guard. Only those in the Council know of its existence and location, due to the danger that magic poses should it fall into the wrong hands. Did Saar ever intimate what he planned to do once he'd opened the gateway to the Third World?"

Carey was silent for a moment, her mind racing with the possibilities. "You don't think he would try to obtain it, do you? He never said as much but, if he still had the Dragon's Heart, it would've been all too easy for him to wield Malevolence's magic. Is that what you're thinking?"

Robert gestured for her to join him. "Come. We have something to show you."

Carey followed her parents to the back of the chamber, where Jenny pulled aside a towering tapestry to reveal a blank stretch of stone. Momentarily perplexed, Carey watched as her mother presented her hand to the wall. After a moment, the stone shimmered oddly, and Jenny stepped right through it. Carey inhaled sharply as her father did the same. Cautiously, she raised a hand to the wall and felt an odd sensation prickle her palm. It spread warmly through her body, and just as it filled her, covering every inch of her, the wall rippled again and she, too, stepped into it.

It felt like silk running over her bare skin as she passed through the wall. Blinking, Carey found herself in a long, dark hallway lit by low-burning torches. There were no windows and only one door, at the very end. A single castle guard stood watch before it – Jensen, with whom she was friendly.

As they approached, he stood to attention, his heels clacking together and the butt of his poleaxe thudding hard on the floor by his toes.

"Your majesties," he said sharply, his eyes forwards.

"Jensen," Jenny acknowledged before placing a hand against the large, heavy door.

Usually jovial, Jensen seemed drawn and distracted. He pointedly ignored Carey's attempts to capture his gaze, and as she drew closer, his expression remained rigid. It was most unlike him, and so Carey turned from him with a frown, instead concentrating on what her mother was doing.

At Jenny's touch, a great number of clicks and thuds sounded. It was as though the insides of the door were rearranging themselves. There came a final *clunk* and the door swung slowly open. Carey stepped in after her mother, her father following behind, and she found herself in a stunningly designed round room. The walls were of shining marble, the domed roof high and ornately carved, and the room emanated an inexplicably ethereal air. Swirling runic markings were carved into the walls and, as Carey studied them, they shimmered. Veins of brilliant blue crystal were inlaid in the walls; they shot up from the floor, joining at a point in the very centre of the ceiling to form a many-pointed star.

A guard stood beside a table in the centre of the room. He snapped to attention as they entered. The small, round marble table seemingly grew from the floor, its base melding with the cool, white stone. Atop was a dark, polished wooden box with a rounded lid. As her eyes fell on the small chest, Carey felt an odd sense of desire stir deep within her, and she shuddered. She wanted to look away from it but she couldn't. The magic emanating from the centre of the room felt… familiar. She initially assumed it was because she'd encountered it before, but no. It was more like an invisible current was drawing her closer. Carey shook her head, trying to ignore the strange sensation. Blinking, she recognised the guard – Faren, who she often saw accompanying Jensen. He also appeared stern, but at least he smiled at Carey when she approached.

"Thank you, Faren," Jenny said. "Would you mind stepping outside for a moment?"

When he had gone, Carey asked, "What is this place?"

"This," Robert said, "is the Stronghold. It's designed to hold objects of great power. Over the years the Council has needed to hide various objects of immense magic, many being too dangerous to wield. Right now, it holds Malevolence's magic. Since we are yet to discern a way to destroy it, it's kept here under constant guard."

Carey stared at the box. There it was again – that pull. Something roused within her, and the magic she feared so much tingled ominously throughout her extremities, as though it could sense the power contained within that small wooden chest.

Jenny carefully lifted a thin filigreed latch on the lid and opened the box. Leaning closer, Carey could see a delicate tear-shaped globe nestled within. However, unlike Kat's magic, which had shone within the globe that time by the Mystic Falls, Malevolence's magic swirled dark and foreboding. As she watched it, Carey was overcome by intense desire once more. She wanted to seize the globe and… what? She couldn't rationalise the feeling it evoked in her, only that it was absolutely and completely irrational. She took a deep breath, pulling herself away from the box and its contents.

She turned her thoughts to the Stronghold instead.

"Wait. If all the Council members know about this place, then that means Saar does too, doesn't it?" she said.

"Unfortunately, yes," Robert said.

"Then we have to move it," Carey said. "It's too dangerous to keep it now we know who and what Saar is."

"Therein lies the beauty of the Stronghold," Jenny said as she pointed to the many markings upon the walls. "This room is imbued with magic that allows it to be hidden anywhere within the castle."

"We can change its location so that Saar will be unable to find it," Robert explained. "The magic this room was created with makes it the perfect place to hide an artefact like this."

Carey strode across to one of the walls and laid a palm gently upon the carved façade. Magic flitted beneath her fingers like a skittish water beetle skipping back and forth across a pond.

"I can feel it," Carey said in wonder before turning back to her parents. "Has the room been moved already? Could he get in now?"

"It was changed in the days following the opening of the gateway," Jenny said as she closed the chest. "Regardless, we do need to know if he said anything – *anything* – about it. You may not even have noticed at the time."

Carey thought back over all the shadowed conversations she'd had with the former Head Chancellor. "Not that I can recall but, then again, everything he ever said was cloaked in double meaning. He was always just vague enough in his requests and threats to not give away his true intentions. But considering he didn't get away with the Dragon's Heart, he may seek another source of power for whatever he has planned."

"That's exactly what we were thinking, too," Robert said. "That's why we wanted you to know about the Stronghold. You need to be on your guard. Try to go over anything he may have said or did that may point to him wanting to get his hands on this. Tell Kat and Rupert. Kat is a member of the Council and should know based simply on that right, and Rupert may have heard something."

Robert chuckled at Carey's look of surprise.

"Yes, we're well aware of Rupert's penchant for knowing more than he should. There's every possibility he already knows about the Stronghold."

"It serves no one to be secretive about that which could prove disastrous to us all," Jenny said. "Keep your friends close – they can prove invaluable."

Carey didn't need telling twice. She'd struggled with this concept in the past, having never had true friends in which she could confide before Kat and Ji came along. Keeping things to herself was a hard habit to break, but she was getting better at it.

"When do you think I'll be able to make for the Third World? I know that Oliver doesn't seem too keen on the idea, but we can't wait much longer."

She knew she was pushing the subject, given what had just been said in the meeting, but she couldn't accept Oliver's decision.

"As soon as the Vuletians arrive, we hope to be able to secure the gateway. Then you should be able to pursue Saar unhindered," Jenny said.

"What?" Carey asked.

This hadn't been the answer she'd expected. Carey thought they'd push back, tell her they didn't want her to go. After the loss of her sisters, she thought they'd be more protective. Instead, it would seem they were helping her plan a journey that would most certainly be dangerous, if not potentially fatal. It didn't make sense.

Robert frowned. "We know you'd like to go after him as soon as possible, but we need to wait for the Vuletians–"

Carey shook her head. "No, it's not that. Why are you doing this? Helping me go after him?" She tried not to sound ungrateful. She certainly didn't want them rescinding their offer. "I was expecting you to try and stop me."

Jenny and Robert glanced at each other before answering.

"When we saw you last," Jenny said slowly, "you were just a waif of a nine-year-old and as curious as any child I'd ever known. Then, when you saved us, we found you all grown, so strong and full of courage, and we quickly realised that despite not being there to see you grow, to help you along that path, you'd become everything we'd hoped you would." Jenny took her daughter's hands and squeezed them gently. "Who would we be if we told you not to go? Doing so would only serve to put our own fears to rest and nothing else. You are your own person now, with or without us."

A single tear streaked down her mother's face and it surprised Carey to find tears gathering at the edges of her own eyes.

Robert placed a comforting hand on Jenny's shoulder and gazed lovingly at his daughter.

"We want you to go because we know that you have the strength and determination to do so, and that in itself could make us no prouder."

~Chapter Three~

Seramina

"So, let me get this straight – there's a room that can essentially be moved anywhere in the castle and holds whatever dangerous magical artefacts the Council manages to possess?"

Kat leant forwards in the chaise as she spoke, a fire crackling in the hearth beside her. They were in Carey's room, Rupert having joined them after the Council meeting. The sun was sinking below the horizon beyond the open window, a brisk autumn wind ruffling the curtain. Rupert had boldly taken up residence on Carey's bed and was resting with his hands behind his head, his socked feet crossed. His boots, which reminded Carey of swashbuckling pirates, were lying at the foot of her bed. His dark button-down top was untucked from his heavy belt.

Carey stood leaning against the end post of her bed, her arms crossed.

"Yes, and we're not to talk about it to anyone else," Carey reminded them both.

"How the hell did we not know about this already?" Kat asked, flopping back in her chair.

Rupert raised his hand in the air, his elbow still resting on the bed. "I did."

Kat threw a cushion at his head playfully.

"And you neglected to tell us about it?"

He deflected the pillow with his outstretched hand. "It never came up, I suppose."

"You know what, Rupert?" Carey said with a grin. "If it were a genuine surprise – you knowing, that is – I'd be inclined to throw something at that great blue head of yours also."

Rupert ran his hand through his dark-blue tresses. "If yer have grievance with my hairstyle, please, feel free ter take it up with my sister."

Carey let out a laugh. "No, thank you. I quite like my hair how it is." She flicked at the ends of her own sandy hair before getting serious again. "Back to the Stronghold though. What else do you know about it?"

"Only that there are some here whose great-grandparents et cetera worked in the castle at the time of the emperor before Malevolence was in power, an' they said that th' Council possessed some great magical artefact. It was kept in a secret room which bears great resemblance ter the Stronghold. Apparently, this is the magic Malevolence stole in order ter gain power," Rupert said.

He really was in his element, Carey thought, speaking of castle secrets and conspiracies. However, his words took her back to a conversation she'd had with Lady Sirona about Elara, her grandmother's sister. Elara had attempted to steal what had been called the Orb of Power from the Council, and had killed her father in the process.

Carey relayed the story to the others.

"The orb must have been kept in the Stronghold. Elara never got a hold of it, though. She was banished to the Darklands for doing what she did. But what if she told Malevolence about it? Her family was part of the Council and apparently only Council members are supposed to know about it. Malevolence came from the Darklands, right? If Elara told her about it, that could have been why Malevolence came to the Council in the first place," Carey said.

Kat held a finger to her lips, deep in thought. "All I know about when Malevolence came into power is that she did so rather grandly. She was on the Council of a rather powerful emperor, Merilius, and she overthrew him. Perhaps she managed to procure this orb – she would've known where it was by then – and used it to kill the emperor and take the throne for herself. It could explain why Malevolence wasn't completely destroyed, why her magic has lingered."

Rupert shrugged and said, "It's not somethin' I've heard of, but honestly, Malevolence was somethin' else. It might be possible. Who knows?"

"What does this have to do with Saar though?" Kat asked Carey.

Carey leant her head against the bedpost; she could feel a headache developing, but she was far too interested in talking about Saar to want to rest.

"We know that since Saar lost the Dragon's Heart he no longer has the ability to capture the magic of those around him. He was Malevolence's right-hand man – there is every possibility she told him about this magic she stole. I hadn't even considered that he might try to steal Malevolence's magic for himself until today. But, like I've said before, he always alluded to something bigger, some *greater plan* that he clearly needed some powerful magic for. Before, he had mine, Sirona's, and Mizèi's magic, but now he needs something else," she said.

"Even if that were so, the Stronghold has already been moved, and now that the Council knows he's a Shapeshifter there have been additional magics placed on the castle to prevent him using that ability in here," Kat pointed out. "It'll be near impossible for him to obtain it."

Carey signalled for Rupert to vacate. Her headache was growing despite her desire to keep speculating.

"I hope you're right," she said as she lay down, placing a hand over her eyes. "Knowing Saar, though, he'll have a plan."

*

Her head continued to pound long after her friends had left. She tried to ignore the throbbing, unable to stop thinking about Saar and his plans, and wondering about the feeling she'd experienced in the Stronghold. It was as though the magic within her knew something about Malevolence's magic that she didn't. But what? Carey groaned, rubbing at her temples as the pain worsened, and momentarily Carey wondered whether she should ask Rupert for a sleeping draught. He might still be awake, possibly tending to Zacharia, whose condition continued to show no signs of improvement even though Rupert remained hopeful. Zacharia, whose face reminded Carey so forcibly of his brother. She wanted to visit him and yet, at the same time, didn't. She was afraid he'd evoke memories that were still too painful to examine, and she didn't know how she would deal with that. There was barely a moment where she didn't feel Ji's absence acutely. Speculating about Saar and the

Stronghold didn't feel the same without Ji there to be the voice of reason.

Carey squirmed uncomfortably. She could picture Ji sitting by the fire as Kat had, listening to them speak with quiet contemplation. He would ruffle his walnut-brown hair in thought and crinkle his nose. His eyes, once that piercing blue but now hidden behind a haze of white, would find her as she spoke. Carey remembered the last time she'd looked into those eyes and heard that voice. She knew there was hope of seeing him again, that the gateway wouldn't remain closed forever, but at that moment, lying in the dark with nothing but the silence and her memories, it felt like eternity stood between them. It didn't help that there was that constant desire to seek him out, to be wherever he was. As if she was at one end of a piece of string and Ji at the other, tied together by something more than she could ever understand. It was bad enough that she couldn't Travel to speak with him. Apparently, the gateway needed to be open for that to happen, as Lady Marksis had discovered in her archives, so even that avenue was closed to them. Yet, despite this, Carey still tried every night before going to sleep. Perhaps, if she reached him, she could talk to him, see him… Carey thought of Zachariah in the Healer's Ward, oblivious to the broken world around him and the missing part of her heart that was also part of his…

She could hear voices echo from the darkness. There was one she knew – a young girl's.

Seramina.

She was speaking to someone, a man, judging by the low rumble of the voice. It sounded like she was trying to comfort him, her tone gentle and pacifying. Carey moved towards them, though she wasn't sure whether she was moving at all. There were no structures or sources of light – everything was smothered in a deep, pervasive darkness that pressed on Carey's eyeballs.

"Do you think you can do it?" Carey heard the man ask. "Do you really think you can break it?"

"I know I can," came Seramina's voice. "You just have to trust me."

Carey shuffled closer.

"Zacharia, you know you can trust me," Seramina said softly, and Carey halted.

Zacharia?

"Sorry, yes. I trust you. It's been so long... I just want this to end."

As Carey advanced again, a light flared, illuminating two figures – Seramina and Zacharia. Seramina's red hair was aflame against the black and Zacharia stood hunched and unsure, his familiar brown hair ruffled and messed, his eyes wide. They were standing close together, holding each other's hands. The light was shining from within their enclosed fists. Carey stared, transfixed, as a heavy silence fell over them. It was the kind of silence that drew everything else into it and expanded outwards, like the ocean dragging water from the shore before spilling it back onto the sand. Seramina's eyes were closed in concentration and Zacharia was watching her with quiet anticipation. The glow grew steadily brighter, and all around them cracks of light began to appear, splintering the oppressive gloom. More and more slivers cut through the dark, until they were surrounded by a veritable web of the brightest light. Then, with a distant rumble that grew to a deafening roar, it exploded –

Carey woke with a jerk. She'd been asleep, and for the first time in a long time, she'd Travelled without meaning to. Sitting up in her bed, Carey watched the moonlight falling across her blankets shift with the fluttering of her curtains. She could still see the blinding light that had engulfed them, its imprint burned into her eyes so that she had to blink a couple of times to rid herself of the shadows across her sight.

Seramina and Zacharia. She had difficulty understanding what she'd just witnessed. First of all, Zacharia was lying in the Healer's Ward, unconscious. He couldn't physically be anywhere else, and yet... What had Seramina been doing? More importantly, how was she talking to him? She'd spoken with Zacharia as though she knew him, as though this wasn't the first time they'd met. Carey thought of the overwhelming blackness, the absolute oppressiveness she'd felt bear down upon her. Rupert had once described Zacharia as being beyond what his magic could reach, that he was yet to find something that could pull him back from wherever he was trapped by Imperial agents' dark magic. Carey shivered, hugging herself as she hoped very much that she would never experience that darkness again. It left an uneasy feeling in the pit of her stomach, a gnawing that there'd been something else there with them, flitting about in the dark and the silence.

After a long while, Carey lay back down, deciding that if anything had happened with Zacharia, she'd find out soon enough. There were still a few hours until dawn and it made no sense to go barging into the Healer's Ward at this hour. As the haze of sleep stole over her once more, she noted vaguely that her headache of a few hours ago was now completely gone.

*

THUD!

The sound of metal against wood echoed through the training hall and Carey wrenched her sword from the pole. She had woken to the pink tint of dawn sifting through the clouds and, unable to go back to sleep, had decided to come down early for her training session with Kat. Rotating her shoulder, she raised her sword again and brought it down upon the practice pole, slicing a decent chunk off the side. The sound of approaching footsteps reached her ears and she turned to see the doors swing open and Kat walk through, her expression jubilant.

"You'll never guess what's happened!" she said with a wide grin. "Zacharia's awake! I just passed the Healer's Ward and Rupert let me know. Apparently, he regained consciousness sometime last night. Meela and Oliver are in there with him now. Isn't that fantastic news? I mean, Rupert must have finally figured it out!"

Kat's eyes narrowed as she neared Carey.

"Why do I get the feeling you're not particularly surprised by this? What do you know that I don't?"

Carey lifted her weapon and indicated for Kat to do the same.

Eyebrows raised, Kat pulled her long sai from her belt and lifted them into a defensive stance.

Carey lunged, the electric blue flash of her sword's Vuletian blade illuminating them.

Kat parried.

"You know how I've Twilight Travelled without meaning to?" Carey said, striking again. "Like that time I saw Ji in the dungeons?"

Kat grunted her confirmation as she flicked Carey's sword aside with one of her sai and thrust the other forwards.

Dodging, Carey continued. "It happened again last night. I was thinking about Zacharia when I fell asleep and I unintentionally Travelled. Those thoughts were what drew me to him, and the place I found myself in was... I honestly don't know, but Zacharia was there. With Seramina."

Caught off-guard by this revelation, Kat stumbled, only just dodging Carey's blade.

"What? Seramina?"

"And by the sounds of it," Carey went on, swinging her sword over her head, "she had been there before. She was trying to convince him to trust her so that she could perform some sort of enchantment. It was as though Seramina was breaking him out of that place."

Regaining her footing, Kat delivered a number of strikes in quick succession. "What was the place, though? Did you recognise anything?"

Deflecting Kat's attacks, Carey struck again, but Kat blocked with her sai crossed, capturing Carey's blade in the forks of one. For a moment they struggled against each other before Kat managed to free herself, forcing the two of them apart.

"There was nothing," Carey panted, lowering her sword. "It was dark, but not like anything I've ever experienced before. I couldn't see an outline of a building, or any kind of structure for that matter. There was just... nothing. It was devoid of anything, even light."

Kat's brows knitted together, the corners of her mouth twitching down-wards. "And Seramina found him there."

Carey heard disbelief in her tone.

Wiping away the sweat creeping down onto her brow, Carey raised her sword again. "Have you noticed how Seramina seems to possess all these abilities the rest of us could only ever imagine, and yet at the same time she acts as though they're nothing special?"

"Do you think she knows what she did last night?" Kat asked as she leapt forwards again.

Defending herself easily with a great swing of her sword, Carey replied, "Oh, I think she knows. I just don't think she understands the magnitude of what she can do."

Kat dropped low to avoid Carey's defence, swinging around in an attempt to kick Carey's legs out from under her; she almost succeeded, catching one of Carey's ankles. Carey stumbled, unable to return the strike. Kat leapt back to her feet, her hands and sai on her hips as she caught her breath.

"You've read her diary," Kat said. "Did she ever say anything about having powers like this?"

Taking advantage of Kat's moment of stillness, Carey walked to a barrel of water at the edge of the training floor and filled a pewter mug. She took a long draught of the cool, refreshing liquid as she thought back to the diary.

"She only ever wrote about being a Telepath," Carey said. "What are you thinking?"

Kat joined her, picking up her own goblet. "If that's the case, then something must have happened after she was taken by Saar and his lot." She gulped down several mouthfuls.

"But Seramina never said they did anything but question her," Carey pointed out. They could only guess at the kinds of horrors Seramina had endured at the hands of the Imperials. "Do you think perhaps they did something to bring on these powers? Because that wouldn't make much sense given they were prepared to have her burnt at the stake. Why create a powerful witch only to kill her?"

Kat drained the last from her mug. "I can't think of anything else that may have caused these powers to manifest. Unless this is just how she is."

"Then perhaps we're just lucky that she is like that," Carey said, thinking of Zacharia and all the other instances Seramina's abilities had been invaluable.

There was something to what Kat had said, though – at some point between her capture and rescue from Saar, Seramina had changed. Was it really possible that this was simply how she was, like Kat with her ability to know a person's past or Carey's own Twilight Travelling? It could be, or perhaps it was something greater, something less easily defined. There were magics that defied all explanation. Carey's own strange magic proved that, especially in the way it presented itself when she was in dire situations. Perhaps Seramina's powers were something similar. Perhaps she just knew how to harness her magic without trepidation, unlike Carey.

Then there had been that inexplicable attraction… Her mind travelled back to the Stronghold, at how the magic that had once been Malevolence's had called to her. She felt it even now, that desire, how it lured her. In all the times that magic had manifested, not once had Carey felt anything like this. She wanted to know more, to see it again, perhaps without her parents.

"Come," Kat said. "We're not done."

Carey and Kat returned to their sparring, this time without speaking. Carey found her time spent in the training hall almost cathartic, a way of releasing the frustration she felt at being stuck in the castle. Her sword flashed satisfyingly through the air to block Kat's moves, and she found that she was finally starting to match her friend's speed and agility.

Ducking the pointed sai, Carey spun away from Kat, dragging the sword in front of her chest and thrusting it straight up at Kat's throat as they turned back towards each other. She found her mark, the tip of her sword sitting just below Kat's chin, but one of Kat's sai had also found its target. Carey looked down to see the tip lightly grazing her tunic, level with her bottom rib. They grinned at each other, breathless, before stepping back and saluting, signalling the end of their session.

"Nice move there at the end." Kat stowed her sai in her belt and wiped the sweat from her face.

"Would've been nicer had you not been so quick," Carey quipped as she sheathed her sword.

As they walked to the door, Kat said quietly, "Do you think we should go and see Zacharia?"

Carey didn't answer immediately. What would she say when she finally saw him? She only really knew Zacharia through Kat and Ji and their stories from when they were young.

There was also the undeniable fact that Zacharia reminded Carey so much of his brother…

"I don't know. Shouldn't we let him be with his family for now?" she said.

Kat shrugged. "As far as he's concerned, we are family. Besides, Ji isn't here."

They climbed the stairs from the dungeon level in silence. Carey knew what she meant – with Ji gone, they were really the only two in the castle who could speak with Zacharia about him. No doubt he'd have a million questions, want to know about the man his brother had become. What had happened…

Carey's throat constricted, and again she found her hand clasping the hilt of her sword.

"I don't think I can, Kat. Not just yet. It's just… it would be so…"

Kat's head bobbed in understanding, and Carey was both grateful and envious of her strength. Kat had known Ji longer, been with him through some of the toughest times in their lives, and still she wouldn't allow herself to break under the grief Carey knew must be weighing her down. Carey had to remind herself that she wasn't the only one who'd loved Ji, wasn't the only one who'd lost him when he'd been stranded in the Common Realm.

Kat left Carey at the end of the corridor that led to the Healer's Ward, and Carey continued on to her room. Rounding the corner, she found the flame-haired Seramina waiting. She was leaning quietly against the stone wall, gazing down at her feet, deep in thought. She was wearing a snow-white shirt with billowing sleeves that cuffed tight around her wrists and a dark caramel-coloured corset, not unlike the ones Kat wore, layered over the top. A skirt of royal blue ended midway down her calves, and it fluttered gently as she shifted her weight, light brown button-up boots covering her crossed feet. Her hair fell unruly about her shoulders; she rarely wore it up, and it suited her free spirit.

"Seramina?"

She started.

"Carey! I wasn't sure if you'd gone to see Zacharia yet or not, so I thought I'd just wait here until you got back. Can we talk?"

She didn't seem upset or nervous, unlike the other occasions when she'd sought Carey out; she seemed calm, and there was an inflection in her voice that made her sound far more mature than her thirteen years. Carey opened the door and gestured for Seramina to enter.

Carey strode in after her, removing her weapons belt and taking a seat by the fireplace. She expected Seramina to do the same, but she stood in front of the fireplace, the dim glow of the smouldering coals gilding the edges of her skirt and boots. She fixed Carey with a look of absolute seriousness, such a stark contrast to her usual bubbly disposition.

"I know you were there last night, when I was helping Zacharia," Seramina said.

Carey was taken aback. "Seramina," she stammered. "I… how… I mean–"

"I felt your presence," Seramina explained.

Carey blinked. "Oh. Is that so? Well, why didn't you say anything?"

Seramina sat down in the other chair and leant forwards with her elbows on her knees. "I'd finally got Zacharia to trust me. If I'd revealed you, it would've scared him and he'd have run."

"Run? But where? What was that place?" Carey asked.

The dying embers in the fireplace shifted, sending a thin column of sparks into the air as Seramina considered her answer.

"It was the way out of the place Zacharia's been trapped in all this time," she said.

"Wait," Carey said, trying to make sense of her words. "I thought he'd been kept in the Corigliphs. We found him after the fall of the Empire, but he's been unable to wake due to whatever torture he endured there, right?"

"That place *was* the Corigliphs," Seramina said. "They're not a physical place. They're a mind trap, designed to keep the victim in a perpetual nightmare where they face endless terrors. That's why it took so long for me to gain his trust – Zacharia thought I was another illusion created to torment him."

"How did you find him in the first place, though?" asked Carey.

Seramina opened her hands wide, as though she was offering something wordlessly to her. Her brow lifted slightly, clearly expecting Carey to have realised it already. "Just like you do. I heard him in my head, calling out for help. So, I closed my eyes, thought of him, and suddenly I was there with Zacharia."

Carey could do nothing but gape at the young witch for a long moment.

"You… Twilight Travelled?" she said.

Seramina nodded. She made it seem like the most normal thing in the world, completely composed, with no excitement or pride at having accomplished such a task. "I think whoever trapped him there never intended to free him.

The point where you saw us was a sort of breach – the end of the maze, if you will. Despite finding his way there, he was unable to break free of it."

"But you could?" Carey said.

"Of course," she said, without a hint of arrogance. "I knew straight away, like I had the key and all I had to do was unlock the door."

"And that's what I saw last night?"

Seramina nodded. "I broke the seal, opened the door for him. But Carey, could I ask you something?"

"What is it?"

"Do you mind not telling anyone what you saw last night? I mean, other than Kat, that is. I don't expect you to keep it from her. It's not for me but for Zacharia. I think that place has really scarred him and unless he wants to talk about it, I'm not sure we should say anything."

Of all the things Seramina said and did, Carey was the most surprised by these little moments of maturity and wisdom. It was as though an older version of Seramina lay within, one aged by something Carey couldn't understand.

"Of course. My lips are sealed."

~Chapter Four~

The Other Brother

Carey felt the familiar sensation of Twilight Travelling as she closed her eyes. The impression of the duck-down pillow beneath her head vanished, replaced by the crunch of the icy earth beneath her feet. She blocked her other senses so that the bitter wind whipping about her went unfelt. The hem of her thin nightgown flicked and tugged about her legs and her hair flew wild about her face, but still she felt nothing but the warmth of her room back in Centre City.

She opened her eyes.

The full moon hung silver and bright in the sky directly above the gateway. A thin wisp of cloud drifted lazily across it but the heavens were otherwise clear, a deep midnight blue spangled with stars that winked down upon her. By the light of the moon, Carey could make out the guards surrounding the stone archway and the secured encampment that housed their troops some way behind it. Although many of the loyalists had slunk back into the shadows to await sunrise, there were a few taking advantage of the darkness to run the gauntlet. As Carey watched from across the clearing, the guards stopped one loyalist from behind their fortified boundary with a few choice spells, sending the figure flying backwards into the snow. For a moment they lay there, unmoving; then, another loyalist ran forth in a hail of spells and curses. Fending off retaliatory attacks by the guards, the Imperial managed to drag their comrade back to cover.

And so it went on.

She wished their forces were greater so that instead of just defending the gateway against Imperials, they could secure it properly and actually round up the loyalists still roaming the kingdom. It was doubtful that any were powerful enough to take up the mantle of ruler of the Empire, but together they threatened the stability of the realm.

Something her father had pointed out came back to her.

"Just because they chose to follow the Empire," he had said, "doesn't mean they ever lifted a hand to do their bidding. Some people followed to save their families; others were tricked. It is not always a matter of 'good' or 'bad'. Who knows what those attempting to get through were told about the gateway? Unless they attack with the intent to kill, we must only react in kind. As soon as we start using deadly magic, we'll have an all-out war and more people will die. It's how it must be."

Carey had struggled to see his perspective. There'd been so many who had said no to the Empire, so many who had fought that she couldn't believe there'd be those willing to just stand by and observe the atrocities committed by the Empire. True, she didn't know what it was like to have to make that choice – she'd always been a Seeker and therefore had always had the motivation to fight, so perhaps her perspective was skewed. But what other reason could there be for those attempting to get through the gateway other than to join Saar?

"Nice night for a stroll in the moonlight, Princess."

A thrill of terror coursed down her spine and Carey spun around to find herself facing the traitorous former Head Chancellor.

"You!"

Carey could barely find the words as she took a few steps backwards, distancing herself from Saar as quickly as she could.

"Come to admire my handiwork?" he said carelessly, but his eyes flashed with intent. "I see you finally have control over your abilities. Bravo."

That final word dripped with sarcasm and Carey's lip lifted in a snarl.

"No thanks to you," she said.

Her hand moved subconsciously to where the hilt of her sword usually sat against her hip, but of course, it wasn't there.

"Well, I couldn't exactly let you have that advantage now, could I?" he said. "Besides, our proximity always made it so simple to block your abilities. Now, however, I have more important things to focus my energies on. By the way, how is young Master Ji these days? Oh, that's right – trapped in that god-forsaken Common Realm now, isn't he?"

Carey stiffened at the mention of Ji's name but she didn't answer. She knew when she was being baited.

"Pity. That family hasn't had the best of luck, have they?" he continued, moving to her left. "But then again, Seeker is hardly an easy occupation. Your numbers are not exactly what they once were."

Carey could feel the heat rising in her face despite her attempts to remain impassive. He was beginning to circle her, a predator stalking its prey.

"He's awake, though, isn't he? Master Zacharia?"

With narrowed eyes, Carey felt her heart quicken, a race against her ribs. How on earth did he know that? How did he know any of this?

"Is it hard to face him?" Saar whispered against the night wind, his words a sibilant sigh that curled uncomfortably around Carey's ears. "The other brother, so like your beloved?"

"No!"

No.

She wasn't going to just stand there and allow him to torment her. Whatever he wanted, he was not going to get it.

Hands balled into fists, she crossed her arms in front of her then brought them down sharply to her sides. The wind disappeared, as did Saar's cruel sneering face, and she was once again back in her room.

For the second time in as many nights, Carey found herself lying awake in her bed, her heart beating a violent tattoo against her chest. This time, however, there was something to worry about.

They had a mole.

The level of Saar's knowledge demonstrated without a doubt that there was someone within the castle passing information to him. There was no other way he could know about Zacharia or Ji – their situations had been kept a secret, bound to those within the castle.

Carey took a few deep, calming breaths before climbing out of bed. She slipped on a grey silk nightgown and soft leather slippers, then padded into the hallway.

It was well past midnight and there was no one in the hall but for a few guards who nodded and murmured acknowledgement as she passed. In no time, Carey was at her parents' door, which was flanked by two of Oliver's guards. She knocked twice and, at the sound of her father's voice, entered.

Her parents' apartments were far grander than her own. She walked into the main chamber, a lushly furnished room with a large four poster, its heavy, green velvet curtain pulled back and tied with gold braided rope. The floor was carpeted with a thick blue rug inlaid with swirls of golden thread that shone in the dim light. A fire burnt low in the fireplace, casting shy shadows upon the two low couches and carved table before it. To the left was an open door that led to a sitting room, lit only by wan moonlight floating in through the open windows, the cool breeze tickling Carey's bare skin as she passed the entrance to stand at the end of her parents' bed.

Carey's father was sitting up, gazing blearily at her. Her mother was beginning to stir at his side.

"Carey? What time is it?" he said thickly.

At the sound of her name, Jenny sat up, pulling her hair away from her eyes. "Carey? What is it? What's happened?"

A large wooden chandelier crafted from the roots of a tree hung overhead, dim light wavering from the last remaining candles casting shadows on her parents' faces.

"I just had an encounter with Saar," she said.

All sign of sleepiness vanished from her parents' faces.

"It's all right, it wasn't here in the castle," she added hastily. "I was at the gateway again when he appeared. It seems he has someone here in the castle passing information on to him. He knew about Zacharia and Ji."

Jenny pulled herself from under her bed clothes and moved to her daughter's side, placing her hands on Carey's shoulders.

"First of all, are you all right?" she asked, her eyes searching Carey's face as though trying to discern some physical injury.

"I'm fine. It was a surprise – an unpleasant one, for sure – but I had complete control. I got out of there as soon as he started spilling the usual vitriol."

She tried to sound indifferent but her heart was still racing and she wasn't sure she'd pulled it off. Her parents, however, did not press the issue, for which she was grateful.

"What do you mean, *'he has someone here in the castle'*?" her father asked, his brown eyes darkening.

"He knew that Ji was in the Common Realm and that Zacharia had woken up, both of which have occurred since he left. How else would he know about any of that if he didn't have someone here to tell him?" Carey said.

Her parents exchanged dark looks.

"We shall have to see if Oliver has any suggestions on how to deal with a spy," Robert said after a moment's thought. "But either of those events could have been relayed by anyone. We know from Rupert and how fast he receives information that news and rumours spread with speed in this castle."

They fell into thought for a moment, considering the implications of having a mole amongst them.

"Did he say anything else?" Robert asked.

"No. Nothing else."

"Well, in that case, we can't do much about this until morning. Everyone is asleep, and if we were to wake the Council now, it would only serve to alert the mole to our knowledge of them," her mother said, giving her shoulders a gentle squeeze. "We can come up with a solution in the morning."

Carey nodded, but frustration settled within, mixed with an unsettling feeling of betrayal. Someone was in league with Saar, someone they probably trusted, and she silently fumed at the thought.

She hugged her mother and bade them both goodnight before stepping back out into the corridor. Wrapping her arms around herself in an attempt to ward off the late-autumn chill, she began walking slowly back to her room, her mind still darting from one thing to another. Carey couldn't believe how brazen Saar had been – if she'd been bolder, she could've held him there with her mind the way he'd done to her so often. However, to open herself up to him in order to do so would've been too dangerous, and she didn't think she was strong enough yet to face him in a physical fight, let alone one with their minds. From now on, she would guard her mind better against him. She would not let him in unwelcomed again.

Thinking that it was much too early to be awake just yet, but knowing she was unlikely to fall asleep again anytime soon, Carey made her way to the

Healer's Ward. She knew Rupert would be sleeping in the Healer's room at the end of the ward, staying close in case Zacharia needed him. She wondered if she might ask him for a draught to help her sleep, a dreamless slumber – she didn't need her mind reliving what had just happened.

Quietly as she could, she pushed open the door to the ward and tiptoed inside. Her slippered feet padded against the stone. Just as she reached the far end of the ward, someone spoke.

"Carey?"

She jumped and let out a muffled scream that sounded like a mouse being stepped on. She spun around to see Zacharia sitting up in his bed, silhouetted against the stained-glass window behind him. The coloured panes threw muted shades of red, blue, and green onto his sheets. He looked as wide awake as Carey felt and wore a mild look of surprise.

"Are you looking for Rupert?" he asked.

She moved cautiously to join him at his bedside.

"I was hoping he could give me something to help me get back to sleep," she answered, watching Zacharia carefully.

"Nightmares?" he said with a knowing look.

Carey grimaced. "Something like that."

She was feeling slightly unnerved by this conversation; Zacharia was speaking to her as though there wasn't a decade of missing time between them.

"How are you doing?" she asked.

"Other than having just woken up for the first time in ages and sitting by myself in the dark?" He let out a small chuckle and Carey was glad to see he still had a sense of humour. Perhaps it was a family trait. "Surprisingly well."

"So, you can't sleep either?" Carey asked.

He shuddered. "Let's just say I now have a rational fear of closing my eyes."

She'd been afraid Zacharia would remind her too much of Ji, that the very look of him would be enough to break her, but now she was here she found him to be having quite the opposite effect. There were subtle differences in his look and mannerisms that were distinctly his own. His hair was lighter, a few early streaks of grey running through the brown. His eyes were a deep shade of green, more like Kat's than Ji's, and his voice was a few tones lower. And the way he spoke… It was smoother and calmer than she remembered Ji's being.

"Honestly, though," Carey said. "How have you been doing – since you woke up, that is?"

Zacharia didn't reply immediately. Something in his demeanour darkened at her query and for a moment she wondered if he'd answer at all.

"It's been… bittersweet."

A darkness that hinted at deeper emotion tinted his voice. The shadows seemed to grow about them, curling around their ankles and creeping up their spines. Carey took a deep, steadying breath, resisting the urge to pull back from the bed. She understood his pain – he was finally free and back with his parents, but Ji wasn't here, and Carey's insides burned with the injustice.

Zacharia must have seen the resentment on her face for he said, almost apologetically, "Kat told me… you and Ji… I didn't mean to…"

Carey shook her head.

"Don't. My grief at his absence is not only mine and is surely not greater than yours. I know he regrets not being able to be here for when you woke and I can only imagine what he'd say if he were."

"Something smart, no doubt," Zacharia said with the hint of a smile, and the shadows eased. "It's true, though, that not seeing him when I woke was a blow I'd not truly been expecting, but then, we are who we are. It's the nature of our existence to expect and endure the worst."

Carey was slightly taken aback by this dark assessment. She could see where he was coming from, but she wasn't sure if she accepted it.

"Surely that's not all we have to expect?" she said, but Zacharia's mouth twitched upwards at the corners, his eyes glinting with the sight of someone who'd just glimpsed what they thought they'd lost.

"Still the optimist, I see," he said kindly. "If anyone is to change their fate, Carey, I'd believe it of you. You and Ji are so similar, I can see it now."

"I could say the same about you," she replied, feeling it was what he would want to hear, what he should hear, but Zacharia shook his head.

"No. In looks only, perhaps, although I'd imagine even less so nowadays.

I've seen too much not to believe I have not changed beyond the wide-eyed optimism and romantic notions of duty that characterised my brother. From what Kat has told me, you have that in common, and for that I hold no resentment. I was gone too long and cannot expect to be who I once was. We are alike only in blood, and no more."

The shadows had gone now, shrunk back into the recesses of the lonely hall, but a heaviness clung to Carey's heart as she imagined the boy, so much like his brother, all smiles and jokes and messy brown hair, and the darkness that had smothered him. It was true – the longer she sat there, the more she realised that there truly was none of the familiarity she'd been so afraid would break her, only a ghost of something that may once have been. Tentatively she reached over and took one of his hands in hers. She felt him flinch in surprise, but he didn't pull away, and for a long moment they just looked at each other, something like hope and gratitude swelling between them.

"Carey?" A sleepy-eyed, tousled-haired Rupert shuffled towards them. "What are you doin' here?"

Zacharia's hand slipped from Carey's as she stood up, finally pulling her gaze from his.

"I was looking for you, actually, but I ended up talking to Zacharia. We're both having trouble sleeping."

Once she'd procured a draught from a grumpy Rupert, she said a quiet goodnight to Zacharia, who nodded politely before letting his gaze wander out beyond the window, a far-off expression falling over his features. As she lay back on her pillow and allowed the effects of the draught to overcome her, she wondered if Zacharia believed what he'd said and if they really were destined as Seekers to endure only the worst.

<h1 style="text-align:center">~Chapter Five~</h1>

<h1 style="text-align:center">Drawn In</h1>

Carey woke the following day with an ache in her right temple and an unease in her stomach that wouldn't go away. She recounted her confrontation with Saar to a meeting of the Council, but then only vaguely managed to listen to their plans on weeding out the possible mole. She wanted to give her opinions on the matter but her mind was clouded by distracting thoughts. At one point Kat tapped her gently on the arm questioningly, but Carey merely shook her head.

And the unease continued to grow.

As she sat there, the voices of the other Council members washing over her, Carey's attention drifted to the far wall. Her gaze fell upon the tapestry that hung there, the one that hid the entrance to the Stronghold, and she felt again the strange attraction, the inexplicable desire. And the magic she held within stirred.

Her unease mixed with the sense of longing.

Carey sat, staring, not hearing a single word anyone was saying. She only knew that behind that tapestry, within that marble temple, there lay something that she needed. Something she wanted. And it called to her.

*

"Carey!"

She dropped her sword and it clattered against the stone floor of the training arena. Blood began to soak the right sleeve of her blouse, the sharp sting of the cut bringing her back to her senses. She moaned in pain and clutched at her wound. Kat cursed, dropping her sai and rushing to her.

"Are you all right? Where's your head at?" she said, hands hovering over

Carey's as she tried to see the damage. "It's like you aren't even here today. Come on, let's get you to Rupert."

Carey didn't say anything as they walked, teeth clenched against the shooting pain in her arm. It was true – she was distracted. She couldn't stop thinking of the Stronghold. She'd tried to think of something else, anything else – it was the reason she'd agreed to a session with Kat – but that had obviously been a bad idea.

Kat swore again.

"Don't let Rupert hear you," Carey said with a grimace.

Kat snorted. "Let's just get you fixed up first and worry about Rupert's sensibilities later."

Rupert was chatting with Zacharia when they arrived at the Healer's Ward. He rushed over when he saw Kat and Carey enter.

"You an' yer pointy things," he tutted as he inspected Carey's wound.

"Yes, well, one day you might be grateful for those *pointy things*," Kat retorted, though she did look remorseful as Rupert cleaned the deep cut running across Carey's upper arm.

Rupert gave Kat a quick, cheeky glance at her words, as though he wished to say something more, but immediately returned his attention to Carey.

"It's not too bad," he murmured as he looked closer. "It might ache fer a day or two, but I should be able ter fix it up fairly decently."

He placed a hand over the top of the wound and closed his eyes. His lips moved, uttering a silent enchantment. Carey felt her skin tighten beneath his hand, an odd pulling sensation, and when he opened his eyes again, she found her skin smooth once more. The only evidence of the incident was her blood-soaked sleeve, which hung torn from her shoulder. Rupert ran a thumb across the top of her arm, his other hand holding her wrist. Once he was satisfied with his work, his gaze dropped to the brand on her left hand.

"Pity I can't do anythin' about this one," he said, grimacing. "Sorry. I shouldn't–"

Carey gave Rupert a smile and a gentle punch with her uninjured arm. "It's fine. It's just a mark. It's not like it hurts or anything."

Rupert didn't look convinced. He wiped his hand on a cloth. "I'll get yer a tonic fer the pain."

As he walked away, Carey's eyes fell on Zacharia and she gave him a small wave, a gesture he returned happily.

"So, you've spoken, then?" Kat asked as she sat beside her on the bed. "Sorry again about the arm."

"I'll live." Carey rolled her shoulder, feeling the slightest of aches instead of the searing pain of a few moments before. "I actually spoke with Zacharia last night. It was... good."

Kat nodded slowly. "So, what's distracting you, then? If it's not Zacharia, then what? Saar? The gateway? Because you've been somewhere else all day."

Carey groaned, flopping back on the bed to stare up at the ceiling. Kat's mess of black wavy hair came into sight as she frowned down at her.

"Carey..."

Letting out a heavy sigh, Carey clutched her hand to her chest. "It's the Stronghold. Or rather, what's *in* the Stronghold. Malevolence's magic. When I got close to it, I felt something... strange."

"Strange?" Kat frowned. "How so?"

Carey dropped her eyes from Kat's. "It's like I'm drawn to Malevolence's magic. It's this intense desire pulling at me, urging me to, I don't know... touch it? Take it? All I know is that it's calling to me and I cannot, for the life of me, stop thinking about it."

"And you don't know why?"

"No idea whatsoever."

Kat looked covertly about the ward. Zacharia was reading a book and Rupert had yet to return.

"Why don't you go back and see, then?" she whispered, excitement alight in her eyes.

Carey propped herself on her elbows. "Go back to the Stronghold?"

"Yes. Why not?" Kat said as though it was the most logical thing in the world. Perhaps it was.

Carey couldn't deny that the prospect of going back there was incredibly enticing. Excitement rippled inside her.

"I can get us in," she said.

*

Moonlight streaked the floor of the Council room, piercing the dark that surrounded them. Carey and Kat moved quietly across the flagstones, eyes darting back to the door as they moved.

"Tell me again why we're doing this in the middle of the night?" Kat whispered.

Carey stopped at the tapestry, glancing once more over her shoulder at the main entrance. "I don't know. I feel like this is something I need to do by myself, present company excluded of course. I want to see what this is without anyone else knowing first. I don't want to have to deal with any expectations or questions or… rumours."

Carey pushed back the tapestry, and Kat stepped up beside her. "I don't even know what this is really. I didn't want to have to try to explain it to anyone else."

Staring at the solid wall, Kat gave a nod. "All right, then. Shall we?"

Taking a deep breath, Carey placed a hand upon the wall as she'd seen her mother do. There was a rippling, tingling sensation beneath her palm, and the solid wall shimmered in the dim light. She gestured for Kat to step through. Kat shot Carey a dubious look before pressing through the barrier and disappearing. Calming her racing heart, Carey stepped through after her.

Flickering torches illuminated the long windowless corridor. Kat was waiting for her, eyes fixed on the door at the very end. It wasn't Faren standing guard tonight – it was a female guard Carey only had seen training with the others in the castle grounds. She came to attention as they approached, bringing her heels together and straightening her poleaxe at her side.

"Your Highness," she said in acknowledgement. "Lady Katrina."

Carey paused, half expecting the guard to ask what she was doing down there so late. But then she remembered that she was, in fact, the Princess *and* a Council member. The guard had no reason to ask. Lifting a hand to the door, Carey felt the same magic shiver through her as the locks and bolts within shifted before the door slowly swung open.

Carey gasped.

The sensation that had been so distracting before now exploded within her, and she had to stop herself from stumbling forwards. It was almost a physical pull that drew her forth, an all-consuming desire to be nearer to it. The small box stood innocuously upon the table at the centre of the room, its simple appearance belying the power within.

A second guard stood at attention beside the table, eyes straight ahead.

"You're Highness. My lady."

"Excuse us, but do you mind giving us some privacy?" Kat asked.

With a sharp nod, the guard strode from the room. As the door thudded shut behind them, Kat let out a low whistle.

"This is something else," she said as she looked about the room, turning on the spot as she took in the majesty of it. Her attention settled upon the wooden chest at its centre. "Is that it, then?"

Carey was before it now, her hands resting on either side, her palms flat on the cold marble. Her heart was pounding. Her breathing was harsh and ragged. Unable to hold back any longer, she flicked the latch open and lifted the lid. There, nestled within, was the Tear Globe containing Malevolence's magic.

"Carey? Are you all right?" she heard Kat say somewhere at her side.

"I can feel it," Carey rasped. "It's so… strong…"

She grabbed the Tear Globe.

For a long moment, it sat warm and smooth in her palm. Then there was an explosion of light behind Carey's eyes and suddenly she was seeing things beyond the marble Stronghold. Shadow and light swirled around her in an onslaught of confusing shapes and sounds. Her hand fused to the glass globe and she felt her magic surround her.

A scene solidified before her, the edges still a blur of colour and shadows. Forests and streams and villages appeared, and magic – magic everywhere. Carey couldn't just feel it, she could *see* it. Streams of silver illuminated the land, the structures, and the people.

A woman appeared before her. She was as dark as Carey was pale, her black hair flowing down her back. She lifted a palm and the magic surrounding them surged towards her, drawn to her like a moth to a flame. The woman pulled it into her and Carey gasped. She felt it as though she were the woman, the magic burning hot and devastating in its power.

The scene shifted, a flash of light and shadow again, rearranging to show Carey the woman standing in the centre of a raging battle. Carey could see the magic; she could *feel* it.

All magic.

She could see it flowing through the woman, bright and strong. The woman was reaching out, gathering the magic around her like a cocoon. Then, with an almighty scream, she unleashed it onto her enemies, the power she commanded felling them where they stood. Carey clutched at her chest, the sensation echoing there, and a sob rose in her throat. The woman stood, undefeated on the field strewn with fallen warriors, and her expression darkened.

The scene changed again.

The woman was cloaked in darkness, the magic that flowed through her darker still. Carey saw flashes of light flicker and die within the shadows; the smothering black pervaded all. Carey recoiled from the sensation that was both foreign and familiar.

A flash of magic split the darkness and the woman fell. A man stood over her, murder in his eyes. The man drew the woman's magic from her, the light of it separating from her body. Then, with a deadly stroke, the man slew the woman, and her magic, freed from its holder, passed into him. Carey watched as the man wielded his ill-gotten power, the magic streaming through him, a maniacal glint in his eyes. It was both mesmerising and horrifying.

The magical ability the woman had possessed, which had been stolen from her… The truth of it lay on the edge of Carey's mind, just out of grasp. It felt as though she should've known what it was, understood it, the reason why she felt such a connection to it–

She screamed. The magic inside her burned red hot. It was pain beyond belief, spreading through her veins, her body. Carey dropped to her knees, holding her hand over her heart, feeling as though that strange magic she held was trying to force itself free of her body.

Someone grabbed her by the wrist and the Tear Globe was wrenched from her hand. The darkness dissolved, the dying witch and her murderer disappeared, and Carey found herself lying on the cold marble floor of the Stronghold. Kat was standing over her, the globe containing Malevolence's magic in her hand. She looked stricken, angry, and she shoved the globe back into the chest and latched the lid shut.

"Carey." Kat crouched down beside her, searching her eyes. "Are you hurt? What was that?"

Running her hands over her body, Carey shook her head. The agony that had seared through her was gone as though it never had been.

"I…" Carey was unable to describe what had just happened, what she'd seen.

She sat up, running her hands through her hair. The desire that had been growing within her all day had been dimmed by whatever had just occurred. She looked down at her hands, remembering the feeling of all that power.

"Take my hand," Carey said.

Kat looked at Carey's outstretched palm. "Are you sure?"

Carey swallowed, then nodded. "I can't describe it. It's the only way I can show you."

Biting her bottom lip, Kat knelt and lifted her hand to Carey's. On contact, Kat's eyes fluttered shut. Her eyes moved behind her eyelids, seeing everything Carey had just witnessed. Carey's heart was still pounding, and she watched with growing dread and anticipation. With a shuddering breath, Kat pulled her hand from Carey's grasp, her eyes flying open. She fell back, her breathing as rapid as Carey's, and together they just sat, staring at one another.

"That… magic…" Kat stared up at the box on the stand. "What the hell was that?"

Carey swallowed hard, wiping at the sweat covering her face. "I don't know. I feel like I should, but it's like a memory that I've half-forgotten."

"But you were drawn to it, so does that mean that whatever you have inside you has something to do with what you just saw?" Kat looked Carey up and down as though she could see the magic within.

Carey dropped her head to her hands. Her whole body was trembling. She didn't know what to think. What had the visions been trying to tell her? Was it connected to the magic she possessed or was it a warning of some kind?

And what if it was a warning?

"Carey?"

She looked up from her hands, seeing Kat's worried expression, and shook her head. "I don't know."

Rearranging her features into her usual stoic countenance, Kat got to her feet before reaching out to Carey.

"Well, you don't have to find out on your own," she said, pulling Carey up. "We'll deal with this together."

Carey wanted to find more comfort in this sentiment, but the vision of the dying woman played on loop in her mind, and she shivered. The magic that dwelled within her had always been a source of fear. She didn't know where it came from, but she knew that it wasn't hers. It was powerful and unpredictable, and when it showed itself, she had very little control over it. The witch in the visions wasn't afraid; she wielded that power with absolute conviction.

Perhaps it wasn't a warning. Perhaps it was telling her something else.

To finally take control.

~Chapter Six~

Fight and Flight

"You seem tired, and coming from me, that's saying something," Zacharia said, watching her over the rim of his cup.

Carey was sitting on his balcony, the city sprawled below them. With Zacharia having been discharged from the Healer's Ward that day, Carey had come to visit, tea tray in hand.

"It's nothing. I just haven't been getting much sleep lately, what with everything that's been going on."

It wasn't a lie exactly, but it wasn't the entire truth either. After the incident in the Stronghold, she'd barely slept at all – Carey couldn't help but think about what she'd seen and what it meant. She and Kat had taken to the Archives, but after almost two days of searching, they'd found nothing. Even with Lady Marksis' help they'd been unsuccessful. If there'd ever been any information about the magic Carey possessed, there was a very real possibility that Malevolence had had it destroyed, which did not bode well for Carey. That magic, which she'd felt deep within, could be helpful in finding and defeating Saar, but without knowing how or if she could control it, it was useless. This knowledge, or rather lack thereof, made Carey anxious.

Zacharia looked unconvinced.

"I'm sure," he said, taking another sip of tea. "Speaking of everything going on, the Vuletians are arriving today, or so I've heard."

"I'm guessing Rupert?" she said with a smile, glad for the change of subject.

"Who else?" Zacharia grinned wearily.

Carey laughed – awake for barely a week and he already knew where to get his information.

"He also said you're hoping they'll help you get through the gateway," Zacharia added.

She sobered quickly. "They're good at this sort of thing – fighting."

"Who will you be taking with you if you go?"

Carey looked at his gaunt face, aged beyond its twenty-four years, and wished she could say his name.

"Kat, of course, and probably Rupert. We could've used his expertise last time," she said, hoping he wouldn't be insulted at being left behind, but he simply nodded before turning to look out over the city. From his balcony, Carey could see the mountains in the far distance where the Vuletian city of Hilarus was nestled.

Zacharia sighed softly.

"And if Ji were here, he would've accompanied you and I'd have felt no enmity. I came to accept a long time ago that I'd no longer be able to fulfil my duties as a Seeker and I will certainly not be responsible for holding back anyone from fulfilling theirs."

His words, so similar to those in Ji's letter, caught her by surprise, and Carey's heart tugged painfully as it always did when she thought of Ji.

"Has Rupert figured out a way of helping you get your powers back?" she asked.

Zacharia sighed. "No, and I'm not holding my breath. Whatever took them in that… place, I think it may have been for good."

"Don't say that," Carey said. "I'm sure Rupert will work it out."

Zacharia grimaced at what he must have thought to be unfounded hope. "Ever the optimist."

"Yes, well, someone has to be," said Carey.

"Indeed. Well, never mind me. I'll be fine in your absence. Just, when you see that baby brother of mine, tell him to get his arse back here. I have words for him."

Carey laughed, thinking that despite everything he said, Zacharia did have some optimism left in him.

"I will, and in those exact words," she promised.

*

The sky shifted subtly from a brilliant blue to an ombre of pinks and pale purples. The sun, sinking towards the horizon, blazed a brilliant orange, signalling the beginning of a particularly cold evening. Carey gloried in its brilliance as she flew out and over the walls of the castle. She revelled in the escape she felt on the back of her pegasus, Firefly. Whenever she felt the burden of duty and expectation to be too much, Carey would take to the skies. This was particularly true of late, and the anxiety she'd felt since the incident in the Stronghold lessened as they flew. Carey leant forwards and stroked Firefly's mane. This evening, however, was no joy ride; Carey was flying out to meet the Vuletian delegation and to lead them into the city.

The first of the evening stars glimmered over the fields and Carey instinctually grabbed at the pocket of her cloak to feel the small cube she kept there. Along with her sword, Carey had taken to carrying the small glass box that contained Ji's parting gift – a star – and his farewell letter to her. They were both a comfort and a reminder. Despite the intensity of her grief at losing him and the uncertainty of ever seeing him again, Carey had taken the words he'd written to her to heart, so much so that they'd become a sort of oath. She was not going to wallow in her despair and waste his sacrifice. Thinking on his promise to see her again, Carey gripped the box in her pocket as tightly as she dared.

It was why she longed to begin her pursuit of Saar – capturing Saar and stopping his plans had become inextricably linked to being able to see Ji again. They would bring Saar back to the Mystic Realm, close the gateway to the Third World and in turn reopen the gate to the Common Realm where Ji was trapped. Carey imagined going through to find him waiting with his wide, cheeky grin and a glint in his eyes. She wished, not for the first time, that her Twilight Travelling wasn't inhibited by the gateways. As long as the gateway was closed, Ji would remain out of reach.

Trying not to let her frustration ruin her moment of enjoyment, Carey gazed down at the expanse of earth below and saw the familiar shapes of four enormous wolf-like creatures with riders heading towards the city. She gave Firefly a pat and the pegasus glided down to where the Vuletians had come to a halt, having spied her overhead. With barely a flicker of nerves, Firefly landed before the four great vuk with a thudding of hooves on soil, giving her wings a rustling shake before folding them against her sides.

Carey looked over the great beasts, taking in their fur of greens, greys, and blues, their dark eyes glittering intelligently in the half-light. Their riders slipped from their backs and made their way over to greet her. Carey knew them – Efren, who now wore the cloak of captain, the same one Marjen had donned; the commanders Riist and Ueran, who'd escorted her most of the way back to Centre City; and Marjen's close friend, Versi. Carey was ecstatic at the sight of Efren and the commanders.

"Efren!" She threw her arms about him.

Efren embraced her tightly in return. "Carey. I'm so glad to see you safely back with your people," he said, though Carey noticed the glint of sadness in his eyes. He leant in so that only she could hear and said in a lower voice, "He was farewelled with full honours. He's at peace now."

Despite the short amount of time in which they'd known each other, Carey's friendship with Captain Marjen Tutari had been as close and personal as any she'd had. An intense trust and mutual bond had been evident from their first encounter and she'd felt his loss deeply.

Carey gave Efren a grateful bow of her head, and perhaps he was able to feel the gravity of what she meant to convey, as he gave her shoulder a gentle squeeze in solidarity before moving aside for the others.

Daaren Riist and Fiika Ueran stepped forwards, both wearing bottle-green half cloaks over their dark armour. With short curly hair and tanned skin marked with the tattoos of the Vuletian people, they greeted Carey with a formal salute. When they moved to apologise, Carey held up her hand, cutting them off.

"You have nothing to apologise for," she said with a wave of her hand. "I left *you* behind, so really, it should be me apologising to you. I'm just glad you're both still alive."

The commanders accepted her words with bows and smiles, and Carey turned to Versi, tall and slender in her fitted leather armour. Her wiry hair had been pulled back into an elaborate plait that fell between her shoulder blades, and the markings on her face shone like wet ink in the light of the setting sun. Her eyes, dark and shrewd, were averted from Carey's, her face wearing a careful, closed expression. She turned to Efren.

"We should make for the castle before dark, Captain," she said, nodding to where the last of the sun could be seen, and without another word, leapt onto her vuk.

Not knowing what to say, Carey glanced at Efren, who gave her an odd sort of grimace and said apologetically, "Versi is right. There will be time to catch up once we're at the castle."

Carey mounted Firefly, and, keeping to the ground, they made for the city, the vuk keeping pace easily.

Their strange procession slowed as it entered the city. Lanterns were flaring to life, their wicks breaching the gathering darkness with soft pools of light, and the cobblestones and white-washed walls of the houses glittered in their glow. Townsfolk paused to take in the newcomers and their wolf-like mounts. Some waved and called out, others stood still, mouths agape. Children ran alongside, laughing and squealing with delight but not daring to come too close. Carey smiled at the people of the city – her people – and revelled in their joy. She glanced back at the Vuletians. Efren was grinning upon his great grey vuk, clearly enjoying himself; the commanders rode straight-backed behind him, their eyes straight ahead and unwavering, clearly the consummate soldiers they'd been trained as; and then there was Versi, her brows pinched and eyes narrowed, as though she wasn't entirely sure what to make of the situation. Even though it appeared that she was simply unaccustomed to such displays, Carey had a feeling it was something more.

They passed through the castle gates and found the Council waiting, Carey's mother and father at the fore. Valets rushed to take Firefly to the stables as Carey dismounted, but they hung back, unsure of how to approach the four vuk. With a grin, Efren whispered something to his vuk and gave it a pat, and the four beasts followed the alarmed stable attendants as they led Firefly back to her stall.

"Mother, Father, may I introduce you to Captain Efren Theron of the Vuletian army, commanders Ueran and Riist, and Lady Versi," Carey said, stumbling a little as she introduced Versi, hoping she had it right.

She'd thought that, despite Versi's chilly demeanour and hesitance towards her, she and Versi had parted on amiable terms. Versi walked past Carey to greet her parents with a cold look on her face and fire in her eyes, and Carey briefly noticed how Versi gripped the sword at her hip much the same way she did when she was working to hold something back. There was something wrong, and evidently Versi blamed Carey for it.

"Lieutenant Cort," Versi corrected, bowing low before the Council.

Her voice was calm and void of emotion, though the white of her knuckles where she gripped her sword's hilt said otherwise. Rising from her bow, Versi gave Carey a singular scathing look before moving back to join Efren. Kat, who'd moved to Carey's side, whispered, "Well, that was friendly."

A touch shaken by Versi's obvious sentiments towards her, Carey shook her head. "That's Versi. She was a close friend of Marjen's, and I think she's angry with me."

Kat snorted. "Really? Never would've guessed."

They watched as Efren spoke with her parents, bowing and offering his greetings from Hilarus. His greying curls reminded her of Marjen's, and Carey suddenly remembered her final conversation with Versi before leaving their city – a promise concerning Marjen. A promise she'd been unable to keep.

Carey's heart caught painfully in her chest, pinching against her ribs. "Oh…"

Kat glanced sideways at her. "What is it?"

"Versi. I swore to her I'd watch Marjen's back, since she wasn't riding out with us. It was one of the last things I said to her."

"But surely she doesn't blame you for his death?" Kat said as the others greeted members of the Council in turn. "It's not as though you had much control over that situation."

Carey grimaced, remembering the moment the Imperial had thrust his sword into Marjen's stomach and the events that had followed. She hadn't told Kat any of this – that was one moment she wasn't prepared to share just yet.

"Yes, well, Versi doesn't think the way everyone else does," Carey murmured, watching Versi's back as she stood at attention at Efren's side.

"Well, this should be interesting then," Kat said, any further discussion cut off as the Vuletians approached to greet her.

Interesting was definitely not how Carey would have described it.

*

Carey couldn't help but grin; Kat may be good, but Commander Ueran was something else. She watched from the edge of the training hall as Fiika's blade flashed and flicked, barely a sound reverberating from the contact with Kat's sai. Carey marvelled as she angled her weapon in such a way that Kat's merely glanced off of it with the slightest *shik*. She kept Kat on the defensive for most of their fight, and Carey could tell from the intense expression on her best friend's face that Kat was equal parts frustrated and impressed. Daaren stood at Carey's side, watching his comrade and commenting on how she could improve. Carey couldn't see how, but then it wasn't her job to be the very best combatant in the Vuletian army.

"Come on, Kat! Get her on the back foot!" Carey shouted, and she saw Kat's eyes narrow, as though the thought of doing so hadn't already crossed her mind.

"Yes, thanks for that pearl of wisdom," she said, her breath coming hard.

"Do you always talk when you spar?" Daaren asked.

Carey shrugging. "Not always. It keeps us on our toes when we do, though."

Daaren gave a thoughtful grunt, then turned his attention back to the fight.

"I wonder how much longer Efren and my parents will be," Carey said, clapping as Kat managed to finally get one up on Fiika, causing the Vuletian to stumble back a step.

In the day since they'd arrived, Efren had spent much of his time in talks with Carey's parents and Oliver Binx regarding the security of the kingdom and the gateway. The Council was set to convene the next morning to go over their decisions.

"They were meant to be discussing border defence strategies so it may take a while," Daaren replied, not taking his eyes from the match.

Carey hadn't spent much time with Commander Riist before leaving Hilarus and found him to be a little more aloof than Fiika and Efren. He

50

stood ramrod straight, as though constantly at attention, and his manner was of calm impassivity. He looked upon everything as though it was only mildly interesting and spoke in much the same way. He wore his hair in similar fashion to how Marjen had – tight curls cut short and of uniform length – and his cool grey eyes were shrewd and considering.

His demeanour, however, was bright and sunny compared to that of Versi, and Carey was not looking forwards to speaking with her again, although she knew she must at some point.

The great wooden doors to the chamber creaked open and Seramina and Kyna entered, their arms linked as they came striding over to Carey.

"And what are you two doing down here?" Carey asked.

"Rupert said Kat was gettin' her backside handed ter her on a silver platter, so we just had ter come see," Kyna said with a mischievous twinkle in her eye.

Kat called out, "I can hear you, you know!", and pushed Fiika back off her once more with a grunt of effort.

Carey tittered. "Of course he did."

One day she'd find out how Rupert knew every single thing that happened in the castle.

Kyna pulled Seramina towards her and whispered in her ear. Seramina chuckled nervously, shook her head, then pulled back and gave Kyna a playful punch to the arm.

One of Kat's sai went flying from her hand and Carey could read the curse on her lips as Fiika's sword flashed at her throat. The four spectators clapped appreciatively as Fiika lowered her weapon and the two women shook hands.

Kat puffed as she picked up her dropped weapon. "Carey, care for a round?"

Before Carey could answer, Kyna spoke up. "Seramina would like a go!"

Seramina stared daggers at Kyna, but followed up with, "If you don't mind, that is."

Fiika raised an eyebrow at Carey, who glanced at Kat.

"You've seen her spar before," Kat muttered. "I say let her have a go."

Carey waved Seramina on. The girl walked over to the wall where the weapons hung and pulled down a short scimitar. Seramina gave it a cursory swing across her body, and as she walked onto the floor, Carey heard Daaren murmur to himself, "Interesting."

She understood the sentiment – to him Seramina looked like a scrawny thirteen-year-old with fly-away red hair, but Carey, Kat, and Kyna had seen what she was capable of.

Seramina approached Commander Ueran and they bowed to each other before taking their beginning positions. Fiika swung her sword back over her shoulder, two hands on the hilt and her feet planted in a wide stance, one foot slightly in front of the other. Seramina, on the other hand, held her sword almost limply at her side, the tip pointed downwards. If Carey hadn't noticed the subtle shift in her weight and the way her free hand tensed ever so slightly, it might have seemed that Seramina was simply waiting casually for Fiika to strike. Yet, as Fiika made to move, Seramina darted to the side and, almost lazily, knocked Fiika's weapon away from her. Fiika's eyes widened in surprise as she whipped back around. She made to strike again and this time Seramina stood her ground – their swords met with a loud *clang*. Seramina's movements came with a fluidity and grace that made it look as though she was barely trying. Her face was calm as she blocked every strike, and there wasn't a moment where she appeared caught off guard by the commander's moves. Fiika, on the other hand, was visibly unnerved by this display of swordsmanship, her brows knotted in mix of fierce concentration and confusion. As the two fighters danced about the training room, Carey watched on, impressed as always by Seramina's skill, while Kyna whooped and cheered. Daaren was sufficiently gob-smacked, and Carey noticed that his amazement was so complete that he wasn't even commenting on Fiika's form.

The session became more and more intense as Fiika tried to best the young girl, but she couldn't get past her perfect defences. After a series of quick blows and blocks, Seramina flicked Fiika's sword out of the way with a graceful pirouette, and in the blink of an eye, her blade was at the commander's throat.

Kyna screamed her delight at her friend's victory while the others clapped.

Daaren finally found his voice and said with a slight warble, "Where did that come from?"

Kat laughed. "We'd all like to know that."

Seramina had re-hung her sword and was now talking excitedly with Kyna, who had bounded over to her to, eager to replay each exhilarating moment of the fight. Fiika joined Carey, Kat and Daaren, still staring at Seramina, who was gabbling away as though she hadn't just beaten a senior commander of the Vuletian army.

"Where did she learn to fight like that? I thought our way was elegant, but she just made me look like a blundering cave troll," Fiika said.

"Honestly, we don't know," Carey said. "She has a number of *natural* talents, our Seramina."

"Yes. Kicking everyone's backsides at sparring being one of them," Kat added with just a hint of jealousy.

The idea of someone being naturally talented at swordplay, especially as talented as Seramina, was clearly something Fiika had a hard time comprehending, but she respectfully said no more.

That evening proved a welcome distraction for Carey as the Council members dined with the Vuletians. The strain of the past few days had become all-consuming, what with the Stronghold and the building tensions at the gateway. Efren proved to be just as entertaining as he'd been back in Hilarus, laughing and recounting amusing stories. Daaren ate mostly in silence, sitting as straight as a poker and answering Kat's attempts at conversation with overt politeness. Kat seemed to find this hilarious and tried, with ever increasing ridiculousness, to get him to break. Versi sat at Efren's side, staunchly ignoring Carey and jabbing at her vegetables as though they'd personally done her wrong. Carey didn't try to broach the awkwardness between them, thinking that if she tried, that fork might end up aimed at her instead of an undeserving tuber. And then there was Fiika, who sat in low conversation with Lady Marksis, who seemed absolutely enraptured by it all. No doubt she was gathering tales of Vuletian warfare to add to the Archives.

After dinner, Carey invited Efren for a walk about the castle gardens. The air was chilly, and Carey pulled her coat around her as they wandered about the grounds. Lanterns hung at intervals, their glow a soft warmth against the darkness. They spoke of Hilarus and the aftermath of their battle in which

Marjen had paid the ultimate price. Efren described the outpouring of grief that followed Marjen's passing.

"You should've seen it," Efren said, pride evident in his voice. "White petals falling on the wind and every colour of silk flying in his honour. He was loved, Carey, and our people ensured that they celebrated him and his life the way he deserved."

And while her heart swelled at his words, Carey couldn't help the guilt they brought, too.

"I'm so sorry," she said, regretting the inadequacy of the sentiment. "If it hadn't been for me–"

"No." Efren shook his head. "You know well that he fought for you willingly, as did we all. He saw something in you that was worth protecting, and he wouldn't thank you for blaming yourself for his death. Marjen did not die in vain."

It was very much the same attitude Marjen had shown before the battle – that by blaming herself she was dishonouring those who had died fighting for her – and Efren was right. She couldn't do that to Marjen. She couldn't disrespect his sacrifice like that.

Carey gave Efren a small smile. "You're absolutely right. He doesn't deserve that."

The rest of the evening was spent in reminiscences and laughter, and when she finally went to bed, it was with a full heart.

*

The next morning was spent once more in the training hall, mostly watching Kat try to best Fiika. When the deep boom that signalled midday sounded, they headed for the banquet hall where they were to go over the discussions regarding the gateway.

The main entrance was flooded with midday sun as they made their way up the wide staircase. Faren stood at the top of the landing; the guard was looking up and down the hall impatiently as though he was waiting for someone.

"Faren?" Carey called. "Are you looking for something?"

He turned, startled. "No – I mean, yes, Carey. I'm looking for Jensen. He and I are meant to be guarding the hall for your meeting, but I can't seem to locate him."

Carey frowned at Kat, who mirrored her expression. It was most unlike Jensen not to be punctual.

"Is everything all right with him?" Carey asked, thinking back to the day at the Stronghold and Jensen's less-than-friendly countenance.

For a moment, Faren looked as though he was considering whether to say anything, but then set his mouth in a thin determined line.

"Honestly," he said, "I can't get him to tell me what's wrong, but he has seemed off these past few weeks. Anytime I ask he gets rather shirty with me and changes the subject."

Daaren's voice came from behind them. "Sorry to interrupt, but we're late for the meeting. We don't want to keep the Captain as well as the Emperor and Empress waiting. Perhaps we can find your missing guard afterwards?"

Only just noticing the Vulctian's presence, Faren snapped to attention, the look of worry disappearing from his face as he recognised the man's superiority. "Yes sir. Of course. This way." And he marched off down the corridor, the group of Seekers and Vuletians trailing behind.

Carey stared at the back of the guard's head, unable to shake the feeling of unease she felt at Jensen's absence, but as they entered the banquet hall, she turned her mind reluctantly to the Vuletians waiting for them. The commanders moved over to where Efren and Versi stood, while Kat wandered over to speak to her father. Carey's parents had chosen the banquet hall for the meeting because it was airier and far grander than the main Council room. The view beyond the balcony was of blue skies and green countryside, and Carey let herself marvel at its beauty for a moment before returning her thoughts to the meeting. Her parents were at the head of the long table in the centre of the room, and Jenny turned at her approach.

"Sorry we're late," Carey said, but her mother waved away her apology.

"We've only just arrived ourselves. Now before I forget, I need to return your pin." She drew from within a pocket a tiny golden "S" – her shapeshifting pin.

Jenny had borrowed it the week before, though considering it had been hers to begin with, Carey hardly thought of it as *borrowing*.

"Did it come in handy?" Carey asked, attaching it to the inside of her lapel so it was hidden from view.

"Once or twice," Jenny said with a smile, and gave Carey a pat on the shoulder.

Everyone took their places at the long, carved wooden table, Efren and his cohort sitting across from Carey. Versi sat directly across from her, and at this range Carey found it incredibly difficult to avoid Versi's accusatory glare. She instead took to gazing about the room in what she hoped was convincing interest.

Jenny stood and all eyes turned to her.

"Thank you all for being here today," she said. "More so, we are extremely grateful to Captain Theron, his commanders, and his lieutenant for meeting with us. Following our talks, we've managed to form a number of plans regarding the gateway."

Carey glanced down the table as her mother spoke. Kat sat upright next to her father, Peter, who always appeared a touch worn in the face these days. Oliver and Meela, Ji's parents, were listening intently; Carey saw the intensity in Oliver's gaze as he watched his empress, the same sense of duty that drove Ji apparent in his demeanour. The attention of the other members of the Council were equally as focused, except Lord Carron, whose eyes were downcast, his fingertips steepled in front of him. Carey frowned; Lord Carron was usually one of the more attentive and yet here he sat, ignoring the proceedings. Apprehension reared its head as she continued to watch him.

Slowly, he placed his hands flat on the table; Carey could see his lips moving silently, barely a whisper escaping them.

"Lord Carron?" Carey called. "Are you well?"

She ignored how everyone turned their gaze to her, keeping her attention locked on Lord Carron. He didn't reply, and his sister, Lady Marksis, looked from Carey to her brother, bewildered.

"Jacom?" She placed a hand gently on his shoulder.

It happened in the blink of an eye and an eternity at the same time.

Lady Marksis' hand flew from his shoulder, thrown by an invisible force.

Lord Carron stood up and looked Carey straight in the eye. The browns of his eyes were clouded over and she knew at once that Lord Carron was not in control. She felt the magic without even thinking of it – that dark, incredible power that sat deep within her crackled at her fingertips, rushing through her body. Without a second thought, Carey flung out her arms, releasing it.

She wasn't fast enough. Lord Carron's magic burst forth a split second before her own, blocking her attack. His assault hit the rest of the Council members and the Vuletians. Carey's mother fell to the floor, while the others crumpled in their chairs. Only Carey remained untouched thanks to the power tingling through her extremities.

"What have you done?" she screamed, terror gripping her chest. "Did you just–"

She gave a quick glance down at her father by her side – his chest still rose and fell, and relief rushed through her. They weren't dead. Lord Carron stood completely still, his breath coming in rough, shallow pulls. His arms were still outstretched towards her, but he didn't move to advance or attack. For a moment they simply stood there, Lord Carron watching with those strange, dulled eyes, and Carey with her mind racing, body tense. What was going on here?

There came urgent banging at the door, followed by Faren's urgent shouts. "My lords! My ladies! What's happening?" There was a further rattling of the door. "I can't open the–"

Screaming erupted in Carey's head, drowning out Faren's words, and she cried out in agony. Clutching at her skull, Carey fought to remain on her feet as the screams tore at her, filling her with their terror.

It was Seramina, her shrieks frantic in Carey's mind: *"No! No! What are you doing? Stop it! Leave me alone! Kyna! Kyna!"*

"Seramina!" Carey groaned against the mental onslaught. She stumbled towards Lord Carron. "What are you doing to her?"

Lord Carron began to back away, drawing his hand over him in a great arc as he did so. He was casting a spell, and as Carey saw the angry red line grow across the ceiling, she knew he was sealing the room. He was trapping them all in there.

Not if Carey had anything to say about it.

Magic still tingled at her fingertips, and at the thought, it surged forwards once more. Carey threw her hands out, knocking Lord Carron to one side and halting his enchantment. The man fell against the wall, his head hitting the stone hard enough to render him unconscious. Without a second glance, Carey darted past him, desperate to find Seramina. She was still screaming, her shouts intermingled with grunts and snarls as she fought her attacker. She was still alive. Still here.

The door burst open as Carey ran towards it, a surprised Faren in the act of trying to pry it open with his poleaxe.

"Carey–"

"Seramina! We have to find her," Carey managed to say through the pain building in her head.

"I can hear her too," Faren said as he sprinted after Carey.

The screams were building to a crescendo inside her skull, and Carey shook her head against them. "They're getting… louder…"

"Help! Someone! Someone, please stop him! Jensen, please–"

The pleas stopped abruptly and Carey's head cleared at once.

"Carey…" Faren puffed behind her, the worry in his voice spurring her on.

They skidded to a halt at the top of the main staircase. There, striding towards the main entrance, was Jensen. Faren called to him and he turned at the sound, revealing an unconscious Seramina in his arms. Carey froze, not believing what she was seeing.

"Jen?" Faren managed to choke out.

Jensen ran for the entrance.

Carey broke from her shock and ran down the stairs after the guard, shouting for him to stop.

With Faren close behind, Carey burst into the courtyard to see Jensen almost at the main gates on the other side. There were two guards standing sentinel, and Carey shouted for them to stop the man, but as they advanced, Jensen cast a spell. The guards fell like puppets with their strings cut. Jensen ran straight past them, Seramina limp in his arms.

A ripple of magic washed over Carey and she staggered, almost losing her footing. The hairs on the back of her neck prickled and the very sensation brought her magic rushing back to her fingertips.

Faren swore.

Another man had appeared, just outside the castle.

Saar.

As Jensen passed through the gates, a burning red line drew itself from one side of the entrance to the other. Ignoring the shock and panic, Carey threw all she had at Saar, only for the magic to explode against an unseen barrier.

"Really?" Saar said. "I doubt that will be of much help."

Carey and Faren stopped just before the red line.

"You're not really here," Carey breathed, dropping her hands and letting her magic extinguish. It was no use to her now.

His silver eyes gleamed at her. "No. Just overseeing my handiwork."

Carey clenched her jaw, her fists so tight at her sides her nails bit into her palms. "I should've known. What have you done to Seramina?"

"Oh, we haven't doing anything to her… *yet*," he said with a malicious grin.

Faren was breathing hard beside her, staring at Jensen on the other side of the barrier. His expression was one of absolute betrayal.

"Jensen. What have you done?"

Jensen didn't reply, his expression lifeless and dull. In his arms, Seramina's head rolled back, revealing the glint of a metal band around her neck. It was the kind used by the Empire to suppress a person's powers. That's why her screams had stopped – the collar had cut off her telepathy.

Saar turned to Jensen. "I shall meet you there."

"Oh no you don't!" Carey flung herself at them, landing hard against the barrier. Panic flooded her, making her heart race and her mind whirl. This wasn't happening again. She had to save Seramina, *needed* to save her. She couldn't let Saar win again. "Don't you dare take her, Saar! Stop right there!"

"Or what?" he asked, the corner of his mouth twitching upwards.

Her palms flat against the seal, she screamed at him, her restraint giving way to fury. Carey had always tried to hold her composure in front of Saar, always refused to give him the satisfaction, but she was so angry at the injustice, so desperate to save her friend that she couldn't contain it any longer. Saar grinned back, apparently relishing the effect he was having on her.

"I'll find you," Carey snarled, her chest heaving as she glared at him. "I will hunt you down and there is nothing that will stop me this time."

Saar quirked an eyebrow. "Oh, my dear Princess. I expect nothing less."

He turned back to the guard and gave Jensen a sharp, expectant look. Jensen hefted Seramina over his shoulder before reaching into a pocket and withdrawing a coin the size of his palm.

Faren punched at the barrier. "Jensen, don't do this!"

Carey saw the guard hesitate, his gaze catching Faren's. Something unspoken seemed to pass between them and Faren gave a whispered plea. "Think about what you're doing."

Saar leant down and whispered to the guard, and in the moment before all three of them disappeared, Carey saw the regret and fear in Jensen's eyes.

"Jensen!"

But they were gone, and she knew Jensen hadn't wanted to do this. It was evident in his terrified expression as Saar had spoken those secret words to him. He hadn't wanted to help Saar, and for all she knew, he'd never had a choice.

~Chapter Seven~

Cross Over

upert. I have to find Rupert.

Carey ran pell-mell through the castle, her heart pounding harder against her chest than her feet on the flagstones. Her mind was racing, terror was constricting her throat, and she gasped in desperation as she flung herself around a corner.

"Carey!"

She collided with someone tall and fell hard to the floor, almost winding herself. Looking up, she saw bright yellow hair with red streaks and a face full of freckles.

"Rupert! Oh my god, Rupert. You have to come now. Something terrible has happened," she panted as she scrambled to her feet.

Rupert helped pull her up, his face stricken. "It's Seramina, isn't it?" he said, and at her look of consternation said, "I heard it too, them takin' her. She must've sent out ter everyone. What happened? Do yer know where Kyna is?"

"I don't, I'm sorry, but please, come with me."

Dragging Rupert back towards the banquet hall, Carey hastily recounted everything. As they entered, Rupert gasped at the scene. Hurrying over to the limp forms of her parents, Carey glanced at Faren, who she'd sent ahead. He was searching the room for any further dangers, and yet even as he moved about in his usual swift manner, his expression was a kaleidoscope of emotion. Pain, confusion, anger, betrayal – but there was something else that Carey couldn't decipher. It was the same look he'd given Jensen just before the man had disappeared, and it tore Carey's heart in two.

Rupert bent over Jenny and Robert, muttering to himself as Carey paced at his back. Kat was still slouched in her chair, her hair fluttering gently about her face as she breathed in and out, looking as though she'd merely fallen asleep at the table. Carey turned her gaze from her best friend and concentrated on what Rupert was doing.

"Good news. They've only been knocked out. I'll be able ter revive them easily enough."

"Rupert! Rupert!"

Kyna's screams echoed down the corridor outside, and Rupert jumped to his feet at the sound of his sister's distraught cries.

"In 'ere! In the hall, Kyna!"

Rupert's little sister came rushing in, bouncing off one of the doors in her haste, before flinging herself into her brother's arms.

"It's Seramina," she cried, tears streaking her face. "Someone's taken her! I heard it!"

"Wait, Kyna," Carey said, striding over. "How did you not see what happened? You two are practically inseparable."

Sobbing, Kyna gripped the front of Rupert's shirt as though he, too, might disappear.

"We were in th' kitchens – Cook always saves us the best pastries – an' a servant boy came for Seramina sayin' she'd been requested in the Council Chambers an' ter go immediately. And… and… she went!"

Kyna buried her face in Rupert's chest as he stroked her hair.

"The Council Chambers?" Carey said. "But we were here. There was no one–"

Her heart raced. "Oh no." She took off out of the hall, paying no heed to Rupert as he called after her.

Busting through the doors to the chambers, Carey raced to the wall at the far end. Slamming her hand against the stone, she felt the tingling sensation as the magic allowed her entry into the hidden Stronghold beyond. She stumbled in the dark – the torches had been extinguished. With her heart in her throat, Carey felt her way through the darkness until her eyes adjusted to the dim light, then let out a stifled gasp.

The Stronghold guard lay crumpled at the foot of the door. Carey knelt beside the man, searching for signs of life; she felt a tiny wave of relief as she heard him release a short, sharp breath. The door stood ajar. She pushed it open. Dread coursing through every inch of her body, Carey stepped inside, afraid to discover what she already knew to be true.

The second guard lay propped against a wall, but Carey's eyes lingered only long enough to discern the rise and fall of his chest. Her eyes cut to the centre of the room, to the empty pedestal.

She sprinted back to the banquet hall. Jenny and Robert were standing not far from where they'd fallen, looking shaken and disorientated.

"It's gone," Carey panted. "Malevolence's magic…"

Her words penetrated her parents' confusion.

"Faren told us Saar did this," Robert said. "He was somehow controlling Lord Carron and Jensen. And now you're saying they have Malevolence's magic as well as Seramina?"

There was nothing accusatory in his voice, but Carey flinched regardless. She nodded, gasping to catch her breath.

"Yes," Carey replied. "Jensen must've taken it for him. He had access, after all."

"Why did Saar reveal himself, though?" Jenny said angrily as Rupert revived Kat. "What was he hoping to achieve?"

"He wanted me to know it was him," Carey said, her chest aching with adrenalin and fury. "He needed me to know so I would go after him."

Jenny looked at her, her brow furrowed. "A trap?"

"It doesn't matter if it is. There's no way I'm sitting here any longer. Saar has Malevolence's magic and, more importantly, Seramina. I *have* to go after him before he gets too far ahead. If he wants me to come after him, then that's exactly what I'm going to do."

"Well, if that's the case, count me in," Kat said groggily as she struggled to her feet.

She nodded to Carey solemnly, her hand at the sai at her hips.

Jenny and Rupert glanced at each other and for a moment Carey wondered if they would go against their word. However, when Jenny spoke, her voice was steady and commanding. It was that of an empress, not her mother.

"Once Rupert revives the Vuletians we shall request their assistance in getting you to the gateway. In the meantime, be sure you have what you need. We shall stay here and wait for Lord Carron to wake. Perhaps he can shed more light on what just happened."

Carey dipped her head in acknowledgement before joining Kat.

"So just us, then?" Kat said, her eyes aglow with what was clearly excitement, and despite the fear and anger, Carey felt it too – the spark of adventure.

"I guess so," she answered, striding from the hall. "Let's get what we need and hopefully Efren and the others will be willing and able to help us by the time we get back."

Carey hurriedly changed into a pair of grey breeches and a white blouse. The chill of winter was beginning to bite, so she donned a pair of wool-lined boots and a dark-green velvet riding coat that hung low at the back and sat high against her throat. She tucked her Seeker's necklace down her front and transferred her mother's pin to the inside of her lapel before placing Ji's letter and the box containing his star in a side pocket. Other than her sword, now strapped to her back, she carried nothing else. With a trembling breath, she took one last look around this haven of hers, a trickle of fear rippling through her at the thought of leaving it all behind. There was no choice, though.

This was her life. From the moment she'd fled the orphanage in Ireland, she'd started down the road on which her decisions were never going to be completely her own. And as she stood there, eyes lingering on the city beyond her window, she knew she did not regret it. She would never choose the safety of the castle if it meant forsaking a friend. With a final look, Carey took her leave.

In the hallway, Carey met Kat who, like herself, had dressed for the winter. She wore a pair of dark-blue breeches with her customary lace-up boots, cream blouse and wine-red coat that tapered in at the waist and fell just above her knees. It had a wide lapel and a fur-lined hood, reminding Carey of a children's tale she'd once heard at the orphanage. Her sai were crossed at her back, the hilts poking up over her shoulders.

"Shall we?" she said, and they began to make their way back to the banquet hall.

Footsteps echoed behind them and they turned to find Rupert running towards them. He was wearing the heavy blue coat he sometimes wore to pick herbs from the garden in cooler weather.

"You going somewhere?" Kat inquired as Rupert came to a halt beside them.

He raised an eyebrow as though wondering whether she was trying to be funny.

"I'm comin' with you lot, of course," he said, a pack over one shoulder, the strap across his chest.

Carey glanced at Kat, who rolled her eyes in a resigned way.

Taking this as approval, he quickly added, "Besides, I heard what you lot got up ter last time an' I reckon yer need a healer taggin' along."

"You're not goin' if I'm not!"

Carey looked over Rupert's shoulder to see Kyna staggering up, struggling to pull on a fitted winter doublet as she walked.

"What?" Kat said.

"Kyna, no. Yer stayin' here," her brother said firmly, his usual smile sliding from his face. "Yer can't come this time."

"Like hell I'm not," Kyna said. "Wherever you go, I go. Besides, Seramina is my best friend. If yer think I'm gonna sit here an' wait fer you ter bring her back, you've got another thing comin'."

"This is way too dangerous, Kyna! You have no idea what we'll be facin'," Rupert said, gripping her by the shoulders, but she shook him off.

"I'm at least three years older than what Kat an' Ji were when they had ter make it on their own! Plus, I'll be with you and Carey and Kat, *and* I can help, I can!" She crossed her arms and stuck out her chin as she glared up at Rupert. "In other words, I'm comin' an' there's nothin' you can say that'll stop me!"

Rupert made to retort but Carey flung up her arms to stop him.

"We don't have time for this," Carey said in frustration. The longer they took, the farther Saar got away from them. "Kyna – you come, you keep up. All right?"

Kyna nodded fervently and Rupert let out a long-suffering sigh while Kat just clicked her tongue and said, "Let's get a move on. We need to get back to the Vuletians and make a battle plan."

Faren was speaking to Carey's parents when they entered the hall. From what Carey could tell, he was pleading with them, trying to convince them of something, and when she approached, Faren turned to her.

"You were there, Carey. Jensen didn't do this willingly, he couldn't have."

Jenny Lee placed a hand on the guard's shoulder. "Faren, we believe you. You've known Jensen longer than anyone here in the castle, so if you say he didn't, then we take your word. Meela?"

Meela Binx rushed to their side.

"Could you and Faren check on our other guards? Jensen managed to get all the way to the gate without interference. I want to know how."

Faren's expression relaxed slightly, and then he straightened, saluted, and followed Meela from the hall.

Efren, the commanders and Versi stood near the doorway, observing as the Emperor and Empress took their seats at the table. Lord Carron and Lady Marksis had finally been revived and they looked across at Carey's parents, their expressions masks of concern.

"My lady," Lord Carron said, hands grasped penitently before him on the table. "I beg your forgiveness. I became weak in my arrogance – I allowed that man inside."

"Can you remember what happened, Lord Carron?" Carey asked. She knew what Saar was capable of and was certain it had nothing to do with weakness on Lord Carron's part.

Lady Marksis gazed at her brother with a look of deep unease, her hand on his arm in a show of solidarity. "My lady, I'm afraid he has no recollection of what has occurred in the past day," she said soberly, and Lord Carron nodded in affirmation, his eyes downcast.

Carey frowned, then turned to where Kat stood a few feet behind her. "Would you be able to see?"

"Perhaps. I could give it a try."

Lord Carron looked up with fearful eyes as Kat approached him. She no longer needed to be touching someone to see their past, but it did help. She sat beside Lord Carron and held out her hand, palm up, in invitation. Lord

Carron gave a cursory glance towards his sister, who gave him an encouraging nod. He took a deep breath, set his features in a determined grimace, and then took Kat's hand.

The room seemed to still as Kat's eyes fluttered shut. Her eyes moved behind her eyelids as though she was asleep and dreaming, before suddenly flying open. Her pupils were constricted to pinpricks amidst deep green pools that slowly returned to normal as she released Lord Carron's hand.

"Kat?" Jenny asked.

Turning slowly from the brother and sister, she shook her head. "It wasn't his fault."

Lord Carron, despite his previous declaration, let out a breath of relief. "When?"

"You passed Jensen in the hallway, early yesterday morning," Kat said. "When your back was to him, he hit you with an enchantment – the one that possessed you just now, I'm guessing."

"Jensen?" Lord Carron said, his gaze cutting across to Jenny and Robert Lee.

Jenny nodded gravely. "He's working alongside Saar."

"We don't think he did so willingly, though," Carey added hastily. She needed to ensure everyone knew this. "Faren is sure of it, which means Saar must have something on him. He wouldn't have helped him otherwise."

"Leave that to us," Robert said. "For now, let us get you to the gateway. You're ready?"

He seemed stoic enough, but there was the hint of sorrow in his voice.

Carey gave her father a steady smile.

"Yes, we're ready," she said, adjusting the sword at her back. "What's the plan, then? No doubt Saar sent Jensen and Seramina to the gateway – I can't imagine him staying in this realm for long. Jensen had this coin, about so big." She outlined on her palm the shape of the coin the guard had used to disappear. "It must've had some sort of enchantment on it to move him and Seramina."

Jenny waved for everyone to follow her as they left the hall, leaving Lord Carron and Lady Marksis to speak in low, worried voices at the table.

They moved quickly to the stables. Efren and his companions approached their vuk, gathered at the far end of the building, too big to be in stalls, though Carey thought it may be an insult to put them in one anyway. She was hard-pressed to think of another creature as intelligent as a vuk.

A whinny echoed to her right, and Carey saw Firefly pawing nervously at the ground in her stall.

"Hey, hey girl," Carey cooed.

She made soothing sounds as she stroked Firefly's forehead. "I'm going away for a while," Carey explained in a low voice, continuing to pat her. "I wish you could come, but this trip is for people only."

She looked to the Vuletians, who were turning their vuk towards the mountains, sending them back to Hilarus without them.

She moved closer so that her forehead rested against the bridge of Firefly's snout. "I'll come back, I promise," she whispered, and yet, even as she said it, Carey felt the pang of uncertainty.

Heading into an unknown realm after a dangerous adversary presented the very real possibility that none of them might make it back.

This, however, was not the time for hesitation.

Carey took a deep breath, gave Firefly a last stroke of her mane, then turned from the reproachful gaze of the pegasus, whose dark brown eyes followed Carey as she walked away.

Steeling herself, Carey grappled for a sense of composure, reaching back to grip the hilt of her sword for reassurance as she so often did nowadays. The others were waiting for her.

Efren was holding a small, ornately carved box that appeared immensely old. When she reached him, he opened it, revealing three gold medallions about the size of her palm nestled on worn velvet lining.

"What are we lookin' at?" Rupert asked, leaning in.

The medallions appeared innocuous enough. They were thick with smooth edges, and as Efren took one from its bedding, she saw that there were deep, intricate engravings on the face.

"Much like our weaponry, these medallions are enchanted objects, given to the captain of the Vuletian Guard by the queen we first pledged our protection to. There were once ten, but now only three remain," he said, holding it up for all to see.

"Why only three?" Kat asked.

"Because the magic they invoke is so great that the medallion, acting as the conductor, can only endure it for a short time before disintegrating. That's why we've used only seven of them over the centuries," Efren answered, indicating the indentations within the case where the other medallions must have lain.

"What kind of magic?" Carey asked, intrigued despite her desire to get moving.

"Wayfaring."

Carey felt a thrill run through her. Until that moment, chasing Saar had seemed increasingly one-sided given his ability to travel great distances in an instant. Yet here was a relic that could possibly turn the tide in their favour.

"Is this what Jensen used? Or something similar?" she said, interrupting the awed silence that had fallen over the group.

"I'd have to agree with you," her father murmured. "It makes sense given that Jensen never displayed any Wayfaring abilities of his own."

"Well, perhaps now we can even the playin' field a bit," Rupert added, and there were nods all around.

"These ones," Efren continued, "can send the holder and anyone they have contact with to any place they desire within a single realm."

A single realm.

"This will only take us as far as the gate, then," Carey said.

Efren nodded. "Unfortunately, yes. That is our plan. Use one of the medallions to get you, Lady Katrina and your friends to the gateway where we will aid you in getting through."

Kat looked at her in a way that said, *Well, it's better than a punch in the nose.*

"All right. Sounds like a plan, then," Carey said, squaring her shoulders.

"Then this is where we shall say farewell," Jenny said.

Carey wasn't sure what to say as she moved to her parents' side, but she was saved speaking as her mother drew her into an embrace.

"Be strong. Be courageous," she said quietly so that only Carey and her father could hear. "I will not say *be safe* as you're about to head into dangers unknown. Just know that you have our pride and we're confident that you will see this through."

"You're speaking as though we'll never see each other again," Carey said, pulling away. Robert gripped her shoulder, accompanying the gesture with a sad sort of smile, and Carey's voice cracked slightly as she spoke. "We will, won't we?"

The others were gathering around Efren, but Carey didn't move her gaze from her parents' faces, their expressions filling her with unease.

"What aren't you telling me?" she asked as she felt someone grasp her arm. Why did this suddenly seem so absolute?

Her parents didn't answer.

"Mother!"

There was a strange sensation and they were suddenly swept away. Carey could feel the grip of whoever was holding her tighten as everything sped past her, her hair whipping about her face in the confusion. Her parents were gone, lost as the world raced by, making her feel dizzier by the second.

And then it stopped.

The landscape solidified around her and she stumbled a little at the abrupt absence of forwards motion. The rigid cold, shockingly different to what they'd left behind, hit her exposed skin; flakes of white snow swirled about them, catching in their hair and on their faces. It was dark and the only light came from torches by the gateway, their inconsistent glow flickering and flaring in the icy wind.

Before Carey could get her bearings, a war cry split the air and she spun around to see a hulking figure running straight at her. It raised its arms over its head before throwing them out in front, sending a violent shower of sparks hurtling at her.

Carey didn't have time to react, stunned by the suddenness of the attack.

A sword appeared before her, flashing electric blue as it deflected the magic, but not before she felt the heat of the spell touch her face. Efren had blocked the curse with his enchanted Vuletian blade.

With a single swift movement, he felled the Imperial loyalist.

"Hurry! Make for the gateway," he called as Carey saw, to her horror, hordes of loyalists burst from the tree line behind them.

There were more – so many more – than what Carey had expected. In the short space of time between her last visit and now, they'd become organised. Much more organised. She wondered momentarily how so many had rallied, or rather, *who* had rallied them, but the need to survive crowded her senses as she ran for the distant gateway. Deflected curses and spells hissed in the snow at their feet as the Imperials charged after them.

Carey reached for her magic and felt it buzz eagerly at her fingertips as she raced after Efren, throwing it back over her shoulder haphazardly at their pursuers. The four Vuletians had their weapons drawn and they flanked Carey and the others protectively.

Kat grunted as she flung a protective barrier about the group, the magic flaring bright blue in the dark. It was, perhaps, not the best idea – the luminescence of the spell caught the attention of more Imperials, and Carey heard shouts of surprise and fury as they sighted the group.

Kat swore loudly.

"Charmin'," Rupert shouted as he held onto Kyna, urging her on as they stumbled through the snow and onslaught of magic.

"I think the situation calls for it, don't you?" Kat screamed back, drawing her sai, her hair flying out behind her as she kept up with the Vuletians.

A great flash of magic hit Kat's barrier and Carey felt it like a sledgehammer between her shoulders. She heard the crackle of Kat's magic dissolve around them. Kat swore again. They were close to the gateway now, the Imperials slowing as they met the spiked barrier surrounding it. The guards who lined the stone steps held their positions, weapons and magic blazing as they defended the gate. With Kat's protection gone, they began to fight their way through. Sword in hand, Carey joined the Vuletians in striking down the loyalists who attacked them.

The melee pressed in on them from all sides. Shouts and screams filled the air, the sizzle and boom of magical assault filling Carey's ears. A flash of blue rushed past Carey and Kyna squealed in pain. The curse sliced through the girl's shoulder and blood spattered the snow at their feet. Rupert caught her as she stumbled, one hand raised over his head to stop another curse as it soared towards them. The Vuletians' swords left bright arcs of light against the darkness.

There was a shout from the enemy ranks and more turned towards them. Carey wasn't sure whether they knew who they were or simply that they weren't Imperials. The more that came for them, the more that flutter of panic rippled against Carey's ribs. Efren and the others would be overwhelmed soon enough, and her own protective magic wouldn't stand against the onslaught that threatened them. Kat and Rupert were hurling all they could at the enemy, but it seemed to be making little difference. It was like throwing a pebble at an oncoming wave.

A jet of green hit Kat and she doubled over in agony, coughing blood onto the snow. Rupert roared in anger as he shot back at the offender, but his rage was swallowed up by the horde. Kyna was attempting to help despite her injury. Sweat glistened at Daaren's brow, an angry red welt under his left eye, and Fiika's armour bore deep gouges from magical blows. Efren and Versi were trying desperately to fend off the magic flying at them, but even as Carey watched, Versi was struck in the knee, causing her to stagger.

The battle surrounding them was deafening, and the wind and snow turned to sleet, striking at Carey's skin like flint on stone. The archway loomed ahead. The guards were fighting frantically, trying to hold back the Imperials.

We are so close, Carey thought. They were so close and yet, give it another minute, and they'd be completely overwhelmed. They would be taken and Saar would escape.

With Seramina.

"No."

Determination unlike anything she'd felt before flowed through her. It was no longer just her own magic lighting her fingertips; that mysterious other magic had awakened and was now coursing like fire through her veins. She could feel the force of it trying to escape her, as it has after Marjen had been mortally wounded, but Carey did something she'd never done before – she held it back. The effort made her gasp. As she did so, something shifted within her. Like a lock sliding into place. Now the magic moved with her thoughts, rather than of its own volition. It was listening to her. It sparked behind her eyes, enveloping her in endless power, and it was something beyond anything she'd felt before.

She was an oncoming storm, lightning at her fingertips.

Visions of magic flowing through her burned in her soul, streams of blue and silver, and Carey lifted an arm over her head. With a swiping movement, she knocked a group of loyalists to the ground like they were skittles in a child's game.

"No," she grunted again, and she drew a hand through the air once more, knocking another group of assailants off their feet.

More Imperials began to realise what was happening, and while some began to back away from Carey, others shouted in anger and surged forwards. It did little to deter Carey. To her, they seemed but flies. She lifted both arms above her head and, in one emphatic movement, brought them rushing down to her sides. A great blast of wind burst outwards, knocking all but a few outliers to the ground, snow swirling in a frenzied flurry about them.

Magic bloomed within her and Carey groaned with the effort of controlling it. It was enough, what she'd done – she'd given them a way through – but that power within her demanded more. In that moment, a kernel of fear planted itself in Carey's heart, but she pushed it back until it receded. It was unlike anything she'd yet experienced – her limbs had felt like they were on fire, and even now they felt raw and sensitive.

Rupert clasped her shoulder, almost bringing Carey to her knees, and asked, breathily, "You right?"

Carey nodded, unable to speak.

Efren looked about at their fallen foes and, without skipping a beat, shouted, "Onwards!" Even as they ran, Carey could see many of the loyalists dragging themselves up from the snow and giving chase, their faces contorted in rage.

Efren signalled for Daaren and Versi to take point, leading Carey and the others towards the gateway. Hands reached out to trip them and spells and curses began to fly as more loyalists regained their footing. As they reached the fortifications, Carey's heart skipped a beat as she saw the guards beyond it hesitate, but then one of them shouted "Seeker!" and a gap in the battlements appeared, creating an opening for them.

A shout echoed from behind and Carey looked around to see Rupert and Kat. Loyalists were trying to pull them back, but they lunged at the opening the guards had made, only just escaping. Efren and Fiika were cut off from the rest by at least a dozen of the enemy. They were holding them off valiantly, but on seeing the swell of Imperials once more, the guards closed the opening, separating the pair from Carey and the others.

"Efren! Fiika!" Carey cried, fighting to get back to them, but the guards refused to let her through their defences.

Over the roar of the wind and the sounds of magic being thrown all around, Efren called to Daaren and Versi: "Get them through!" He thrust a fist in the air, something glinting between his fingers. One of the medallions.

With a flash of bright light, Fiika and Efren were gone, leaving the loyalists gazing about in dumb confusion.

Daaren called to her. "Now! Carey, let's go!"

The guards protecting them were beginning to strain beneath the weight of the loyalists' attacks, curses flying at the Seekers. Carey turned to the archway, its white smoke swirling before her. Ji's face flashed before her eyes at the sight of it. Her heart pounded in her ears and she swallowed hard against the overwhelming urge to run away, despite the only other prospect being a horde of vicious loyalists. She raised her sword, hand clenched tight on the hilt, and stepped up to join Kat, Rupert and Kyna. Versi led the way and Daaren covered the rear. Helped along by Kyna, Kat went through behind Versi, disappearing into the swirling mist. Rupert motioned for Carey to go ahead of him; she looked up at the stone gateway with mounting dread, but there was no choice. There was no turning back now. She had to follow.

Without a backwards glance, Carey stepped into the whirling mist and the unknown.

~Chapter Eight~

Eternals and Innocents

Carey stirred.

A pungent mix of damp, mould, and something less easily defined reached her nose. Something metallic. She scrunched up her face against the sudden assault on her senses. Her brain scrambled to make sense of it. She was lying on hard, cold stone; she could feel it against her aching hip and shoulder. She must have been asleep a while for it hurt so much, but Carey couldn't think of why she'd even be asleep in the first place.

She groaned, lifting her hand to her head. There was a sore spot at the base of her skull and she touched it gently, the area tender.

"Carey? Are you awake?"

It was Kat, but her voice sounded weak. Pained. Something was wrong.

Carey's eyes snapped open.

She was lying in what appeared to be a cell roughly hewn from stone. There were no windows, and thick, rusted bars surrounded her on three sides. It felt like a cage. She and Kat were in the same cell. She sat up slowly. The others were spread out in the adjacent cells.

They faced a long stone wall, a walkway passing in front of their cells, and the roof hung low, making the space feel cramped. Light shone from cracks overhead, and Carey noted vaguely that it was much like the lichen she'd seen in the underground city with Sirona. She looked over at Kat, sitting against the wall at the rear of their cell. Her face was pallid and drawn, and she was holding a hand to her side. She was clearly in a lot of pain.

Carey crawled over to her. "Kat? What happened? What's wrong?"

A memory of bright sparks and blood skipped across Carey's mind, but her head was still too befuddled to remember anything concrete. Rupert, who was in the cell to the right of theirs, leant on the bars separating them.

"Don't move her. I think she has some broken ribs. Move her an' they might pierce somethin'."

"Broken ribs?" Carey echoed, looking down at Kat's hands helplessly and noticing her rapid breathing.

"The curse… that hit me," she gasped. "It did some real damage."

Carey remembered now.

In the chaos at the gateway, Kat had been hit. They'd managed to escape the Imperials – Efren and Fiika had held them off and used one of the medallions to get away. Carey recalled stepping through the gateway, the fog whipping about her as she'd been transported to the Third World, how they'd stepped out into darkness, stars glittering overhead.

Then pain.

"Someone attacked us." Carey lifted a hand to her head once more.

Sitting back on her knees, she looked over at Rupert and Kyna. The young girl's eyes were on Kat, concern etched on her face, a hand outstretched through the bars as though she was attempting to comfort her. She had a piece of cloth wrapped around her bicep, blood seeping through.

Daaren and Versi were in the cell to Carey's left. Daaren paced his enclosure, his movements impatient and frustrated like that of a caged animal. Versi, on the other hand, sat cross-legged on the floor, her back ramrod straight, her hands in fists upon her knees. She was gazing around with a look that suggested she was doing some calculated thinking; her face was set with a grim look, her lips a tight thin line.

They were still wearing their leather armour, but their weapons were gone. Carey's hand flew to her back but she found herself grasping at thin air. Heart pounding, she thrust her hand into her pocket, silently pleading that the familiar shape of Ji's gift would meet her touch, but it too was gone. All that remained was his letter, the piece of worn paper clearly too inconsequential to be worth taking.

She swore loudly.

"'Hey, enough of that," Rupert chided with a small smile, but his face fell quickly as he looked back at Kat. "Someone got th' jump on us, all right. As soon as we came through. None of us saw who it was."

Kyna shook her head.

Daaren growled. "We were so distracted by escaping the other side that we were caught off guard."

Trying to focus on their current situation rather than her lost memento, Carey thought she heard the commander murmur words like "humiliated" and "never" as he continued to pace.

Versi fixed him with a stare. "This is hardly the time to allow your ego to get the better of you, Commander."

Daaren stopped pacing, held her gaze for a long moment. Then he gave a curt nod and straightened his armour with a tug at the waist.

"You're right, Lieutenant. This is hardly the time for regret. We need to focus on how to get out of here."

Carey was beginning to think that Daaren had more in common with Versi than she'd first thought when Rupert said, "Where is *here*, though? We don't even know where we are, an' even if we did, how are we supposed ter move Kat as she is?"

Looking at the rusted metal hinges and the mundane appearance of the bars, Carey frowned. These cells looked innocuous enough, so what was it about this place that was keeping them trapped?

"Is this place Bound?" Carey wondered aloud.

Kat tried to say something, but her words came out quiet and slurred. Carey shuffled beside her and let Kat rest her head against her shoulder.

"Don't try to speak," Carey said, noticing how Kat had her eyes squeezed tight against the pain.

"I tried healin' her while you were still out." Rupert shuddered. "It's not that we can't use magic – we can – but instead of flowin' outwards, it works its way inwards. It felt like I was placin' a curse on m'self."

Carey turned Rupert's words over in her head as she tried to soothe Kat. No one spoke, and she let her eyes roam about their quarters as thoughts rushed through her head. The bars were dotted with moss that glowed the faint green of the lichen above. Each bar was almost the thickness of her forearm. She swore under her breath. It was true that Carey had been able to use magic where no one else had before. And she'd effectively decimated an entire army. If these cells had been no more than Bound, she might have been able to work the same magic to enable their escape. But they weren't just Bound, and the thought of having that strange magic of hers backfire and feed back into her made Carey blanch.

"Who are we dealing with here?" she whispered, her voice cracking.

A low voice answered from the far side of Daaren and Versi's cell. It came from the shadows in the far corner of the rock cavern where the dim green light didn't reach.

"An immeasurable evil."

Kyna let out a muffled squeal; Rupert started so badly he almost fell backwards; Versi was at Daaren's side at once, their bodies moving subconsciously into defensive positions; and Carey jerked upright, cursing as Kat gave a muffled cry of agony with the sudden movement.

From the shadows came a tall, dark-skinned man clothed in a fitted tunic of brilliant teal over light-tan pants and high-laced boots. Gold thread gilded his clothing, the intricate patterns of vines and leaves reaching across his chest and arms. However, small tears and smudges of dirt gave him a slightly derelict appearance. His long dark hair was partially braided, pulled back so that half was tied in a knot at the top of his head, leaving the rest to cascade down his back. His face was sharp with high cheek bones and a strong chin, and his eyes were a piercing green that shone through the darkness.

As he surveyed the group, his hair shifted to reveal delicate pointed ears studded with elegant silver piercings and rings, and Carey had to bite her tongue to suppress a gasp of surprise.

He stood a foot from the commanders' cell, and while they remained tense, the stranger merely stood with his hands clasped behind his back, exuding serenity. His peaceful composure was in such stark contrast to their own that it disturbed Carey. This place hardly inspired a peaceful temperament.

The man looked at her, considering her with his bright, otherworldly eyes.

"I am Ilvisar," he said in a low, measured tone. "I would tell you where I am from if I thought it were pertinent, but I observe you are not of this realm."

None of them spoke as Ilvisar observed them, head tilted to one side. It occurred to Carey that he would've heard every word they'd spoken. She could see no use in denying it.

"No, we're not," she said.

Carey wasn't about to accept that he was a prisoner. Trust was not something she gave freely anymore – she'd learnt that the hard way.

"I assume you came through the Opening?"

Carey gave him a nod.

"The Opening lies on the border between my country and another – Truav Skain. That is where you find yourselves now," Ilvisar said.

"Since you're of this realm, then, can you tell us why we've been taken prisoner by these people," Daaren asked, his eyes narrowed.

Ilvisar shifted his gaze to the commander. "The people of these lands are superstitious and do not appreciate intruders. However, you are *here* because you are practitioners of theurgy." He eyed Carey's out-stretched hand, the hand she'd not realised until that moment she had raised against him.

"Of what?" she asked, but it was Rupert who answered.

"Magic."

Kat groaned weakly. Carey shifted to try to make her more comfortable, and Kat's dark hair fell across her ashen face as she settled.

Rupert said, "It's an old term from the Common Realm I came across durin' my studies."

"What's so special about bein' able ter do magic?" Although Kyna's voice wavered as she spoke, clearly her curiosity was greater than her fear.

"*Magic*, you call it?" Ilvisar answered. His face softened as he looked at Kyna, a sadness creeping over his features, and Rupert moved protectively towards his sister.

"Magic – theurgy – is practised by only a few in our world. It is not rare, per se, but it is uncommon, and usually only the gift of women. Male practitioners," he said, shifting his gaze to Rupert, "*are* rare, and are generally power hungry, driven to cruelty by their abilities. You will find this particularly true here, in Truav Skain."

The tone in which he said this last part was so ominous that Carey couldn't help but feel a deep sense of foreboding.

"Why are these people so interested in magic, then?" Rupert asked with a note that suggested he didn't appreciate the insinuation.

"What is it that men with power want more than anything else?" Ilvisar said.

Carey answered. "More power."

There came the bang of metal on stone from somewhere past Rupert and Kyna's cell. A flicker of pale light grew brighter as someone made their way down the dungeon. The dancing tongues of flames illuminated more and more of the cavern as they approached, the green of the lichen subdued by the burning glow. Carey shifted into a crouch, laying Kat on her side as gently as she could, and glanced back at where Ilvisar had stood; he slid back into the shadows of his cell, but not before giving Carey a sharp look of warning. She knew perfectly well what it meant.

Say nothing. Do nothing.

Rupert had crouched down next to Kyna, his arms wrapped around her as she watched the approaching light with wide, fearful eyes. Daaren and Versi had retreated to the rear of their cell but stood straight and watchful, careful to keep their body language neutral.

Carey stayed by Kat's side but repositioned herself so she was facing the walkway beyond her bars. She watched with bated breath as their gaolers approached.

The two figures wore red and black. At first glance, they looked much like Ilvisar with their pointed ears and angular features, but that was where the similarities ended. Where Ilvisar exuded a peaceful energy, there was something menacing and violent about these two. Their clothes were roughly made, pieces of leather cobbled together with tarnished studs and crudely made chainmail. Their hair was sleek and oily, held back from their faces by burnished metal headpieces that tucked behind their ears and came down to a point between their eyebrows. Strange tattoos covered their skin. Unlike the elegant, curving tattoos that graced Daaren and Versi, the guards' markings were pale and raised, like scars rather than ink. Some were series of dots, others crude symbols. Carey couldn't help but feel nauseated.

They came to a halt just beyond Carey's cell and she noticed the long gleaming scimitars hanging at their waists.

BANG.

The taller of the guards slammed the iron torch against the bars, sending a shower of red sparks onto the stone floor.

"*Gabeh!*" he shouted at them. "*Gabeh!*"

Carey looked at the others in confusion.

"What now?" Rupert said, confusion and alarm upon his face.

"*Mek gabeh!*" the other guard said, louder than the first.

Carey felt a frisson of fear as he glared at her.

He turned to the other and said something unintelligible, clear disdain in his tone. Then he turned back and said clearly, "Get up, now!"

So stunned by her sudden ability to understand him, Carey stumbled to her feet but moved no farther. Rupert and Kyna followed suit.

"Get her up, too!" the tall guard spat, motioning at Kat.

"No, she can't," Rupert said. "She's injured."

The guard's gaze shot to Rupert and he moved slowly to stand in front of his cell. He glowered at Rupert as he hissed, "She will stand, or we will make her."

For a moment, Carey thought Rupert might argue, but then he swallowed whatever words he wanted to say after a quick glance at Kyna. He nodded to Carey, whispering, "Take it easy. Lift 'er gently. Don't pull 'er up."

Slowly and carefully, Carey helped Kat to her feet. Kat grimaced and whimpered, but she managed to stand, albeit resting most of her weight on Carey.

Seemingly satisfied, the guard moved back to his companion. "Practitioners of theurgy, you have trespassed on the sacred lands of the Eternals of Truav Skain. For your transgression, your gifts will be given to the Eternals in penitence. Your sentence will be carried out at dawn tomorrow."

The guard spoke with a lilting accent. This, however, did nothing to distract Carey from his words. Sentence? Penitence? She couldn't understand what he was saying. What were the Eternals he spoke of?

It seemed, however, that he would not be elaborating. His lip curled in an arrogant sneer before he turned to Ilvisar's cell.

"Kasek! Moragenau. Toka bin zakindeh."

The guard spoke with obvious venom and spat on the ground in Ilvisar's direction. Straining to keep Kat standing, Carey's knees buckled slightly as she watched Ilvisar's tall, dark form emerge from the shadows. His eyes, emerald green not moments before, had turned dark, almost obsidian as he stared coolly back at the guards.

"Bikha dun, jakin kech bekrani."

His voice was low and dangerous, barely a whisper, but Carey heard it clearly across the dungeon. The shorter of the two guards, clearly angered by what Ilvisar had said, made to advance on his cell, but his companion stopped him with a hand on the shoulder. Ilvisar smirked almost imperceptibly as the guards glowered at him. Carey had no idea what they had said, but it wasn't amicable. There was absolute loathing there; the air was thick with it. Ilvisar was more than a simple captive like themselves – there was a history there, something she couldn't see. Ilvisar seemed calm in his taunting, unlike the impassioned guards, but his eyes burned through the darkness with an intensity that scared her.

The guard shrugged clear of his comrade's restraining hand. "You think you can save them?" he asked, his words shifting back to a language Carey understood.

Carey tensed, hearing the danger in his voice. His eyes flicked from Ilvisar and ran, one by one, over the Vuletians, Carey and Kat, then to where Rupert and Kyna stood. Slowly, he unsheathed his sword, the sound of the steel slicing through the silence with metallic menace. Carey's heart beat faster, a swirl of adrenalin enveloping her as she watched the guard's deliberate movements. The scimitar held her gaze as the guard ran it across the bars, clanging loudly on each rung.

They were all watching him, transfixed with growing dread. Ilvisar's disposition of calm defiance was slipping; his gaze darted between the guards and the other prisoners, apprehension slowly creeping over his features.

The guard was landing each hit of the bars with intentional malice, his face turned towards Ilvisar as he attempted to illicit a response. Kyna followed the sword with terrified eyes, flinching every time it hit a bar. Rupert's knuckles were white on his sister's shoulders. Daaren was tense, his hands flexing ever so slightly, and Versi stood at his side, her eyes narrowed.

No one made to break the stand-off, everyone waiting to see who would make the first move. Carey could almost hear the pounding of her heart through the growing silence when a soft moan shattered it.

Kat.

Carey doubted she even knew what was happening, but at the sound the guard stopped pacing and his head whipped about to face her. He slammed his palm against the latch of the cell door and Carey heard the *CLUNK* of the lock. She turned to the other guard to find him leaning lazily against the far wall, watching the proceedings with the bored air of someone who'd seen this before and who didn't much care for it. The rusted hinges screeched loudly as the door swung open. Carey's heart lurched, blood pounding in her ears as the guard strode towards her, his scimitar flashing at his side. She stood rooted to the spot, unable to move with Kat leaning on her, and she knew she'd have no chance of stopping him without using magic.

"Carey," she heard Rupert say in a low, desperate voice.

She saw Daaren move defensively out of the corner of her eye, impeded by the bars separating them, but the guard paid no heed. He reached Carey, seized Kat by the neck and threw her to the ground. Carey tried to pull her back as he tore her away, but the guard was too strong. Kat cried out in agony as she hit the stone floor and the others screamed and shouted, fear and indignation reverberating around the cavern. Carey flung up her arms to shield her face as the guard advanced, and his fist connected hard with her stomach.

Pain rolled through her body, causing her to double over and drop her arms to her mid-section. She fell against the bars, her back hitting the metal hard. Winded and trying to regain her footing, Carey felt the guard's hand grab a fistful of hair at the base of her skull; he ripped her head back roughly so that she was forced to look up at him. Her eyes watered as she felt hair separate from her scalp. She dared not move. The man's eyes danced maliciously as he leered at her.

"Kasek."

Panic filled her, and with it, Carey felt her inner magic rising unbidden. She shook uncontrollably as she struggled to hold it back, but it had a will of its own.

"No…"

The word escaped her lips as it spread to her fingertips, ready for the attack. Before she could say or do anything else, fire ripped through her body.

Carey let out a long, guttural scream as waves of agony rippled through her. She collapsed, thrashing uncontrollably on the floor. She couldn't form a single thought; the only thing she knew was that in that moment, she would have been glad to die. Anything, *anything,* would be preferable to this torment.

At the thought of death, however, the pain extinguished. Carey found herself drenched in cold sweat and panting at the leather-bound feet of the guard, all vestiges of the agony she'd experienced moments before gone. The others were watching intently. She glanced up at the guard and saw a satisfied grin on his face. Her breath hitched as he slowly raised the tip of his sword to her chin, keeping her from turning away from him. He moved his dark eyes overhead to where she guessed Ilvisar was standing. He gave a huffing sneer before dropping his blade and striding from Carey's cell. He slammed the door shut, signalled to the other guard, and together they left without a backwards glance.

Shaking violently, Carey waited until the sound of their retreating footsteps had faded away completely before crawling shakily over to where Kat lay motionless. She could hear the others talking, whether to her or about her she wasn't sure. All she could think of was Kat. Her friend lay motionless, her black hair splayed out around her pain-stricken face. Her breathing had become shallow and uneven, and blood trickled from the corner of her mouth.

Carey called out to Rupert without taking her eyes off her dearest friend. She'd been barely conscious before, but now…

"She's not going to last like this," Carey said, her voice breaking.

Rupert reached through the bars, his outstretched hand on Kat's wrist. After a long moment he let out a sigh.

"Her heartbeat is steady at least, but unless we can get out of here, there is nothin' much I can do."

His face was downcast, his voice filled with regret. Daaren, who until this moment had been watching quietly, face filled with indignant rage, strode towards Ilvisar. He slammed his hand furiously against one of the bars, the sound jarring Carey from her reverie.

"What is this place? Speak, now!"

They all waited, silently watching the tall dark stranger whose exchange with the guards had impacted them so acutely. Ilvisar's bright eyes flicked from where Carey and Kat lay to Daaren's furious face, the calm indifference he'd exuded before having dissipated.

"We are in the bowels of the Arena, a great structure in the heart of Truav Skain. Those with the gift of theurgy are brought here as sacrifices for the beings that call themselves the Eternals. They take the powers possessed by the gifted and absorb them, extending their lifespans far beyond that of a normal Skanian, hence their name."

"Men with power," Carey echoed, and he nodded solemnly.

"They are cruel, degenerate old men who, through a mixture of *magic* and manipulation, have their entire country under their influence. It is at the point where their people's reverence of them borders on the divine, and their loyalty is fanatical. Because of this, the Eternals order their forces to seek out and capture any practitioners of theurgy as threats to their nation in order to sacrifice them for more power."

Carey felt a chill run down her spine. How many people had been in her place, held behind these metal bars awaiting their fate?

Running her hand across Kat's forehead gently, Carey despaired at the thought that they may not escape this. She wanted to speak with her friend, martial her thoughts and strategise, but now she felt nothing but a great well of anxiety that threatened to swallow her whole.

"If these Eternals are so powerful, how is it they've not gone beyond their own borders?" Daaren asked.

"Oh, they have tried," Ilvisar said. "But they lack a military presence. Mercenaries, yes, but they are few, and despite their abilities, they are not so strong that they can overthrow an entire country, especially given the countries beyond these borders are far larger. However, given what I have learnt here, I'm not about to say they'll never try again."

"And you? You seem ter refer ter us as though you are not a wizard," Rupert said. "If yer not one of us, then why are you here?"

Carey saw a flash of something akin to agony flit across Ilvisar's features. His bright eyes dimmed much as they had done before and she realised what it was.

Grief.

Ilvisar seemed to be steeling himself when his gaze fell once more on Kyna and his jaw stiffened. "No, I am not gifted as you are, but I was not captured alone. I was taken because of my daughter."

His features glazed over and he seemed to disappear into himself, remembering something they were not privy to.

"She was a witch, then?" Rupert asked, though his tone was softer, with just a touch of fear.

With a small shudder, Ilvisar came back to them, the distance retreating from his eyes. "Yes, but she was not just a simple practitioner. She was what the Eternals crave the most."

When he didn't go on, Carey coaxed him gently. "What was she?"

Ilvisar looked directly into her eyes, lifted his chin and squared his shoulders in pride.

"She was an Innocent."

~Chapter Nine~

Facing Truths

"My daughter, Terienn, was a *witch*."

He said the last word slowly and deliberately, as though to ensure that he was using it correctly. "As was her mother. They were considerate and kind, strong and wilful." Ilvisar took a deep, steadying breath as his expression turned stony. "When Terienn was barely twelve years old, she witnessed the brutal murder of her mother. My wife. She managed to escape the same fate, but from that day on, she was different.

"Her abilities grew exponentially. She became stronger, but at the same time wiser and more compassionate. She would learn a new skill without any hindrance or setbacks. Despite these developments, however, she remained grounded and humble, almost unaware that she was any different to how she had been before. She also stopped aging, something everyone but she seemed to notice. I was amazed, but I was also afraid. I was worried by what these new abilities meant for her, so I sought out others like her, travelled to distant lands in search of answers."

"And did you find any?"

Kyna's voice was small and timid compared to Ilvisar's deep commanding one, but it was clear. His face softened again, and Carey wondered what he was thinking.

"I did. I found two others like Terienn, and their situations had been much the same. They had both experienced a terrible trauma at the same age, and as a result, their abilities had grown, just as Terienn's had. They, too, remained oblivious to the truth of their situation, a crucial element, I was told, of them being able to maintain and wield such power. One old man referred to them as *Innocents*, simply because that is what they were – innocent.

"It was on my return to my city that I learnt of the Truav Skain and their obsession with Innocents. For years they had been little more than a collection of rumours and stories – a civilisation that worshipped three powerful beings. As much as my people longed to know the truth of the country we bordered, none managed to cross into Truav Skain and return. I came upon a woman who herself was a powerful witch. She told me that the Eternals were obsessed with the power of Innocents, so much so that they sent out mercenaries to track down and kidnap children who displayed the qualities of one. If they were unable to find one, they would take a child of the right age and make one instead."

Carey's stomach swooped sickeningly at the implication. *Make one?* Rupert and Kyna were listening transfixed, and while Kyna's brow crinkled with confusion, Rupert's expression was one of disgust.

Versi, who had retaken her seat at the back of her cell, voiced what Carey was thinking.

"I assume in order to create an Innocent, the children are subjected to unspeakable suffering?"

She said it in such a matter-of-fact way that Daaren's head snapped in her direction and he hissed admonishingly, "Versi!"

Ilvisar, however, did not react to her cool assessment other than to nod. "I will not disturb you with the process, but yes, they would traumatise young practitioners in the hope they would produce an Innocent. When it did, they would have the child sacrificed so they could absorb their power."

If the thought of maniacal wizards slaughtering people for their power wasn't already disturbing enough, this made it so much worse. Carey swallowed back the bile that rose in her throat. Children. *Children.* And she thought Saar was bad.

"How is it you came to be here, then?" she asked. "And where is your daughter?"

A deep, aching feeling spread across her chest as she gazed into Ilvisar's green eyes. There was absolute devastation there, a chasm so dark and endless that Carey was suddenly very afraid of what he was going to say. When he spoke, his voice was quiet and husky with barely concealed emotion.

"They found us. They took us as we rode for the mountains. I knew they would discover what she was one day, and when they did, they would seek her out. So, I took her away from our city. There was a monastery in the hills where she was to hide, but we weren't fast enough." He paused, as though to steady himself for what he was about to say next. "I knew I could not save her. I looked for any way of escape, begged, bribed, but nothing worked. So I decided to take away the magic they so craved. An Innocent is only an Innocent so long as they remain oblivious."

Everyone stared blankly at him, bewildered, so he added: "I told her the truth."

"And that took away her abilities?" Carey asked.

"It did, but that only made them angrier. I failed in saving her," Ilvisar murmured, his voice barely a rumble, regret and pain filling every word. "But at least they did not get what they wanted."

In the thick silence that followed, Ilvisar turned away from them, leaning his back against the bars of his cell. "I deserve this. I could not protect my wife or my child. It is better this way."

He spoke his words to the air, a resigned acceptance of his fate at the hands of the people who had taken his child. Carey couldn't think of anything to say, partly because Ilvisar's demise meant theirs also, but mostly because she'd thought she was used to the terrors wrought on others for the sake of power. It took a certain type of evil to tear a child from their family and claim their life for its own benefit. For weeks she'd been haunted by her actions that had destroyed an Imperial army and had vowed never to allow that kind of magic to inhabit her again. Surely, she'd told herself, she was better than the Imperials that hunted her. She didn't want the ability to kill indiscriminately, to be capable of that sort of destruction. She hadn't wanted that, she had no desire to wield it.

But this...

Carey wanted nothing more than to decimate these so-called Eternals as thoroughly and completely as the lives they themselves had destroyed. This was evil at its most profound and she felt bound to do something about it.

However, they were trapped and Kat was gravely injured. Their dire situation did not exactly lend itself to exacting vengeance.

There was something else, however, that Ilvisar's words had stirred – realisation. Everything that had happened to his daughter had happened to Seramina. The trauma, the power, the skills… and now Saar had her. Fear burned through Carey as her imagination triggered myriad possibilities.

"I have a question," Rupert said, breaking the silence and dragging Carey from her terrifying thoughts. "What was it that those guards said ter you before? I've never been under the impression that prison guards were particularly educated, let alone bilingual."

Ilvisar turned back to them, considering Rupert and his question for a moment.

"Bilingual?"

"You know… they spoke two different languages?"

Ilvisar cocked his head. "They weren't. They spoke but one language."

"But we heard two," Kyna said.

Ilvisar paused, his eyebrows knitted together pensively. "No… you don't speak Ethellen, do you? *Santau?*"

Rupert answered, a touch gruffly. "Clearly not."

Ilvisar's face lit with sudden understanding.

"If you do not speak Ethellen… unless I want you to understand what I'm saying, you won't," Ilvisar said.

"But how can *you* understand us? We're not speaking… *Ethellen*, did you say?" Rupert said, suspicion in his voice.

"Generally, we would only be able to understand you if you wanted us to," Ilvisar said, and Carey couldn't help feeling like he was hiding something.

"But we didn't know you were here before," she said slowly. "Yet, you still understood us then."

She could see him considering his answer.

"I can understand all languages," he said. "A gift afforded to someone of my birth."

Despite how pretentious this sounded, Carey waited for him to say more, but Ilvisar seemed reluctant to elaborate.

"So?" Versi said, and when Ilvisar did not reply, "What did they say? Or are we going to continue speaking on the finer linguistic points of our verbal understandings?"

They all waited for him to answer; his jaw tightened.

"They said I am to die with you."

There was an uneasy silence, one, it seemed, Versi was unconcerned with breaking.

"And you said?"

Ilvisar squared his shoulders defiantly before answering.

"That I would see them in hell."

Versi nodded.

Carey put her hand to Kat's forehead, then leant down to listen to her breathing. She was pulling long, ragged breaths with some effort.

"Rupert," Carey said in a quiet, strained voice. "Tell me what I can do. Anything. We need to keep her well enough for when we escape."

As Rupert instructed her on how to best position Kat, Ilvisar said, "I have already told you – there is no escaping from here."

"Then you know nothing of us!"

Carey's voice echoed around the dark chamber. She wasn't sure why she was suddenly so angry, but at his words, Carey's blood had surged, boiling in her veins. Perhaps it was the prospect of finding herself once again at a complete disadvantage. She was so tired of being clueless, of being unlearned in the dangers and positions she so often found herself in. She wanted to be the one in control, one step ahead instead of two behind. This man may know all about this world but he did not know them or what they were capable of.

Carey stood, gritting her teeth. She knew how it had sounded, snapping at the only person to have shown them any compassion since arriving in this hell of a place, but she was not about to take it back – it was the truth and she would not apologise for it.

"This punishment tomorrow – what does it include?" she asked. If they couldn't escape beforehand, then perhaps their execution would provide them with an opportunity.

Ilvisar was considering Carey with considerably more curiosity than he had previously.

"We will be taken to the Arena. There, we will be stood before the Eternals."

Carey narrowed her eyes. "Will we be Bound, as we are in here? Will we be able to use magic out there?"

Ilvisar paused. "I am unsure. Sorry. I only ever witnessed my own daughter's slaughter within the Arena, and she was too afraid to fight back."

Carey paced back and forth, contemplating her options.

"Carey, what are yer thinkin'?" Rupert was gripping the bars between them. She crossed over to him and spoke so only he could hear.

"Not much, but there was something that happened while I was away from Centre City that makes me think that we might just stand a chance against these tyrants."

*

Hours later, the two guards returned, banging at the bars of their cells and shouting for them to stand. Despite all they'd endured and the exhaustion that dragged on Carey's body, she'd barely slept. Fear and adrenalin hummed through her limbs, preventing her from any decent rest. The others also had languished in varying states of unrest, speaking very little as the night wore on. Kat hadn't woken, but even with the sweat beading on her brow and her pale waxen skin, her breathing remained steady, which was, as Rupert assured Carey, a good sign. Carey knew Rupert was a skilled healer, but she found it difficult to take his word right now – they felt like the words of someone comforting the dying with *everything's going to be fine*.

One thing the rush of adrenalin had not been able to overcome was the hollow emptiness of her stomach. She knew they must all be feeling the pangs of hunger, Kyna having said as much at least four times, but it seemed their captors didn't require their prisoners to have full stomachs before they were sacrificed.

The guards barked their orders again and Carey, pushing against the fear rising within her, stepped forwards, her face set with determination.

"I need help with my friend." She motioned at Kat on the floor. "Let him carry her."

She pointed to Rupert, trying not to let her hand shake as she did so. The taller of the guards narrowed his eyes at her, but then gave a grunt and a sharp nod that Carey took for assent. The other guard opened Rupert and Kyna's cell and led them roughly into Carey and Kat's. As Rupert knelt to lift Kat into his arms, Carey whispered to him.

"Remember, stay close."

Without meeting her gaze, Rupert gave an almost imperceptible nod. They turned back to the guards, who had brought Versi, Daaren and Ilvisar from their cells to stand before them. Carey, Rupert and Kyna joined them, and they were led from the dungeon, the shorter guard in front, the other close behind. They walked up a steep set of stone steps, the dimly glowing lichen winding its way through the crevices in the walls. They moved in single file, Carey at the front. The air, which had been stale and damp, was replaced by the smell of cold stone, metal, and a hint of something that reminded her of a butcher's shop. It did little to calm her nerves, but she kept her jaw tight against the constricting feeling building within her ribcage. She couldn't tame it until she knew what they were facing, until she knew they had a chance of escape.

At the top of the stairs, they came to a door of heavy steel. Dim light crept through the gap between the door and the wall, orange though, not like the greenish hue they'd grown accustomed to in the dungeon. The guard opened it, then steered them into a wide hall with an arched ceiling. The wall opposite them was broken at regular intervals by low entrances from which the orange glow filtered – sunlight. The causeway they now found themselves in was bare and silent but for a muffled roar, like the sound of a rushing waterfall.

Carey wasn't given much time to think on this; she was grabbed roughly by the guard in front and hauled towards one of the entrances. His grip digging into her skin, he shoved her through the opening. Carey stumbled but caught herself before she fell. The others were being similarly herded through the opening, the guards shouting from behind.

"Move!"

They forced them down a tunnel, light streaming in through the opening at the end. This sight, however, brought Carey no comfort. Danger lay beyond this passage; she felt it shiver through her, her instincts tingling. The roaring grew louder as they advanced. Rupert was at her side now, Kat limp in his arms. His eyes were set on the opening, his brow creased.

"Are yer sure about this?" he said in a low rasp.

Carey wished she had something a little more comforting to say. "We don't really have a choice."

He let out a slow, low sigh. "Then I guess we shall see soon enough."

Rupert adjusted Kat in his arms, her head resting against his chest. Her skin was white as parchment and her hair stuck to her face with sweat. Carey's heart lurched as she observed Kat's eyes flutter feverishly, and she suddenly realised how ridiculous this plan seemed. She was risking everything, *everyone*, on something she'd managed only once before. But what else could she do? This truly was their only hope. It was a flimsy fly-away hope, but as Rupert had said, *they would see soon enough.*

The roaring was growing louder and louder as they crept closer to the end of the tunnel, and as they stepped out into the open, Carey looked up to find the source of the commotion. Hundreds upon hundreds of Skanians stood in tiers that rose up around them. They were shouting and screaming, stomping their feet in demented excitement. Carey and the others found themselves at the edge of a massive clearing with a dais in the centre. The guards jabbed them hard from behind, shunting them towards the middle. This must be the Arena Ilvisar had spoken of. Carey heard Kyna whimper in fear and felt the tug of her coat as the girl grasped a handful of material.

"Keep close, Kyna," Carey told her.

The circular stage of carved stone before them matched the outer curve of the Arena so that it was perfectly proportioned. As Carey stepped onto it, she noticed elaborate markings around the edge in a language she couldn't understand. Trying to appear inconspicuous, she moved to Ilvisar's side.

"Do you know what the markings say?" she asked.

Ilvisar gave a jerk of his head. "They speak of the honour of our sacrifice."

Carey's stomach clenched but she also felt a jolt of triumph. "So, not magic."

Her eyes met his intense green ones, and in that moment, she knew they had a chance.

There came the boom of a gong and an unnatural hush fell over the Arena.

Carey turned to find three tall figures standing halfway between the edge of the Arena and the dais. The two guards had retreated to where they'd come from, leaving the prisoners alone.

The three figures bore the pointed ears and dark skin of their guards but their eyes gleamed an unnerving silver that reminded Carey unpleasantly of Saar. They stood barefoot, and their long flowing garb was ornately embroidered with the same markings as those at her feet. Their unbound hair fell down their backs, and while Carey had been able to easily distinguish Ilvisar and their guards as male, there was an undefinable quality about the three before her.

"The Eternals," she said under her breath.

As though they had heard, all three Eternals turned their gaze to her. Their unsettling stares set her nerves on edge and she balled her hands into fists in an effort to steady them. She felt the others move subtly, positioning themselves closer to her. Their proximity was imperative.

The middle of the three Eternals raised their arms out wide as though in greeting and addressed the crowd. Their voice was thin but commanding, and every eye in the Arena was upon them.

"Beloved people, as Eternals, we exist to serve you, the great people of Truav Skain, to give you power over those who would oppress you and protect you from outside forces who would do you harm. Just this past day, our loyal guard stopped this horde of magical scourge as they attempted to enter our lands. They came with ill-intent, seeking to spread discord and enmity throughout our country. But we have managed to stay their wicked plans."

Carey heard Daaren shift uneasily behind her, but only barely; anger rose up within her at the Eternal's words. So, this was how they got away with sacrificing all these people. Lies and fallacies. But why the performance?

The Eternal to Carey's right spoke, their voice much like the first's, except pitched a few tones higher.

"As punishment, their strength will become ours so we may continue to protect and serve the great people of Truav Skain."

And there it was.

Carey shook with repressed fury. These power-hungry degenerates were justifying their actions with threadbare promises of safety and power, yet as her gaze moved over the citizens of Truav Skain, more than one of them wore tattered and torn clothing. It was her bet that they were still waiting for those promises to come to fruition. Either that, or they'd long ago been coerced into believing their lot to be the very best that could be afforded them.

Carey decided it was time to test her plan. As the Eternal droned on, Carey reached inwards, allowing her eyes to glaze over as she concentrated on bringing forth the magic within. As though it had been waiting, she felt the spark of immeasurable power flicker at the corners of her mind. She felt it spread down her arms, shooting through her body to her extremities. Taking care to hold it back, Carey took a deep breath and allowed a single spark to alight her fingertips.

Nothing happened. She didn't collapse, nor did she find herself writhing in pain. She was completely unbound.

Fighting back a grin of satisfaction, Carey held the power ready, feeling it buzz within her expectantly. It took a great deal of strength to hold it back like this, but she had to control it. Just a little bit longer…

The Eternal to the left took over the orating.

"Bear witness, our children! Bear witness and behold!"

The Skanians erupted with cheers and shouting.

The sounds were her signal. Carey closed her eyes, concentrating on Rupert and Kat, Kyna, Versi and Daaren, and finally, Ilvisar. She visualised each of their faces, willed her magic to feel each connection, then let it flow from her slowly. Her hands shook with the effort, but she opened her eyes and looked around at Rupert. He gave her a nod and she knew he could feel the magic enveloping him and the others. She turned back to the Eternals, who were still too busy revelling in the ill-gotten love of their people to notice her intentions. Carey took a deep, steadying breath and felt the protective magic billow from her, stronger now, and evidently more noticeable.

The Eternals' heads whipped towards her in unison like that of hunting dogs who'd suddenly caught a scent.

"What are you doing?" the middle one asked over the roar of the Arena. "How dare you defy us!"

Their eyes flared red then black, the colour spreading until the whites of their eyes were no longer visible. All three Eternals spread their arms out wide, palms towards Carey. She could sense their impending attack – her magic vibrated and surged as it always did when she found herself in danger.

"Who are you to assume you can stand against us?" cried the Eternal to their left. "You are but children. We are eternal, all-powerful. This is our domain!"

Sparks flickered about them and the Eternals chanted words Carey did not understand.

But she didn't need to understand.

She could feel their magic building, and her own magic burnt in response. Her arms were aching from holding back and she bit her bottom lip as she strained against it. Carey staggered slightly as the first wave of their magic hit them, but it did no harm. Her magic was doing what she wanted – protecting them, like it had done when they were nine and she'd protected Ji and Kat and herself from Malevolence's cronies. A bead of sweat rolled down her forehead.

"Relinquish now!" called the final Eternal on their right, their magic building up around them in a wild display of blue fire and sparks. "You cannot deny us!"

Carey stared back at them.

"Want to bet?" she snarled, and with every last bit of energy, she directed her magic at the Eternals.

She had decided on entering the Arena that the people of Truav Skain did not warrant the ire of her abilities – the Eternals alone deserved what was coming. And so Carey watched with grim satisfaction, and the merest touch of guilt that came with such reckless destruction, as her magic whipped towards the Eternals. She saw their eyes widen as their own mortality was presented to them. There was a great explosion of blue flame and the three Eternals were gone, consumed by Carey's magic.

The force of the blast knocked spectators over. The bright flames rushed over their heads, illuminating the stunned and confused faces looking down upon the prisoners. Carey felt a hand upon her shoulder – Daaren's hand –

and she released her hold on her magic. As she relaxed, she felt it retreat, the prickling under her skin receding, and she took a deep, gasping breath.

Yet as she did so, the familiar blinding pain shot up into her temples, causing her to cry out. She felt like falling to her knees, giving into it, but they still had to get out of there somehow, and get their weapons back. And Ji's gift.

Daaren caught her by the elbow as she staggered. No… she couldn't lose it now. The others were counting on her for their escape, which was seeming less likely by the second. Her skull was pounding and her eyes watering. Through the tears, she saw people rushing onto the arena floor, the growing sounds of the crowd buzzing in her ears like a swarm of angry bees. The gathering horde was blocking their escape routes and they'd soon be on top of them, yet no matter how much she tried to focus, Carey couldn't recall her magic from a few moments ago. She heard Rupert curse as he spun around, Kat in his arms, searching for an alternative exit while Kyna, sobbing, raised her hands protectively.

"Carey!" Versi said. "What do we do?"

Her face was set with a stony grimace and her body was tense, as though she expected to be able to physically fight her way out of this.

With Daaren still holding her up, Carey reached for the magic again, but just the thought sent excruciating pain rocketing around inside her head. She'd tried to control it, and now it seemed it wasn't going to allow her to do so again.

"I can't…" she whimpered as the masses neared.

They were so close now, and Carey saw Ilvisar step down from the dais in front of her, putting himself between Carey and the advancing Skanians.

"You did what you could," he said without taking his eyes off the mob before them.

The angry swarm was feet away and stars began to pop in Carey's sight, threatening to carry her away from this nightmare. Her head felt heavy and her knees were buckling.

Then there was a blinding light so intense that it burned through Carey's eyelids as she shut them against it. It surrounded them, wrapping them in warmth, erasing the screams and cries of the Arena. It blazed bright and hot for a moment longer, and then it was gone as suddenly as it had come.

Carey gasped painfully as her knees hit soft, green grass.

~Chapter Ten~

Ilvisar

arey stared at the lush green grass between her fingers. She was on her hands and knees, the pain still throbbing at her temples somewhat diminished by the shock she felt at this sudden change in their situation. Everything was quiet except for the heavy breathing of her companions and the occasional twitter of some bird.

"What the hell was that?"

Rupert's uncharacteristic cursing snapped her back to her senses.

They were in a large clearing edged by tall fir trees on all sides. The woods were bright, the foliage shimmering with every conceivable shade of green. The grass rippled as a breeze played about them, the dark emerald of each blade glimmering in the bright sunlight. Barely a cloud obscured the periwinkle blue.

Rupert knelt beside her, staring about in confusion with Kat still clutched to him. Kyna was gripping her brother's shirt sleeve so tightly that her knuckles were white, and Ilvisar bore an expression of mingled shock and delight. Versi and Daaren stood battle ready, as though they expected a fight. Their weapons glinted at their sides.

"Your swords," Carey cried as she shakily got to her feet.

Carey's words triggered a flurry of movement and exclamations as they found their weapons and possessions had been restored to them. Once she'd confirmed that the solid, reassuring weight upon her back was her sword, Carey fumbled desperately in her pocket for the box containing Ji's star. With a jolt of joy, she brought it slowly out of the folds of her coat. Hot tears pricked at the corners of her eyes as Carey gripped it tightly to her chest.

Until that moment she hadn't allowed herself to consider the loss of this invaluable gift. The dire circumstances of their capture and impending executions had required all of her energy and attention; she'd pushed the loss of Ji's star to the back of her mind. If she'd allowed herself to acknowledge it, she was sure the despair would've taken her over.

"Carey? Was that you? Did you bring us here?" Rupert asked.

Carey replaced the box. "That wasn't me." She was surprised to hear the calm in her voice. "I'm not a Wayfarer like Seramina or... or like Saar. I can't Send people anywhere. Besides, it didn't feel like being Sent, and that light..."

Rupert turned his gaze upon Ilvisar, who was standing silently by himself, looking about the place as though he'd never seen anything so wonderful in his life.

"Do you know what that was, then?"

"I am no *wizard*," he replied. "I thought that was your doing."

"Well, since it was clearly not us," Daaren said, indicating himself and Versi, "I'd say someone helped us back there. Either that, or we just all got incredibly lucky. I'm predisposed to think the former as I've never believed much in luck, but I wouldn't say we're completely out of danger. It would seem we're still in the same realm, though how far we are from the Arena is unclear. We need to move."

"No," Rupert snapped. "We can't. Not until I have Kat stable."

As he moved to lay her down upon the grass, Carey was stunned to see that Kat had paled even further, her skin standing in stark comparison to the dark hair that framed her features. Her chest hitched painfully with every breath, and when Carey held her hand, Kat's fingers were limp and cold.

"Rupert..."

"I know." He tenderly brushed Kat's hair away from her face, then laid a hand on her forehead. They all stood silent as Rupert muttered enchantments, his eyes closed and his brow furrowed in concentration. Kyna knelt beside them and let her hand rest upon Carey's forearm in a show of comfort, but Carey was shaking. She'd never seen Kat so weak and vulnerable. She'd almost lost her once before and it had been heartbreaking. Carey could not endure it again; she gave Kat's fingers a light squeeze.

"Please, Kat. Come on."

Rupert finally ceased his murmuring and sat back on his heels. His expression did nothing to ease Carey's worries. "She's bad. I need medicine, potions, none of which I have."

Carey felt her heart tighten.

Ilvisar knelt beside them. "I can help."

Rupert looked at him with a doubtful expression. "But you have no magic."

"No, I do not, but I have this." Ilvisar drew a small, elaborately wrought silver flute from under his shirt. It dangled from the end of a fine silver chain. "As you appear to have your weapons returned, so do I."

He played a short, lilting melody, far louder than would be expected from an instrument of such size.

It was no ordinary song; Carey felt it reverberate through her body, wrap itself around her heart. It was trying to tell her something but she couldn't understand what, its notes a foreign language. The others watched Ilvisar intently, expectantly, until the tune ended and its enchantment lifted.

There was a moment of silence, and when nothing happened, Rupert cocked an eyebrow.

"Was that it, then?" His voice dripped with sarcasm and impatience.

Kyna shot him a disapproving look, which quickly turned to surprise. "Oh!"

Whipping around to follow her line of sight, Carey saw eight fast-moving figures appear from among the trees. They were shifting blurs, ghosts of beings on horseback that faded in and out of view. As they cleared the tree line, they slowed to a halt, and Carey could finally make out eight pure-white steeds with armoured riders, their plating an odd obsidian metal inlaid with brilliant gold.

The riders surveyed the group, then, on spotting Ilvisar, one of them gave a sharp command and the riders approached, surrounding them. Unsure of their intentions, Carey moved closer to Rupert and Kat, shielding them against the towering riders.

"Ilvisar?" She raised her hand in anticipation of an attack, although the riders were yet to raise their weapons.

In one swift movement, they dismounted and fell to one knee, their heads bowed, one hand tucked behind their back and the other covering their heart.

"*La' in eweh,*" they said reverently. They remained on their knees, looking up at Ilvisar expectantly.

"Ilvisar? Care to explain?" Carey asked, not lowering her hand. "What are they saying?"

Ilvisar moved to the front of the group, his eyes brighter than Carey had seen them.

"*La' in eweh* means *Your Highness.*"

*

From the back of a silver stallion, Carey gazed up in awe at the glittering palace that loomed before them. They'd been riding at break-neck speed for the past hour, the others little more than a haze in her peripheral vision, and each riding behind one of Ilvisar's men. The steeds they rode wove in and out of the trees with impossible grace and agility, clearly more than just ordinary horses. Two of Ilvisar's guard had remained behind so Rupert and Kat could share a horse and Ilvisar had his own mount. Rupert had refused to allow any of the men to carry Kat, keeping her strapped carefully in front of him. He held the reins with one hand while he cradled Kat's head protectively against his chest with the other. She'd regained a modicum of colour in her cheeks but was still unconscious. One of the guards had produced a satchel of medicine and equipment, and after some convincing, Rupert had allowed them to treat Kat. She was far from healed but had been well enough that Rupert was unafraid to move her.

Ilvisar's palace was a glimmering spire rising from the heart of the lush green forest. It broke from the rock at its base as though it had grown from the forest floor like the great trees that surrounded it. Ivy crawled over its surface, white flowers dripping from the vines. Instead of the angular lines and sharp edges of the castles Carey was accustomed to, the palace towers curved and swirled upwards, with graceful archways reaching out from the main spire. Elegant carvings gave the illusion that the sparkling surfaces were moving before her eyes.

As they drew closer, Carey saw that crystalline dwellings had been sculpted into the massive fir trees surrounding the palace, looking like shimmering chrysalises. Balconies protruded from the iridescent hives, their railings resembling the twisting ivy that clung to the strange abodes. Long gravity-defying bridges stretched between the trees, appearing to have grown from the trees themselves. Glittering crystals crowned each door, and doorways and windows were curtained with brilliant fluttering silks.

Kyna sighed in wonder as she peered out from behind her guard, and Versi and Daaren regarded it all with quick assessing looks. Curious faces peered out at them, their features as strange and beautiful as their king's. The citizens rushed to offer a strange salute as their monarch passed, pressing a hand over their heart, then reaching up to their brow before offering their outstretched palm. There was much Carey wished to discuss with Ilvisar; they'd all been taken aback by the revelation of his true identity, but she couldn't blame him for hiding it from them. They were yet to tell him who they really were or about Seramina and their mission. And although he was the king of these lands and his knowledge could prove helpful, he was still, for the most part, an unknown quantity and would be afforded the right amount of caution and suspicion. He may not wield magic of his own, but that flute he'd used was clearly enchanted. Magic wasn't completely beyond his reach.

Their procession came to a wide crystalline bridge that led to the palace, its low balustrades dripping with ivy, the sweet smell of the white blossoms wafting about them. The bridge stretched across a deep crevasse that ended in a river far below. Long, thin rivulets gushed from the walls of the ravine, the breeze catching the water and carrying it away, creating a dreamlike haze as they rode across. Beyond the etched gateway of the palace, they found themselves in a circular courtyard that was more like a miniature version of the forest beyond the walls, with passages leading through the trees and other startlingly beautiful flora into the glass structure.

As soon as they'd come to a halt, a swarm of Ilvisar's people rushed from the palace. Ilvisar called out to them, waving away their attention and directing it to Rupert and Kat. If they were surprised by the return of their king, they didn't show it, nor did they seem perturbed by his strange company. They helped Rupert down from his mount as he held onto Kat before whisking them away. Carey and the others followed, Kyna holding tight to her arm as they walked down high-ceilinged hallways and up sweeping staircases. The entire palace was overrun by the white-flowered ivy and other plant life, but it didn't feel derelict – in fact, the whole place felt ethereal. The presence of nature gave the impression that the palace was a part of it rather than an intrusion upon the land on which it was built.

The halls and passages were a blur as they were ushered into a spacious bedroom. A spectacular four-posted bed stood on a dais, its frame carved from a pale wood; instead of curtains, ivy fell from its canopy. At the other end of the room there stood a crescent-shaped divan carved from the tangled roots of a massive tree. Cushions and blankets were draped over it, their bright colours standing in stark contrast to the brilliant white of the rest of the room. The wall opposite the doorway was made completely of movable glass panels, their white gossamer curtains pulled back to reveal a magnificent view of snow-capped mountains beyond the forest below.

Rupert laid Kat gently on the bed, and then began conversing with two of Ilvisar's people – obviously healers by the way they spoke and gestured towards Kat. Carey and Kyna stood back, watching anxiously as Ilvisar's healers produced unusual plants and sparkling liquids in stoppered crystal bottles for Rupert to inspect. He watched them closely as they worked. The three of them spoke in hushed tones, Rupert laying a hand on Kat's forehead and chest from time to time as he murmured complicated enchantments.

Versi and Daaren stood by the door, their hands on the hilts of their weapons. Despite everything, they seemed intent on fulfilling their duty as escorts. Beneath the exhaustion and anxiety, Carey was grateful for their watchful eyes. Ilvisar had been gracious, but this was not their castle and they needed to be wary.

Finally, as the sun began to dip behind the mountains, throwing brilliant shades of pink and orange onto the growing indigo of night, Rupert drew away from Kat's bed and wandered exhaustedly to where Carey sat with Kyna on the lounge. Carey had long disposed of her heavy travelling coat, the palace spring-like in its warmth and aroma. Rupert flopped down next to his sister, whose head was lolling sleepily. Gently, Rupert pulled her against his chest and Kyna snuggled into him, mumbling nonsensically. After a moment, he looked up at Carey with tired green eyes.

"How is she?" Carey asked quietly, passing him a piece of flatbread, which he accepted gratefully.

Food had been brought for them shortly after they'd arrived, and while Versi and Daaren had taken a moment from guarding them to eat, Rupert had refused to leave Kat's side for even a moment.

"She's healin'," he said through a mouthful of bread. "Their methods are different here – most of the potions an' remedies I don't recognise – but along with my magic, I think she'll make a full recovery."

Carey watched the two healers fuss over Kat. "How long do you think?"

"Before she wakes up? A few days – three perhaps. Until she can move again? Four days, five tops." Kyna stirred in his lap and he dropped his voice lower. "Perhaps if we'd been able ter do somethin' sooner…"

Carey knew what he was thinking; his summation had her stomach roiling and she clenched her eyes shut at the ramifications.

"He already has a head start." She groaned, her head in her hands.

Earlier, as Rupert had worked on Kat and Kyna had dozed fitfully on the lounge, Carey had taken herself away to a quiet corner. There, she'd attempted to find Saar. She knew without even trying that he would've already thought to block her, was already a step ahead, but she needed to try regardless. Clearing her mind and reaching out for him, she found herself snatching at nothing but darkness, a thick fog holding her back.

He wasn't about to let her find him; she'd only be able to if he let her.

Rupert swallowed the last of the bread. "Look. I know we don't know Ilvisar well enough, an' I know I have my own doubts, but honestly? We don't have much choice right now."

Carey lifted her head from her hands. "You're saying we should ask him for help?"

Rupert's lips were a tight thin line. "We don't know this realm, Carey. Saar could be anywhere, we have no way of trackin' him, and by th' time we work somethin' out, it could be too late. I'm sayin' we need to trust someone, an' given what Ilvisar has already told us, plus the fact that this is *his* country, I'd say he's our best bet."

"A moment ago, you were all suspicion and sarcasm, and now you want me to trust him?" Carey quirked an eyebrow and Rupert shrugged.

"Perhaps not trust him, but we could use his knowledge. If we'd had more time, I'd have been able ter use my skills, befriend some of those in the castle and find out what we needed, but we don't." His gaze drifted over to where Kat lay.

Rupert was right. They had nothing to go on and Saar already had the advantage on them. They needed to ask for help, and Ilvisar was their only hope.

"Let me go talk to him. Will you be all right here without me?"

Rupert jerked his head towards the door. "We've got those two out there. I'm sure we'll be fine."

Upon Carey's request, one of Ilvisar's healers summoned a palace guard to escort her to the king's chambers. Carey motioned for Daaren to follow – if Ilvisar decided to try anything, then perhaps having a trained Vuletian commander by her side wouldn't be such a bad idea.

Now they weren't hurrying to save Kat's life, Carey was able to appreciate the splendour of the palace. The passageways were lined with arched windows and doorways, vines and plant life dripping from every surface. Vibrant blooms scented the air, their petals and leaves a riot of colour. The floor was of polished wood, and dark whorls ran along the grain.

They passed several people, some in bright gold-trimmed attire that spoke of status and wealth, others in plain yet equally beautiful clothing that Carey realised must be the uniforms of the palace servants. And all of them had the same startling bright eyes and long, pointed ears. They reminded Carey of the fairy stories she'd heard as a child. Growing up in an Irish orphanage she'd heard all the tales, but she'd always imagined those pointed features to belong to small, pesky creatures. She wondered if this was where those stories had originated, as the Commoners' tales of witches had come from the Mystic Realm.

Rounding a corner, they came upon a towering doorway, its opening covered by a thick curtain of flowering ivy instead of a door. A small silver bell hung beside the archway and the guard lifted a hand to tap it. Somewhere deep inside, Carey perceived a musical ringing before a low calm voice called "Enter".

The guard motioned Carey and Daaren towards the doorway. Carey glanced at the Vuletian and nodded before parting the floral curtain and stepping through.

Ilvisar's quarters were magnificent. The high, arched ceiling glittered with the light of dozens of candles on dazzling chandeliers that, much like the divan in Kat's room, had been crafted from the knotted roots of a tree. The wood was polished and carved, delicate swirled etchings covering the dark surfaces. The room was large and round, walled by twisting crystal archways supporting the roof. Gossamer pearl curtains were pulled back from the arches, creating an open-sided pavilion. Delicate wooden furniture was scattered around the room – a low, carved bench looked out towards the snow-capped mountains; a rack of weaponry glinted in the candlelight; and a small table held a platter of food and drink. The king was standing on a balcony, gazing out over the forest below.

Ilvisar wore a long, sleeveless tunic unbuttoned at the front to reveal his bare chest. The flowing crimson fabric was delicately embroidered with gold stitching that mimicked the ivy curling about the palace. Beneath he wore a pair of champagne-coloured silk pants, wide legged and equally as adorned with golden thread. His feet were bare and Carey wondered if this was a normal state of dress for a monarch in this realm.

Ilvisar turned at their approach, and Carey and Daaren gave short bows. He raised an eyebrow.

"Is that a form of greeting where you are from?"

"It's the way one greets a member of royalty in our realm, yes. How is it done here?"

Ilvisar lifted a hand to his chest, just over his heart, then to his brow before extending his arm, palm facing upwards in offering. It was the same gesture his subjects had made when Carey's party had arrived.

"It is an offering of wisdom," he said, dropping his hand. "A king's people wish only for a ruler with the good judgement to lead them wisely, so they offer wisdom upon greeting them."

"Well," Carey said, copying the motion. "I cannot argue with you there."

Ilvisar gave Carey a small smile before motioning for her and Daaren to join him on the balcony. Daaren hung back, as though sensing that this was a conversation best observed, and Carey joined Ilvisar at the railing. They were high above the canopy of the towering trees below, though not so far away that Carey couldn't make out the twinkling lights of the city clinging to the tree trunks.

"How is your friend?" Ilvisar asked.

"Kat is recovering, thanks to your help," she said. "Without your medicines and your healers, Rupert would've had a much harder time. He brought the basics with him, but I feel Kat's injuries were far beyond anything he'd expected. He said she should be recovered enough to travel within five days."

Ilvisar gave a nod of acknowledgement. "I must thank you for what you did back at the Arena. I must say, I'm afraid I underestimated your strength."

"That tends to happen," Carey said with a wry smile. "I have a feeling those Eternals never expected anyone to stand up to them. Considering their usual targets were children."

She watched for Ilvisar's reaction. She wanted to be sure that what he'd said to them in the dungeons was true, that he hadn't just said all of that to gain their trust. The noticeable pain that flickered across his features, however, could not be manufactured.

"What you said about your daughter," Carey said cautiously. "There's a reason why we're in your realm, why we came through that gateway."

She waited for Ilvisar's attention to return to her before continuing. "A man – a very powerful and dangerous man – took a friend of ours. Her name is Seramina, and from all you said last night, it would seem that she, too, is an Innocent."

The King's eyes snapped up to meet hers, his gaze blazing. "What did you say?"

"Our friend, Seramina, is an Innocent, like your daughter," Carey repeated, and she saw the panic and regret flare in his eyes.

"What are his plans for her?" he asked, moving closer to Carey, a ripple of fear punctuating his words.

Carey shook her head. "We don't know, but he also stole a powerful magical object, and we can only guess that his intentions are of the dominating sort."

There was no reason to confide everything about Malevolence's magic to Ilvisar. Carey knew they could trust him to help them find Saar and Seramina – this was his country after all – but to tell him everything was unnecessary. Better to keep it vague.

"Do you think he has similar aspirations as the Eternals of Truav Skain?" Ilvisar said, his brows knitting in thought.

"Honestly, he could be planning anything," Carey answered. "What we need is a guide, someone who knows this realm well. We also don't know in which direction he went, but perhaps someone has heard or seen something."

Carey gazed at Ilvisar hopefully; his face transformed, resolution smoothing the sadness from his features.

"I will send out riders for you – it is the very least I can do," he said, and he moved to one of the columns nearby to tap a bell similar to that at the door.

The ringing of bells echoed around the chamber. The guard who'd escorted Carey and Daaren to the king's chamber marched in, his hand on his weapon; he gave the salute Ilvisar had shown Carey. Ilvisar relayed a set of orders to the man before sending him away. Daaren watched the exchange with interest.

Once the guard had disappeared, Ilvisar turned back to Carey. "It is done."

Carey was about to thank him, but he cut her off. "Before you leave, though, I must ask you something. You hunt this man like a king's mercenary, dress like a lady of the court, and speak with the authority of someone much older. May I ask your title?"

Carey gave Daaren a quick glance, her hand fastening around the small box in her pocket before lifting her chin confidently. Now was not the time for weakness. He'd guessed at her lineage and she wasn't about to lie about it.

"My name is Carey Lee, Duchess of the Mystic Realm, Princess, and Seeker of the Order of the Rose."

Ilvisar lifted a hand to his heart then his brow, before extending his palm towards her.

"Then welcome, Princess Carey, to Suvheil, land of the Aoifein."

~Chapter Eleven~

A New World

Carey held the magic at her fingertips, the buzz of such power electrifying every inch of her body.

"Are you sure about this?" Rupert asked.

He was standing at the head of Kat's bed, Kyna by his side. Versi and Daaren stood with them, looking down to the end of the bed where Carey stood.

"Saar has hidden himself, but that doesn't mean he can't find us using his abilities," Carey said. "I've done this before, to hide Seramina. I can do it again. It's sort of how I protected you all in the Arena, except this way, I don't have to actively protect you all of the time. I take a small part of the magic I control and instil it in each of you."

Briefly she wondered if *control* was the right word for what she could do with this magic, but she pushed that thought away. Now was not the time to be doubting her abilities. It was just as she'd done before, except this time she didn't have Kat's help. Last time, Kat had used a spell to extract the essence that had protected Seramina. It'd been uncomfortable, feeling the magic forced from her body. She wasn't keen on repeating that process. That said, Carey hadn't had the confidence she had now, or the strength. No doubt this time would be different.

The magic was already at her fingertips, eager to be used. She'd concentrate on each of them. Envision its protection over them from Saar. Feed into them the magic that flowed through her, giving them just enough to keep them hidden.

Carey took a deep breath as she withdrew a small part of her magic.

Yes, this was going to work.

Carey looked at each of them, and her companions nodded in return. She closed her eyes, doing just as she'd planned. She concentrated on Kat, Rupert, and Kyna. She captured Versi and Daaren in her mind's eye. She saw them protected against Saar finding them, blocking them from view. Carey lifted a hand and, as she opened her eyes, saw ribbons of gold magic unfurling from her upturned palm. They snaked through the air, reaching for the others, who stood watching in awe. Carey directed a ribbon towards each of them, sweat beading on her forehead at the effort. The others gasped in shock as the magic made contact. It sunk into their skin, threading through their bodies as it wove its enchantment. Kyna giggled nervously at the tingling sensation Carey knew she must be experiencing. Kat lay perfectly still, too unaware to show any effects. When Carey felt she had done enough to protect them, she closed her fist on the flow of magic and the ribbons cut free, the magic receding inside her once more.

She sunk to the carpeted floor, steadying her beating heart and willing the pain in her temples to go away. Carey couldn't understand why the magic kept hurting her when it never had before. But she'd done what she'd set out to do – they were protected against Saar finding them. She felt sure of it. Some intuition deeply entwined with her power told her so. The thought gave her comfort. Perhaps they wouldn't be two steps behind this time.

Someone gripped her elbow and pulled her to her feet.

"Come. Take a rest. I have it from here."

It was Rupert. He steered her to the divan and Kyna brought her some water. Taking it gratefully, Carey stared out to the mountains, their snow-capped tips bright in the moonlight. Somewhere out there was their quarry. As much as she wanted to take off into the night in pursuit, Carey was thankful for their current situation. Kat would heal. They would rest. And as soon as Ilvisar's scouts found anything, they would ride. Carey smiled to herself as Rupert returned to Kat's side and the guards to their posts. This time she was not alone. This time she was stronger.

This time, she was prepared.

*

As Kat continued to heal – her ministrations given by Rupert and nobody else – Carey and Kyna became more acquainted with the country of Suvheil and its king. Versi and Daaren took turns watching the duo, the other keeping a vigilant watch over Kat and her healer. On the second day, they came upon a library – a dazzlingly bright room, unlike the dusty dark caverns of their own realm – and they set to reading and memorising the maps on the walls and deciphering tomes. Much as with the spoken language, no sooner had Carey or Kyna opened a book than the strange swirling symbols that made up Ilvisar's language rearranged themselves into something they could understand. It seemed that the books wanted to be read. Carey managed to pull from the towering shelves a thick book simply labelled *Suvheil*, which appeared to be a history of the Aoifein. The pages were lined with silver, and intricate illustrations wove around the words as they shifted before her eyes. It appeared that, even though the people of this realm did not wield magic the way Carey did, magic seemed to manifest in subtler ways here.

"Look at this, Kyna," Carey said as she turned a page of the enormous book.

"Oh," Kyna said. There was an illustration of the gateway they'd used to come here. Surrounding it was a swarm of people. Ilvisar's people. Their pointed ears and bright eyes were expertly painted onto the brittle page, visible under black helmets. Some rode white horses while others were on foot, weapons in hand. The unmistakable spark of magic littered the air, colliding with riders and soldiers alike. Two symbols marked the warriors' armour – silver with two crossed swords of red, and black with a golden star. They were fighting before the stone archway, blood staining the ground, the chaos of the fight evident in the minute details.

"A war…" Kyna said. She read out the words curling down the side of the page.

A danger and a menace, those of theurgy were forced back from the land, back to the realm from which they had come. Though the great King Ralheir succeeded in turning the theurgists upon themselves and sealed their entrance, their remnants remain – children of Suvheil's people created with cruel intent and dark purpose. They were cast aside, their propensity to display the attributes of a theurgist excluding them from the life of a true Aoifein.

Carey frowned. If she was understanding this correctly, the king had sealed the gateway to his realm and any born of a witch or wizard that were left behind were made outcasts. She gritted her teeth. Was it still like this?

Kyna furrowed her brow. "Wait. Does that mean they hate witches and wizards?"

Carey read more of the passage, but it merely hinted at the other conquests of the time against neighbouring countries and people. It had to have happened a long time ago as not even Lady Marksis or Lord Carron had been able to say when the gateway to this realm had been opened last.

"Once upon a time by the looks of it, Kyna," Carey murmured, turning the page.

The door behind them creaked open.

Ilvisar strode in, with Versi lingering by the door, her hand on her weapon.

"Princess." Ilvisar acknowledged her with the salute he'd given her the night before.

Carey shook her head. "Please. Just Carey."

Ilvisar smiled and gave a small nod. "*Carey.* I see you have found the palace library. Has anything piqued your interest?"

He looked at the book she and Kyna were reading. "History. Were you wanting to know more about my country? You could have just asked me – these old books can be rather dull and long-winded."

Carey ran a finger over the words as they shifted for her to read. "You said that there weren't many people with magic in this world. Why is that?"

She wanted to see what he would say. Despite his promises to help them, Carey remained cautious about the non-magical king who'd fathered a magical child.

Ilvisar considered her for a long moment before answering, his words slow and deliberate.

He gestured at the book. "You wish to know whether the sins of the past have followed through to the present?"

Carey held his gaze and waited for him to answer. Ilvisar released a long sigh.

"The gate you came through – my ancestors were convinced that the evils of the world were caused by it and anyone who had used it. People like you –

practitioners, with your stunted ears and strange ways."

Kyna lifted a hand to her ears, pouting.

"For a few years, your kind came and went, trading with our people, showing them magic. Many objects we have today carry the magic from that time – our bells, my flute – but as with any, there were some who caused trouble. So, when the trouble became too much, my ancestors drove your kind back through the gate and, using their own magic against them, managed to close it. However, there were those among us who had taken practitioners as partners, and their families were left behind."

His face hardened as he spoke, anger clear in every syllable. "Instead of fostering these children, caring for them, my ancestors cast them aside, making them outsiders. Generations passed and slowly we worked to rebuild a country united, but there are, I'm sorry to say, still those, magical and not, who seek to keep those they consider enemies from rising above them."

Ilvisar took a deep breath, straightened his back and clasped his hands behind him. "I'm proud of my country, Carey, as I imagine you are of yours. But we all have our problems. I like to think that I do not run from mine. I want only the best for my people, magical and non-magical. Besides, my daughter would never have forgiven me if I had done otherwise."

Carey smoothed the page of the ancient book. Although the actions of his forbears had been callous and unforgiveable, it truly seemed that Ilvisar sought to rectify those wrongs.

"You say you still have troubles?" she asked.

Tension faded from Ilvisar's shoulders. "When you leave, you must take care. You will attract attention and there are some who will not take kindly to you. Most of my people are hardworking and generous, kind and forgiving, but–"

"There are always the few who are not," Carey said. "Thank you. Have you heard anything about our man?"

Ilvisar shook his head as he moved to a nearby table and rummaged through the papers piled on it. "Nothing as of yet, I'm afraid. But it has only been a short while since they rode out. My legionnaires are skilled in tracking and gathering information. They will find him, or news of him."

He freed a scroll from the pile and unrolled it in front of them. It was a map, newer than those hanging on the walls, its edges smooth and unweathered. The palace was evident near the top left, surrounded by forests. The border between Suvheil and Truav Skain cut off the upper right corner. Mountain ranges wound through the entire map, villages dotted amongst them, many next to lakes and rivers. It showed a difficult landscape to traverse, especially for the uninitiated.

"This is the most recent plotting of our lands," Ilvisar said, holding down one side. "I am happy for some of my legion to escort you when you leave, but I find it's always best to take a map, just in case."

Kyna pulled it towards her, her eyes raking over every detail. "I'll take this, Carey. Rupert taught me how ter read a map when I was little. Seemed useless at th' time given we were in an *underground city*, but it looks like those skills are finally goin' ter come in handy."

Ilvisar's expression brightened at her enthusiasm, a smile tugging at his lips.

"Well, shall I leave you to it then, Kyna?" Carey said.

When she didn't answer, Carey gave a wry chuckle and turned to Versi. "Do you mind staying with her?"

Versi gave her a sharp nod before moving to sit next to the girl. They made an odd pair amidst the towering crystal shelves, yet as Carey turned to leave, Kyna reached over to show Versi something on the map, pointing and explaining in excited tones.

"I was surprised when you said you were hunting this man. I would never have considered something like that what with your young friend here," Ilvisar said as he closed the door behind them.

"It wasn't my intention to bring her along, trust me," Carey answered. "But Rupert is her brother and sole remaining family member, so she was reluctant to let him go without her. Besides, Seramina is her best friend. We mightn't have planned for her to come along, but she's here now."

Ilvisar led her back towards Kat's room. "She reminds me greatly of Terienn – curious and bold. I watched her in the Arena. She listened to you, stood her ground. She was scared, of course, but I have seen stronger men break in lesser situations. My daughter was the same. When they came for her, she didn't shed even a single tear."

To have seen his daughter suffer must have been torturous, but to have watched as a horde of onlookers called for her blood… Carey shuddered. As they rounded the corner near Kat's quarters, Ilvisar came to a halt.

"I want you to know that you are welcome here, Carey, despite what you read or the suspicions you might have. I know you do not trust me fully, and I understand – a strange land, a strange palace – but you saved my life, intentionally or not. If you had not been in that cell with me, I would have perished that day and my people would be without a king. A life debt is not something I take lightly. So please, all I can ask is for you to trust that I will do everything in my power to help you."

They stood for a moment, Carey weighing his words as she thought back on Rupert's suspicions of the day before. However, the sincerity in Ilvisar's voice was palpable, and there was an almost pleading look in his eyes. She bowed her head, the way she would to a monarch of her realm.

"You have our trust."

A lightness spread over his features and he offered his customary gesture, extending his hand out towards her with a smile. "Then I shall leave you. Should I hear anything regarding your quarry, I shall let you know immediately. In the meantime, I shall have horses and supplies arranged for when you depart."

With a word of thanks from Carey, Ilvisar turned and strode back the way they'd come, leaving Carey to return to Kat's room to await news that might bear them forth.

*

Unwilling to leave Kat and Rupert, Kyna slept on the lounge under a heavy fur blanket. When Rupert and the healers weren't attending to Kat, Carey snuggled up on the opposite side of the bed, watching Kat's chest rise and fall, taking comfort from the slow return of colour to Kat's face. When she did sleep, she dreamt of bright flashes of light and the rustling of feathers. There was also the intense feeling of being watched, which she couldn't shake, even after waking. Rupert managed a few hours here and there, though the pronounced shadows beneath his bright eyes told her he wasn't sleeping well either. Versi and Daaren took turns watching the room, one or the other camping just within the doorway, weapons within reach. Carey had tried to convince them to take one of the rooms Ilvisar had set aside for them, but they refused. Their commitment to their captain's orders was unwavering and commendable, but it didn't stop Carey from feeling guilty. It wasn't as though she couldn't look out for herself. But she knew better than to press them – the Vuletians were proud of their status as warriors. She didn't want to insult them – any further, at least. Carey still hadn't managed to talk to Versi about Marjen, but she knew it would be best to do so before they left Ilvisar's palace. Carey needed to know where Versi's head was at before they set out.

Her chance came on the morning of their third day in the palace.

Versi was heading for the training grounds, and Carey, seizing the opportunity, hurriedly picked up her sword and called for her to wait. She ran lightly past Rupert and Kyna who were asleep on the couch, Rupert's now bright purple hair peeking out from beneath the blankets, and joined Versi at the door.

"Do you mind if I join you? Sitting around is really starting to get to me."

For a moment Versi just stared at her, then she gave Carey a short nod.

Carey gulped back a wave of uncomfortable nerves before following her.

A guard escorted them onto a balcony, down a twisting set of steps and out to a wide stretch of clear ground edged on three sides by towering trees. A few guards were already training with long silver spears with lethal tips that gleamed and flashed as they fought. Others were throwing daggers at pock-marked poles, the thin blades burying themselves deep into the wood with a *thunk* as they hit.

Heads turned at Carey and Versi's arrival and the guards paused to watch the two women cross to an open patch of grass and unsheathe their weapons. Versi's sword was similar to Carey's, long and curved, and she swung it across her body a few times, warming her muscles. Carey, acutely aware of everyone watching, rolled her shoulders before raising her weapon.

She hadn't had the chance to fight Versi yet, but she remembered Marjen saying she was a formidable warrior. Given her experience with other Vuletians, Carey was not about to underestimate her.

Versi faced Carey, looked at her calmly for a moment as though assessing her, before raising her own sword.

"Don't hold back," Carey said, adjusting her grip on her hilt.

Versi narrowed her eyes. "I wasn't aware that I should."

Then she struck.

Her first blow was staggering, the vibrations shuddering through Carey's arms as she blocked it, their Vuletian blades sparking blue on contact. She danced backwards as Versi swung again, this time her sword glancing off Carey's instead of it taking the full brunt. Versi was quick and nimble. She didn't stumble as Carey attacked, her feet moving with a grace that reminded Carey of Seramina. The two women worked their way around the clearing, their weapons flashing and sparking. The guards had stopped training completely in order to watch and she heard low murmurs as they passed, no doubt brought on by the magic swirling about their weaponry. Versi's features remained calm but focused, the slightest crease in her brow the only sign of exertion. Carey frowned in concentration, trying to keep up with her opponent's strikes. She dived out of the way, rolling on the grass, sword still in hand, as Versi's blade swung low at her head. Darting to her feet, she moved out of range, trying to give herself a moment to breathe. Versi took her lead and drew back a little, adjusting her footing and holding her sword at the ready, waiting for Carey to strike.

"Did Marjen teach you how to fight?" Carey asked, taking the chance to broach the subject.

Versi frowned. "You wish to speak as you fight?"

Carey shrugged. "I find it's a good way to talk things through."

"You have something you wish to *talk through?*"

Carey stepped forwards, thrusting her sword at Versi's chest. Her opponent blocked her. "Yes. We need to talk about what happened with Marjen."

Versi showed no reaction, simply slashed at Carey.

"Why do we need to talk about Marjen?"

Carey spun away, moving out of Versi's reach before attacking with a series of quick, glancing blows. "Because I believe you blame me for his death."

Versi missed a step and Carey noticed a flicker of emotion in her eyes. "Blame you?"

Carey took advantage of Versi's moment of hesitation and knocked the tip of Versi's sword away before drawing her own up through the space between them. Versi recovered almost instantly and skipped out of the way.

"Yes," Carey said, panting as she drove Versi back. "Marjen is dead and you blame me."

Versi stopped Carey's blade inches from her face and shoved back with more force than she'd used so far. Her passive expression was breaking, a hint of something like fury peeking through.

"You promised to watch out for him. You promised me," she said striking hard, making Carey work defensively.

A group of onlookers scattered as Carey and Versi carved a path towards them. Suddenly, this didn't feel like training anymore.

"I know I promised," Carey said, ducking as Versi lunged at her, then turning to face Versi as she stumbled past. "But you have to understand. He wouldn't let me fight alongside him. He made me stand back. And I tried to get to him, but–"

Versi whipped around and charged at Carey, determination etched in her face. Her sword came down heavy and Carey felt the force of it shudder through her body.

"You. Promised," Versi spat.

With all the strength she could muster, Carey pushed her off and swung her sword around, level with Versi's throat, a move that Versi knocked aside easily.

"You're not listening!" Carey's voice rose as she tried to get her footing, struggling against Versi's furious attacks.

Her foot caught on a patch of uneven ground and Carey fell hard, her sword flying from her hand. Versi levelled her sword tip at Carey's throat. They stared at each other for a tense moment, neither of them moving, chests heaving.

"Marjen was the best man I ever knew," Versi said. "My best friend. You promised to watch out for him. You failed. There is nothing more to say about it."

Anger was etched across her face, but there was a deep anguish in her voice that tore at Carey. Marjen had said that Versi didn't often see things the way everyone else did, but, despite her differences, she was incredibly loyal. A true friend.

Suddenly, Carey saw what she was doing. She was trying to make excuses for what had happened, trying to make Versi see it from her point of view, when she should've been trying to see it from Versi's. After all, it was hers that mattered the most here.

Carey took a deep breath before slowly getting up. Versi did not lower her weapon despite Carey being disarmed.

"I'm sorry."

It was all Carey could offer. No more convincing, no more fighting. She waited until Versi lowered her sword, her gaze searching Carey's face for insincerity. She wouldn't find any – Carey had never been more sincere in her life. Marjen's death had changed her, broken her then remade her, and Carey would no sooner forget him than join Saar.

Finally, Versi sheathed her sword before holding out her hand. Not willing to give Versi any reason to doubt her, Carey raised her own and they clasped forearms.

"Come," Versi said with a small nod before releasing her arm. "We mustn't stay away from the others too long."

And without even acknowledging the gathering still staring at them, Versi turned on her heel for the palace, and Carey felt they had finally reached an accord.

*

It was uncomfortably still and quiet.

Carey swore.

The windows were shut against the cool night air – "To keep out the winter chill", Ilvisar had said, though Carey could barely call this winter. If flowers could still hold their bloom, it wasn't winter. With no windows open, the curtains hung motionless, and the flames of the candles wavered lazily without a draught to make them dance.

She tossed where she lay across the bed from Kat, who still hadn't woken up. Everyone else, save for Daaren standing outside their door, was asleep. Rupert had declared Kat fully on the mend earlier that day, and so there were no healers bustling about her bedside, which made for an eerily calm room. Kyna was curled on the lounge once more, the nearby table covered with maps, ink, and pens. Her brother lay on a rug at her feet, purple hair lost among the pile of cushions he'd pilfered from the divan. And Versi slept by the door, sword held to her chest like a child with a favourite teddy bear. A very deadly teddy bear.

All had fallen asleep hours ago, yet for some reason Carey lay wide awake, her mind racing.

Saar was never far from her thoughts, and tonight he dominated them with a vengeance. Her heart was racing at the notion that every day they remained in the palace meant he got farther away. Ilvisar's people were yet to find any sign of him and she was starting to fear they wouldn't. He was, after all, highly skilled at concealing himself. At least they were hidden from him too – one advantage they had taken from him.

Carey shivered in the near dark. She wished Kat was awake so she could talk strategy.

She wished Ji was there to calm her.

Neither of these thoughts eased her mind and Carey turned over and punched her pillow in frustration.

"Well, this is new."

Carey whipped her head around to find Kat watching her with bleary eyes. Her voice was croaky from disuse, but she was awake.

"Kat!"

Carey hadn't meant to say it so loudly. Daaren charged into the room, weapon drawn. Versi was on one knee, wide awake and alert. Kyna sat bolt upright as though Carey had shouted in her face, and Rupert lifted a mussed head, his hair flopping in his eyes as he gave a confused, "What now?"

The moment he realised Kat was awake, however, the sleep disappeared from his face. He stumbled to his feet, tripping over pillows in his haste.

Kat gave him a puzzled look. "That's certainly not the reaction I was expecting," she croaked.

"How are you feeling?" Carey asked, shuffling to Kat's side, elation wiping the frustration from her mind.

Kat turned to her. "Feeling?"

"Yes," Carey replied. "*Feeling.* You… well, you took a pretty bad hit."

Kat was silent for a moment, her eyes going distant. "The clearing… wait, that really happened?"

She looked around, taking in the strange new surrounds. The realisation that she wasn't in their own castle had her struggling to sit upright, pushing away Rupert's insistence that she should take it easy.

"Where are we? What happened?"

Sitting on the edge of the bed, Rupert asked, "What do yer remember?"

"I remember the clearing, the gateway. I got hit." She clutched at her side, glancing down as though expecting to see the injury. "Then… I'm not sure. Somewhere dark." She scrunched up her nose. "Pain."

Kat's gaze found Versi and Daaren.

"Where's the captain and Commander Ueran?" she asked.

Daaren gave Kat a short bow before answering. "They were unable to follow us through the gateway. The captain tasked us with your protection."

Kat turned to Carey. "What happened?"

Carey recounted their time under the Arena and everything that had happened thereafter. Her eyes grew round as Carey spoke of her defeat of the Eternals, but then grew confused when it came to their escape.

"But, you're not a Wayfarer," she said

"Not that I know of," Carey said, wishing she knew how they'd managed that small miracle.

"And this place is?"

"Ilvisar's palace," Kyna said from her spot at the end of the bed. "He has the most fantastic library."

"The other prisoner? This is his palace?" A mix of awe and suspicion drifted across Kat's features.

"He is the reigning monarch of these lands," Carey said. "We can trust him."

Kat held her gaze for a long moment. "If you say we can…"

"How are you feelin'?" Rupert asked, looking his patient over. "Any pain? Aches?"

Kat moved her hands over her upper body. "I feel a little stiff, but otherwise not too bad." She smiled wryly up at Rupert. "Well, aren't I glad you decided to tag along."

Rupert relaxed, relieved to know Kat had healed as he'd hoped. "Lucky, more like."

"Does this mean she'll be right to travel?" Carey said.

Rupert squinted, considering. "Give it one more day. Better ter be safe than sorry. Besides, even if we could start movin', Ilvisar is yet ter find out anymore on where Saar might've got to."

Kyna gave a loud yawn.

"All righ'," Rupert said, moving over to her sister. "Back ter bed. Kat, you'll be all right now?"

"I'll stay up," Carey said. "It's not like I was asleep anyway." She turned to Kat. "Are you hungry?"

"Absolutely starving," she said with a grin.

Daaren moved back to his post as Versi made to lay back down and Rupert and Kyna returned to their makeshift beds. Carey called for some food, and for the rest of the night until the early light of the morning, they sat on the bed and ate, talking in low voices of Saar and this realm and of plans. And for the first time in days, Carey was content.

~Chapter Twelve~

Into the Wild

A series of knocks jerked Carey awake. She'd finally fallen asleep just before sunrise, leaving Kat to finish off their midnight feast on her own, the remnants of which were still scattered about the bed covers. Kat was now padding quietly over to the door where Versi was getting to her feet, hand on her weapon. She opened the door a crack ahead of Kat, and Carey could hear her speaking in a quiet voice to whoever stood on the other side. There was a low, urgent answer, followed by the rumble of Daaren's voice, then Versi opened the door wider. Ilvisar stepped in, his face alight with triumph. He stopped short, though, when he saw Kat standing before him. She crossed her arms and regarded him shrewdly, taking in his silver-embroidered green tunic and his long, braided hair.

Carey rolled off the bed, blinking the sleep from her eyes, and hurried over to where they stood, her exhaustion fading at the sight of the king.

"Kat, this is Ilvisar, King of Suvheil," Carey said, gesturing in introduction. "Ilvisar, this is Katrina Lawrence."

Ilvisar gave Kat his usual sign of respect followed by a bow. "Carey tells me bowing is customary in your realm. I am elated to see you have recovered so well. Your friend is quite the healer."

Kat returned the greeting with a slight bow of her head. "And I hear you're the one to thank for these accommodations."

Ilvisar gave her a warm smile. "It is the absolute very least I could do. However, I came with news."

He strode to the divan where Rupert and Kyna were sitting. Kat looked Ilvisar up and down before giving Carey an appreciative glance, one sharp eyebrow raised. Carey shook her head, trying not to laugh as she took a seat at Rupert's side.

"I have news of your quarry," Ilvisar said.

Carey's laughter died in her chest. The tension in the room drew tight like the string of a bow; silence fell over them, and Carey waited with bated breath for Ilvisar to continue.

"I've been told that there have been others coming through the gateway, and they are heading for the mountains to the south," he said. "Once my warriors discovered the intruders, it was not hard to follow them. They are carving a wide path of destruction through my country, wreaking havoc as they go."

Carey felt a stab of guilt. "Ilvisar, I'm so sorry."

The king's face hardened. "If you manage to catch this man you seek, what will this mean for my people?"

Kat strode to Carey's side and held her chin high with confidence. "We'll catch him, and once we do, we can close that gateway. This man has supporters, but ours are more. If you can, station some of your people at the gateway and force them back. That will help. Those who are coming through are vicious and power-hungry, just like the man we seek. Don't take any chances with them. If your people face them, they must show no mercy."

Carey stared at Kat. *No mercy?* But Ilvisar didn't seem to take issue with this, and clearly, neither did Kat.

"When will you be departing?" Ilvisar said

"As soon as possible," Carey said. "Rupert, is that all right with you?"

"Yes, that should be fine," Rupert said.

"In that case, I will provide you with two of my own people." Ilvisar turned his attention to Daaren and Versi. "They will be able to show you the way, provide some extra protection, though I know you are more than capable. They will take you as far as you need to go."

Carey wasn't sure how far that would be but she was immensely grateful, nonetheless. "Thank you, Ilvisar. We'll get ready and meet you and your guards in the main courtyard."

The king gave Carey a small bow and left. There was a flurry of movement as the others started grabbing clothes and boots, weapons and bags. Before

Carey could say anything about Kat's advice to the king, Kat was behind a divider, stripping off her bed clothes. In hardly any time at all, the six of them were gathered in the courtyard, coats on and weapons readied.

Two tall, armoured men stood before them, along with eight white steeds. The horses reminded Carey of Firefly and she wished the pegasus was with her. Long rapiers hung at the soldiers' waists, and an assortment of lethal, thin-bladed knives were sheathed at their wrists. Long silver feathers emerged from the pointed tips of their gleaming helmets, which extended to cover the bridge of the nose. As the group drew close, the soldiers removed their helmets, revealing smooth mahogany-brown skin and brilliant violet eyes. Their hair was knotted into a thousand tiny braids woven with silver thread and gathered at the base of their necks. Their long, pointed ears were edged with intricate silver cuffs, making them look fierce in their beauty. Carey caught Kat staring and her friend leant over to her.

"If we weren't witches..." she said in awe, and Carey gave her a playful nudge with her elbow.

There was something about the people here – an easy elegance and beauty. It was ethereal, unlike anything Carey had encountered. But Kat had not yet met that one person whose destiny entwined with hers, so the appeal was easy to see. Carey, on the other hand, couldn't compare. The only one who brought light to her world was an entire world away, but his voice, his eyes, his touch were all memories that never waned. She couldn't appreciate the people here as Kat did, not when she ached for another.

Ilvisar appeared and the two guards dropped to one knee, hands performing their salute to their king, offering him wisdom.

"*Bahsh*, Hillfren, Dolvein," he said, and the two guards stood straight and alert. "This is the princess and her companions. You know what is expected of you. *Safeh, Suvheil fa'hi.*"

"*Suvheil fa'hi!*" the soldiers replied in unison.

Ilvisar faced the group of Seekers and Vuletians. "You have my best wishes and eternal gratitude. Beware, however – once you leave the confines of the palace and its city, my guards will be the only distinguishing quality between you and the marauders terrorising my people. Stay close to them.

The mountains to the south are the domain of Magorian – a warlord who is ruthless and powerful. If your intruders are going anywhere, I would guess that they are travelling to his lands. I will try my best to stem the flow coming through the gateway, but for now, you go with only my word."

Carey held her hand to her chest before lifting it to her brow, then extending it out. "And we'll be forever grateful for the help you've given us."

One of the guards handed Carey the reins to her mount and she pulled herself up effortlessly. The others took their places, Rupert helping Kyna onto her horse, and with a final nod towards Ilvisar, they rode from the palace, flanked by their escorts. They passed over the ivy-strewn bridge, rode through the tree-city beyond, and then headed towards the mountains. Despite the flowering woods and general green of the land, there was a chill in the air, and Carey wondered if this was winter for them or if their seasons were something completely different here.

The guard who led their procession, Hillfren, was a stoic, straight-backed soldier with shrewd eyes. A four-pointed blue star adorned the right side of his chest-plate, and when Kyna, ever curious, asked him about it, he told her it was the sigil of his *Ozeuli*, the group of soldiers he belonged to within the legion. Dolvein was wary at first, but after continued badgering from the youngest of the group, his expression softened and a smile twitched at the corners of his mouth. He, too, wore the star, though it seemed Hillfren was the more senior of the two.

As they travelled through lush farmland with bright-red crops, Daaren took the time to familiarise himself with the new guards, asking them about everything from strategy to weaponry. Dolvein rode near Versi, and when he did eventually speak to her, she replied with short, closed answers, and Carey hoped he wouldn't take it personally. Kat rode alongside Rupert, just behind Carey, their playful conversation making her smile. Seeing her best friend well and happy did more for Carey's confidence than anything else, and it helped quell the anxiety and helplessness of the past few days.

They passed the occasional village, the houses just as colourful as those around the palace, though firmly set upon the ground. The presence of Hillfren and Dolvein seemed to dispel any suspicion towards them, but the party kept their hoods up. Children ran alongside them, laughing and calling out in Ethellen and trying to catch a peek of their faces. Rupert allowed one little girl a flash of his now forest-green hair, and Kyna laughed at the stunned look it rendered.

Just past noon, as they travelled through a sparse woods, the sound of frenzied running, cries of pain, and cracking branches reached their ears. Hillfren and Dolvein, along with Versi and Daaren, drew their weapons, encircling the group. Carey instantly brought the thrum of magic to her fingertips, Kat following suit at her side.

There came a child's cry.

"Oh no," Rupert murmured.

A man appeared, dragging a struggling woman by one arm. A small boy clung to the woman's hand, tripping on branches and brambles as he tried to keep up.

"*Shadun*, Jinalla!" the man said, before stopping short at the sight of the travellers.

The woman stared wide-eyed and panicked, panting hard as her gaze ran along the weapons pointed at them. The boy gave a terrified whimper and buried himself in the woman's skirts.

"What is the meaning of this?" Hillfren asked.

The man dropped to his knees. "*Suvheil fa'hi!* My lords! We did not see you."

"That is not what I asked," Hillfren said, his weapon still raised. "Why are you here and what are you doing?"

The woman spoke up in a thin, shrill voice. "Our village was attacked, my lords. Strangers, theurgists – they destroyed everything."

Her voice cracked on the last word, and Carey felt her blood turn to ice in her veins.

"And who are you, sir?" Hillfren asked the man.

"I am Kaif, and this is my sister, Jinalla, and her son, Sifé. My sister, she wants to go back to our village–"

"Our friends and family are back there!" Jinalla said. "We need to go back!"

"No!" Kaif pulled her closer. "We go back, there's no telling what will happen. I can't... I won't... You cannot go back."

Rupert leapt from his horse and approached the cowering family. Daaren and Versi tensed, but held back once they realised what he was doing. He knelt before Jinalla and Sifé, speaking in a calm tone. Sifé, moving from behind his mother's dress, showed a large cut down his right arm, the sleeve torn free. The young boy was slight, his pointed ears appearing almost too big for his thin face, and his piercing blue eyes stared at Rupert as though not sure what to think.

"I'm a healer," Rupert said to the mother. "I can help."

Jinalla looked to the palace guards, then back to her son before bringing him to stand in front of her. Rupert lowered his hood and Kaif went to wrench his family back, but Rupert held out a placating hand.

"Please. I'm not one of them."

With a frightened scowl, Kaif gazed back up at Hillfren, who gave him a nod. Sifé looked at Rupert in wonder. "You have funny hair," he said in a small, light voice, his fear drifting from his face.

Rupert grinned mischievously. "It is. My sister is quite the trickster," he said with a wink, pointing to Kyna. "Do yer mind if I have a look at yer arm, Sifé?"

Biting his lip, Sifé looked down at his injured arm, then presented it to Rupert.

Rupert inspected the wound gently. Then, he passed a hand over the cut, muttering an incantation as he did so. Sifé gasped and his mother cried out when they saw the wound had been completely healed.

"Theurgist," Sifé's uncle growled as he inspected the boy's arm.

"Wizard," Rupert amended. "And we are *not* with those who attacked you."

"Which way is your village?" Carey asked.

Kaif pointed back the way they had come. "To the east. But they came from the north."

"Meaning, they're heading south, just like Ilvisar said," Kat said in a low voice.

Dolvein put away his weapon and dismounted. He took a small, white silk bag from his saddlebag. He retrieved a handful of golden leaves; they clinked together as he handed them to Kaif, who accepted them gratefully.

"My lord..." He gazed at the leaves, which Carey realised must be the currency of the realm.

"Go," Dolvein instructed him. "Seek refuge at the palace city. Tell the King what you have seen."

Jinalla, holding her son tight against her chest, thanked each of them before bestowing upon Rupert the gesture Carey had seen granted to the King. Sifé smiled at Rupert with watering eyes as they hurried down the road that would lead them to the palace.

"Monsters," Rupert snarled as soon as the family was out of sight.

"We need to keep going," Versi said.

They continued along the road, a distinct feeling of unrest amongst the group. The forest didn't seem as bright anymore.

When they finally emerged from the trees, they saw great plumes of black smoke rising in the east. Kyna moaned in despair, and Kat cursed colourfully, something about a dog and a plague. Carey gripped her reins so tightly she felt the edges of the leather bite into her palms. She felt responsible for these attacks, for the evil that now spread through these lands. The darkness was spreading, and soon it would be absolute.

All three realms, touched by Malevolence's malice.

"Is there anything we can do?" Carey asked, though she was sure she knew the answer.

Dolvein answered from the rear. "The King dispatched riders to defend the villages, my lady."

Kat grimaced by her side.

"What are you thinking?" Carey asked her quietly so the others couldn't hear.

Kat glanced towards the dark smoke. "How many of the King's riders do you think have magic enough to fight what awaits them?"

Carey's set her jaw, fighting back the anxiety that gripped her chest. "I don't know. Which is why we need to find Saar. Perhaps in stopping him we can stop the rest."

Kat nodded slowly. "Head of the snake..."

As the afternoon waned, the road narrowed and became less worn. Weeds poked through cracks in the surface, and they hadn't passed a village or even a house in some time.

When Carey pointed this out, Hillfren said, "We're taking a lesser known route to avoid trouble. If we continue on this trail, we will come upon the forest of Kalaren by nightfall. Beyond the forest, we will pass through a city that lies at the edge of the mountain pass."

There was a hesitance to his voice at the mention of this forest.

"Kalaren?" Carey asked, wondering what Hillfren was holding back.

He cleared his throat, his eyes darting to his fellow guard.

Dolvein sniggered. "There are stories about the forest," he said, as Hillfren looked thoroughly embarrassed. "It's a strange place, which has led to many a rumour over the years. Superstitions surrounding it tend to keep most people away."

"Superstitions?" Kyna asked.

Hillfren nodded. "Ancient stories of beings that visit in the night. They say the forest is full of them."

"I, however," Dolvein said, "am yet to experience any. Hillfren will say otherwise."

He said this with a smirk, and Carey had the distinct feeling he was poking fun at his comrade.

Hillfren ignored the jab. "Like Dolvein said, they're just superstitions."

Kyna's eyes bulged and Rupert coughed, grinning. "Exactly, Kyna. Yer can't actually go lookin' for them."

Kat snorted in laughter. "You just know that if Seramina was here, those two would go looking for the damn things."

Carey smiled, but it was bittersweet, because if Seramina were with them, they wouldn't be there at all.

"What do you think Saar has planned for her?" she said, her smile falling away as soon as it had come.

"I don't know." Kat chewed her bottom lip in thought, her brow creased. "If he knows what she really is, it could be anything."

Saar with the power of an Innocent at his disposal. Carey shuddered at the thought.

"Plus, he has Malevolence's magic," she added.

"What if you used your Twilight Travelling to try to find out what he's up to?" Kat suggested.

Carey scrunched up her nose in frustration. "I tried, back at the palace when you were out. He's blocking me. I can't even feel a sense of him. Sorry."

Kat fell silent and the group rode on, each lost in their own thoughts.

The sun was low on the horizon when they reached a wide field of tall purple flowers, swaying and rippling in the breeze. Before them loomed a dark wood.

Carey thought it must be the forest Hillfren had spoken of. She couldn't imagine a wood being any less appealing than the one before them. Gnarled tree trunks, twisted and warped, reached upwards, their dense canopy blocking any and all light. Their bark was soot black, streaked with luminous red sap that made Carey think of blood, and their leaves were iron grey. She could see how it had inspired the stories Hillfren and Dolvein had spoken of.

"We're sleeping *here*?" Kyna said when they finally came to a halt.

Dolvein dismounted and tied his horse to a stump at the very edge of the wood. "The trail we will follow winds around the edge of the forest. It is another half day's ride to Reistahl, the city before the pass, and it is best we rest now. In the shadow of the forest, we are less likely to attract attention."

Kat, Rupert, and Carey shared a hesitant glance before dismounting. Rupert helped Kyna down while Versi and Daaren pulled supplies from their saddlebags. As the sun set, they worked to erect their campsite, and by the time the last vestiges of light had disappeared, they were all sitting by a low fire, eating bread and meats from the palace kitchens.

By the dancing light of the fire, Dolvein and Hillfren told them the stories of the forest. Speaking in low, hushed voices intended to scare and thrill, they spoke of the ten-tailed fox who took the shape of a woman – a kitsune. She was bone white and would show travellers visions of their deaths, driving them mad with the knowledge. Then there were the tengu – mischievous tricksters that wore long cloaks and hats to hide their bird-like beaks and wings. Kyna listened with rapt attention, taking in every word. When she finally started to yawn, Rupert declared that it was probably time to turn in. This earned him some half-hearted protests on Kyna's part.

Looking at the dark trees, Carey wondered if any of the stories were true, or if they were mirrored in any of the other realms. It seemed that so much that was legend or myth in one was reality in another. A simple story from a long-forgotten truth.

Versi took the first watch, standing knee deep in the swaying flowers and gazing out into the darkness. Kyna curled up next to Rupert, Kat stretched out near their feet, and Carey pulled herself in under her sleeping roll, facing the flames. Daaren, Dolvein, and Hillfren were opposite them, and as they settled in, Kat lifted her hand to the fire and it dimmed to just glowing embers.

"We don't want to make it easy for people to find us," she said before rolling onto her back.

It didn't take long for Carey to fall asleep, surrounded by the slow breathing and occasional snore of her companions. Even the stories Hillfren and Dolvein had entertained them with hadn't been enough to keep her awake. She had her magic protecting them from Saar and no forest dwellers could compare to him.

~Chapter Thirteen~

The City of Black

Carey let out a long, low moan.

It was early – much too early – to be on the back of a horse. The sun was barely up, and Carey was clutching the reins of her mount, hoping she wouldn't fall off. She'd slept badly. Carey had dreamt of bird-like tricksters jumping from the shadows to wake her and lithe fox-women showing her vision after vision of terrible deaths. More than once she woke to find herself tucked inside her sleeping roll only to be pulled mercilessly back into the nightmares by her tired body. Perhaps there was some truth to the guards' stories.

And then there were the dreams of feathers and wings, always just out of sight…

Judging by the heaviness in her head and the scratchy, unrested feeling in her eyes, Carey had managed only a few hours of decent sleep before Kat shook her awake in the early-morning darkness. Apparently, Hillfren and Dolvein had insisted they get an early start, and although she knew they were right, it didn't mean Carey couldn't resent them for it.

"Carey."

She jerked at the sound of her name, Kat's voice pulling her away from her nightmares.

"What?"

Kat eyed her with a narrowed gaze, and Carey had a feeling she'd been talking to her without her realising.

"I said, you look a bit drained. Did you even sleep last night?"

Carey ran a hand over her face. "Not really. I…" She groaned. "I had a few nightmares. Those stories Dolvein and Hillfren told didn't help."

Kat eyed the forest around them. "Hmm. I didn't get the best sleep either. No wonder people tell stories of this place. At least they were just dreams. Just try not to fall off your horse."

Carey scrunched up her nose, but tightened her grip nonetheless.

Around noon, they found themselves cresting a hill, and below it, a great city sprawled before them. Reistahl, Hillfren told them. It sat in the shadow of a great mountain range, snow dusting their jagged tips. The city was a mass of black stone buildings, reminding Carey more of the towns in her own realm. It was surrounded by a high stone wall, the blocks the same obsidian hue as the dwellings.

Rupert frowned in contemplation. "Black?"

Dolvein nodded as he pulled up beside him. "The black orinite comes from the mountains. It is said to have magical properties, and so our ancestors built the entire city from it."

"Huh," Kat said. "That's all very interesting, but I'm guessing those plumes of smoke are less common."

Carey followed her pointing finger to where a number of smoke columns rose from within the city. They were black and thick and much too large to be chimney smoke.

Hillfren's eyes narrowed. "No, they're not."

They started off down the hill, and as they drew closer to the black gates leading into the city, Carey heard screaming.

As they cantered through the gates, the roar of flames and the splintering of wood added to the cacophony of shrill cries and shouts. People were dashing about, harried and panicked, tears streaking blackened faces.

Magic flew through the air, sparks erupting against buildings, flames flaring from the impacts. Screaming people ran from the horror or rushed towards it, fury contorting their faces. Those who seemed prepared to fight wielded axes, rusty swords and other makeshift weaponry. There seemed to be two sides fighting, though neither was Imperial loyalists, as Carey had assumed they'd be. They were of this realm, their pointed ears and tall frames making it obvious. Carey's mount reared as a man charged at them with a hunk of splintered wood, and she only just managed to hold on. Hillfren intercepted the man before he could reach her, his blade at his throat.

"You will back away now," Hillfren growled as the man dropped his weapon, his eyes manic, fear and fury warring within. For a moment Carey thought he might try to attack them again, but he backed away slowly before turning and running.

"What is goin' on here?" Rupert shouted over the noise.

Kyna rode close by his side, her eyes darting from one horror to the next. Mothers dragged terrified children away from the fighting, their cries tugging at Carey's heart. One woman staggered from within a building, her long-braided hair falling across her distraught face. She seemed to be looking for something or someone as she scrambled awkwardly to her feet. A shout rent the air and her head snapped towards it. Carey followed her gaze and saw a tall, muscled man storming towards her.

Before Carey knew what she was doing, she'd leapt from her horse and flung herself between the man and the cowering woman. The man roared with anger, raising his arms; magic flickered about his hands, and Carey threw up her arms before he could attack. She wanted to force him back, and the resulting magic hit him in the stomach with such power that he flew backwards, hit a wall and crumpled to the ground.

"Carey!" she heard someone screech, but she'd already whipped around to where the woman stood, stunned.

"Are you all right?" Carey asked.

The woman's bright green eyes shifted from Carey to where the man lay groaning, then back to Carey. "You… you are a practitioner. You saved me."

Carey frowned at her. "Why wouldn't I?"

An explosion rocked the earth and rubble rained down upon them. Carey shielded her face and the woman ducked, as though bracing for something larger. Carey heard Kyna scream her name, and she turned to see a horde of people thundering towards them, weapons raised The woman Carey had saved gave her a fleeting look, then took off in the opposite direction. Carey ran to her mount, gripped the saddle, and pulled herself up onto the horse's back.

"This way," Dolvein called, and the eight of them galloped away.

They wound through the city, dodging panicked townspeople and shots of magic. None of them had bothered to pull on their hoods, which, Carey thought, was probably a major mistake. As far as she could tell, the feud raging about them consisted of two types of people – magical and non-magical. The group took a deserted street, the sounds of fighting echoing down the narrow corridor from both ends. A young man darted out in front of them, looking over his shoulder as he ran straight into Hillfren's horse. He fell hard to the ground and began to say something when his eyes fell on Rupert at Hillfren's side. He raised a shaky hand.

"Theurgist," he said with a shudder. He looked about as though to call for help, but Hillfren alighted at his side.

"What is happening here, boy?" he said in a stern voice, pinning him with a piercing glare.

The boy swallowed hard, looking at each of the travellers in turn. They must have seemed a motley crew, their differences so incredibly stark that Carey couldn't blame the boy for being confused.

"There were attacks. In the villages to the north. They say theurgists destroyed them," he managed to squeak in a terrified voice.

"And?" Hillfren said.

"And – and there were people in town here. They wanted to drive out the theurgists, make them leave, but the theurgists didn't like that. And they started fighting."

Kat swore under her breath. Kyna watched the boy keenly, her chest rising and falling rapidly.

Rupert said to Carey under his breath, "We need ter get out of here."

Hillfren told the boy to go, and he ran away from them as fast as he could, glancing over his shoulder as he disappeared into the fray. Daaren, Versi, Dolvein, and Hillfren drew their weapons.

"Our duty is to keep you safe," Daaren reminded her, sword in hand. "This is not our fight. We must get away from this city."

As much as she hated to walk away, Carey knew he was right. There was no way they could help here, even if she did feel responsible for what had started it. It was too much and their party was too small.

"Hillfren, get us out of here," she said.

Flanked by their four protectors, Carey, Kat, Kyna, and Rupert rode swiftly through the city. Hillfren tried to keep them away from the main fighting, but the entire city seemed to be at war with itself. More and more buildings went up in flames, and the streets were choked with people trying to flee or fight, and soon it became impossible to ride with any speed.

"How far do we have to go?" Kat shouted over the chaos at Dolvein as she deflected a spell with a flick of her wrist.

A mass of people surged from a street to their right and the party swerved, narrowly missing trampling some of them.

"Not far now," he yelled in return, slashing at a man trying to attack his horse with a long shard of jagged metal.

Their hopes of an easy exit were dashed, however, as they rounded a corner and, to their utter dismay, found the courtyard before the gate teeming with people. It was absolute madness. A fire was climbing a tower to the right, sending billowing black smoke over the melee below. Magic sizzled, and the noise of battle assaulted Carey's ears. Dozens of injured lay sprawled on the ground or propped against houses bordering the courtyard. Some appeared to be fatally wounded.

Kyna whimpered.

Carey turned to Kat, who lifted a hand, magic already sparking at her fingertips. There was a mad glint in her eye, and Carey knew she relished the idea of a fight.

"Ready when you are," she said.

A man shouted "Hey!" and pointed straight at them. He yelled to the mob and a large number broke away from the main fight. They ran at Carey and the others, weapons raised. Non-magical folk.

"Kat! Force them back! Don't hurt them," Carey cried as her group moved to meet them, Hillfren in the lead with his sword raised.

Kat raised her hands and swept the front row aside as though she was drawing back a set of curtains. This blatant use of magic seemed only to anger them further. Many of those Kat had knocked down sprang eagerly to their feet, reclaimed their dropped weapons and re-joined their fellows.

Carey attempted to force them back, repeating Kat's spell. The crowd parted again, more of their aggressors tumbling to the ground, weapons clattering across the cobblestones. But more townsfolk surged forwards to take their fallen comrades' places. Carey hit the crowd again, trying to give their guards some support, but there were so many. She felt her heart tear as blood sprayed, knowing that at least one of the townsfolk had gotten too close. They kept coming, spurred on by their anger and hatred. The fact that Dolvein and Hillfren, clearly non-magical folk themselves, were protecting Carey and the others did little to placate them. Kyna screamed and Carey turned in time to see her blast an attacker away from her. This was basic defence, but Kyna had never been in a real fight before. Basic was not going to be useful for long. The crowd swelled around them and all too soon she saw Dolvein struggle as he was pulled from his horse. He managed to shrug off his assailants, but Carey knew he'd not be able to hold them back for much longer. Rupert and Kat were trying desperately to fight off grabbing hands, and Versi and Daaren were doing all they could to help. They were clearly overwhelmed.

Carey's darker magic flickered inside her, humming in her chest before shooting down to her fingertips. She reeled it in, focusing on what she wanted it to do. She didn't want a repeat of the Dead Plains – she wouldn't be the cause of that kind of destruction again. It was almost impossible, though; there was so much power pushing for release. Pain was building inside her head, as though the magic was punishing her for holding it back, but she refused to just let it go. She closed her eyes, took a deep breath, and focused.

Knock them down, don't kill them.

Knock. Them. Down.

She let loose.

Her magic exploded from her. It rushed past her companions and, with a mighty force, flattened the townsfolk surrounding them. They were knocked to the ground, hard – hard enough that they wouldn't be getting up right away. There were cries of shock and pain as the magic hit them, and then fell an unnatural silence. Carey sat atop her horse, arms outstretched. Adrenalin was coursing through her. She set her jaw and looked out over the astonished crowd.

"Now listen here," she bellowed into the quiet, her voice strong and commanding. "We are *not* your enemy! Your kin who practise are *not* your enemy! Your realm has been invaded by people who wish no more than to create chaos. By fighting amongst yourselves and destroying what you have, you make it that much easier for them to take control! We are trying to right the wrongs created by these invaders, so you will let us pass, *now*. I will not give you another warning!"

Her chest was heaving and her head was pounding from the exertion. When no one made to move, Hillfren started forwards, leading their group through the startled masses. Carey, Kat, and Rupert kept their hands raised, and Kyna held her head high, biting back the terror Carey most assuredly knew she was feeling. Their guards didn't lower their weapons, even though the townspeople seemed too scared or stunned to try attacking them again.

As they crossed the city's threshold, they set off at a canter, eager to put as much distance between themselves and Reistahl as possible. No one pursued them, however, and as the city disappeared from view and the path began to climb towards the mountains, Kat turned to Carey with a bright grin.

"Well, that certainly was different."

~Chapter Fourteen~

The Mountain Door

They stopped to gather themselves at the foot of the mountain range. Kyna was still shaking, and Rupert administered a draught he'd made from ingredients in his satchel. He spoke to her in low, soothing tones and rubbed her back. Kat and Carey stood a short distance away, watching the exchange.

"Do you think she'll be all right?" Carey said softly, rubbing her hands together against the brisk air. It had turned cold as soon as they'd stepped into the shadow of the mountain, and a sharp wind bit at their exposed skin. Her head was still pounding, though the cool air seemed to be doing it some good.

"She'll have to be," Kat said, handing Carey a pair of gloves from her bag. "I have a feeling that this is just the beginning."

Carey pulled on the gloves. Kat was right. She and Ji had weathered much worse when they'd been left to fend for themselves as children. She wished they'd made more of an effort to dissuade Kyna from coming. Just because she, Kat, and Ji had endured hardships at a young age didn't mean she had to. It wasn't a rite of passage that she needed to experience. Carey wondered if Rupert was having the same regrets and whether he would've been as keen to join them had he known what they would face. Carey gripped the star in her pocket, wishing once more that Ji was there with them.

"How's your head?" Kat asked.

Carey raised a hand to her temple. "How did you know my head was hurting?"

Kat gave her a wry smile.

"Fine," Carey huffed. She should've known she'd be unable to keep this from Kat. "It's fine now. Just… whenever I try controlling that magic of mine, it makes my head hurt, as though it doesn't like being held back."

"And if you don't control it?"

Carey shuddered. "That's not an option."

Kat released a long breath. "Perhaps you're going about it the wrong way?"

Carey had no idea how she might go about it otherwise, but it was clear that neither of them had any real answers. "Perhaps…"

Daaren approached them, his sword sheathed, and said, "My lady. We should keep going."

Carey gave him a grimace and a short nod.

"No rest for the weary," Kat said.

They pulled themselves back up onto their horses, Kyna with Rupert's assistance, then started up through the mountain pass. Carey rode up beside Kyna and she gave the young girl a sympathetic smile.

"How are you?" she asked.

Kyna gave her a shaky smile. "Better. It was…" she searched for the right words. "I wasn't prepared." She sat up straighter and pulled her chin up. "But you don't have ter worry about me, Carey. I'll be tougher next time."

Carey wanted to tell her that it was all right to be afraid, that she had nothing to prove, but as she took in Kyna's defiant expression, she knew she shouldn't. Kyna was trying to show that she could be trusted, that she was just as confident as the others. Treating her differently would only break that confidence and that would benefit no one.

"I'm glad, but just know you can be afraid and be strong," Carey said. "I'm scared a good part of the time, you know."

Kyna's eyes widened and her brows furrowed, as though the idea of Carey being afraid was something she couldn't quite fathom. "Really? What about before when yer did all that magic an' told everyone off?"

Carey chuckled. "Honestly? I was terrified. But I didn't let it overwhelm me, if that makes sense."

Kyna mulled her words over. "All right. I suppose I can try ter be like that." She smirked. "Maybe I'll get so good at it I won't be scared at all one day."

Carey laughed, admiring her cheek. "Maybe. In fact, I don't doubt it."

Kyna cantered up to join Rupert, who looked over his shoulder and gave Carey a grateful smile. She raised two fingers to her brow and gave him a small salute with a flick of her wrist.

The mountain pass was a wide, rough trail cradled between high rocky cliffs. Carey gazed upwards, following the sheer faces of the rock to where they disappeared into low cloud. It was quiet except for the occasional shrill cry of a bird and the clip-clop of the horses' hooves upon the stone. They continued like this for some time, the path winding through the mountain, until they came to a fork in the road. A forest of tall, thin trees with broad green leaves crowded the hillside. The foliage enveloped the paths and clung to the steep inclines of the mountain. How the trees managed to stay imbedded in the sharp slope, Carey couldn't fathom, but there were some where she could see the roots poking out from the rocky walls.

They stopped to try to discern the better path. They'd followed signs of the invaders' destruction until they'd reached the mountains, but now there were no signs or tracks to follow.

"Perhaps we flip a coin?" Rupert suggested, to which Kat gave him a withering look.

"Wait! I have a map!" Kyna pulled a folded piece of paper from her bag.

She smoothed it out against her horse's neck. "Where are we?"

Dolvein pointed to a spot low on the page. "There. That's where we are."

Carey craned over Kyna's shoulder and saw where Dolvein was pointing. The intersection at which they stood was only a short way into the mountainous region. The path to the right led farther south until it disappeared off the side of the map, while the one to the left headed east, towards the border between Ilvisar's country and another smaller one. Neither presented any true advantages for the Imperials coming this way, and Rupert's suggestion seemed more and more like a viable option.

"What do you think?" she said, looking from Kat to Rupert.

Kat was about to say something when the pounding of hooves reached their ears. The sound reverberated off the cliffs around them, sending tiny avalanches of pebbles and stones cascading down the steep ridges. They all turned towards the noise coming from behind them. The four guards drew their weapons and Carey brought forth her magic.

A rider on a midnight-black mare thundered towards them around the bend. The rider was shrouded in a long, dark, hooded cloak, and when they spotted the group, they raised their right hand and whipped it across in front of them. A horizontal arc of red sparks flew towards Carey's group. Carey and Kat raised their hands at the same time, casting a defensive spell. The sparks crashed against it, making Carey's arms shudder from the impact.

Undeterred, the rider made a whip-like motion, and their horses broke into a skittish frenzy. Carey and the others gripped their mounts tightly as the animals wove in circles and reared. The rider dodged through them and galloped down the path to the left. Their hood fell back as they passed, revealing rounded ears – an Imperial.

Rupert shouted an enchantment over the neighing and nickering of the horses, and in an instant their horses settled.

Carey pointed down the path after the rider. "He was an Imperial!"

With a shout, Hillfren nudged the flanks of his horse and took off, the rest in hot pursuit. They sped along the mountain path at a perilous speed, the trail twisting and turning, sharp corners and sudden drops testing their reflexes. Carey was desperate to keep the Imperial in their sights. Several times she spotted their flapping cloak as they whipped around a corner or over a rise in the trail, and she urged her mount on, Carey flattening herself to her horse's back, eyes searching and heart racing.

She was close behind Hillfren, and she hoped the others were not far off. She didn't want to look around; their speed made it too dangerous. Carey heard a shout from behind – Dolvein, his voice sharp and panicked.

"Ahead!"

Rocks were tumbling towards the track. Carey could only guess that their quarry had cast some spell in an effort to slow them down.

"Kat," she cried over her shoulder, and she heard Kat shout in reply.

A whoosh of magic raced over her head. It hit the rocks, shattering them into tiny shards, but they were still careering down the cliff towards the path. Carey urged her horse faster, and she and Hillfren managed to pass under the falling debris just before it hit the ground. She gritted her teeth, knowing the rubble would slow the others down, but not stopping regardless. She and Hillfren were still in pursuit of the Imperial, which was all that mattered at that moment. They could not afford to lose this lead.

Carey saw the tip of the Imperial's cloak disappear to the right as the path split in two again. As they followed, Carey grazed her palm against the mountain's rock, leaving a trail of bright red sparks for the others to follow. They rounded another sharp corner to find the path disappeared into a dark cave. The Imperial jumped from their horse and sprinted straight into the yawning mouth. If they knew they were still being followed, they didn't seem to care.

Hillfren pulled up his horse next to hers. "It could be a trap."

"We can't let them go." Carey raced towards the cave, but as she reached its threshold, her horse reared back, whinnying in distress. She tried to rein in her mount, but the more she tried to steer it towards the cave, the more it backed away, eyes wide and hooves stamping.

"Damn it," she exclaimed, realising she'd have to follow on foot.

Carey leapt from her horse and snatched up her bag; she wasn't about to wander into a dark cave without supplies, regardless of the urgency. Hillfren followed, drawing his weapon as he joined her. They took off at a run, Carey hoping there weren't too many deviating tunnels.

Her fears were unfounded. A glow emanated from deep within the cave and they made towards it, keeping their footsteps light and their breathing quiet. The cave narrowed into a low tunnel. In the dim light, Carey could make out symbols on the walls. They were of the same language she'd seen in Ilvisar's palace, only this time they did not shift to intelligible script. Hillfren had noticed it, too, and slowed to read.

"What does it say?" she whispered, barely breathing.

"This is a doorway, a way of stepping from one place to another within our world." He paused, reading some more. "This one leads to a place called Thyenasera. That's halfway around the world."

He sounded awed, as though he'd never heard of such a thing. Carey moved towards the light.

"Clearly this is magic," she murmured, stepping carefully. "What's in Thyenasera?"

Hillfren shrugged. "I've never been. It's not part of our kingdom and it's far beyond those we trade with. All I know is that it is a vast country with a very unusual landscape."

Before Carey could ask what he meant, she heard a low voice ahead and, at the same time, from behind them, the sounds of the others approaching. She was afraid they would alert the Imperial to their presence, so she told Hillfren to intercept them. He hesitated for a moment, but then Carey brought a few sparks of magic to her fingertips and said in a hushed voice, "Don't worry. I can handle this. Hurry."

As he rushed off, Carey crept forwards, careful not to make any noise. The tunnel opened into a small, rounded cavern lit by a single torch. Carey flattened herself to one side, keeping to the shadows, and inched towards the opening. On the opposite wall was what looked like a mirror. A round, oval-shaped section of the wall shimmered almost imperceptibly, reflecting the light of the torch and the face of the Imperial standing before it. He was young – not as young as Carey, but not much older either – and his dark, messy hair fell about his rounded ears. He was consulting a crumpled piece of paper in his hands. His thin lips moved as he spoke the words written upon it. As he read, the mirror rippled, like water when a hand was dragged along its surface. As he continued, the movement grew more and more violent, until a whirlpool began to form on the rock face. The pool deepened in the centre, growing darker as Carey stared, transfixed – this must be the doorway the glyphs spoke of. The Imperial raised a hand and stepped towards it, the movement jolting Carey from her trance.

"Stop," she shouted, and the Imperial spun around, dropping the piece of paper as he raised a hand to cast.

Carey charged; she dropped to slide beneath his magic, heat flaring overhead. The rock wall behind her cracked under the impact. Carey fired a spell at him, willing pain but nothing fatal – she needed him to be able to talk. But the Imperial managed to deflect her spell. He snarled at her as he swiped the air, causing the ceiling to crack and rubble to tumble down. Carey only just managed to duck out of the way, but not before she saw the Imperial lunge for the doorway and disappear.

She swore loudly, scrambling over the fallen rocks just as the others came sprinting into sight.

"Charmin'," she heard Rupert say, but she ignored him.

The doorway had flattened once more to a still, glass-like pane. Unwilling to touch it, Carey picked up a stone and threw it at the reflective surface. It bounced off. Frustrated, Carey looked around, trying to find anything that might help them, and saw the piece of paper the Imperial had dropped. She snatched it up to find words written in a script she could somehow follow, even though it was not any language she knew. Carey sounded out the first word, then glanced up at Dolvein and Hillfren.

"What did I just say?"

Dolvein answered her. "Open."

She looked back at the paper. This was how an Imperial was able to open a magical doorway in this realm. Someone had made it possible for him to speak Ethellen.

Carey held up the paper for the others to see. "This is some sort of spell, words to open the doorway to Thyenasera. This is how we'll follow him."

Kat took the paper from her and scanned the script. "Do it."

The others stepped up to join them. Rupert gripped Kyna's shoulders protectively.

"Yer do know this is probably a trap," he said, eyeing the mirror.

Carey adjusted the strap of her bag and gripped the hilt of her sword over her shoulder in reassurance. "Oh, I know. But this is our only lead."

Carey took back the paper from Kat, reading over the strange words in her head before speaking them aloud.

"Shin'heh, un, ifeynah handun

theurn miss, simeh inrakni."

The mirror shimmered as it had done for the Imperial. She repeated the verse, careful to say each word clearly. The mirror rippled more violently as the whirlpool began to manifest. Kyna and Rupert muttered exclamations as it deepened, and she continued to speak the words of the enchantment.

Finally, it widened as it had done for the Imperial, and Carey could see a shimmering landscape beyond.

She made to step through, but Daaren intercepted her.

"I insist," he said, ignoring her protests.

He turned, weapon in hand, and made to step through. It was though he'd hit a wall, stumbling backwards and almost knocking Carey over.

"What?" he said, rubbing his arm.

"Theurgy," Dolvein said. "The enchantment you spoke. It translates to *'open door, for we are true, with magic, we'll go forth'.* With magic – theurgy."

Kat took a tentative step towards the doorway and slowly reached out her hand. It slipped through without resistance.

"Only those with magic can pass through," she said, looking at Carey.

"No." Versi stepped forwards. "We made a vow to protect you. There must be another way, where we are able to remain at your side."

Carey stared at the doorway and the land beyond and felt her stomach drop at the idea of having to find another way. They couldn't afford the delay – they'd already lost so much time at Ilvisar's palace, and that had been unavoidable. This came down to a choice – try to find a way to Thyenasera that meant being able to stay with Versi and Daaren or leave their guards behind. If what Hillfren said was true, Thyenasera was half a world away. They couldn't afford to spend weeks or months travelling when there was a far more immediate option right before them. Seramina's face swam before Carey's eyes, her screams in her ears, and she shook her head.

"No, there isn't. Not if we want to catch up to Saar," Carey said firmly, meeting Versi's gaze. "We can't waste this chance."

Versi's nostrils flared and her mouth thinned into a hard line. "I cannot protect you if you walk through that doorway." Her voice was strained.

Carey let out a sigh. She knew what was going on. Versi didn't want to go back on her word to Efren. She was determined to see this through – to her, there was no choice. Versi wouldn't go through the doorway if their roles were reversed. Carey wished she saw the world as black and white as Versi. It would make things so much easier.

"Versi, I'm releasing you from your duties. Go back to our realm, tell Efren you did what you could. He'll understand. Please."

Versi began to protest, but Carey cut her off.

"I will not hold this against you. You and Daaren have done what you were ordered, but we must go through this doorway. There is no other way for us."

Carey looked into Versi's dark eyes, willing her to understand. Versi stared back fiercely and for a moment Carey thought she might continue to argue.

Instead, she reached into the pouch at her waist. "In that case, you will need this." She handed the final Wayfaring medallion to Carey, who stared at it, gratitude swelling within her.

"Thank you," she said as Versi stepped back from the doorway.

"One last thing, my lady. I…" Versi took a deep breath. "I understand about Marjen. You tried your best. Sometimes… sometimes it's hard to do what needs to be done."

A smile tilted Carey's lips. She hadn't realised she'd needed to hear those words until Versi had said them. The Vuletian walked over to join Daaren, Dolvein, and Hillfren, the latter two giving their realm's customary salute.

"We will carry word back to Ilvisar of what we have seen," Hillfren said as he raised his hand to them. "May you find what you are looking for."

Rupert, Kat, and Kyna stepped up beside Carey. She handed Rupert the medallion for safe keeping.

"Shall we?" Rupert said as he tucked the gold coin into his saddlebag.

Carey turned to the doorway, took a deep breath, and stepped through.

It wasn't like stepping through one of the gateways. Rather, it was like walking through an ordinary doorway. Carey had been expecting wind, strange sensations, sounds – anything – but there'd been nothing. She blinked as she tried to adjust to the sudden brightness when there came a sharp pain to the back of her head. The ground rushed up to meet her as the world erupted around her.

~Chapter Fifteen~

The Warlord and the Empress

"Bring her in here."

She heard the creak of a door and saw the change in light from behind her eyelashes. Pain, sharp and all-encompassing, wrapped around her head and she winced. There was more murmuring, words she couldn't make out. She was being dragged, two hands, one under each arm, hauling her along as her feet lagged behind her, toes scuffing flat stone.

"Here she is, General. She had companions – three others."

Carey tried to lift her head, but it, and all her limbs, felt as heavy as lead. Something tugged at her neck – the strap of her necklace – as though someone was pulling down on it.

"That's her. Leave her here. Watch the rest," came a gruff voice, and the hands let her fall roughly to the ground.

Carey's cheek struck the floor – hard. The impact, along with the skull-wrenching pain in her head, forced her eyes open.

"Ah, she is awake."

She was rolled onto her back by what felt like the toe of a boot. Carey tried to move but found herself incapable of shifting even a finger. It wasn't that she was sluggish from the hit to her head she'd received coming through the doorway – she couldn't move at all. She blinked a few more times, trying to bring her eyes into focus, and flinched.

A man with wiry black hair and a long, braided beard was looming over her, staring intently with eyes so dark they were almost obsidian. His face was wide set and his complexion was pale and smattered liberally with freckles, as though he'd stood in the sun his entire life. His ears were pointed, like

Ilvisar's, the very tips poking through his dark hair. And he had piercings. Not small and unobtrusive like those on the inhabitants of the palace, but large and obvious. Thick, carved rings hung from his earlobes followed by others that ran up to the tip of each ear, each smaller than the last. At his throat hung a heavy silver chain with links shaped liked dragon scales, and he was clothed in a slick high-collared coat.

His mouth split into a wide grin that showed startlingly white teeth – the sight brought Carey little comfort.

"Come. Sit up." He gave a casual wave of his hand, and Carey lifted from the ground.

Her spine stiffened. Magic. This man had magic. What had Ilvisar said about men wielding magic in this realm? That's right. *Rare and dangerous.*

Carey glanced around. She was in a small room, its stone walls black with age. Two small windows on either side of the wooden door allowed the smallest amount of light to permeate the grimy darkness. It was furnished with fur-lined lounges and rugs, candles burning low in the corners. Weapons were piled by the door, and a table beside one of the chairs was covered in bottles and platters of food. It was unlike any of the dwellings in Ilvisar's kingdom, the bright crystalline buildings a far cry from this dingy room. It felt derelict and old, as though it hadn't been lived in for some time.

Carey realised she was entirely alone with this man. Her heart skipped.

"Where are my friends?"

She was glad to find her voice strong and sure. The man, who was quite stocky and broad across the shoulders, slumped into a large fur-trimmed chair.

"They are fine for now. My people are watching them." His low, rumbling voice sent shivers down her spine.

Carey didn't miss the implications of his words. *For now.*

"What do you want from me?" Carey tried to move her legs again, tried shifting her weight, but the spell held tight. She was trapped.

"Oh, I wouldn't do that if I were you. Trying to resist my bonds has never ended well for anyone. And whatever other powers you think might supersede my work, I would advise you against trying that also. You might escape, but your friends will not."

He said this so calmly and with such indifference that Carey stilled immediately. There was a current beneath his words, a violence she could sense that she was unwilling to test. Not, at least, until she could be free of his magic. The man continued to watch her, his expression impassive and observant as he looked her over.

"What do you want from me?" Carey repeated.

He narrowed his eyes. "It's not so much a question of what I want from you, but what having you will get me."

Carey frowned. "*Having* me?"

A dark smirk crossed the man's lips. "I've heard about you and your friends. Practitioners, the lot of you. And not of this world, either." He pointed at her chest where her necklace sat. "*Seekers*, I've been told."

The word made Carey freeze, her breath catching in her throat as though it sought to strangle her. This man knew who they were, which meant only one thing. She kept her features impassive, breathing slow and deep.

"He's here, isn't he? Saar?" Carey asked, trying to keep herself from looking away from him.

"Not *here*, exactly, but he's close. He wants to see you, made sure to let me know exactly who you are and how to deal with you."

A bead of sweat trickled down Carey's back beneath her coat despite the cool air. "Who are you, exactly?"

Picking up a goblet, he took a great gulp, a thin rivulet of liquid spilling down his chin and into his beard. His eyes stayed locked on Carey and she could practically see him deciding how much to tell her.

"My name is Magorian."

Magorian. The name stirred a memory.

"You're a warlord – Ilvisar warned me about you."

Magorian's lip tilted into a sneer as he grabbed a handful of small round fruits. He shoved a couple into his mouth, crunching down on them and chewing noisily. Carey's stomach turned.

"I would be insulted if the dear king did not. After all, it's not like he hasn't spent the better part of the last century attempting to keep me at bay."

Carey wished she'd asked Ilvisar more about this man. He was clearly a wizard, though how powerful, she couldn't tell.

"You're very clever to have found your way through my doorway," Magorian said, leaning forwards and propping his elbows on his knees. "Saar, however, seemed to know you'd find it."

"Your doorway? How is it yours?" Carey willed him to keep talking. Perhaps he'd give her an out.

Magorian ran his tongue along his bottom lip in thought. "I found it – some relic from centuries past – and I've used it ever since to pass from my lands to here, Thyenasera."

When Carey didn't say anything, he continued. "I suppose it's not as impressive to someone who doesn't realise the scope of the matter, nor the kind of abilities needed to do so." Magorian glared at her. "What I'm saying is, you are very calm for someone in my presence."

She raised an eyebrow at this display of arrogance. Carey knew she shouldn't poke a bear, but she couldn't help herself. "What is it that people usually do in your presence?"

Magorian grinned at her daring. "They are not so bold, that's for sure."

The truth of him danced in his eyes, challenging Carey to ask, but she was certain that was one thing she didn't want to know. Instead, she forced the conversation down another avenue.

"How did Saar find you?"

Magorian scratched his chin, winding his finger around one of the braids in his beard. "He approached me. He'd discovered my fortress in the mountains and killed every one of my sentries to get my attention. Suffice to say, he got it. He told me about his plans. Told me of the power he could give me. You see, those with abilities in this world are shunned, cast out. Your friend, Ilvisar, might be all idealistic in his perfect palace and his utopic city, but beyond that, practitioners are suffering, and with everything Saar is promising me, I'll be able to reclaim what is rightfully ours."

Despite herself, Carey understood Magorian's desire to help his people, though she had a feeling his approach would be less diplomatic and far more violent.

"If you're such a mighty warlord, why do you want Saar's help?" Carey asked carefully, sensing danger in his words. "Saar doesn't just *help* people, he doesn't just give them power."

"Help? Who said anything about help?" Magorian sneered. "What he wants is someone to lead his army when the time comes. He's told me all about his plans to resurrect some great magic. If the magic he speaks of is as powerful as he says, then we'll have no trouble crushing Suvheil's forces. He's willing to give me power beyond anything I've ever possessed in order to do so. He just needed me to deliver you to him when you finally made it through the doorway."

The world slowed around her at the implications, the true meaning behind them. Resurrect some great magic? Resurrect…

Sweat broke out on her forehead as connections began to weave. Stealing Malevolence's magic from the Stronghold. Kidnapping Seramina. It all made sense now. He didn't want Seramina's power for himself. He wanted to resurrect Malevolence and, given what she'd learnt from the Eternals of Truav Skain, that was how he was going to do it.

He was going to kill Seramina to bring the empress back.

Carey felt the world tip dangerously as she felt a wave of nausea pull at her consciousness.

"No," she heard herself whisper as she struggled to keep herself from losing control completely. "No…"

"All we have to do now is wait for the time to come and we'll take back the land that is rightfully ours."

Carey looked at Magorian through weary eyes, her head pulsating in agony. Magorian's hot breath wafted across her face. He lifted a hand, magic twisting around his fingertips as he grazed her cheek. Searing heat trailed her skin.

"It's a pity I have to hand you over – you've been rather entertaining. I would've been intrigued to see what you can do. But fate has finally dealt me my hand, and I'm not about to deny it. I will get what I want, and so will he."

Magorian tapped between her eyes, hard and purposeful, and Carey's vision went black.

*

Carey emerged from unconsciousness once again, this time lying flat on her back on something hard and cold. She was staring up at a grey stone ceiling, unadorned except for a spider web of cracks. She wriggled her fingers experimentally and was relieved to find she could move again. She turned her head and found herself lying on a raised stone platform; beside her were Kat, Rupert, and Kyna. She couldn't see Rupert or Kyna's faces, but she could see Kat was staring up at the ceiling with a furious expression. Carey was just about to speak when she noticed the metal band around Kat's neck. She made to raise her arms, made to grasp at her own neck, only to find some invisible binding holding her arms down. It wasn't like with Magorian where her body had felt so heavy it was impossible to move. With this it felt as though her limbs were being pinned down.

"Kat!" she whispered.

Kat turned to her, relief replacing her fury. "You're awake!"

"Where are we? What happened to you all?"

"We were in some dingy little room at one point, then they brought us here."

"We're all right, though," Rupert said. "Not overly thrilled with th' current accommodations, mind you."

Kat looked away, then back to Carey. "Carey, he's here. Saar's here and he's working with people from this realm."

"I know." Carey closed her eyes, willing the pain in her head to go away and for her mind to stop racing. The aching in her skull, however, was nothing, absolutely nothing, compared to the shock and realisation of what Saar was planning to do. Magorian clearly had no idea what he was actually planning, that the magic Saar spoke of was not a power he could partake in, but a single, dominant being. Malevolence, reborn, and with Seramina's unlimited abilities… Carey felt overwhelmed by the thought. What was worse, she couldn't believe she hadn't figured this out earlier. It all seemed so painfully obvious now.

Before she could say another word, a voice echoed through the vast chamber. "I'm so glad you've finally decided to join us."

Saar appeared in Carey's line of sight, stepping out from behind a pillar in the far corner. A burning sensation flared in her chest at the sight of him and she felt immeasurable fury scorch her flesh. She was beyond being careful when it came to this man; she was past playing his games. She wanted to scream, to rage. She wanted to burn this place down and decimate him. She wanted to pin him to the flames and watch the life bleed from his eyes. Carey had never felt such violent anger, but she knew it was futile as long as this metal clasp around her neck held her magic at bay. Oh, to be on equal footing.

"Sorry to have kept you waiting," Carey spat as Saar drew closer, halting when he was only a few feet away.

The dais where they lay was perhaps only a few feet off the ground, not even reaching his waist. Saar looked down at her, mock pity on his face.

"I know what you're thinking, dear Princess. That you would dearly like to teach me a lesson if it weren't for the binding around your neck."

"Why don't you let me free and we'll see just how much you know," Carey retorted. She knew she was being reckless, but she didn't care. She was done holding her tongue.

The corner of his mouth lifted in a sneer. "As amusing as that would be, I prefer to keep you where you are. After all, you've managed to keep me at bay since arriving here – so nice to see you've progressed with your Travelling abilities – therefore I've had very little opportunity to *speak* with you."

Carey glared at him, though beneath her anger, she felt relief at knowing the magic she'd performed to keep him away had worked.

"Well, you have the chance now. Why don't you tell us what you're really doing in this realm, *Saar*?"

He stepped closer and crouched low, bringing his cold silver eyes level with hers. "You really think I'm going to tell you?"

They stared at each other for a long moment, Carey hoping he would say something that would give away his true intentions.

"Let me tell you something, Princess. I worked *very* hard to make Malevolence what she was, to build the empire that she had. And what, with your little friend… I've always found her so intriguing. Such power for someone so young. Who's to say she won't be my next project?"

He looked straight into Carey's eyes; Carey refused to turn from his gaze.

"What are you saying?"

Saar cocked his head to the side, considering her. "You always just assumed that I was simply a follower, a mere lackey. What you failed to realise was that I *made* Malevolence. I saw her potential as a young child, worked and manipulated her until she became the most powerful sorceress in the known realms." An evil smile stretched across his features. "So, tell me, Princess, how could I leave my greatest achievement to rot in some dark part of the castle?"

Kat muttered something, but Saar merely raised a finger, never taking his gaze away from Carey's face.

"It would be best if you remained silent, Miss Lawrence. The Princess and I are speaking."

Obviously, Kat didn't enjoy being told what to do and raised her voice in answer. "You arrogant piece of–"

Saar clicked his fingers and Kat fell silent, though Carey could still hear her trying to speak, her words muffled by the spell Saar had just cast. Carey continued to stare at the man before her, mind reeling.

"What do you mean, *'made'* her?" she asked, trying not to let her voice shake.

A malevolent spark lit his cruel eyes and Carey's stomach dropped, as though by asking that question she'd just inadvertently thrown herself off a cliff.

"You could have been so much more, so much like her, if you'd just joined me. You have no idea just how much you and Elara Parnell have in common."

He said the name with clear emphasis and a flush of panic lit Carey's face, scrambling her thoughts.

"What did you say?" She could barely get the words out. He hadn't just said that. He couldn't mean what she thought.

"*Elara. Parnell.*" He touched a single finger to her chin. Carey was so caught up in his words that she didn't even flinch at his touch. "I was her tutor, the one who saw her true potential. I showed her what she could do, what she might achieve if she simply took that step and got out from under her sister's shadow. I convinced her to steal the orb from her parents, show them her power. But she got carried away, killed her own father. She was banished, but I travelled with her, helping her learn everything she could. She changed her name, changed her appearance, became Malevolence, and together we returned to the Centre City. The rest, as they say, is history. Once she finally got her hands on the orb, she became *unstoppable.*"

Carey felt numb. Words eluded her. Her thoughts were a mess. Elara Parnell was *Malevolence*? Her grandmother's sister had become the monster who'd brought darkness down upon them all. She, who had captured and tortured their families, killed and enslaved countless others. How was this even possible? How could Saar have done all of this?

She forced the words from her mouth, swallowing back the bitter-tasting bile that had risen in her throat. "If that's true, then why didn't you rule with her?"

Saar let out a laugh of derision. "Ruling that which had been denied her as a young girl had been the Empress' dream, not mine. There is something to be said about revelling in that kind of power but never being the focus of it. You might notice, Princess, that I am still here, whereas Malevolence is not."

And Carey understood. Saar had never wanted to rule, never wanted the crown. He liked to pull the strings and watch from the shadows. It made him less of a target but no less powerful. Suddenly the scope of his abilities made sense. If he'd been there from the beginning, then he was older than she'd assumed, more powerful than she'd given him credit for, and she'd given him *a lot* of credit.

This revelation though… With everything she knew about Malevolence and everything she'd been told about Elara Parnell, she'd never made the connection. How had she never realised it before? And what did that mean for her?

"Did Fianna know about this? My parents?"

Saar stood up, looking down on her. "Your parents, no. But your grandmother… Fianna discovered the truth when Malevolence finally convinced the Council to let her use the magic of the orb. But instead of revealing her identity, she kept it a secret and fought against her. Your grandmother knew, even in her benevolent state, that to tell the truth would've been devastating. Distrust would've formed around her and her family simply by association, and Fianna knew she was the only one who could face her sister."

Shock and confusion slammed into Carey, stealing her breath from her lungs. This was too much. Malevolence was Elara Parnell. Her grandmother had known and kept it a secret. And Carey... she'd been predicted to destroy her, to be the downfall of her empire. The weight of this pressed down upon her, wiping any other thought from her mind. She forgot about Kat and Rupert and Kyna. The fact that they'd just heard everything didn't quite register either. There was something in the back of her mind that hinted at worry about what they might think of this familial connection, but at that moment, it didn't matter.

She couldn't breathe. It felt as if something was trying to force its way out of her throat and she couldn't swallow it back down. It was choking her, making her eyes swim with panicked tears. Saar sneered, enjoying the effect of this admission. He turned away.

"I tire of reminiscing, Princess. I have more important things to attend to. I leave you in the capable hands of Master Liseau. I believe you've met before."

A stooped man limped to Saar's side and Carey recognised him immediately. It was Ji's torturer, the man Carey had seen in the dungeons when Ji had been held captive, and she gasped for air. She was losing control. She was drowning in panic and terror, black spots forming in the corners of her vision as she struggled to take a breath. Saar said something to the man before looking over his shoulder at the four of them.

"We'll see each other soon enough," he promised, then disappeared.

Of course, he'd never truly been there at all.

Liseau hobbled over to Carey, a twisted sort of glee forming on his face as he stood over her. As he pressed a knobbly hand to her forehead, his palm soft and clammy against her skin, he rasped, "Now, this will hurt."

Chapter Sixteen

Nightmares

Carey opened her eyes and her immediate thought was that she'd gone blind. She could see nothing but absolute darkness. She sat up, feeling along the ground in an attempt to discern where she was. Hard, cold stone, uneven with sharp, jagged edges, met her fingertips. She squinted, trying to focus on something, anything, but the darkness pressed in on her eyeballs in an oppressive way. She forced herself to be still, listening intently.

"Kat?" she whispered hoarsely. "Rupert? Anyone?"

Nothing.

Carey took a deep breath, willing herself to stay calm. This was nothing. She'd find a way out of here. All she had to do was stay calm and–

The sound of something being dragged broke the silence, the direction hard to fathom in the dark. Then footsteps – the heavy, thudding footsteps of something big.

Carey shrank back as light flared all around, and she found herself in a high-ceilinged cavern of black stone. The cave was so wide she could barely see the edges. Above her, stalactites dripped long and thin and sharp. She scrambled to her feet just as a loud roar echoed through the space, rattling her bones. She whipped around.

An enormous hideous creature stood across the cavern from her. It was easily ten feet tall, with broad, hunched shoulders and limbs as thick as small tree trunks. Its head was shaped like a wolf's but with a stunted snout and protruding, yellowed fangs glistening with saliva. Its arms were long, its knuckles dragging on the floor, and foot-long claws, curved and lethal, graced its hands.

Carey had no idea what this creature was. She stumbled backwards, her head a mess of panic and adrenalin as the creature fixed its blood-red eyes on her. It lumbered towards her, bringing its massive claws up in anticipation. Carey ran, only to find that there was no way out of the cave – the walls were completely smooth, not a single tunnel or doorway to be found.

Slamming up against the wall, she turned and ducked just as the beast swung. Its claws dug deep into the stone, leaving four long gouges, and Carey screamed, losing all sense of control. She stumbled out from under its shadow, smelling its reeking breath. Trying not to heave, she sprinted away from it. Desperately she tried to summon her magic, but something was blocking it. Try as she might, she could not reach her powers.

"No," she panted, chest heaving as she ran from the pursuing beast.

Something sharp connected with her ankle and she came down hard, her shoulder hitting the stone floor painfully before she felt something wrap around her leg and tug. The creature had caught her. It was dragging her back. Its eyes flashed in triumph as it roared excitedly. Carey kicked and flailed, trying to escape, but the beast's grip only tightened the more she fought. It stood over her, lowering its snout until it was barely a foot from her face.

Carey was frozen in place, petrified beyond anything she'd ever felt. This was it. This was the end. Then the beast roared. It was so loud that her ears popped painfully. Rearing, the beast drew one clawed hand back, then brought it down. Carey raised her arms over her head in a useless attempt to protect herself. Its claws sliced into her stomach. She screamed as she felt the white-hot pain of foot-long claws cut into her, and the heat of her blood as it began to pour. Carey dropped her hands to her stomach, but just as her fingers fell to the sticky red mess, the beast shimmered from sight and the cavern began to shift.

She found herself atop a cliff overlooking the lights of a city. Carey peered through the night-time gloom as her fingers probed her stomach – she was once again whole. Not a spot of blood was to be seen, and the pain that had been there not a moment before had completely vanished, nothing but a memory.

"What on earth?" Carey gasped, her chest still heaving from the fear racing through her body.

She whipped around, thinking she'd see the monster again, but she was completely alone. Stars sparkled overhead, and the dim lights of the city cast a corona against the night. She squinted down at the sprawling mass of buildings, picking out a familiar castle at the centre.

It was the Centre City.

For a moment she thought she was home, back where she was safe, but then a voice sounded in the still night air and she froze.

"Beautiful, isn't it?"

It was voice she'd know anywhere, a voice she had dreamt of almost every night since he'd left. Slowly, Carey turned to find Ji sitting at her side, legs out in front of him on the grass as he leant back on his hands, gazing up at the stars. He looked calm, his eyes a bright blue.

Carey's heart sank.

"Hmm?" He turned to her, his eyes catching hers. He lifted a hand to her cheek, and even though Carey knew it wasn't real, she didn't move away. As soon as his finger touched her skin, though, she howled in pain. She clapped a hand over the searing sensation cutting at her skin. Ji, however, didn't react.

"I've thought of this moment for so long," he said, his eyes on hers. "What I'd say if I ever saw you again."

Carey's eyes watered as the burning sensation spread beneath her fingers. She couldn't see what was happening, but could feel her skin turning rough. She tried to back away from him, but he grabbed her by the forearms and she screamed as her skin blistered.

"Stop! Ji, please stop!"

She knew it wasn't him, knew this was nothing more than some twisted nightmare, but her heart still broke. He didn't seem to notice what was happening as his lips met hers softly. Carey stiffened in agony as they burned against her own, unable to pull away, unable to push him off.

The pain spread throughout her body, burning her inside and out. She squeezed her eyes shut in anguish, wishing for it to stop, and found herself falling backwards. The pressure of Ji's hands on her arms disappeared.

She was tumbling down an incline. Cold bit at her bare skin as she rolled over and over, finally coming to a halt in a snow drift. Carey panted as she slowly inspected herself. No trace of the angry red blistering remained on her arms; the burning pain had vanished. It was no longer night, but a bright, cold winter's day. She was sitting in a snow-covered forest, a veritable winter wonderland.

What was going on here? It was like she was bouncing from one nightmare to the next – incredibly vivid and painful nightmares – and she couldn't make sense of any of it. She thought of Ji and tears sprang to her eyes, hot against the cold air. She wished he were truly here and not the monster she'd just encountered. She wished she knew where the others were, and if they were trapped in this nightmare as well.

"Hello?"

A voice came from behind her, somewhere within the trees. The crunch of snow sounded through the silence and Carey's breath caught in her throat. She ducked behind a thick tree trunk and tried to hold in her ragged breathing.

The voice came again. "Is anyone out there?"

It sounded familiar. Carey bit her bottom lip before making the decision to peek around the side of the tree. A figure stood only a few trees away, searching as they called out.

Carey gasped.

Zacharia.

He wore a thick coat and woollen pants with high black boots and mittens. He continued to search, his brow furrowed. Carey swallowed hard, her mouth suddenly dry. This was another apparition, like Ji before him. She wasn't about to reveal herself to him and end up with a knife in the back or her throat cut. Carey flattened herself against the tree, hoping Zacharia would head another way.

Something shifted ahead of her, movement amongst the white. Squinting, Carey tried to make out what it was, but the white of the snowy landscape was almost blinding. A tumble of snow fell from a branch to her right, followed by the flitting shadow of something quick to her left. Whatever it was, it was fast. Carey wished she had a weapon, if not her magic at least her sword, but she wore only the bare minimum of clothing. Her gaze darted about as she tried to follow the thing's movements. With a shudder of horror, she realised it was closing in on her. She crouched, prepared to defend herself, when something wrapped around her fingers. Jumping, she turned to find Zacharia's hand in hers.

"Run."

Something about the look in his eyes decided it for her. Carey didn't hesitate. They ran. She let Zacharia lead the way, tightening her grip on his as they pelted through the trees, her feet slipping on the uneven ground. The snow was shallow, thankfully, but it was still hard to run, and she hazarded a glance backwards. She wished she hadn't. She could see it now, a thin, gangly creature barely a shade darker than the snow, darting from tree to tree in pursuit of them. It had tiny beady black eyes and rows of sharp, needle-like teeth dripping with blood.

"Don't look back!" Zacharia puffed out, pulling her onwards. "Don't acknowledge it. The more you look, the more real it becomes."

Carey didn't have the mental capacity to decipher any of this, but took his advice, looking straight ahead and focusing on not running headlong into a tree. Leaping over a fallen trunk, Carey screamed as the ground dropped away beneath their feet. Next thing they were sliding down a steep incline, kicking and flailing in an attempt not to hit any trees on their way down. Carey swore she heard a snarl from behind them, but kept her eyes ahead, resisting the urge to look back. Another drop was coming up fast, the ground giving way to what appeared to be a cliff.

"Take my hand!" Zacharia reached for Carey's outstretched hand as they slid towards the drop.

Carey flung herself sideways, just as they went over the edge, and her fingers closed around Zacharia's. They fell, straight towards an icy river, raging rapids a piercing blue against snowy shores. Carey wanted to scream but she used her energy to tighten her grip on Zacharia, and he pulled her into him just as they hit the frigid water. She expected pain, expected agonising cold, but it never came.

Carey had closed her eyes just as they'd hit the water, and she opened them now to find herself standing in the dark again. Zacharia was still with her, his right hand in hers and his other around her shoulders. He looked down at her through the near pitch-black darkness.

"Carey. Are you all right?"

She didn't know what to say, how she might even begin to answer that question. And how was Zacharia here to ask it of her in the first place? Regardless, she didn't pull away. Somehow, she knew he wasn't an apparition, ready to burn her as Ji had.

"I don't know," she finally said, her voice shaking. "What is this place? And how are you here? Have you seen the others? Are they here too?"

Zacharia kept his arm around her, keeping his eyes on her face. She had a feeling he was resisting looking anywhere else.

"I don't know how you got here, Carey, but I'm always here. This is the Corigliphs."

Carey narrowed her eyes in confusion. "What?"

Zacharia's frown deepened, as though confused by Carey's reaction. "The Corigliphs. This is it."

They were silent for a moment, their eyes never leaving each other's.

When Carey finally spoke, her voice was quiet and uneasy. "But that was the place the Empire kept you. You're not there anymore. You're in the Centre City, in the castle there. How are you suddenly back in the Corigliphs?"

Zacharia gave a small shake of his head. "The Corigliphs isn't a physical place, Carey. The Corigliphs is a nightmare-scape. An ever-changing labyrinth of your deepest fears. It's not somewhere they trap you physically. It's where they trap your mind. The Empire found that a tortured body could heal, but the mind... the mind can be broken irreparably if bent the right way. So they created this place."

Eyes wide, Carey made to look around, but Zacharia stopped her, clasping her face between his hands. "Don't look away. You don't want to do that. Just keep your eyes on me. Tell me, what was the last thing you remember?"

Carey lifted her hands to Zacharia's. "We got caught. Saar was there. He was talking about..." Carey stopped, unable to bring herself to say aloud what he'd revealed, merely shaking her head. "It doesn't matter. But then there was another man. He was the one who'd tortured Ji back before we defeated Malevolence. His name is Liseau."

Zacharia nodded gravely. "He was the one who created this hellscape. He was the one who trapped me here to begin with."

"But how are you here *now*? Didn't Seramina help you escape?"

Zacharia closed his eyes and took a deep breath. "She did. She helped me understand what I had to do to release myself of this place. But my mind… it'd been tethered to this place for so long that unfortunately a part of me will never be free of it. This is where I find myself when sleep finally takes me."

Sadness rolled over Carey at his words. "This is why you don't sleep."

She wanted to turn away. She hated the look of anguish in his eyes, the ones that reminded her so much of his brother's. "Why can't I look around? You said I shouldn't." Carey squeezed his hands lightly, still holding her face towards his. "Why?"

"As soon as you look around, the landscape will shift to fit what will terrify you the most. This place – it takes what you fear and it makes it manifest. I didn't realise this at first. I thought it was a test, something I had to fight, which only increased my fear more."

"So how do you escape?"

Carey didn't like the sound of this place. Without magic or weapons, she couldn't see an advantage.

"Seramina helped me. She knew at once what kept me here, that my fear was my prison and nothing more. She showed me how to own that fear, use it as my strength," Zacharia explained. "That's how she set me free."

Out of the corner of her eye, Carey could still see the all-consuming black, a blank slate waiting to call on their deepest fears to fill it.

"All right. I suppose that makes sense," she said. "Although, I don't seem to remember having a fear of giant, clawed beasts or snow monsters. I suppose the one with Ji was understandable…"

Zacharia gave her a pensive look. "So, you saw monsters you'd never seen before?"

"Yes, I'd never seen anything like them."

They were both silent for a moment, neither looking away from the other. Carey desperately wanted to turn away from his intense scrutiny but she stayed still, waiting.

"You said, once, back at the Centre City, that you were so frustrated with always being the last to know, not having the knowledge everyone else seemed to already have. This must be what it's drawing on – your fear of what you don't know."

Carey was stunned. Had she really said that to Zacharia? She couldn't remember those exact words, but perhaps she had at some point. What surprised her more was that he'd remembered, and that despite herself, it was true. She'd always been afraid that the day would come where her inexperience and lack of knowledge would be her undoing. Only, she'd never thought it would be so literal.

"Wait – if this man Liseau created this place, why did he make it so you could escape it?"

"He didn't. He created a place that fed off a person's greatest fear. But if that person faced their fear, accepted it, then it wouldn't have anything to hold onto. He never considered that someone might actually find out how to overcome his prison."

Carey wondered if she *could* face her fears.

"Don't worry. I'll help you get out of here," he said.

"But the others," Carey said. "They're here too, they have to be – Kat, Rupert, and Kyna. How did you manage to find me before? Could you do it again?"

Zacharia closed his eyes, silent in thought before opening them once more. "I can try. You can too. I wasn't trying to find you before – it must've been something you'd been thinking that drew me into your fear-scape. If we think of the others, one at a time, perhaps we can bring them to us, or us to them."

Carey nodded. "It can't hurt to try. Kat first?"

Zacharia brought his forehead to hers. "All right. Kat."

They closed their eyes and Carey focused all her thoughts on Kat. Repeating her name over and over again in her head, picturing her face, hearing her voice. She called Kat to her, reached out into the darkness of this place with her mind… and felt a snag. She pulled.

The dark that had surrounded Carey and Zacharia exploded into chaos. They found themselves in the middle of a battlefield. The sky was blood red tinged with black smoke, and the sounds of war surrounded them. Zacharia pulled on Carey's hand, yanking her out of the way of a rider who'd been about to run her over. Ducking and swerving, avoiding swords and spears, they found themselves with their backs against a giant boulder, looking at a bloody landscape from the shadow of the stony outcrop. A faceless army of black-armoured warriors was hacking and screaming at a smaller opposing group. The battle was downhill from where the two of them stood, and even from there Carey could see Kat's wild hair fly as she swung her sai about desperately, her face spattered with blood. Yet despite her skill and ferocity, Carey could see that she was close to being beaten. Her movements were slower than Carey had ever seen, and the small group she seemed to be commanding was being slain one by one.

"We have to get to Kat. When the final blow comes, we must be within reach," Zacharia said urgently.

Carey thought back to how he'd grabbed her hand as they'd plunged into the icy river of her own nightmare.

"Right," she said. "Let's go then."

They ran. The army seemed focused solely on Kat and her band, so Carey and Zacharia were able to wend their way through without any challenge. It made sense – this was Kat's nightmare. The army wasn't there for them. As Carey and Zacharia burst through the final row of soldiers, Kat swung her sai wide just as the sword of the opponent in front of her sliced through her side. Carey screamed her name and she saw Kat register her with wide eyes. They dived for Kat. Carey grasped her forearm as she fell, blood coursing from her wound. Just as Carey knelt at her side, the battleground whipped from sight, the darkness taking over once more.

Grabbing Kat's face as Zacharia had done to her, Carey knelt over her friend, who was frantically scrabbling at where she'd been wounded moments before. Her breath was ragged and her chest was heaving, but Carey knew she'd be all right despite what she'd just seen.

"Kat, Kat! Look at me! Look, please!"

Kat's green eyes caught on Carey's face and she stilled, but her breathing remained hard and fast. "Carey? Is it really you?"

Carey doubted she'd ever heard Kat so scared in her life. She was always the stoic one, the one who laughed at danger and sought out adventure. The Kat before her was close to losing control, and Carey finally began to understand the power this place possessed. Worse still, if this was how bad Kat was, then they needed to find Rupert and Kyna fast.

"Yes, yes it's me. And Zacharia is here too. Just, don't look away from us. Don't look anywhere else but right at us."

Zacharia was at Kat's other side, his eyes trained on the two of them. Around them, the canvas remained blank. Darkness prevailed.

"But, how?" Kat sat up slowly, keeping her gaze on the two of them. Her breathing was starting to even out, but she was still shaking. "Explain."

And they did. Zacharia did most of the talking as he quickly relayed to Kat everything he'd told Carey. Kat spoke very little, listening intently, her face set. By the time he'd finished, she had regained her usual composure.

"What now, then?" she asked, staring straight at Carey.

"Kyna." Carey knew they had to find Kyna first. Rupert would never forgive them if they didn't. "We find her, then we go for Rupert."

Zacharia and Kat clasped hands before taking one of Carey's each. They leant towards each other, thinking of their youngest companion. Carey thought only of Kyna, pictured her in her mind, and reached out. It took a moment longer than it had with Kat, but she finally felt something catch, dissolving the darkness around them once more.

They found themselves in a vast, stark desert. A white sun burned relentlessly overhead, causing heat waves to ripple over the sand. There was nothing but flat sandy plains in every direction – no hint of a mountain range, city, or oasis. Here and there stood dead trees, burned black by age and heat, not a touch of foliage on their bare branches. Carey's eyes fell on one in particular, its branches twisted towards the sky in supplication. At its base was a small, prone figure.

"There!"

Carey sprinted towards the tree, the other two in hot pursuit. She skidded to a stop in a spray of sand and dropped to her knees by Kyna's side. The girl was pale and clammy, as though she was suffering a fever, and her eyes struggled to focus as Carey turned her onto her back. Carey propped Kyna up against her, brushing her long hair from her face and speaking gently. Kat and Zacharia were there now too, each with a hand on Carey's shoulder, waiting for the moment when the proverbial blade fell on Kyna. This was the catalyst with each new hellscape. They had to die for it to reform. It was, indeed, a special type of torture.

"Carey?" Kyna's eyes were filled with tears, and her voice was rough. "I didn't think anyone was goin' ter come. I thought… I thought I was all alone."

She was struggling to speak, and although Carey knew this wasn't real, that Kyna would inevitably be fine, she still felt her heart break at the pain in Kyna's voice.

"It's all right, Kyna. We're here. We're all here. You can rest now," she said soothingly, embracing the girl tightly.

Carey's breath caught in her throat as Kyna's chest fell for the last time. As she exhaled, the sand whipped around them, extinguishing the sun and turning the landscape black one more.

Back to the beginning.

Kyna jerked awake, gasping for breath, and before Carey could stop her, she was flailing about, twisting and turning to see where she was. Carey tensed, waiting for some nightmare to envelop them, but nothing happened. The darkness remained.

"Zacharia?" Carey said as she helped Kyna to her feet. "Why is nothing happening?"

Zacharia turned on the spot, searching. "I don't know. This has never happened before. Something always forms."

"Based on what you fear most, right?" Kat looked Kyna over and pulled her into a hug. "What if there's too many of us? What if it can't do that with all of us here together?"

It was a possibility. There were four of them now, and they all feared different things. How could a nightmare form if they were all projecting vastly unique fears?

Kyna was still shaking, clutching Kat's arms. "Where are we? What is this place?"

Kat quickly told her about the Corigliphs and what needed to be done to escape. As she finished, Kyna looked around. "Where's Rupert?"

"We still need to find him," Carey said, stepping up to them and holding out her hands.

Standing in a circle, hands clasped, the four of them took a deep breath.

Kat nodded. "Think of Rupert. Find him."

Carey closed her eyes, squeezing Zacharia and Kyna's hands gently as she thought only of Rupert.

She heard his nightmare before she saw it.

Screams.

People screaming, running. Carey and the others found themselves in a tunnel swollen with people. They were running from something, their voices and footfalls echoing against the cavern walls. Carey, Kyna, Kat, and Zacharia flattened themselves against the side of the tunnel in an effort not to be trampled. It was poorly lit, adding to the chaos, and amidst the screams Carey heard the cries and wails of children. She was reminded of the underground city she and Sirona had hidden in, and she wondered if they were somewhere similar. Her gaze flitted over the heads of the panicked crowd, searching for Rupert's bright hair.

"We need to get out of here," Kat shouted.

They edged along the wall, going against the flow of terrified people. More than once, Carey was slammed back against the rock or elbowed in the side, but she kept moving until they came to a cavern. People were rushing towards them, trying to escape through the tunnel. The cavern looked as though it was a marketplace. Upturned stalls and produce lay shattered and crushed on the floor. A statue had been smashed, its stone appendages scattered around its torso. People stumbled and ran, dirty faces streaked with tears. A fire burned in the far corner, filling the space with toxic black smoke.

More tunnels fed into the marketplace, and people streamed in from them. Kyna's hand flew to her mouth. "This is our city, where we used ter live."

A thunderous explosion sounded down one of the tunnels, followed by more screams and a renewed frenzy in the people around them. Carey looked towards the sound, searching the faces of those surging from the passageway. Still no Rupert. This was his nightmare, however, and even though Carey didn't intimately know his greatest fear, she knew he would be at the centre of the turmoil. She turned to Kyna.

"Are you sure that this is the underground city you lived in?"

Kyna's face was stricken, but she nodded in affirmation. "I'm sure of it."

"What's down that way?" Zacharia pointed towards the explosion.

Another explosion boomed from the tunnel, followed by a flare of light. A woman fell at Carey's feet and she rushed to help her up. The woman's face was wild with terror and she pushed away from Carey, stumbling away from the noise.

Kyna seemed to be steeling herself, taking deep breaths, her hands in fists at her sides. "That leads farther in ter the city. But this…" She looked around at the people rushing past. "This looks like the day the Imperials invaded. We were in this cavern. I remember Rupert wantin' to stay and help." Kyna pointed towards the explosions "That was where they came from. A hidden back entrance."

As Carey followed Kyna's outstretched hand, she saw the flash of bright hair as Rupert's form disappeared down the tunnel. "There!"

They ran towards the echoing booms of what was surely magic. Carey wished she had her own magic and that they weren't about to run into an Imperial ambush without any weapons. She just hoped that, as in Kat's nightmare, their enemy's focus would be on Rupert and not them. If something happened and they were pulled apart again…

Carey fought her way towards the magical destruction. The exodus was starting to thin when, as they rounded a corner in the passage, they came on a smaller cavern crammed with witches and wizards exchanging blows. Carey could make out the Imperials – Essedarian in their distinguishable robes, their hoods raised and arms outstretched. Figures lay prone on the floor, some clearly dead, others with magical injuries.

Carey's heart leapt as she spied Rupert. He was darting about, trying to tend to the wounded. Sparks flew overhead, and more than once they almost hit the healer. He was frantic and pale, his hands flying over the bodies of those before him, but no magic flowed from his fingers. A witch Rupert was trying to help emitted a high-pitched wail before collapsing, her eyes rolling back in her head. Rupert fell back, gripping his hair in distress. He held his hands in front of his face, looking from one to the other, shaking his head desperately. He didn't see the Essedarian come up behind him.

"Rupert," Kyna screamed, and he looked up to see them just as the Essedarian lowered his hand in a sweeping motion.

An arc of red flashed across Rupert's back and he roared in pain, falling forwards onto the ground. Zacharia didn't hesitate. He ran for the Essedarian, catching them by surprise as he rammed his shoulder into their chest. They fell to the ground in a tangle of limbs, and with one swing, Zacharia knocked Rupert's attacker out cold. Carey and Kat followed Kyna as she flung herself on Rupert. Carey helped Kyna roll Rupert onto his back as Kat hauled Zacharia to his feet. Huddling around their fallen friend, they held tight to each other, waiting for the inevitable. Rupert was dazed, barely able to focus on any of them as a thin trickle of blood ran from his mouth. Kyna was sobbing, and as Rupert closed his eyes another booming explosion rocked the cavern. Clutching each other tightly, Carey watched as Rupert died in his sister's arms and the world faded to black once more.

~Chapter Seventeen~

Facing the Darkness

"**K**yna!"

Rupert's eyes flew open as he cried out his sister's name. He found Kyna and they threw their arms about each other, sobbing and heaving for breath.

Watching the siblings' reunion through the inky dark, Carey felt Kat squeeze her hand.

Zacharia came to them, turning his back to Rupert and Kyna before leaning in and speaking in a low voice.

"We need to get out of here soon. Otherwise Liseau will begin to notice that you're no longer immersed in your nightmares and he will change the game."

"You said we have to face our fears, accept them and make them our strengths," Kat replied. "How do we do that exactly?"

Rupert pulled Kyna to her feet and the five of them stood facing each other.

Rupert ran a weary hand over his face, his eyes bloodshot. "This is a nightmare, isn't it?" he said. It had clearly taken its toll on him, and Carey regretted not getting to him sooner.

"We're being tortured," Kat said. "Short story – this is the Corigliphs. They're nightmare hellscapes that trap us inside our worst fears. This is where Zacharia was held, and in order to escape them, we need to face our fears."

Rupert stared hard at Zacharia, clearly struggling. "*This* was where yer were all that time?"

Zacharia gave him a reluctant nod and Rupert let out a long sigh. "No wonder I couldn't get ter you. So, our fears then?"

Carey held a hand to her chest. "Mine is the apparent fear of what I don't know. Kat?"

Kat looked around the circle, clearly uncomfortable with having to say it out loud. She let out a reluctant breath. "Fine. Honestly, was it not obvious when you found me? I was getting my backside handed to me and it wasn't even that difficult a fight."

"So, defeat, then?" Carey supplied, trying not to smirk despite the gravity of the situation. She knew it was exactly what Kat feared and why she always trained so hard.

Kat glared at her.

Carey shifted her gaze to Kyna. "You were alone when we found you. Is that what you're afraid of? Being alone?"

Kyna averted her eyes and Rupert gave her arm a comforting rub.

"And if yer must know, mine was clearly bein' found useless at what I'm supposed ter be able ter do."

They all turned to Zacharia, who was running his finger along his bottom lip in thought. "Now, think of how you can embrace them. Accept that some things can never truly be known; that at some point you will find yourself defeated, alone, and, heaven forbid, useless in a crisis."

They all nodded slowly, though Carey was still not sure how this would work.

"We need to face those nightmares once more, one by one. But we'll face them together. Everyone take a hand," Zacharia instructed, and they grasped each other's hands again. "Kat? Care to go first?"

"It's probably best," she said, "in case someone is waiting for us to wake on the other side."

"Right. Then Kat, take us back to where we found you. Everyone else, think of Kat, and Kat only."

"How do you know this will work?" Carey asked as Kat closed her eyes.

Zacharia grimaced. "Like I said, this place is a part of me now. There are some things I just know. And honestly, I wish I didn't."

Pity crept into Carey's thoughts as she closed her eyes, but she pushed it away for now. *Kat.* Kat was who she needed to concentrate on right now. For a moment there was just the heavy breathing of her companions and the unnerving silence that surrounded them.

Then, with a tug and a rush of sound, they found themselves back on the blood-soaked battlefield of Kat's nightmare. Now, though, they were all holding weapons. A quick glance around told Carey that their band of five was all that stood against the advancing army of black-clad warriors. Kat was at the fore, sai in hand and staring down the enemy. Her knuckles were white as she gripped her weapons hard, and Carey could see it was taking all her willpower not to raise them. Kat began shaking from the effort, and Carey wondered whether this place was forcing her to act.

With two swift steps, Carey was at Kat's side. She placed a hand on Kat's shoulder; she felt Kat flinch at the contact, as though her presence had startled her out of some reverie. Kat looked at Carey, eyes manically searching, before turning back to the bloodcurdling screams of the army before her. The ground thundered beneath their feet, rattling them to the core. There were hundreds, maybe thousands charging towards them, murderous intent foul upon the air, bloodied axes and spears raised.

"You can do this," Carey whispered.

With barely a few feet between them and the enemy, Kat knelt to the muddy ground and lifted her sai over her head in supplication.

She was accepting defeat.

That single movement, as simple as it was, was all it took. The blood-thirsty screams of the oncoming horde grew to a high-pitched scream. The landscape around them shook, then shattered into dust. Kat looked up at Carey a moment before she, too, became nothing more than a wisp of smoke, and then it was darkness once more. Kat was no longer with them.

Carey whirled around to find Zacharia. "Did it work? Did she escape?"

Zacharia closed his eyes and Carey could see a flicker of movement behind his eyelids. He opened them and met her gaze with a smile. "She did."

Relief washed over Carey and she turned now to Kyna. "Your turn. Do you think you can do it?"

Despite the horrors this place had already shown her, she lifted her chin defiantly. "I'm ready."

Again, they took each other's hands and Kyna focused on her desolate stretch of desert. The sun was just as hot as it had been before, and Carey lifted a hand to her eyes to shield them from the glare. Kyna stood a short distance away, her back turned to them. Her chest was rising and falling rapidly as she took in the bleak view. Then, she turned to Carey, Rupert, and Zacharia, a look of absolute determination on her face.

"I was afraid ter be alone before because I thought that I wouldn't be able ter survive. But yer know what?" she said, her voice strong and resolute. "Seramina is out there right now, all alone, with no one ter help her. If something were to happen ter all of you, it would be up ter me ter save her. I didn't think I could do it before, but now I have ter believe that being alone is not what will stop me. Being alone is not going to break me." And with that, Kyna turned on her heel and sprinted into the desert.

Rupert made to go after her, but Zacharia grabbed hold of him.

"Don't," Zacharia said. "If she can keep going, demonstrate her conviction, it'll work."

For a moment Carey thought Rupert might actually fight him, but then he pulled back, giving them a curt nod. "Yer right. Yer right."

They stood in silence, watching as Kyna ran farther and farther away. When she was no more than a shimmering dot on the heat-hazed horizon, there came a mighty crack and the world shattered around them. Kyna vanished along with everything else.

Back in the blackness, Rupert stood frozen, fear for Kyna etched on every part of his face. Carey gave his hand a squeeze of reassurance. "Your turn now. So you can make sure she's all right."

Holding tight to Carey and Zacharia's hands, Rupert closed his eyes and they followed him back to the underground city.

At once he was at a wizard's side, immediately looking to see how he could help the mortally wounded man. Carey and Zacharia ducked out of the way, flattening themselves against a nearby wall as deadly magic flew overhead. She could see Rupert struggling, trying to help the man she knew could not be helped.

"Rupert! You can't help him! You need to stop trying," she shouted over the screams and shouts and magic.

Rupert looked stricken, and for a moment it seemed as though his resolve would break. But then he stopped, clenched his hands into fists and pulled them back from the wizard's body. The injured man's bloodied hands streaked red down Rupert's shirt as he grabbed for him in his panic. Rupert was about to pull away when sudden realisation lightened his features, and instead he took the man's hands in his. Amongst the chaos of flying debris and thundering noise, the two men sat in a bubble of their own. Rupert spoke low words only the dying wizard could hear, and Carey watched anxiously as the man took his last breath. Rupert closed the wizard's eyes with gentle hands.

An explosion shook the cavern, and it took Carey a moment to realise it was the enchantment breaking. The rock cracked and the Essedarian shimmered from sight. Zacharia gripped Carey's hand tightly as Rupert disappeared.

Zacharia and Carey were left alone, clasping hands once more in the dark.

Carey looked into Zacharia's eyes, her heart in her throat.

"Once I'm out of here, will you be able to wake again?" she asked, her voice shaking.

Zacharia gave her a strained smile and pulled her into a hug. "Unfortunately, I'm an old hat at this now – it's just like waking up."

Releasing an unsteady breath, Carey hugged Zacharia tightly, dreading what was coming next.

"All right then," she said quietly, finally pulling back from him. "Let's get this over with."

Carey wrapped her fingers around Zacharia's wrists and closed her eyes, thinking of the great beast she'd faced in her first nightmare. The air around her shifted.

Zacharia's hands slipped from her wrists. Carey's eyes flashed open just in time to see him being pulled away into the darkness, a look of surprise on his face. Carey lunged for his outstretched hands, but before she could grab them, he was gone.

"No." Carey's voice was small and terrified. What had just happened? Zacharia hadn't left by choice, that was for sure. Something had stopped him from helping. Something, or someone. The only possible answer was that Liseau had realised what was happening. She just hoped the others would stop him before he changed the rules of this place completely.

Carey spun around, searching for the beast she'd meant to conjure, but it was nowhere to be seen. She was once again in the dark cavern she'd first arrived in, but it was completely devoid of any signs of life. Her ragged breathing echoed around the chamber – it was the only sound to break the unnatural silence.

She was all alone.

Carey tried to think of a way out of this place, but nothing came to her. Her fear was of the unknown, but there was nothing there to face, nothing to conquer.

Something twitched inside her chest; she clutched at it, thinking her panic was starting to manifest. But then a great tug behind her ribcage had her stumbling forwards.

"What?"

The feeling was growing, spreading out from her centre. It was reminiscent of that other magic that lay within her, the darkness that showed itself when times were tough, but that couldn't be. She'd been unable to use magic the whole time she'd been trapped there, so what was it?

Carey peered at her arms and her breath caught in her throat. Her veins were turning black, the inky lines spreading rapidly towards her hands. She began to shake, her pulse quickening. Sweat gathered at her brow as the darkness reached her fingertips. She expected sparks to form, but instead smoke began to rise from her palms, bringing forth the darkness from her veins. It was like the witch she'd seen in her vision of the Stronghold. The darkness had surrounded her, flowed through her just as it was doing to Carey now. Carey stumbled back, but the smoke continued to force its way from her hands, as though she herself was conjuring it.

She stopped, blinking as a thought struck her.

That magic within her. Carey had always believed it was something dark and powerful. And although she'd tried to control it, she was ultimately just as afraid now of what it could do as when she'd first felt its power. It had always seemed different, a magic apart from her own that she often felt possessed her rather than the other way around. That was it. Whether it was Liseau controlling her narrative now or this place, it had gone beyond her dread of the unknown and shown her her ultimate fear.

The darkness within.

The plumes of smoke grew, encircling her and blocking the meagre light of the cavern. She knew that if she didn't do as Zacharia had said and accept this power and the fear it instilled, she'd never escape this place. Carey looked down at her hands, thinking of all the terrible things that magic had enabled her to do. The power she possessed didn't feel like her own, but that didn't mean she couldn't bend it to her will. And she *would* bend it to her will.

She thought of Saar and the magic he was able to wield and thought of everything she could do if she could only harness this. They might truly have a chance at defeating him and Malevolence once and for all. After all, she'd almost done so once before without even meaning to, so perhaps, just perhaps, taking control of this power and accepting it might give them the edge they needed.

Carey held up her hands, watching as the smoke surged forth, and focused only on the power that possessed her.

No more.

She was done letting it use her.

It was time *she* possessed *it*.

Carey closed her hands into fists, drawing the smoke back inside. Slowly, it began to withdraw, then quicker. It whipped around her, blackening her veins as it coursed through her body. She felt it grow within her, strengthen her, and, as the last of the smoke disappeared, Carey let out a mighty gasp and fell to her knees as the darkness claimed her.

~Chapter Eighteen~

Above the Clouds

Carey woke, gasping for air. Lying on the stone dais, she immediately felt the lack of bindings holding her down. Her hand flew to her throat – nothing. The collar was gone. Perhaps it had never been there, an illusion to trick them into compliance. For why try magic if they knew they were Bound?

"Damn him!" Carey cursed.

The first thing she saw as she sat up was Kat fighting a stooped figure in the centre of the hall.

Liseau!

Magic flew from Kat's hands, and Carey could see the fury on her face as she fought. Rupert stood by the entrance to the hall, doubled over with his hands on his knees. He looked out of breath, as though he'd been running.

Kyna appeared at Carey's side.

"Oh, thank goodness, yer back," she said with relief. "We don't have long. Rupert managed ter fight off the two guards that were here, but they've gone ter get more."

Carey leapt to her feet and ran for the entrance. They appeared to be in the throne room of a dilapidated castle. Pillars stood at intervals on either side of the great hall. With Kyna hot on her heels, Carey reached the others, summoning her magic as she went. Spells and curses, hot and fierce, flew past them and she threw up a hand to deflect. Liseau moved nimbly for someone so frail looking, and his face contorted with savage pleasure as one of his curses slipped past Kat's defences. A scream of equal parts pain and fury ripped from her throat as her sleeve was slashed open and blood spattered the floor.

Rupert dived to shield Kat as Liseau continued his attack.

Carey grabbed Kat by the arms, steadying her.

"Oh, finally decided to join us, then?" Kat joked feebly through gritted teeth as she grasped her wounded shoulder.

"Yes, well, sorry I was late," Carey retorted, relieved; if Kat could joke at a time like this, her wound wasn't that bad.

"I'm fine," Kat said with a grimace. "Help Rupert."

Carey released her. Taking a deep breath, she raised her hands, palms upturned. She closed her eyes. There it was, the magic she'd been afraid of for so long. It rippled down to her extremities, coming to rest at her fingertips. It tangled with her own magic – the dark with the light. She felt the beginnings of a headache forming as she reached for a small part of the magic, but she no longer feared the power. She was in control of it now, rather than at its mercy.

Carey opened her eyes and stepped in front of Rupert.

Liseau's beady gaze fell upon Carey. As he raised his hand to cast, a look of malicious joy spread across his face. Carey crossed her arms at her chest then flung them out in front of her. *Knock him out,* she thought. Magic burst from her, a bright blinding blue that slammed into her enemy's chest and knocked him to the floor. Liseau came to rest against a wall, eyes closed and face slack.

Ignoring the others' cries of surprise, she ran over to the man, who was stirring faintly. As she approached, he opened one eye and attempted to raise a hand in defence. With no effort at all, Carey pinned him down, imagining the same bindings he'd used on them. He flattened to the floor, his wrists held at his side. Groggily, he shook his head, muttering something that sounded like curses. Colourful, but not magical.

"Let me go," Liseau slurred, as though he could command such a thing from his position.

A headache was blooming in Carey's temples but she didn't waver in her resolve. She held tight to that small drop of magic and forced the rest back. The tide of magic swelled, wanting to take control, but it was her turn now. Carey leant over the man, her hand still outstretched towards him as she held him there. She hated this man. For everything he'd done to them, to Zacharia. For what he'd done to Ji. This man deserved their ire. But not before he told them what she needed to know.

"Where is Saar?"

Liseau clenched his jaw tight and glared back at her through hooded eyes. Carey flexed her fingers, forcing herself to remain in control. This man was a murderer, a sadist. She was not going to sink to his level in order to find out what he knew. But the magic at her fingertips was making that option hard to resist and the pain was building in her head; she couldn't keep this up much longer.

Carey felt a hand on her shoulder.

"Let me," Kat said with a reassuring squeeze.

The rush of magic coursing through her made it hard to pull back, but Carey knew Kat could get the information they wanted far more effectively than she could, so she nodded. She kept the Imperial in place as Kat crouched at his side. Liseau glared at Kat, and Carey kept her grip on him firm. Closing her eyes, Kat began sifting through Liseau's memories, her eyes flitting about beneath her eyelids. Chest heaving, Liseau looked from Carey then back to Kat.

"What's she doing?" he said, and Carey was glad to hear uncertainty in his voice.

"Getting what we need," she replied, her hand beginning to shake from the effort.

The sounds of people running came from outside the hall.

"Carey," Rupert muttered nervously, just as Kat's eyes snapped open.

She straightened up, moving her neck as though to relax stiff muscles. "He's heading east."

Carey released Liseau from his bindings, then shot a bolt of magic between his eyes, sending him to sleep. As much as he'd done, she wasn't about to kill him in cold blood. No – he'd be facing Saar soon enough with the news that they'd escaped, and Saar was not the forgiving type. Surely that would be punishment enough.

They ran from the hall, Kat at the fore, Carey at the rear, and turned into a hallway. It was a mess of stone and vines, walls crumbling as nature made to reclaim it, and they had to dodge piles of dislodged bricks.

They came to a halt as a group of Magorian's men rounded a corner ahead of them.

"Duck," Kat shouted as she dived for cover in an alcove.

Carey, Rupert, and Kyna followed suit as magic flew at them, followed by a volley of arrows and daggers.

"Kat! We need to get our weapons and supplies back," Carey shouted. "Do you know where our stuff is?"

Kyna shouted over the sound of curses being fired and arrows hitting stone. "Down this hallway and to the left! The room they took yer into when we were first brought in is jus' around there."

Rupert let fly a curse before ducking back into his hiding spot. "An' how exactly do yer know that?"

Kyna rolled her eyes. "Because, big brother, they weren't quite as good at knockin' me out as they were you, apparently. I was awake when they dragged me past."

Kat raised an amused eyebrow at Carey, then shouted, "Well, let's head that way. Carey?"

Carey knew exactly what to do. The magic still at hand, she looked around the edge of the alcove, waiting for the right moment. As a flash of red hurtled past, she flung herself into the hallway, sliding to its centre and raising her hands over her head. Before the guards could react, Carey brought her arms down, slamming her hands to the floor and sending a shockwave along the corridor. The stone rippled out from where her palms made contact, and the guards cried out in shock as the floor crumbled beneath them, all of them dropping from sight in a shower of rock and dust.

Kat gave a bark of disbelieving laughter. "Brilliant! Now let's go!"

Kat, Rupert, and Kyna joined Carey, skirted the gaping hole in the floor and sprinted around the corner. Two more guards stood ready at a door, spears out.

"That's it," Kyna said. "That's where Magorian took our weapons,"

Without even breaking stride, Kat hit one hard in the chest, sending him tumbling in pain, while Carey pinned the other to the wall. Slowing to a halt outside the door, Rupert looked up at Carey's petrified prisoner.

"Is yer boss inside?" he asked casually, as though they were there for a simple visit.

The guard gave a series of frantic nods. Rupert gave him a wry smile. "Thanks," he said, before thumping him hard over the head and knocking him unconscious.

"Really?" Kat asked in a whisper as she grabbed the doorknob, to which Rupert gave her a wink.

Kat paused, then on Carey's nod, she pushed the door open and they rushed in.

They found Magorian sitting in a chair, sipping a drink as though he'd been expecting them.

"I see you escaped. How very... interesting," he said, taking another sip from his goblet.

Unnerved, but not about to drop their guard, all four Seekers kept their hands raised.

"Where are our weapons?" Carey asked, taking a step forwards, her magic sparking at her fingers.

Magorian looked at her hands, then back to her face. "By the door. All of it is there."

Carey muttered, "Rupert, Kyna – grab our stuff. Make sure everything is there."

She felt them leave her side, then heard the rustle and clink of weapons and bags. She and Kat kept their eyes and hands trained on Magorian.

"Why aren't you fighting us?" Kat asked.

"Who says I won't?" he said. "I was intrigued when Saar first told me of you. Little more than children, yet he seemed determined to have you caught. He seemed so sure that whatever little trance he had his man put you under would hold you – guess he was wrong." He took another long draught of his drink, considering them closely.

"Why didn't he just ask you to kill us?"

Magorian picked up a piece of fruit and popped it in his mouth. "I got the feeling you're worth more to him alive than dead. I didn't ask. He wanted you held – I saw no reason to say no."

"Will you let us go then, since we're of no concern of yours?" Carey asked, wondering where this was going.

A slow smirk rose to Magorian's lips. "And if I did, would you hunt Saar down?"

When neither Kat nor Carey answered, Magorian placed his goblet on a small side table and got to his feet. They tensed, and Carey felt Rupert and Kyna do the same behind her.

"Now, you see, should you hunt him down and it ends with his blood on your hands, then how would he fulfil his promises to me, hmm?" Magorian clasped his hands behind his back, asking the question as though of a stubborn child.

"You're stalling," Kat said.

Magorian's face broke into a wide smile. "Too bad you're not inclined to join me – I would've liked to have seen what you're capable of."

Blindingly fast, Magorian brought his hands around. Ropes of burning red magic extended from them. They whipped around Carey and Kat's outstretched wrists and he yanked them towards him, the magic searing their skin. Carey cried out in pain. Rupert managed to grab onto Kat, hauling her back from Magorian, but the ropes were strong and, after a quick contest, she was torn from his grasp. Carey heard a commotion outside the room. Of course – reinforcements.

She pulled against the binding around her wrist, the pain of it threatening to overwhelm her the more she struggled. A flash of magic flew past her shoulder, hitting Magorian square in the face. He stumbled backwards, clasping at his head as blood poured between his fingers. The ropes binding Kat and Carey dissipated as Magorian pulled a hand away from his face, a wide gash running across the bridge of his nose. Carey didn't wait for an invitation – she sent a bolt of magic at the warlord's chest, aiming to knock him aside, but he was quick in his deflection. Releasing his bloodied face, he threw a wild retaliatory strike, hitting the wall by Carey's head. The stone crumbled down upon her. A chunk of rock struck her hard in the side of the head and she saw stars, stumbling sideways into Kat.

Magorian stepped towards them and Rupert charged to meet him, pushing past Kat and throwing up a buffer. It momentarily halted the warlord's progress, but then he threw up his arms and flung them back down again, the gesture dragging down half the roof. Rupert moved just in time, covering them protectively as stone rained upon them. Seizing his chance, Magorian attempted to grab Carey. Her head was pounding, the entire situation nothing but a blur before her eyes. She felt rather than saw Magorian's fingers close around her wrist. Before she could even attempt to jerk free, she felt it – the magic within her rushed to her fingertips and toes, raising goosebumps on her skin. It was so fast, and in her addled state, Carey didn't have time to react. She was swallowed up by the power. She didn't even have to raise a hand. She had just enough time to shield Kyna, Kat, and Rupert from the onslaught before it tore from her body. With a deafening blast, the walls and ceiling exploded. Magorian was ripped from Carey's arm and disappeared under the rubble that rained down around them. Kyna's screams were lost in the thundering of the collapsing castle.

As the dust settled, Kat's hands tightened around Carey as she looked about in shocked wonder at the devastation outside their circle of protection.

"We, er… we need ter go," Rupert stammered. "I have our stuff. Kat, you help Carey. Kyna – with me."

The ache in Carey's head was starting to clear and she gave Kat's hand a pat as they got to their feet. "I can handle it from here."

Kat stared hard at her for a moment. "Carey, what was that?"

"Not right now. Rupert's right. We need to get out of here."

Kat didn't argue. Carey had effectively obliterated an entire side of the old building. It was as though a giant had scooped away part of the structure and left them standing at its centre. Magorian was nowhere to be seen, and a few paces away were the half-buried bodies of the men who had come to his aid.

Carey stared, unable to take it all in. However, there would be time later to think about what had just happened. Right now, they needed to get away from this place. She took her sword from Kyna and strapped it across her back as Kat holstered her sai. Rupert threw his bag onto his back. Kyna picked up a shining dagger and tucked it into her belt. She noticed Carey watching her and said, "What? You've all got weapons."

Rupert didn't seem inclined to argue with his sister's argument and Carey had to concede she had a point.

"Let's get out of this place," she said, and without another word, they ran from the rubble.

They emerged, blinking, into bright daylight. The castle was perched upon an outcrop – what lay beneath, Carey couldn't tell as the edge rose upwards and she could see nothing but sky beyond. . Behind it the land sloped away to a green field that disappeared into a dense, dark forest. The field was lined with row after row of tents.

"Oh," Kat muttered, taking in the city of tents and following with a rather colourful expletive. The sight was so overwhelming that Rupert didn't even chastise her for it.

"Magorian said he had an army," Carey said as people emerged from the tents and turned towards the damaged castle. "A deal with Saar."

"Well, assuming that's the case," Kat said, slowly starting to back away towards the castle, "that would include loyalists who've made it through."

A shout came from the people making their way towards the castle, and it quickly spread, the soldiers starting to run towards the Seekers.

"Go," Carey cried.

They ran, darting through the ruins of the castle towards the cliff at its back. Carey was hoping it was water they were running towards – she could handle that, if they had to jump. Instead, what they found made them stop dead.

Clouds. They were above the clouds.

Instead of blue water, there was a great drop then nothing but white, fluffy clouds. Kat spun around, drawing her sword and readying herself for a fight. Rupert grabbed Kyna's hand, muttering about frying pans and fires.

Carey gazed over the cliff edge, looking for something, anything, that would help them escape.

Tethered to a great oak growing close to the castle's foundation was something that made her pause. A rowboat. She rushed over to it. It was bobbing just above the ground, suspended in mid-air as though floating on a gentle current. The others followed, Kat with her back to them, sai flipping anxiously in her hands.

"What is that?" Kyna said. She laid a hand upon the white, weathered wood and it stilled.

"I think it's our way out of here," Carey said.

The sounds of thundering feet and furious voices were coming closer.

"You think?" Rupert said.

Carey grabbed onto the edge with two hands, hesitating for only a moment before jumping in. "Got any better ideas? Get in."

Her body was aching and she didn't think she had the strength to ward off their pursuers. The magic was doing something she hadn't noticed before – it was taking a toll, and she didn't want more blood on her hands. The confidence she'd had not a moment before was quickly evaporating, along with her control. This little rickety boat was their only hope of salvation.

Rupert swallowed hard before lifting Kyna into the vessel and then scrambling in. Kat backed up, sai raised as the first of Magorian's army came into view. Reluctantly, she sheathed her weapons and leapt in after them, sitting at the back of the boat with Carey. Unsure of what to do next, Carey place a hand on the boat and looked around.

"Go! We need to go!" Kat cried as the army barrelled towards them, curses beginning to fly in their direction along with blood-curdling screams.

At her words, the boat lurched forwards, rushing towards the edge of the cliff at an alarming speed. Carey gripped the edge tightly; Kyna and Rupert, who'd been facing her, were pitched from their seat onto the floor. They raced towards the verge. Carey's stomach lurched painfully with fear. She had no time to regret the decision to get in the boat, no time to wonder if they were rushing to their deaths, as the expanse of sky and cloud opened up before them and they plummeted over the edge.

Kyna screamed. Kat swore. The nose dipped straight down towards the clouds, an ominous groan sounding from the planking. Carey's hands were clenched in a death grip on the side of the boat, and her heart leapt to her throat. Then thankfully, mercifully, it levelled out, gliding smoothly away from the castle. The angry shouts and curses of Magorian's men followed them, accompanied by ill-aimed shots of magic.

"What in the ever-livin' hell did we just do?" Rupert stuttered as he pulled himself and Kyna back onto their bench.

Kat tutted from where she sat. "Charming."

*

Carey and the others were silent, trying to catch their breath and gather themselves as the boat left the castle far behind. Knuckles still white on the side of the vessel, Carey dared a glance over the edge; there was nothing but white fluffy clouds below and brilliant blue sky above. The boat swayed as though riding a current borne on the breeze as it slowly sank lower. All they could do was sit and wait, hoping that it guided them somewhere safe.

It reached a layer of soft white clouds and Carey gazed about, momentarily forgetting the pain in her head and the hammering of her heart. It was beautiful. They were surrounded by great white plumes and swirling turrets tinted blue and grey. It was a kingdom unto itself, its majesty beyond anything Carey could imagine. Then the view was cloaked in a thick mist as they entered the cloud layer. Droplets of water coated them in a fine sheen of moisture and then, as though a curtain had lifted, they emerged beneath the clouds and were able to take in the land below.

"What in the name…?" Kat murmured aloud in wonder.

A brilliant green land spread before them: emerald mountains topped with snowy caps and wide, pristine valleys with glittering blue rivers. Villages dotted the landscape, their farmlands and buildings ordered patterns against the splendour, their people miniscule from this height.

"But, weren't we on some mountain? How high up were we?" Kat looked behind them.

Carey twisted in her seat to look back the way they'd come, but there was no mountain, no cliff. Just clouds. Carey's mind struggled to understand. Where was the castle they'd just escaped from?

"Perhaps it was… floatin'?" Rupert suggested, his brow furrowed with confusion as he too tried to come up with a plausible explanation. "A floatin' castle?"

Kyna laughed nervously.

"I suppose anything is possible," Kat said, looking forwards once more. She gave Carey a grin.

Carey frowned at her, nonplussed. "What?"

"It's ridiculous, but–" she let out a sigh that seemed almost content "–would it be mad to say that I missed this?"

Carey stared at her, deadpan, and Rupert chuckled.

"For you, no. For th' rest of us..."

The boat continued to float towards the ground. Below them, a long sapphire-blue river ran lazily through a valley. Carey braced for the impact as they approached the water, only to have the boat skim along its surface like a graceful water bird. Letting out a breath of relief, they all turned to face the bow and the riverside village that loomed ahead. Birds chirped in the trees, and the bubble and gurgle of the river lifted Carey's spirits. Kat scanned the surrounds with wary eyes, while Rupert and Kyna shifted about in their seats, taking in the sights.

The village teemed with life. It looked as though Saar's influence had not yet tainted this part of the realm. Carey grimaced to think what would happen if he succeeded in resurrecting Malevolence. She hadn't yet told the others about what she'd learnt back in Magorian's chambers – she hadn't had the time – but she held no doubt that that had been Saar's plan all along. Like he'd said – he was happier working from the shadows, pulling the strings. He wasn't about to put himself out there as Malevolence's replacement. Besides, should he succeed, Malevolence's powers combined with Seramina's would make her stronger than even he was. Than even Carey and her wayward magic.

The very thought made her blood run cold.

"Carey?"

Kat's voice interrupted her reverie and she blinked, refocusing. They were coming up to the village. As they neared a pontoon, Rupert reached for a frayed rope hanging from a pole. He tied it off at the bow and brought the boat alongside the dock. The boat rocked from side to side as they disembarked. Rupert slung his bag over his shoulder, passing the others theirs, and Carey readjusted her sword. It was then that she remembered Ji's star and her hand flew to her pocket. In all the commotion, all the rush and panic, she hadn't thought to check. As her fingers closed around the familiar shape, relief flooded her, closely followed by guilt. She hadn't even thought of it until now. She took it out and clutched it to her chest, thankful that it was still there, promising herself that she wouldn't forget it again. Wouldn't forget Ji.

The others had started walking up the jetty. Rupert stopped and turned.

"You comin', then?" He jerk his head towards the village.

She took a final glance at the glowing star within its glass box, then pocketed it carefully before raising her chin, straightening her coat, and striding to join them.

Onwards.

~Chapter Nineteen~

No Rest for the Wicked

Villagers paused to stare at the foursome as they strode up the short jetty. A few looked out from the windows of their quaint stone houses. The walls were built with mortar and that shiny black stone, orinite. The rooves were steep and slanted, made from perfectly shaped rods of wood lashed together and gleaming with a lacquered shine. Carey marvelled at the workmanship. The doorways were arched, and the doors brightly hued – greens, reds, yellows, and blues – and marked with elegant script.

Carey and the others surreptitiously pulled their hoods over the heads as they entered a bustling marketplace. They were covered in the vestiges of their recent fight and didn't want to attract any further attention. Heads low, they made their way through the crowd, keeping their eyes downcast. Their senses were assaulted from all sides by the shouts and conversations of the market goers, the tantalising smells of cooking food, and the bright colours of the wares. Carey found her mouth watering and her stomach grumbling, and she suddenly realised that she hadn't eaten since before Reistahl. How long had that been?

"We should find somewhere to rest," Kat said, looking around at the stalls. "An inn or something."

Rupert inquired at a nearby stall and they were pointed towards the far end of the square where a small inn sat tucked into the corner. A bright-green door, carved with symbols, sat beneath a small sign that read *The Strider*. Pushing it open, they found themselves in a dimly lit bar. Small globes of yellow light hung in intervals along the ceiling, and the walls were painted with elaborate murals of a long-haired woman on a silver steed. The paint was peeling in places, but the artistry was apparent. Small, low tables crammed the long, thin room, cushions piled beneath them for patrons to sit upon. A few customers talked in quiet voices that, combined, made the room sound like it was emanating a low rumble. The bar itself was sunk into the floor, just the bartender's head and torso visible above ground level. He watched the four enter before continuing with his task of pouring a lurid blue drink into a large silver mug. Rupert withdrew Dolvein's drawstring bag of leaf-shaped coins, and at Carey's enquiring look, told her, "Dolvein passed it on ter me before Reistahl, just in case."

If the bartender had been wary of them before, the sight of the golden leaves immediately wiped away any doubt, and he showed them upstairs without questions. They climbed a spiralling staircase at the back corner of the barroom and came to a floor with a narrow hallway down one side that led to six separate boarding rooms. A washroom sat at the very end, and Carey felt a strong desire to make use of the ivory bathtub in the middle of it. A nice hot bath would certainly take the edge off the aches and pains she felt all over.

Kat and Carey took one room while Rupert and Kyna took one next door. The rooms were small but neat, with brightly coloured blankets and more murals of the same horse-riding woman from downstairs. Kat walked to the small window between the two beds and threw open the shutter. The building next door was lower, giving them an unimpeded view over the top. In the distance was a set of mountains, three distinct peaks dominating the horizon. The very tops were capped with white. The soft white clouds they'd descended from covered the sky. Carey wondered about Magorian's castle and whether there were more up there.

"We need to rest and regroup," Kat said, shutting the window and plunging them back into semi darkness. The only light came from two yellow light globes dangling from the ceiling. "And then we need to keep moving."

She poured water from a jug into a shallow basin, removed her jacket and began washing the blood and filth from her face and arm. The wound had stopped bleeding, but her jacket and shirt were a mess.

Carey kicked off her shoes before flopping onto her bed. "Agreed. But first, there's something I need to tell you all. Something Magorian let slip about Saar's plans."

Kat stilled, water dripping from her face. "Are you serious?"

Carey nodded. "And, it's big."

Unwilling to have this particular conversation down at the bar, Carey summoned Rupert and Kyna, who sat facing her on Kat's bed. Kyna tucked her legs beneath her, silently anticipating what Carey had to say. Kat leant against the wall by the window, wiping the last of the water from her face with a towel. She dropped it by the wash basin before folding her arms, waiting.

Carey clasped her hands in her lap. "When Magorian had me in his quarters, he let something slip about Saar's plans. I have trouble believing it was a mistake on Saar's part, given he never does anything without a purpose. However, when I asked Saar about it at the castle, before the Corigliphs, he didn't confirm my suspicions – instead he side-stepped my questions, which makes me believe that what I suspect is the truth. I doubt he thought the Corigliphs would hold us indefinitely, nor that we wouldn't escape Magorian. I think those obstacles were simply there to stall us and give him time."

She paused, and no one spoke, three pairs of eyes waiting patiently for her to continue. Carey swallowed.

"He's going to bring back Malevolence, and he's going to use Seramina to do it."

Kyna gasped, a hand to her mouth. Rupert frowned, and Kat sat down next to Carey.

"Are you sure?" Kat asked.

"Magorian said that Saar would give him power, lands and armies once he'd *resurrected some great magic*. They were his exact words. And given the fact that Saar has Malevolence's magic *and* Seramina…"

"She's an Innocent," Rupert said, staring at some indeterminate point in space as though he was working through a problem. "What the Eternals did in Truav Skain with those Innocents there… He's goin' to use Seramina's magic ter resurrect Malevolence?"

Carey let out a dejected sigh. "Yes. I believe that's what he has planned. He was in this realm for weeks before he came for Seramina. He could've learnt what the Eternals did in that time *and* made the connection with Seramina, just as we did."

Kat cursed loudly.

"Charmin'," Rupert replied automatically, though with no real conviction.

They fell into an uneasy silence, each lost in their own thoughts.

Kyna looked absolutely stricken, eyes unfocused as she said, "When?"

"I don't know," Carey said. "That's all he said."

Rupert put an arm around Kyna's shoulders and gave her a hug. "Don't worry, Kyna. We're here ter find her. We are not about ter let him hurt her." He turned his attention to Carey. "Can you find out anythin' else?"

"I'll try finding Saar again," she replied. "I doubt he'll have let his guard down, but you never know."

They lapsed into silence again, and Carey rubbed at her aching temples, wondering what they'd do if she couldn't find Saar. Perhaps someone in this town had seen him, but that was a big perhaps.

Kat sniffed. "I say we get some food, clean up, and if Carey finds out anything, we'll move on. But until then, I say we take a well-earned rest."

Rupert nodded and Kyna wiped her face with her sleeve. As they made to go downstairs, Carey headed for the washroom, feeling that a warm bath and clean clothes might fortify her mood and help her to rearrange her thoughts.

Once the water had heated on the stove by the tub, Carey filled the bath and added a sprinkling of the salts from the bowl beneath the shuttered window. A single light globe hung in the corner of the room, shrouding her in near darkness. She sighed appreciatively as she slipped into the tub, the warm water soothed her aching body. Carey washed away the dried blood and dirt and sighed again, releasing the tension in her shoulders. Leaning back and letting her head rest on the edge of the tub, Carey closed her eyes and attempted to clear her mind. The room was silent except for the slight shifting of the water around her and she took a deep breath, centring herself.

She focused on Saar, reached out with her mind, thinking of nothing else. But at the point where she usually felt that pull towards her target, she was met with an immovable wall. Carey pressed against it, tried to force her way past, but the more she focused on the wall, the less she focused on Saar, and that disconnect sent her reeling backwards. Her eyes flew open as she came back into herself.

Pulling on her hair in frustration, Carey let a few choice curses fly before flopping back once more, causing some of the tub water to spill over the sides. She squeezed her eyes shut, rubbing at her eyelids with the heels of her palms, then let her arms drop.

There was no splash.

Startled, Carey opened her eyes to find she was no longer in the tub. Fully clothed and blinking, she stood in a void of blinding white. There was no ground beneath her feet, no sky overhead, and she spun around, mind racing with the possibilities.

"Carey!"

Her name rang in her ears just as her eyes fell on the red-headed figure of Seramina. Carey froze, heart racing. What was this? A dream?

But then Seramina came crashing into her arms and she knew at once what was happening, though she couldn't understand how.

"Oh Carey, I'm so glad this worked," Seramina said. "I'm not sure how long I have until he realises."

Carey pulled back, gripping Seramina's forearms and looking her straight in the face. "You're doing this? But how?"

Seramina shook her head frantically. "No time to explain. I finally managed to get around his binding magic, but I doubt I have much time. I need to tell you something."

Carey bit back her protestations, hearing the frantic tone in Seramina's voice. "What is it?"

"He's going to open the final gateway."

Carey blinked. "What?"

"He found the final gateway and we're there now," Seramina continued, gripping Carey's arms as though her life depended on it. "It's just like the one we came through to get here. He's going to open it and we're going through; I heard him say it."

For a moment Carey couldn't think, couldn't understand this. If Saar had wanted to go to the Common Realm, then why hadn't he just gone through the one in the

Mystic Realm? Why had he even bothered opening the doorway to the Third World in the first place?

"Where are you right now? Can you tell me exactly where the gateway is?"

Seramina closed her eyes as she spoke. "It's in a cliff face on the side of a mountain. There are two other mountains, one on either side of us. I can see the snow caps from where we are. And there are symbols – symbols all the way along the track leading up." She opened her eyes to look back at Carey. "My blindfold slipped, just enough so I could see. But Carey, he's going to do it, and he's going to do it soon. You have to come. You have to–"

Seramina blinked out of existence, and a moment later, Carey found herself gasping and heaving in the lukewarm water of the tub.

*

Carey rushed down to the bar, her hair still sopping wet and her feet bare. She'd barely managed to pull on clothes before darting from the washroom. She found Kat, Rupert, and Kyna at a table at the back of the bar, and they all looked up in surprise as she came skidding to a halt beside them.

"Seramina," she gasped, out of breath and heart racing. "She just… Twilight Travelled. I saw her…"

Carey put a hand out to brace herself against the wall, willing her frantic heart to slow. Rupert jumped to his feet and guided her to a chair. He placed a hand over her heart and murmured a lyrical enchantment. A warm haze spread through her body and she immediately began to relax. When he opened his eyes again, he asked, "Better?"

When she nodded, he said, "Now start from the beginnin'."

Carey breathed deeply. "Seramina just summoned me using Twilight Travelling."

Kyna's eyes went round. "But she's never done that before! How can she do that?"

"She's an Innocent, remember?" Kat said, a piece of bread in her hand abandoned as she looked at Carey. "Her magic is essentially limitless. What did she say?"

"She didn't have a lot of time," Carey said, drawing her shaking hands into fists. "But she did manage to tell me this." She lifted her head to gaze at the others. "Saar's opening the final gateway, and he going to do it soon."

"Are you serious?" Kat said. "Could this day get *any* worse? All right then, I'll bite. Where is this gateway? Did she say?"

"She did." Carey got to her feet and strode towards the front door. The others followed hurriedly, passing a slightly annoyed bartender and some curious customers.

Carey pointed to the three peaks of the mountain range on the horizon. "Right there."

*

Carey closed her eyes, knowing that if she didn't do this now, who knew when she might get the chance again.

Focusing on her parents' quarters in the castle, hoping they'd be there, Carey Travelled from the Third Realm back to her own.

She blinked.

Standing on their balcony, their backs to her, were her parents, talking quietly to each other against the glow of a brilliant sunset.

"Mother! Father," Carey called, and they whipped around, eyes wide with surprise.

"Oh, Carey,!" her mother cried, dashing over to her. "You're not really here, are you? Has something happened?"

Shaking her head, she spoke quickly, knowing that the others were waiting for her and that time was firmly against them. "We're all right for now. I don't have much time though. We know what Saar's plans are and where he is at this very moment. He's found the gateway between the Third World and the Common Realm, and he's planning on opening it. Not only that, but he's going to resurrect Malevolence."

There was a beat of silence and Jenny and Robert's expressions hardened.

"So, it's as we thought," Jenny said softly, dangerously. "With the theft of Malevolence's magic, we considered this a possibility, though we'd hoped we were wrong. Do you know where or when?"

"No. But I don't plan on giving him the chance to go through with it," Carey said firmly. "If we can't stop him from opening the gateway, it will throw the realms into chaos, like it did last time."

Robert placed a comforting hand on his daughter's shoulder and Carey could feel the warmth of his hand, allowing the contact. "If that happens, we'll be ready. You just concentrate on what needs to be done on your side."

Carey would've gladly stayed, talked through strategy and possibilities with her parents, but time was short and the longer she took, the closer Saar was to opening the final gateway. She drew herself up to her full height.

"You can count on us," she said, and she drew her arms up in front of her, crossing them before bringing them down at her sides, severing the connection.

She opened her eyes to find Kat waiting. "Did you speak to them?"

Carey adjusted her sword straps and rolled her shoulders. "Yes, they know what Saar's planning to do. We just have to do our part."

Kat turned and beckoned with her head. "Let's do it then."

~Chapter Twenty~

The Final Gateway

The foot of the mountain range looked like something from a nightmare. A crumbling stone archway framed a walking path that wound up the mountainside. Dead trees lined the pathway, black and skeletal as though they'd been burnt and never regenerated. The emerald-green grass of the valley behind them stopped a few feet from the archway, the blades withering away to a grey sand-like soil.

Rupert craned his neck, looking up at the mountain.

"Well," he said, readjusting the bag on his back that was now laden with extra food and supplies from the inn. "Doesn't this just look fantastic." He turned to Kyna and gave her shoulder a squeeze. "You up fer this?"

Kyna squared her shoulders. "If Seramina is up there, then I'm ready fer anythin.'"

They'd hitched a ride on a wagon to cross the valley before hiking to the base of the mountain, their exhaustion overridden by their renewed desire to catch up to Saar. Carey had forced down a hurried meal of flatbread and meat that they'd procured on their way out the door, and her stomach was not appreciating it. It squirmed with nerves as she approached the pathway.

The same symbols that had adorned the doorways of the village wound their way around the broken arch. They'd been etched into stones and tree trunks along the edges of the pathway as well.

"Symbols…" Carey muttered, recalling Seramina's words. This was definitely the place. The old farmer who had given them a ride on his wagon had grumbled about the symbols being an ancient superstition, something about keeping otherworldly beings away. Now she realised that they were in response to the gateway. How long had it been since that gateway last opened?

Kyna snatched at Carey's sleeve.

"Stop," she whispered fearfully, her bravado from a moment ago replaced with a stark look of uncertainty.

"What?" Kat looked around in expectation of some threat, but there was nothing.

Only the whistling of the wind reached Carey's ears.

Kyna bit her bottom lip, her gaze roving across the deadened mountain path before her. "There's just… somethin'. Can't yer feel that?"

Kat, Carey, and Rupert turned back towards the mountain, but still… nothing.

"Are yer sure?" Rupert said.

When Kyna continued to look concerned, Kat drew her sai, giving them an expert spin before tucking the points back flush with her forearms, hands tight on the handles. Carey tucked her hand inside her pocket, fingers alighting on Ji's star for a moment before she too drew her weapon from its sheath. Kyna gripped the handle of the dagger at her waist, and Rupert pursed his lips before giving a nod.

"All right, then."

Carey knew what Kat was thinking – better safe than sorry. She wasn't sure whether what Kyna had felt was merely a bout of nerves or something more sinister, but she wasn't about to brush it off. Nothing good ever came of being complacent.

They stepped through the ancient arch and began walking the path, the strange grey grit beneath their feet crunching with every footfall. Kat took the lead while Carey followed from behind. The protective symbols were repeated over and over, on rocks and trees and mountain face. As they climbed, the valley spread before them in all its glory, the greens and blues beckoning. It stood in stark contrast to the black trail they now trod. Carey wondered if it was natural or something else, for it reminded her terribly of the Dead Plains. The thought sent an involuntary shiver down her spine.

The lands below were momentarily blocked from view as they entered a tunnel. The walls were like dripped wax turned to stone, a structure built over millennia, and the same kind of lichen that had lined the walls of the Arena cells and Ilvisar's castle glowed in cracks and crevices. As soon as they had all entered the tunnel, however, Carey knew they'd made a mistake.

Before she could say anything, Kyna screamed: "Run!"

Before they'd moved a step, a figure appeared at each exit, blocking their escape. Magic flew at them from both directions, and Carey's sword flashed blue as it deflected. Kat retaliated, Rupert lining up beside her to fight. The attacker at Carey's end ran at her, a wild war-cry tearing from his throat and he flung his arms out towards her; the curse struck her sword with such force that Carey's knees almost buckled. The tunnel shook from the impact and dust trickled from the ceiling as a crack opened up. The man produced a long, thin sword as he ran, swinging it down over his shoulder to connect with Carey's.

Behind her she heard Kat and Rupert battling the other assailant, and a crack like lightning echoed around them. She didn't need to look up to know that the roof of the tunnel was beginning to fold under magical pressure, and she swore loudly as she pushed her opponent from her. Magical defence was out of the question if she wanted to keep the whole mountain from coming down on top of them.

As the man hacked at her again, Carey shouted to the others.

"Stop! Don't use any more magic – we'll collapse the tunnel!"

She grunted as she deflected the man's blows, her sword flashing with every strike. They were equally matched, but Carey feared her exhaustion would get the better of her if this went on much longer. She ducked, hoping Kyna was staying out of the way, and tried to relax into the fight, anticipating her enemy's moves. She took herself back to the training hall of the castle and sparring with Kat and Ji.

Something flared inside her, and Carey began to attack with renewed force. She could hear Ji in her head, urging her to not give up, to keep going. The letter in her pocket and the gift he'd left were not empty gestures; she'd thought she'd known their purpose, but she hadn't, not really. This right here, this fight for her life and those of her friends, was why he'd left them, and there was no way Carey was going to let him down.

She unleashed a series of blocks and thrusts with such speed that she saw her attacker's eyes widen. She dodged a blow to her side, skipping backwards out of his reach, and he sprang forwards, sword raised overhead. Their weapons collided and Carey groaned under the strain, his sword pressing down on hers. She wanted so desperately to use her magic, could feel it tingling beneath her skin, but even as they fought, more cracks appeared, showering them with dust and pebbles.

Her attacker pushed harder, bearing down on her, and for a moment Carey thought he might win as her arms started to buckle. She couldn't dive to the side – there wasn't enough room – and she could feel Kyna close behind her. Carey had to keep this man in front of her; she had to shield Kyna from him. His brutal eyes were locked on hers as they fought for dominance, and he was winning. A dagger flashed in her peripheral vision, thrusting up from under her arm to drive deep into the man's chest.

With a short gasp of surprise, his eyes going round, the man dropped his sword and clutched at the shiny hilt sticking from his body as blood began to stain his front.

"Don't," Carey cried without thinking as he pulled the dagger from his chest, letting it fall to the ground with a clatter.

She spun around to find Kyna staring at the man as he fell to his knees, her hands clasped over her mouth and tears shining in her eyes.

"I… I was… I just wanted ter…" she stuttered.

Carey drew her in protectively, shielding her from the sight of the dying man on the ground, blood spreading across the rock.

There came a loud ominous crack as a great fissure began to slither from one end of the tunnel to the other, heading towards their escape. As Carey turned to Kat and Rupert, she saw the second man fall, whether out cold or dead, she didn't have time to discern. Behind her, the tunnel began to cave in.

"Get out of here," Carey screamed, one hand in Kyna's, the other clasping her sword as she ran for the exit.

They sprinted towards the light, dodging bits of rock, the tunnel falling in around them. The mountain roared as it broke down, chasing them towards the light, and Carey could feel a rush of wind behind them as they ran, finally diving for the opening.

They burst into the daylight, tumbling out onto the rough path as rock and dust exploded from the collapsed passageway. Carey barely managed not to skewer herself with her own sword as she hit the ground, releasing Kyna's hand as she went down. Kyna skidded to a stop beside her, curling up against the pain of falling so hard. Rupert and Kat heaved and coughed nearby, the dust coating them in grey as it settled. Carey dragged herself to her feet, staggering as she surveyed their surroundings. It wouldn't do to escape one ambush only to stumble into another, but all was quiet.

Carey sheathed her sword and helped Kyna to her feet.

"Are you hurt?" she asked, letting Kyna lean against her.

Kyna buried her face in Carey's side.

Rupert rushed over, taking Kyna by the shoulders and giving her a quick once over. "Kyna?"

She was still hiding her face in her hands as she began to shake her head. There was a splatter of blood on Kyna's sleeve, blood from the man she'd stabbed, and Carey gently pulled Kyna's hands from her face.

"Kyna?" She looked into the shell-shocked face of the young witch. "Is it that man?"

Rupert looked at Carey sharply; clearly, they'd been so busy fighting that they hadn't witnessed what Kyna had done. Kyna nodded, her eyes never leaving Carey's.

"I know what just happened was terrifying and horrible. I know what it's like to do something like that, but you listen to me," she said, still holding Kyna's hands. "If you hadn't done what you did, that man would've overpowered me, and then who knows what might've happened. You saved me, possibly all of us. It's… hard, but we're right here with you."

Kyna stared at her for a moment before nodding, her eyes still shining with unshed tears.

Carey gave her a small smile. "Now, let's get moving. We need to get to that gateway."

The mention of the gateway seemed to snap Kyna out of her daze. She shook her head, blinking. "Yes. Yer right. We have ter get ter Seramina."

She let go of Carey's hands, straightening up and dusting the dirt from her clothes. Rupert and Kat looked at Carey curiously, concerned, but Carey simply shook her head and mouthed, "Later", before setting off once more.

Thinking of the ambush, Carey remembered Kyna's words from the beginning of their trek.

"Kyna, did you know they were going to be there?"

Kyna slowed. "What?"

"At the start of the trail. You said you felt something?"

Clearly, and justifiably, Kyna was still wrapped in the shock of what had just happened, because it took her a moment to register what Carey was talking about. "Oh… I don't know. It was just a feelin'."

She said this as though everyone had such premonitory feelings, but Carey had a suspicion it was more than that. She glanced back at Rupert questioningly, but he was still watching his sister with concern and didn't seem to know any more than Carey. Kyna took off at speed, whether to get to Seramina or away from what had just happened, it was unclear, but it gave Kat and Rupert a moment to enquire about what had just happened. In hushed tones, Carey told them, all the while keeping a close eye on Kyna up ahead.

Kat, who Carey knew to have slightly skewed ideals when it came to violence, gave a nod of approval before saying, "Well, at least we know her weapons training with Seramina has had some effect."

Rupert, on the other hand, was not so impressed. He'd never been one for weaponry, given his occupation, and Carey laid an understanding hand on his arm.

"I know what you're thinking, and trust me, I wish it wasn't, but this is unfortunately the reality of our situation."

Carey hated that she had come to accept this so readily, but it was the truth. This was their life, death and all.

Rupert closed his eyes momentarily, taking a deep calming breath. "I know. I just… I wished she'd stayed behind. I mean, it was really only a matter of time before you lot found yerselves in trouble."

Carey recognised his attempt at lightening the mood, but she knew he was struggling with it. Again, she was surprised to find that it didn't affect her nearly half as much as she might have expected it to. They'd killed two men, and yet that knowledge didn't register the kind of mortification it once had. Feeling uneasy, Carey fell into step with Kat as Rupert ran to catch up with Kyna. She might've said something to Kat if she thought Kat might understand, but somehow she knew she wouldn't. Kat had been part of this world for so long that her sensibilities weren't so easily disturbed, and perhaps this is what made her such a formidable warrior. However, there was something to be said for feeling the horrors of war, for knowing one's humanity, and Carey wondered if it was wasn't slowly being stripped away by the life they led.

On they climbed, the pathway to the mountain's summit winding steadily higher, the air growing cooler. They didn't meet any more of Saar's cohorts.

They were coming around a bend when the entire mountain seemed to shudder. Almost losing her footing, Carey felt Kat's hand close around her forearm as she hauled Carey against the side of the mountain. Up ahead, Kyna and Rupert pressed themselves to the mountainside as the ground shook, sending a cascade of rock and snow down upon them. Carey shielded her eyes from the debris as it slammed into the trail, the pathway crumbling as it passed through it.

A violent wind whipped up and Carey squinted against the rush of air and dust. The sky, which moments before had been clear and blue, was now an angry, swirling black. Lightning flashed past them; a deep red glow limned the roiling storm clouds. The mountain shuddered again, and Kat tugged at her arm.

"The gateway! We need to get there, now," she shouted through the din.

They edged towards Rupert and Kyna, the pathway now little wider than their feet in places. Reaching the other two, Kat urged them onwards, Carey hoping there wasn't much farther to go. The fury of the storm threatened to throw them from the mountainside as they climbed, each clutching the one in front. Carey knew what was happening. Saar had opened the gateway, throwing everything into chaos. Two of the three gateways were open and it was creating an imbalance. Carey hoped her parents were ready, that they were at the gateway beyond the Centre City and ready to open it once more. It was either that or close the other that Saar had opened, but Carey knew her parents would never allow it, not after what it had cost them. Ji's face flashed before Carey's eyes and she felt a rush of hope. With a gate to the Common Realm now open, there was nothing stopping them from finding each other again.

A rumble from above signalled more falling rock, and Carey pulled Kat back as it rushed past. Rain and small, sharp shards of ice began to fall, biting at their exposed skin. Slowly, they edged their way up the mountain, gritting their teeth against the deluge and the pain until they found themselves on a plateau.

The gateway was identical to the other two, the three guardians surrounding a swirling mass of cloud and wind. It was set into the mountainside, a step of grey stone at its base. Carey's stomach rolled over; before the gateway lay a single prone figure, red seeping from beneath it.

"No," she rasped, breaking away from the others.

Carey dropped to her knees at the man's side. He was thinner than she remembered, and his eyes stared back at her, blank and unseeing.

"Oh, Jensen," Carey murmured, a lump rising in her throat as she brushed the guard's hair away from his face.

At his throat was a dark red gash; he'd been killed in exactly the same fashion as Sirona. His clothes were drenched in scarlet.

Kat crouched beside her and laid a hand on Jensen's still chest. "He's not yet cold."

She closed his eyes before putting her arms around Carey's shoulders and pulled her friend to her feet. Carey let her. As she looked down on Jensen's body, a wave of regret and guilt washed over her, causing her knees to buckle. Kat caught her deftly and gave her a tight squeeze.

"You've got this," she whispered. "His death won't be for nothing."

"He knew he'd need a sacrifice," Rupert said, glaring down at Jensen. "Isn't this what he did ter Lady Sirona?"

Carey nodded, unwilling to say anything for fear she would start either crying or screaming. The rain flowed at their feet, diluting the guard's blood.

Kyna looked down at Jensen, her expression unreadable. "We should bury 'im before we go through, yes? He was always so nice ter me an' Seramina."

Rupert nodded. "Yes, we can't just leave 'im 'ere."

Carey looked to Kat. She'd once refused to bury a body they'd come across on their travels, but they'd been in hiding at the time and she hadn't wanted to leave a trail for the Imperials to follow. This time was different. This time they were the hunters and their prey had just taken one of their own. Kat gave a single nod.

Rupert scooped up Jensen's body, his thin figure small in Rupert's arms. He then strode beyond the gateway and laid him upon the sodden ground. Carey was aware that, as a Healer, he knew the rituals for the dead, but she'd never seen him perform them. Now, he stood over Jensen and murmured the rite, ignoring the freezing rain. Kyna stepped up beside him, lending her own magic as she raised an outstretched hand to join Rupert's.

As they spoke in unison, their enchantment almost musical, the earth shifted beneath Jensen's body; slowly, Jensen sank beneath the surface, the grey cold dirt swallowing him up, claiming him. When Kyna and Rupert were done, there was nothing to show where Jensen lay – the ground appeared undisturbed, and Carey wondered if they would be able to find him again. Kat seemed to be thinking the same thing, as she reached over to the rock where Jensen's head had rested moments before and held a hand to it. A round scorch mark appeared beneath her palm, and as she drew her hand away, Carey saw that it was in the shape of an open rose.

Kat wiped her hand on her wet trousers and pushed her damp hair from her eyes as she turned from Jensen's grave. "Let's go."

Carey gave Jensen's final resting place one last look, her pain replaced with fury as she turned towards the gateway. She strode towards it, itching to exact some revenge.

"Yes. Let's."

~Chapter Twenty-One~

Old Realm, New City

The four of them stood before the swirling gateway, the rain and sleet pouring down on them. The storm of white clouds and magic within the stone arch never ceased to both amaze and terrify Carey, and she wondered who or what had created the portals. With her right hand deep in her pocket, fingers tight around Ji's star, Carey stepped up to the blinding vortex. Kat stood to her right, Rupert and Kyna on her left. They wouldn't be going through one at a time; instead, they clasped hands, holding tight to one another as though each of them was a life preserver.

"Ready?" Kat asked, looking straight ahead.

No one said a word, but stepped up and through in a singular reply.

Carey's hair whipped about her face, the rain and hail gone, replaced by a ferocious wind. Everything went blindingly white, and Carey braced for it to fade, as it had before, to reveal the new realm. Something heavy and constricting surrounded them, and Carey had only an instant to take a deep breath before she was plunged into a wall of water.

Carey thrashed, feeling Rupert and Kat tugging in panic on either side of her. Her hands slipped from their grasps. Carey saw the gateway behind them, the base buried in dark sand, the swirling mist undeterred by the mass of water surrounding it. Above, she saw the dull, shimmering light of the surface and struck out for it. Kat, Rupert, and Kyna were at least a few body lengths ahead of her already. Kat looked back, then screamed, the muffled noise erupting in bubbles as she pointed past Carey's shoulder.

Carey whipped around to look. Slithering creatures were appearing from the shadowy depths, following them towards the surface. They were easily seven feet long, with sleek bodies of gleaming obsidian scales and fins of bright blue lining their spines. Their heads were snake-like, long and pointed, with blue fins circling their necks like collars. Their eyes shone white, and long, lethal fangs grew down over their thin lips.

Carey's fear spiked; her lungs felt as if they were about explode. With leisurely flicks of their tails, the creatures sped through the water towards them, and Carey only just managed to dodge a set of those deadly fangs as one of the monsters lunged at her. The eel, for want of a better word, whipped past, its tail hitting her hard in the side, knocking the remaining air from her body.

Bubbles escaped from her lips and panic replaced her fear as she felt her face begin to burn from the lack of air. Another two eels made for her friends. Kat raised her hands, stopping mid-stroke to drive a jet of magic through the water towards one of them. It exploded against the eel's body, a rush of bubbles and light causing it to writhe in pain. It lashed in fury, a blue fin flicking across Kyna's back. A gash opened between her shoulders and Carey saw the rush of air that escaped Kyna's mouth as she cried out in agony, blood clouding the water around her.

The blood seemed to act like a beacon for the eels; their heads swung towards Kyna and they surged hungrily. The tingling in Carey's limbs grew stronger and she suddenly realised that it wasn't just the lack of air causing it. The magic surged through Carey before she had a chance to control it, light-headed as she was. It vibrated through her. There was a dazzling light and a muffled boom. A wall of magic rippled outwards and the water monsters fled, Carey's fear now their own. Without stopping to consider any of this, Carey made for the surface, her legs and arms growing heavier and heavier as she followed the other three towards the light.

Carey broke the surface, a cold breeze grazing her face as she took a gasping breath. Shaking, her vision blurred, Carey reached out for the nearest person. Kat. Her friend pulled her in close and slowly they kicked towards the shore, each helping the other struggle through freezing water. It must be winter where they were, and somehow Carey hadn't felt the frigid temperature of the water until that moment. She put it down to shock. Sudden underwater attacks did that to a person.

Rupert was ahead of them, Kyna on his back, her blood leaving a gory trail behind them. As her vision cleared, Carey saw that they'd emerged in a lake. The water was glassy in the dawn light, and small birds flew from the trees that lined the shore as they approached.

Rupert dragged himself up onto the pebbly beach and gently rolled Kyna from his back. She was pale and barely moving, and as Carey and Kat crawled up beside them, Carey saw the damage Kyna had sustained. Her coat had been slashed open, the tail of the water beast having sliced through the thick layers down to her skin. Blood pooled in deep wounds as Rupert desperately tried to remove Kyna's coat, but his hands were shaking almost uncontrollably. Carey could feel his panic, but she couldn't think of what to say to calm him. Kat placed her hands over his and looked him straight in the eye.

"Stop. Stop. Rupert, just take a deep breath," she said.

Rupert stilled, and his gaze lifted to find hers.

"You can do this. Kyna needs you."

They stayed like that a moment longer, then Rupert relaxed a little. "Yer right. Of course, yer right."

He turned back to his sister, his usual focus asserting itself. Removing the back of Kyna's coat and pulling her shirt to the side, he examined the wound, his hand hovering just over Kyna's bare skin. His hands were steady now, and he bowed his head, eyes closed. His lips moved silently, small puffs of warm air escaping with each word. Carey and Kat held their breath, unwilling to make even the slightest sound that would break his concentration. Beginning to shiver from the cold and the wet, Carey gripped Kyna's hand. Her skin was like ice, colder even than Carey's, but she felt Kyna's fingers tighten around her own as Rupert worked. The torn skin began to knit together, blood seeping back into her body, and raw, red lines formed as the wounds disappeared. As the last of her injuries healed, Kyna let out a shuddering gasp, her grip tightening on Carey's fingers.

Carefully, Rupert turned his sister over, sweeping back her hair from her face and giving her a small smile.

Kyna blinked weakly.

"Oh no," she croaked, brows turning down as she took in their concerned faces. "What did I do now? An' why is my back hurtin'?"

Kyna's face was still deathly pale but at least her sense of humour hadn't been lost. Rupert pulled her in for a gentle hug and Kat ran a hand through her wet hair, face tight as she watched. Carey knew what she was thinking – that had been too close. Again.

As Rupert saw to Kyna, Carey stood to take in their surrounds. They were on a narrow, pebbled beach lined with long green grass. Frost tipped the green, and not far from the edge of the sand stood tall poplar-like trees. The sky was beginning to lighten to a navy blue, the thinnest line of pale light highlighting the horizon across the water. It was calm here, far calmer than the realm they'd just left, which could mean only one thing – her parents had re-opened the gateway between the Common and Mystic realms. There were no signs of storms or manic weather but, considering how fast they'd manifested on the opening of the gateway, Carey could only assume that they'd dissipated just as fast.

She couldn't see any buildings, but beyond the lake's edge there appeared to be a cart track. At least they were somewhere close to civilisation. Carey shuddered violently and she wrapped her arms tightly about herself. She wasn't sure if winter had truly begun yet, but it was certainly cold enough. Her wet clothes and hair did nothing to better the situation.

Kat came to stand by her side, shaking. Her lips were tinted blue and her long black hair hung limp around her face.

"Where do you think we are?" Carey asked through chattering teeth, looking out at the quickly rising sun.

Kat shrugged. "Doubt it will matter much if we don't get warm soon."

Rupert looked up. "Oh, sorry, I can probably help with tha'."

He gripped Kat's leg, taking her by surprise, but a warming glow was emanating from Rupert's hand, and within seconds Kat was completely dry.

"That's handy," Kat said, patting herself over as Rupert repeated the process on Carey and Kyna.

"Yes, well, not all of us can be master sai wielders," Rupert said, lifting Kyna up into his arms and getting to his feet. "My talents are a little less showy."

Kat gave him a playful punch to the forearm before turning to survey their surroundings again. "Well, we might want to find somewhere to rest, let Kyna recuperate. Can we move her?"

Rupert nodded. Kyna was slumped against his chest, eyes closed, her skin still pale.

"I have somethin' in my pack that will help, but this weather will do nothin' for her, or us for that matter, if we don't get inside."

"Do we know which way Saar went?" Carey said, looking around as though there might be some clue as to the direction of their quarry.

"Let's just get Kyna better first, then we can figure out where Saar is headed," Kat said. "We don't even know where *here* is, so perhaps we should figure that out first."

From beyond the trees came the clatter of a horse and cart. The vehicle appeared from the tree line, moving slowly, a couple perched on the cart's seat up front; the cart was laden with brown sacks.

"Perhaps we could hitch a ride?" Carey suggested with a nod towards the cart and Kat took off at a run, calling to the driver.

As Carey and Rupert followed, the cart slowed, and Kat spoke with the man at the reins. There was a lot of shaking of heads and exuberant arm waving from both parties. Then Kat pulled a pouch from a pocket and held one of Ilvisar's golden leaves out to the driver. The man inspected it, showing it to the woman beside him, before giving Kat a curt nod towards the back of the cart. Kat jumped up into the back, shifting some of the cargo before helping Rupert lift Kyna up beside her. Once Rupert had taken his place in the back, Carey gripped the edge and swung herself up beside them, quickly ensuring her sword was still in place. If the couple were alarmed by their unusual appearance, they didn't show it.

They were an older couple, probably farmers by their attire. The man's wispy grey hair stuck out from under a brown wool hat perched high on his head, and he wore a worn black woollen coat over a long white shirt. His boots were laced high, sitting just below his knees, and they were splattered with flecks of dried mud. The woman wore similarly muted colours, her cream blouse tucked firmly into a long, dark woollen skirt. A shawl was wrapped tightly around her shoulders, and her fading dark hair was tucked beneath a patterned scarf tied under her chin. She glanced back at the four curiously with heavy-lidded eyes before quickly drawing her gaze back to the road ahead.

"So?" Carey said under her breath to Kat.

Kat shrugged. "I don't know. I couldn't understand him. It wasn't until I gave him that leaf that he seemed interested in giving us a lift."

Rupert grunted. "Can yer blame him, though? Look at us."

Carey couldn't disagree. They were indeed unusual, what with their strange clothing and weapons, not to mention Kyna in her current state and Rupert's bright hair. Rupert had wrapped Kyna in his coat, ignoring the biting chill. They trundled along a wide rough-cut road that ran alongside the lake. The sun rose, the blue water burning orange as the light skipped across its surface. They huddled close in the back of the cart, silently watching the countryside slide past as they reminisced on the past twenty-four hours. So much had happened. So much had been revealed.

Malevolence. Elara Parnell. They were one in the same and the knowledge made Carey feel disquieted. She looked down at her hands, thinking back on every encounter she'd ever had with the Empress. Had there been signs? Should she have suspected it? The magic that flowed through her veins – was it the product of such evil? Perhaps dark magic was part of her bloodline. Perhaps she'd never had a choice…

No. That couldn't be it. Carey knew her magic, felt the difference between her powers and that which simply inhabited her body. It wasn't hers, even if she did have some modicum of control over it now. That wasn't some familial link to Malevolence. She balled her fists and swallowed back the bile that had risen in her throat.

"Carey? What are you thinking?"

Kat's voice floated to her on the cool morning breeze. She was watching her with her bright green eyes as though she could see right through her.

"I was thinking of what Saar said," Carey murmured, closing her eyes against the flood of memories burning through her mind. "About Malevolence…"

Kat growled at the mention. "Don't do it, Carey," she said fiercely.

"Do what?"

"Start thinking you're like her just because she's some relative."

Carey frowned. "I wasn't…"

Kat folded her arms defiantly. "No? You weren't thinking that that magic you have isn't somehow connected to her? That just because she went dark, and your sisters turned on us too, that that means you'll do it too some day? That the darkness will overcome you?"

Carey hadn't even thought of her sisters, and when she said as much, Kat stared back at her, eyes blazing. "I know you, Carey Lee. If you were going to turn, it would've been long before you ever found out about Malevolence. You've said so yourself – Saar offered you a place at his side, all sorts of power, but you turned him down."

"Of course, I did!"

"Then you have your answer," Kat shot back. "Malevolence may have been your grandmother's sister at some point a long time ago, but she gave up any ties to your family the moment she joined Saar. She's proven time and again that blood means nothing to her. She would rather spill it than honour it. So you stop thinking that she has some power over you right this instant. You are a Seeker. She is nothing but an Imperial."

They stared at each other for a long moment. Carey's heart thudded in her chest, and she felt fearful and hopeful, daring to believe Kat's words.

Rupert, who'd been sitting silently, said, "Kat's right, Carey – yer not goin' to turn, not now. Besides, I'm inclined ter let you know that if you ever did, I'm not sure we could be friends anymore."

A wide grin split his face and Kat gave him a shove, her lips tugging ever so slightly at the corners of her mouth.

The knot in Carey's stomach eased as she realised she wasn't alone in this. She'd never been alone. Elara Parnell had felt alone, neglected, and Saar had taken advantage of that. But Carey had always had Kat, and Ji, and Rupert, and her parents. She had never felt the loneliness Elara must have; if she had, perhaps she'd have caved to Saar's offers too.

The sun was well and truly up now, and Carey looked over the hunched backs of their hosts to see a small city before them. Tall stone buildings of cream stone were surrounded by lower buildings in darker shades and the streets were already busy, the road muddy from the cold and the damp. Kat leant over and asked the driver the name of the city. Despite not understanding a single word Kat spoke, he understood her hand signals as she pointed towards the looming buildings.

"Petrovsk-Port," the old man said in a rumbling voice. "Eto Petrovsk-Port."

"Petrovsk-Port?" Rupert murmured, looking around. "Where in the Common Realm is that?"

Carey shrugged, having never heard of it before. Her childhood education at the orphanage hadn't extended much farther than the edge of the European continent.

As they trundled into town, they passed an impressive rail station, the façade of which stretched a good way down the road and stood taller than anything around it. It was built from a light brick that had already begun to stain from the soot of the trains it serviced. The old man pulled up alongside the entrance, clearly believing that they required further transport. Instead of arguing, which would've gotten them nowhere in any case, Carey and the others disembarked, thanking the elderly couple nonetheless, and watched as they joined the morning traffic heading into the town.

Rupert, who was holding Kyna in his arms protectively, pointed across the road. "Look. I think we might be in luck."

A two-storey building bore a sign over its doorway and a wide window that looked into some kind of inn or café. The windows above were open, curtains fluttering, affording the group a glimpse of what might be apartments or, if they were lucky, rooms for board. They crossed over to it, avoiding the people on horses and carts, and entered the inn. Dark wood panelling covered every surface, offset by a moulded ceiling of light cream. Elaborate copper light fixtures lined the walls, globes of yellow casting the room in a warm glow. Booths upholstered in deep green and red velvet ran along the right wall opposite the bar, tables illuminated by dripping candles at their centres. Heavy framed paintings hung at intervals depicting what looked like storybook creatures of this realm in faded colours. None were terribly pleasant to look at. They were angular and almost crude in nature, but gold flecks threaded through each, giving a magic to them they'd have otherwise lacked.

A thin layer of pipe smoke hung in the air and Carey noticed that the few patrons were nursing large mugs of steaming liquid, clearly eager to fight off the chill that lingered around the doorway.

The man behind the bar, thin with dark features and a rather impressive moustache, glanced up with them in alarm as Rupert stepped in with Kyna still cradled against him, Kat with her wild hair and sai at her back, and Carey with her own weapon peeking over her shoulder. He began speaking rapidly in a thickly accented language that Carey could not understand.

Kat stepped forth.

"We need beds," she said, holding her hands up to one side of her face and leaning against them in a mimicry of sleeping. "We can pay."

She produced a single gold leaf, holding it out in the palm of her hand. The man, who'd begun to shake his head, stopped, staring at the leaf. Some of the other patrons were following the exchange. The man gingerly took the leaf from Kat's hand and inspected it as though it might suddenly disappear. When it didn't, he looked back at the four of them with wide eyes, then hurriedly summoned a young man from the other end of the bar.

The fellow couldn't have been much older than Kat or Carey, and at some low-cast words from the moustached owner, he stumbled forwards in a hurry to beckon them up a staircase behind the counter. The boy wore what seemed to be the fashion in these parts – loose-fitting trousers tucked into high brown boots and a loose white shirt cinched at the wrists. His sleeves billowed out in a way that made it look like his shirt was almost too big for him. He had thick dark eyebrows and a mess of black hair, and his skin, despite the cold environment, had a warm glow to it, as though he spent a lot of time in the sun.

He gave them a nervous smile over his shoulder as he led them up the narrow stairs. The hallway at the top was long and lit by more round light fixtures that jutted out from the walls. It was a simpler décor than that of downstairs – the wood less polished and more worn – but it was clean and well kept.

The young man led them to the very end room and opened the door with a set of keys at his belt. As he led them inside, he handed another key to Kat, his eyes flitting over each of them in turn. Kat gave him a small smile.

"I'm Kat," she said, placing her hand over her heart. "Kat. And you?" Kat pointed to the boy, who seemed startled that she would speak to him.

He swallowed hesitantly before answering slowly, placing his hand on his chest. "Misha."

"Misha." Kat smiled wider, holding out her hand. "Nice to meet you."

For a moment it seemed Misha was too scared to take Kat's hand, but in the end, he shook hands. *"Priyatno s vami poznakomit'sya."* Then he left, shutting the door gently behind him.

Carey shot a quizzical glance at Kat.

"Commoner," Kat said. "No magic whatsoever."

"I thought you didn't have to touch a person anymore to know," Carey said.

"If I want to be absolutely certain, it helps. Plus, I'm dead tired. That really makes a difference."

There were two low beds in the sparsely furnished room, one on either side of the room. There was a small window in between and by the door stood a small table with a wash basin. Rough wool blankets were folded neatly at the end of each of the beds and Carey wondered if they'd be warm enough – the room was frigid.

Rupert laid Kyna down on a bed and pulled off his bag so he could shuffle through its contents. Despite their early-morning swim, the contents were dry. He pulled out small bottles of dried plants and liquids, examining each with a cursory glance before laying them on the bed by Kyna. Retrieving a small mortar and pestle, Rupert mixed a number of the ingredients and proceeded to crush them together, muttering as he did so. Once they were combined, he carefully tipped them into a small vial of blue liquid, and, with magic sparking at his fingertips, he swirled the contents gently. Steam rose from the vial. Rupert blew on it, then lifted it to his sister's lip and let a small amount slip between them.

Carey and Kat stood, unwilling to move at that moment, still strapped with their bags and weapons as they watched their friend work. Slowly but surely, colour began to return to Kyna's cheeks. Carey let out a sigh of relief, the action mirrored by both Kat and Rupert, and they all laughed.

They might be in the Common Realm again, in a strange city in an unknown country, but for now, they were all right.

They were not alone.

~Chapter Twenty-Two~

The Ancient

Once they were sure Kyna would be fine, Kat and Carey retrieved some food from the bar downstairs and brought it back up to their room. Despite the chill that permeated the walls, Carey figured that with the four of them all in there together, they should be able to keep each other warm. After they'd eaten and washed and mended their damaged clothes, Kat convinced Carey and Rupert to rest while she took first watch. Rupert, always the watchful Healer, refused, but Carey could feel the exhaustion of the past few days starting to set in, so she gladly wrapped herself in woollen blankets and fell asleep to the hum of Rupert and Kat talking in low voices.

She was standing atop a mountain, overlooking a great expanse of green and brown, snow and grass. The night sky was ablaze with more stars than she'd ever seen, and Carey wondered if this was a real place. Despite the altitude it wasn't cold, and Carey looked around, wondering where she was.

Movement caught her attention and she spun around, stumbling backwards in surprise.

There was someone there with her. An unusual someone.

Carey had never seen anyone like him before. He was exceptionally tall with a muscled torso and broad shoulders. His brilliant white hair stood in startling contrast to his flawless dark skin and he was clothed in nothing but a cloth of midnight-blue that hung low from his hips. Intricate gold patterns woven into the material flashed in the breeze. His electric blue eyes reflected the stars, but it was the wings that took her breath away.

Wings.

Great feathered wings were furled against his shoulders.

An angel?

Her dreams of flashing light and the rustling of feathers...

The man dropped his gaze from the stars, levelling an apathetic look at Carey. He didn't speak but held her with an unflinching stare, his eyes like chips of ice. Unsure of what was happening or if she should speak, Carey stood, unblinking. His face was both young and old somehow; shadows of unspoken things flashed across his features, and an odd sense of magic rolled off of him. It made Carey uneasy, like she wanted to run as far as she could from him.

The man's wings ruffled slightly, the tips of the feathers flashing silver in the moonlight.

"Carey Lee."

His voice was an oncoming storm, a low rumbling she felt to her very core. Carey swallowed nervously. It hadn't been a question, simply a statement, but she felt inclined to nod. The man turned back to look over the valley below and pointed, arm straight towards the horizon.

"North-west. That is where you will find him," he said.

Before Carey could say anything, the world around her, including the winged man, faded away, and she felt herself being pulled back to her physical body.

Carey blinked, the ceiling of the inn in Petrovsk-Port sliding into view in the dim lamplight. That had been the most unusual instance of Twilight Travelling she'd ever experienced. Coming back, it had felt less rushed, almost gentle. She thought of the strange man and his even stranger presence. Who was he? And what had he meant by his words? Kat and Rupert were still conversing in hushed voices, their heads close together. Carey cleared her throat, causing Rupert to jump.

Kat frowned. "Sorry. Were we being too loud?"

Carey sat up, shaking her head. "No, but I just had the weirdest Travelling experience."

She immediately had their full attention.

"It wasn't Saar, was it?" Kat asked. "Where is he?"

"No. This time I'm going to say unfortunately not." Carey rubbed her face.

Kat looked confused. "Then who?"

It took Carey a moment to get the word out. "An angel?"

Rupert raised an eyebrow. "I'm sorry. A what?"

Carey scrunched up her nose, the ridiculousness of it causing her to squirm a little. "An angel. I found myself on the top of some mountain range where it was already night-time, and a… *man* with actual *wings* appeared next to me."

"What did he do, this angel?" Kat asked, scepticism in her voice.

"Well, that's the thing. He said my name, and then, 'North-west. *That is where you will find him'*. Then he disappeared and I woke up."

Carey frowned; she regretted not saying something to the man before he'd disappeared. Anything really, even if just to ask *who.*

After a moment, Kat said, "He meant Saar, didn't he?"

Carey covered her face with her hands and groaned. "I want to say yes. I mean, it would make sense, wouldn't it? Who else are we looking for? But what if this was just Saar trying to throw us off again? I know I've blocked him from finding us, but he could've figured a way around it for all I know. He's a Shapeshifter, after all"

"Wait," Rupert interjected before Kat could say something else. "Yer said he looked like an angel. Yer mean one of those bein's Commoners have modelled in places of worship? Wings, light around their heads, long white robes…"

Dropping her hands from her face, Carey thought about the man's appearance. It was apparent that the wings were the only likeness to the angels she'd seen in the church near the orphanage as a child. Those depictions had been much more modest.

"Sort of?" Carey replied, trying not to blush at the memory.

Kat grinned as though she knew what Carey was thinking. "Sort of? Oh, now this I have to hear."

Trying to keep her voice level and ignoring the flush creeping up her neck, Carey described the winged stranger to Kat and Rupert. Kat's grin grew wider, almost a little wicked, and Carey felt as though she'd have had no trouble talking with the stranger. Rupert's face, however, lit with sudden understanding.

"That's not an angel," he said, his voice quieter, and Carey looked to him, ignoring Kat's smirk.

"You know what he was, then? He had magic, that much I know, but it felt *strange.*"

There really was no better way to describe it. The magic she felt in Kat and Rupert was something she was accustomed to. The magic inside her was different again, though she'd be able to distinguish it if she ever came across another who possessed it. The magic that winged man held, though, was *overpowering.*

Rupert looked around the room, searching perhaps for the words to tell them what he knew.

Kat dropped her smile impatiently. "Just tell us, Rupert."

Rupert bit his lip. "All right then. That wasn't an angel. It was an Ancient."

"An Ancient?" Kat repeated, as though she couldn't quite believe what he was saying.

"Yes. My father used ter tell Kyna and I stories of the Ancients. They were the beginnin' of magic, the first ter bestow it upon the realms. For those who were unable ter possess it like wizards an' witches, they gave them objects imbued with magic ter wield."

Carey looked over at her Vuletian sword, thinking of the magic that coursed through it.

"They are all-powerful, benevolent bein's that watch over the realms. I have a feelin' that's where Commoners get their angels from – there have been times in history where Ancients have helped, intervened even, an' because Commoners have no basis fer magic, or they associate it with evil, they invented angels ter explain their existence."

Kat shifted on the edge of Kyna's bed, eyes closed as she spoke. "I've heard of the Ancients too, but I'd never heard a description or seen a picture of one."

"What do yer know of them?"

Kat narrowed her eyes. "Pretty much what you just said, but they never mentioned anything about angels or wings."

"My father was a scholar of history," Rupert said. "Perhaps it was somethin' he came across, but I remember him always describin' them with wings. Was there anythin' else about him that yer noticed, Carey?"

"No. Which makes me wonder if it wasn't just some diversion set up by

Saar to lead us in the wrong direction. If it'd been an Ancient, shouldn't he have given me more to go on? Told me what he was? Or even that he was there to help?"

"What do yer think we should do, then?" Rupert said.

Kat looked from Rupert to Carey, lips pursed. "Go north-west."

"What?" Carey said, surprised.

"I think we should go north-west. You said this man's magic felt strange. You've never said that about Saar's before, which makes me think this isn't him. And even if this man was sent by Saar to distract us, honestly, we have nothing else to go on. We might as well go north-west and see where it takes us," Kat said.

The thought of blindly following the instructions of the might-be Ancient made Carey nervous, but Kat's argument made sense. They had nothing else to go on – Saar wasn't about to appear and tell them where he was headed – and it was either this or have a coin decide where they should head next.

Carey gave a resigned sigh.

"Fine. I guess we're heading north-west then."

*

By the morning, Kyna had recovered sufficiently enough for them to continue. Helped along by Rupert and Kat, Kyna, still rather sickly looking, made her way across the road from the inn to the train station. Carey trailed them, keeping a sharp eye on their surroundings. It seemed they'd been allowed a reprieve from Imperial attacks and were merely treated to the odd stare or murmur. Their clothing was distinctly foreign, and Carey wasn't terribly thrilled with the attention they were receiving. With their weapons hidden beneath their coats and in their satchels, they managed to buy tickets for the train. Clearly gold was its own currency, and the moment the ticket salesman had seen the golden leaf in Kat's hand, he'd given them first-class tickets to a city called Warsaw that, judging by the maps on the wall behind the clerk, was as north-west as the railway allowed. Carey supposed they would just have to keep an ear out for trouble on their way and find another mode of transport once they disembarked.

They boarded the carriage, the steam locomotive hissing and puffing up front, and found themselves in a rather spectacular private compartment. The seats were lined with red velvet and the ceiling's intricate mouldings matching the carved wood of the armrests. Cast-iron light fixtures sat on either side of the sliding wooden door, which had a glass window lined with gold paint. A privacy curtain was pulled back from the glass, allowing them to see out into the corridor, but given it also gave strangers the chance to peek in, Carey pulled it shut.

Kyna curled up on the seat by the window and Rupert sat close to his patient.

"So," Kat said, taking the seat opposite Rupert and Kyna after stuffing her bag in the rack overhead. "Warsaw?"

Rupert slumped back in his seat. "That's what the man said. Not sure how long that's supposed ter take, but perhaps this is a good opportunity ter get some rest."

Carey smiled. "I doubt I've ever heard you sound so exhausted."

"Yes, well, I blame Ji fer completely understatin' the reality of it all. You lot are straight-up crazy."

Kat snickered, then folded her arms behind her head and kicked her legs out in front of her. "Oh, you have no idea."

There was a loud *CLUNK*, and with a shudder, the train began to move as Rupert and Kat exchanged teasing words and jokes. Smoke billowed past their window as they began to speed away from the station, and soon they were past the outer limits of Petrovsk-Port, making their way through fields deadened by the cold.

They'd brought food from the inn, and in between meals they took turns sleeping on the soft velveteen benches. The ticket inspector came around and gave them a general look of suspicion before leaving them to their own devices.

Carey couldn't remember ever travelling so lavishly and spent the better part of their trip observing their surrounds and enjoying what would probably be their only respite.

Her thoughts drifted between Saar and his plans to the mysterious winged being Rupert was so sure was an Ancient. It seemed strange to her that such a person, if he could be called such, would even be interested in them. If he was indeed helping them find Saar, what were his motivations? She shivered at the memory of him, the way his voice had seemed to vibrate through her entire body. It was both chilling and strangely comforting, which only made her more wary.

"I'd certainly be interested in meeting this Ancient," Kat commented with a smirk.

Carey rolled her eyes at her friend. "I wonder why he only came to me, though? Why not all of us?"

Kat glanced over at Rupert and Kyna, who were propped up against opposite sides of the door, sleeping, and shrugged. "I can't say. Obviously, I've never encountered one. But Carey–" she turned back to face her, all vestiges of humour gone "–this could be either a blessing or one huge curse. For now, we should head north-west. Take him at his word. But anything else... I don't want to fall into another trap. Like you've said before, Saar is always two steps ahead and he'll do anything to knock us straight off course."

Carey didn't need telling twice. She'd been hoodwinked too many times by that man and she wasn't about to let him do so again.

Seramina's life depended on it.

The train stopped a handful of times that first day, and Carey and the others watched as they passed villages and cities. The weather didn't improve, what with the constant grey clouds and weak sunlight, but their compartment remained warm, heat from the engines pumped in through a small iron grate over their heads. Kyna was almost fully recovered by the time night fell and was amazed by the general splendour of their cabin. Rupert seemed much more at ease now Kyna was feeling better, and his joking personality gradually resurfaced. They needed that, the laughter and the jokes, to offset the horrors. Once again, Carey's fingertips met the edges of the star in her pocket. She couldn't believe how lucky she'd been so far, but then perhaps there was a reason she'd not lost it yet. Perhaps Ji had made it so...

Ji.

Carey jerked upright. They were in the Common Realm, which meant she should be able to contact him.

She cursed out loud, thinking of how ridiculous it was that she hadn't thought of that the moment they'd cleared the lake.

"Charmin'," Rupert commented and Kyna giggled as she munched on a chunk of bread.

Kat raised an eyebrow in question.

"Ji!" Carey smacked her forehead.

"Yes," Kat said, drawing the word out. "What about him?"

Carey still couldn't grasp her stupidity. "I can contact him now! We're in the same realm – no closed gateways or anything. I can *contact* him!"

Kat's eyes lit up. "So, instead of just contacting him, you're telling us instead?"

Carey jumped to her feet, nervous energy coursing through her body. She wanted to, so very badly, but the mere thought sent her into a frenzy. Ji. She would finally see him again. Ji. Speak to him. Hold him… Thoughts of their last encounter reeled through her mind and subconsciously she lifted a finger to her lips.

Kat clasped Carey by the shoulders to stop her pacing. "Stop. Carey, just *stop*."

Rupert and Kyna simply watched, bemused. Carey blinked, shaking herself from her memories. Anticipation – that's what it was. It tingled through her body, making her heart race and her hands twitch. But she concentrated on Kat's face as she continued to speak, willing herself to calm down.

"Stop," Kat commanded once more, looking directly into Carey's eyes. "Just take a seat, breathe in, and calm yourself. You can do this."

Of course I can do this, Carey thought. It was just… this wasn't just anyone. This was *Ji*.

"You're right," she said, taking her seat again. Rupert, Kyna, and Kat were all watching her now, and their gazes threatened to flare her anxiety and nerves once more. She looked away, shutting her eyes instead. "I just have to think of Ji."

Carey took a deep breath. She took hold of her memories thinking only of Ji, his ruffled hair, laughing smile, deep, soothing voice… She pictured his face, imagined what he would say, how he would feel…

She reached out into the void, searching for the one person that felt like home, a shining beacon in the dark. She cast out through the darkness, calling to him with her mind, separating herself from her physical body. He was out there. Ji was out there.

Yet, as the moments wore on, anticipation gave way to worry.

The tether that ran between them was there, pulling at her heart, but Carey couldn't find him. Nothing but darkness greeted her.

As panic rose in her chest, she found herself reeling back into her body, the void shrinking. She found Kat, Rupert, and Kyna still watching her. She opened her mouth to speak, but nothing came out.

"Did you find him?" Kat asked, her eyes raking her expression, her smile falling from her face. "Carey?"

Her voice broke. "I couldn't find him."

"What?" Rupert asked.

Carey shook her head. "I couldn't find him. I searched and searched but he wasn't there. He's not *anywhere.*"

She felt hot tears prick her eyes, though she wasn't sure exactly why. This wasn't proof of foul play or anything, but something just didn't feel right.

Kat gripped her hands tightly.

"Don't," she said. "This doesn't mean anything. For all we know, he's hidden himself with some enchantment, just like we have. He knows Saar can Travel. He's probably just protecting himself. In fact, I bet that's exactly what he's done. There are still plenty of witches and wizards still living in this realm, many who are strong enough to hide someone who wants to be hidden."

"But he had to know we'd come," Carey retorted, wiping her eyes with the back of her hand impatiently. "Why would he hide from *us?*"

Rupert cleared his throat. "Kat's right, Carey. Ji wouldn't leave himself exposed. He knows that he can't let himself get caught, not even in this realm. We'll find him, don't yer worry. He's still out there."

Carey took a few deep breaths before nodding. It made sense that Ji would be hiding, especially since he was on his own in this realm. And he had promised he'd find her again. *He'd* find *her.* Perhaps Kat and Rupert were right. Perhaps it was not they who needed to find Ji, but Ji who needed to find them. She forced back her fears, calmed her panic. She still felt that irresistible pull she felt towards Ji. Surely that had to mean something.

Carey held tight to that connection. They would find each other again, of that she was absolutely determined.

~Chapter Twenty-Three~

Hunted

By their second day aboard the train their food supplies were running low, so Carey and Rupert made their way to the dining car to see what they could muster. There was a bar that looked promising, so they made their way down the car, past the diners sitting at tables set with white linen and silver cutlery, earning more than just the occasional stare. The fact that Rupert's hair was now a lurid shade of green streaked with white probably didn't help, and Carey wondered if she could perhaps persuade Kyna to tone down the shades for this realm. By the time they'd reached the bar, half the car was staring, and Carey made a pointed effort to ignore them. Rupert went to order while she wandered to the door separating them from Second Class. The car swayed and rocked as they rattled along, a swirl of white whipping past the windows.

It had begun to snow during the night, and the first light of dawn had shone upon a brilliant landscape of white beyond the frosted window. Even with the heating, the chill of the snow permeated the glass pane, an intricate pattern of crystals spreading across the glass. She looked through to the Second Class carriage, giving it a careful search before turning back to find Rupert chatting eagerly to a young woman by the bar. She was unusually dressed – at least, unusually compared to the rest of the passengers. She wore all black: black blouse buttoned high at her throat, black slacks tucked into black boots, and a long black coat and gloves. The only hint of colour was her long white hair through which a streak of red ran from her widow's peak all the way down her back. Her almond-shaped eyes were a dark blue, almost violet, and they gave her an almost feline look. There was something seductive about the way she was speaking to Rupert – seductive and dangerous. Her red lips curved into a wry smile as she listened to him. Carey edged closer, listening hard; the woman's attention was solely on Rupert, allowing Carey to sidle right up behind him.

"I'm a Healer, Head Healer at the palace. I'm travellin' at the moment with Carey Lee and Kat Lawrence – perhaps yer know of them?"

Carey froze. What on earth was Rupert doing?

The woman spoke, her voice low. "And where are you going?"

Rupert leant against the bar, his body relaxing in towards the woman. "Well, fer now we're headed ter Warsaw, but after that, we're not entirely sure. Perhaps we might see yer there?"

Carey couldn't believe what she was hearing. Rupert was telling a perfect stranger *everything*.

"Hmm," the woman said, and Rupert shifted just enough that Carey could see the smirk twisting her lips. "Perhaps you will."

She left, exiting through the door to First Class with a swish of her hair and long coat. Carey gripped Rupert's shoulder and pulled him around to face her, anger and disbelief creeping through her at what she'd just heard.

"What the hell was that?" she said, losing all sense of decorum and startling several nearby diners who glared at her outburst.

Rupert looked at her, startled. "Sorry? Did I miss somethin'?"

Carey was not in the mood for Rupert's jokes. "Are you serious? That woman that just walked out of here – you were telling her everything! Who you were travelling with, where we were going! We might as well hang a banner with a great big arrow saying, 'Seekers here!' on the side of the train!"

Rupert glanced about nervously before taking Carey by the arm and gently moving her to the very end of the car. "What are yer talkin' about? I was just waitin' at the bar for the man ter get us our food. What woman?"

Carey gaped incredulously. "The woman you were talking with! I saw you – *heard* you!"

Rupert didn't answer, and as the moments stretched between them, Carey started to wonder if she was missing something. Maybe Rupert wasn't lying. Maybe…

"You don't remember her?" Carey asked, a slew of possibilities forming.

Rupert narrowed his eyes then shook his head. "Like I said, I was just waitin' fer the bartender–"

Carey didn't wait to hear the rest. She grabbed Rupert by the wrist and pulled him back towards their compartment, earning a couple more disapproving looks as they raced past the tables. She slid open the door to their carriage and was about to step through when a short sharp quarrel struck the doorframe to her right, cracking the varnished veneer. Carey looked up to see the woman from the bar standing before her, partway down the hall of the carriage. She had a crossbow lifted to her shoulder, another bolt already nocked. Screams and shouts erupted from the dining car behind them but Carey ignored them, slamming the door shut against the noise.

"Who's that?" Rupert cried as Carey shoved him back against the wall as another bolt flew past.

"That," Carey replied, reaching for her magic, "is the woman you just met!"

Before their attacker could fire another shot, Carey flung her hands out, bringing forth just enough magic to knock her off her feet. It flew straight at the woman, but at the last possible second, she stepped aside, dodging Carey's attack. Carey stared. How had she done that? She'd have to be impossibly fast to have timed that so perfectly. But before Carey could get an answer, another bolt landed with a hard thud beside Carey's head.

"We need ter get to Kyna and Kat," Rupert said, eyes darting between the woman and the car door behind him.

Their compartment was only two doors away. Carey just had to distract this woman long enough to get inside. She looked up at the lantern by the woman's head as another bolt was aimed at her. Carey grabbed the lantern above her own head and forced magic into it. With a series of deafening pops, the lanterns exploded down the corridor, one after the other. Glass rained down on their attacker, and under the cover of the distraction, Carey and Rupert darted into their compartment, slamming the door shut and locking it.

Kat and Kyna were already grabbing bags and weapons. As Carey turned, Kat tossed her sword to her. Carey threw it onto her back and buckled the strap across her chest. She turned back towards the door just as the window smashed inwards. Kyna let out a small squeal. Kat stepped up, striking out with a kick as the door slid open. Kat's foot connected with the woman's midsection. The crossbow flew from the woman's hands as she crashed into the wall opposite and slumped to the floor.

Hand out, Kat advanced on the woman as Carey, Kyna, and Rupert slipped past, heading for the dining car.

"Out cold," Kat reported when she caught up to them. "That should slow her down a bit."

As they ran into the car, screams and shouts erupted once more. Passengers scrambled from their seats, pushing back against the windows to get as far away from the Seekers as possible. The barman seemed a little braver and attempted to halt them. Kat flicked out a single sai, spinning it menacingly as she advanced, and the man cowered behind his bar.

"After you," Rupert said, holding the door to the Second Class carriage open and allowing Kat to step through first.

Kyna followed, and Carey nodded for Rupert to proceed so she could watch their rear. No one was following them, but that didn't mean they wouldn't.

They hustled past the plush forwards-facing seats of Second Class; passengers stared in surprise. Stopping at the rear of the car, they cast about for any others that might be in pursuit.

"All right," Kat said, low and fast. "Anyone care to explain?"

Carey glanced at Rupert then back to Kat. "That woman approached Rupert in the dining car. She must have enchanted him because he was telling her everything and then, as soon as she left, he forgot all about her. We came to find you two, and that's when she attacked."

"Is there anyone else with her?" Kat asked.

"We don't know," Carey replied, looking over her shoulder.

"But that doesn't mean there won't be, does it?" Rupert said.

Kat huffed. "No, it does not."

Kyna was peering through the window leading to the Third Class car. "There's no one comin' from this way."

Kat looked back towards First Class before giving a quick nod. "Let's get to the back of the train. That way, if we need to make a quick exit, it'll be easier."

Carey led them through Third Class, the bench seats crowded with passengers and their luggage. Carey's gaze roamed the cramped car – passengers were sleeping, heads propped on their suitcases or travel companions, while others gave the four quick glances. One man, however, sat perfectly straight in his seat, his dark eyes watching them intently. Carey wanted to draw her sword but knew that it was too risky in such a cramped space. Instead, she brought the smallest touch of magic to her fingertips.

"Psst," Carey whispered out of the corner of her mouth. "The man in the green coat looking at us. Dark hair."

Rupert grunted in reply behind her.

Carey flexed her fingers. "Be ready."

Somehow Carey knew this man wasn't just some Commoner, and as they drew closer, he shifted in his seat. The moment she stepped level with him, he leapt to his feet and grabbed for her neck. Before he could make contact, however, Carey hit him square in the chest. The magic crumpled him back into his seat, the woman next to him shrieking in surprise. That sound was enough to awaken the car, and before they knew it, people were shouting and calling out. Not waiting to see what they might do, Carey took off at a sprint, the others following closely behind. A few tried to stop them, but Carey pushed past, knocking them off their feet. She burst through the door at the end into a baggage car, trunks and suitcases piled precariously. They kept running.

Shouts and cries followed them, but they didn't stop to look if anyone was pursuing them. They needed to get off this train, and they needed to do it right now.

"If we have ter jump," Rupert shouted, "it's best if we jump from the rear car. We don't want ter accidentally get caught in the train's slipstream. That could get messy."

Carey shook her head at Rupert's ability to pull humour out at a time like this but yelled her agreement back to him.

They rushed through into a second luggage hold and for a moment Carey thought they might actually escape without their attackers catching up. It was a short-lived moment, for no sooner had the thought formed in her mind than a roar of fury sounded from behind them. It was the woman, and, although she wasn't toting her crossbow, she was moving fast, her companion close behind her.

"Come on!" Carey reefed open the door to the final car.

She stopped, Rupert, Kyna, and Kat coming up short behind her.

Amongst the bags and crates stood three figures. A woman with cropped dark hair and a deeply scarred face stood to the left, her long brown woollen coat covering dark riding clothes. A tall, brawny fellow stood to the right, with a blond stubble of hair and a beard that curled down to his chest. He seemed oblivious to the cold, with a leather vest over a short-sleeved shirt and dark pants. A leather belt lined with daggers hung across his hips. And at the centre stood a young man with shoulder-length white-blond hair and eyes the same shade of blue-violet as their original attacker, now standing behind Carey and her friends. If Carey was to guess, she would've thought them brother and sister. Carey, Kat, Kyna, and Rupert all made to raise their hands in defence when he spoke.

"There'll be no more magic or fighting from you."

At first, Carey thought this was a strange thing to say. She would've thought a better action would be to duck, run, or fight. But then a strange sensation washed over her, and she felt her arm begin to lower of its own volition. Her body was obeying the young man's words despite her wanting to do very much the opposite. Beside her, Kat, Rupert, and Kyna were following suit, Kat's eyes wide with a mixture of fear, anger, and defiance.

"Come closer," the white-haired man said, crooking his finger at them.

No, Carey thought, willing herself to remain where she was, but just as with his previous command, she found herself moving forwards, unable to resist it. She came to a halt just in front of him and he stared at her, his eyes searching.

"Tell me your name," he said.

Carey swallowed hard, trying to fight the urge to speak, but it was impossible; the words came tumbling out of her mouth. "Carey Lee."

Something sparked in the man's eyes and a satisfied grin stretched across his lips.

"Excellent. We've been looking for you, Carey Lee. Now, if you and your friends would like to join us. Ah–" he said sharply as Carey went to speak "–no speaking. That won't be necessary. Follow me."

He walked to the side of the car and his burly companion slid back the door separating them from the outside world. Wind and snow whipped inside, and as much as Carey didn't want to follow this man, she again found herself incapable of denying him. He stepped to the very edge. Out of the corner of her eye, Carey noticed the man's companions move down to the end of the train and out onto the small platform beyond. One by one they swung up onto the ladder by the door that led to the roof. She couldn't fathom why they'd want to climb on top of a moving train, but right now that wasn't important. Their leader motioned to Carey.

"Come," he called over the howling wind and clattering of the train. "Jump."

~Chapter Twenty-Four~

Kings and Pawns

Carey's heart pounded a violent tattoo against her ribcage. She wanted her magic to save her as it had saved her before, but the man's words were binding – her thoughts drew not a single spark to her fingertips as she moved to the edge of the car. The cold, snow-covered ground beyond the tracks raced past, the trees a blur. Carey strained against the command, teeth gritted with determination until a bead of sweat trailed down her forehead. Her feet continued to move. She wasn't sure what happened when one jumped from a moving train, but Carey bet that it wasn't pleasant. Her toes reached the edge of the car. Despite the screaming in her head and the wild pounding of her heart, she closed her eyes and jumped.

The slipstream caught her, throwing her sideways, and she braced for the impact. But before Carey could even anticipate the inevitable crash to earth, something caught her by the shoulders. She was jerked roughly out of her fall and then upwards into the sky. Forcing her eyes open, she saw sharp talons clutching her shoulders. Above her, wings of red and orange flapped hard, pulling her up and away from the train below. Her breath caught in her throat – a griffon. There was no point trying to wriggle out of its grip – the griffon's clutch was like steel and they were climbing rapidly, leaving the ground far behind.

Carey glanced down to see four more griffons following. Each had a rider on its back, and she realised now why her attackers had climbed atop the train.

The cold winter air bit at Carey's exposed skin. She could feel herself shaking, her mind racing as she struggled to calm herself.

Kyna screamed from below and Carey tried desperately to turn in the griffon's grasp. She spotted the young girl, whose griffon was now level with her own, her face clasped in her hands as she tried to block the view from sight. Carey didn't blame her – she herself was trying her best not to look down at the cold, hard ground so far below. Each time she did, her stomach swooped uncomfortably, and she barely resisted the urge to hold on to the griffon's avian legs, instead grasping the strap of her sword.

That man and the way he'd spoken to her didn't imply Imperial or even Essedarian. Carey guessed that he wanted something from them. Perhaps they were to be used as hostages. Or bait. Wouldn't be the first time. That woman and her crossbow though – she'd have to keep an eye on her.

Carey caught glimpses of the others as their griffons rose and fell around her. Rupert was being hauled by one with midnight-blue plumage and he clutched his bag to his chest, his bright hair ruffled by the wind. Kyna was now gripping her griffon's legs so hard her knuckles had turned white and her face was a delicate shade of green, not unlike the colouring of the beast carrying her. Kat, in the clutches of a red griffon with silver-tipped wings, looked positively murderous. Carey knew that if she could reach for her sai, she would, height be damned.

It was late in the day, after her limbs had become stiff and face frozen, when the griffons began to descend towards a forest. Circling, they slowed as they approached the tops of the trees, a clearing visible beneath them, pristine snow covering the ground. Carey's griffon dipped suddenly, and before her feet could brush the ground, it released her, sending her tumbling. The snow stung her face, crystals burning her cheek as she rolled awkwardly, her sword ramming into her shoulder blade as she went. She saw the others dropped unceremoniously alongside her, Kat cursing and Kyna letting out a pained yelp as they rolled, sending white powder flying.

Carey got to her feet as the five beasts landed; the man who'd commanded them rode a pure-white griffon, its ruffled feathers a perfect match for its rider's hair. The group dismounted as Kat, Rupert, and Kyna joined Carey, dusting the snow from their clothes and hair. The white-haired leader stepped towards them, and as Carey and Kat raised their hands instinctively, he again called, "Stop!"

Kat swore as their hands dropped against their will. The man smiled, satisfaction etched in his face.

"Now, if you're quite done trying to kill us, let me introduce myself. I am Maël," he said, holding a hand to his chest. "This is Emilia–" he indicated the woman with the scarred face "–Kaleb–" the dark-haired man who'd tried to attack Carey in Third Class "–Niko–" the tall man with the beard "–and my sister, Reay."

The woman flipped her long white hair and stared at them with disdain. The smiling woman who'd enchanted Rupert on the train was nowhere to be seen.

"So, who are you then?" Kat asked. "Essedarian? Lone Imperials wanting some notoriety?"

Maël sneered at her words. "Imperials? Do we look like Imperials?"

Kat raised an eyebrow. "I've seen a lot of Imperials in my time. They don't always follow a type."

The hulking Niko grunted behind Maël and folded his arms.

"We're not Imperials," Maël said. "We're bounty hunters, and there's a price on your heads."

The statement left Carey mute. This was not what she had been expecting.

"Bounty hunters?" Rupert repeated. "If you're bounty hunters, then why did yer friend there try to do us in with a crossbow?"

The man's gaze flicked towards the woman and she gave an unapologetic shrug.

"She can be... *over-enthusiastic*. That being said, someone wants you so badly that they put out a rather large reward for anyone who could deliver you to a city in Ireland – Monaghan," he said in an almost bored tone.

Carey's ears pricked. "You're to take us to Monaghan?"

Emilia gave a derisive snort. "Not terribly bright, these ones, are they?"

Maël was studying Carey, as though considering her. "Not sure what you expected from a bunch of Seekers, Em. Come on, let's set up camp."

Bunch of Seekers?

His attitude angered Carey and she strode after him. The dark-haired Kaleb stepped between them, eyes hard with warning. Carey stood her ground, refusing to be intimidated.

"You said you weren't Imperials, yet you speak of us as though we're your enemies," Carey said. "Our enemies are Imperials. So, what are you?"

Maël's hand touched Kaleb's shoulder and the man obediently stepped aside. Maël's eyes were like ice as he glared at Carey, pink rising angrily in his cheeks.

"We," he said, indicating his fellow bounty hunters, "are not your allies, *Princess*. And just because we don't support the Order of the Rose or its pretentious cause, doesn't mean we're Imperials either. Some of us don't care for you *or* your war. Some of us just want to live our lives."

He spoke with such vehemence that Carey couldn't help but take a step back. She'd never met anyone who didn't identify with one side or the other. She'd become so used to either being admired as a Seeker or hated by Imperial loyalists that she'd never stopped to think that there might be some who were neither. It didn't make sense.

"How can you not care about the war?" she shot back. "It affects everyone – you included, regardless of what your feelings are towards us."

"Oh, I know very well how your war affects us, thank you very much," he sneered. "Had you stopped once to consider those beneath you, then maybe you'd have seen that." And he turned from her, his team following.

Carey wanted to say something in reply, shout at him as he retreated, but she felt a hand close around her arm.

"Don't, Carey," Rupert muttered, pulling her back towards the others. "It's not worth it."

Niko and Emilia came over to them and threw two sleeping rolls at their feet and a sack containing a meagre meal of meat, cheese, and bread. They then stood guard, their eyes never leaving their bounty.

The Seekers silently set up their inadequate camp, lighting a fire with a flint Rupert had packed "just in case", under the watchful eyes of their captors. Carey had attempted a small bit of magic but found herself still unable to bring forth even the tiniest of sparks. The whole affair had Kat in a dark mood – being unable to fight would be driving her crazy.

"So, what do you think?" Kat said as the sun began to dip below the horizon.

Carey chewed on a piece of crust. "You mean Monaghan?"

Kat nodded.

"Monaghan?" Kyna repeated. "What's so special about that place?"

Carey wanted to say nothing and ignore the gnawing pit in her stomach at the very mention of it, but she knew she couldn't.

"It was where Malevolence kept me all those years," she said.

"So, are you thinkin' Saar fer this?" Rupert said.

"Well, it's certainly not Malevolence," Kat replied. "At least, not yet."

"But, why? He's been tryin' ter stop us from followin' him 'til now, so what would make him change his mind?"

Carey stared out at the dark, trying to fathom Saar's motives. She couldn't think of any reason why Saar would put a bounty on them, but couldn't think of anyone else it could be. She sighed. If it was Saar, at least it meant they were on the right path, and the Ancient had been right.

Carey relayed her thoughts to the others, and while they agreed it was odd, Saar was the only likely possibility. With his desire to always be one step ahead, perhaps this was his way of maintaining an advantage.

"The question is," Kat continued quietly, "what do we want to do about..." She gave a surreptitious nod towards the bounty hunters sitting by their own fire.

Carey narrowed her eyes at Maël's turned back. "We can't fight them."

"And we can't use magic ter escape," Rupert added.

Kyna, huddled against Rupert's side against the cold, was taking in everything they were saying, but Carey could see she was thinking hard.

"Kyna?"

She jumped, as though she hadn't been expecting anyone to include her in the conversation. She hesitated, looked furtively over her shoulder at the hunters, then back at Carey. She seemed unsure, but Carey kept quiet, waiting.

"If it is Saar, and we want ter find him, an' these people want ter take us to him, then why do we have ter fight?" Kyna said.

Carey, Kat, and Rupert stared at Kyna. Then they stared at each other.

"You have a point, there," Kat said, and Rupert gave Kyna a wide smile and a playful nudge. "We don't have any other way of getting there, so if this lot really are just wanting their money, they'll drop us off right where Saar is with no effort on our part."

Carey bit her lip, contemplating this strategy. "Right. So, we use the bounty hunters. Get them to take us to Monaghan. They get their money, we get Saar."

"Unless, where they intend to exchange us in Monaghan is a trap," Kat said.

Carey thought back to Captain Vordeaux and how, despite Saar's promises of treasures untold, he had certainly ended up with a much worse deal. She doubted Saar would pay these hunters their bounty, even if they did make good on their end of the deal. He'd set a trap: take the Seekers and kill the hunters. That being said, would telling Maël and his merry band do the Seekers any good? Or would they think they were too high a risk and ditch them the first chance they got, no matter the price on their head?

"I say we let the hunters take us to Monaghan. I doubt Saar will even pay them, but we can't let them in on that or they might decide to cut and run. We'll work something out before we get there. But until then–" Carey glanced once more at Maël "–we act like the helpless hostages they expect us to be."

"Only, I don't think we really need ter act that hard," Rupert pointed out dryly as he dusted off his hands and made to get into the sleeping roll, and Kat grunted in agreement.

Despite their fire, the night air was frigid and uncomfortable. To keep warm, the four of them tucked into the two sleeping rolls they'd been given. Carey was increasingly thankful for the thick woollen coats they'd thought to wear, which were holding up fairly well against the chill. She lay on the outside of the roll, her back against Kat's, who was right next to Rupert. Kyna was curled up behind Rupert, her face buried into his coat, and surprisingly, in no time at all, they fell asleep under the watchful eyes of their guards.

All except Carey.

She was watching the bounty hunters. Emilia and Niko had swapped guard with Reay and Kaleb, turning in for the night, but Maël stayed by the fire. Carey found herself watching him. Like the Ancient, his magic seemed...

off. She had a feeling he wasn't a wizard, but he most certainly wasn't a Commoner either, not with his ability to command them with a simple word.

Sliding out from beside Kat, Carey started for where the bounty hunter sat, only to find herself face-to-face with his sister.

"Where do you think you're going?" she asked, her lip rising in a sneer.

"I'd like to talk with your brother, if it's all the same to you," Carey answered, trying to look past Reay's shoulder to see if Maël had noticed.

Reay raised one dark eyebrow. "And if I don't?"

Before Carey could answer, Maël spoke, keeping his face towards the fire.

"Let her past, Reay. It's not like she can do anything," he said, sounding almost bored.

Reay huffed out a breath of frustration, then stepped aside. Carey took a seat on the ground at Maël's side – not too close, but close enough to see his face in the firelight. The orange glow danced across his features, making him look young and old at the same time. He was gazing into the flames, his violet eyes almost black. Maël and his sister reminded Carey of Princess Mizéi with their delicate features, rounded faces, and pointed chins. There was something fierce about the siblings, however, something dangerous that Carey couldn't quite put her finger on, and when Maël finally turned his gaze to her, she felt a shiver trickle down her spine.

"You wanted something?" Maël said in the same uninterested tone.

Carey shook off the odd feeling. "Can I ask, who are you, exactly? You're not wizards."

She hoped she hadn't sounded rude or prying, but her curiosity was too strong.

Maël stared at her for a long moment before answering. "Is this so you can figure out how to escape?"

"I think we both know you have that covered. No, I just wanted to know, regardless of what your sister might think." She jerked a thumb over her shoulder towards Reay.

Maël seemed to find this amusing, as the corner of his mouth twitched. "Reay is the older sibling. She can be a little overprotective."

He paused, considering Carey before speaking again. "And you're right. I'm not a wizard, but neither am I a Commoner. I am a little of both, you could say."

When Carey frowned in confusion, he added, "I'm what they call a dhampir. Half-human, half… vampire."

Carey's eyes flicked towards Maël's mouth. She half-expected to see fangs or even blood there, given the stories she'd heard about vampires.

Maël gave a dark chuckle. "Don't worry, Princess. I won't bite. As a dhampir, I have all the strengths of a vampire without their weaknesses. I tend to prefer a good piece of meat to the soft skin of a human's neck."

Carey brought her gaze back up to Maël's, and she resisted the urge to back away from what she saw there. His violet eyes were tinged with red. At first, she thought it was merely a reflection from the fire, but the longer she looked, the more she realised it was more of a glow, a burning from deep within. It made her want to run.

"Is that why you can do what you do?" she said. "Make people do exactly what you say?"

"It's called Persuasion," Maël said with a smirk. "And yes, some dhampirs have that ability. My sister's own style of Persuasion is directed only at the male species and has an almost *amnestic* effect, which your unfortunate friend experienced back on the train."

Maël shifted so that his body faced Carey's, and she stiffened as he leant towards her.

"And yours?" she said, trying to keep her face neutral despite his proximity.

A devious grin spread across Maël's face, a wicked twinkle in his eyes. "I have no such limitations," he purred.

He leant even closer until there was barely anything between them. Carey didn't move, unwilling to do anything that might be misconstrued as an attempt at escape or attack, but his closeness was sending her heart into a frenzy, fear paralysing her just as well as any enchantment. The red in Maël's eyes flared as he closed the gap between them, his body flush against her own. Carey wanted to run, to fight, but Maël's power wouldn't allow her to even push him away, and she felt nauseated. He traced a cold finger along her cheek bone, his face impossibly close.

"I can smell your fear," he said against her lips. "You want to fight, to flee, but you can't because I will it so."

Carey's eyes widened and her stomach turned as he moved an inch closer, his dark, burning gaze still on hers.

"All the power in the world is nothing in comparison. And yet, you still sit here as though you are somehow better than us just because you have magic," he whispered.

Maël glared at her a moment longer before dropping his hand and moving back to his spot by the fire. Carey let out a sob of relief, unable to hold it back, clutching at her aching chest where her heart beat wildly.

"Why don't you go back to your friends, Princess," Maël sneered dismissively, his eyes back on the fire. "I'm not one for abusing my powers, unlike some. Yet, as you so unwittingly just demonstrated, you clearly expected no less of me. We're bounty hunters, not Imperials or brigands. We do our job and that is all."

Regaining her composure, Carey straightened, clenching her jaw as she fumed at his accusations. "It's not like you gave me much room to consider anything else with that little performance. And if that's how it is, then let me make a proposal."

Her words brought Maël's attention back to her, one eyebrow raised. "Oh really?"

"We think we know who put out this bounty on us. Thing is, we want to find him just as much as he wants to find us. So, you take us to him, and we won't fight or try to escape. *And* we'll make sure you get your bounty."

He stared hard at Carey as he ran a finger along his bottom lip in contemplation.

"You *want* to go to Monaghan?" Maël said.

When Carey said no more, he narrowed his eyes.

"Fine. But if I sense so much as a double-cross or an attempt to harm my team, I will consider our agreement forfeit. We won't be pawns in your game. Now go back to your friends. I wouldn't mind getting some sleep."

Carey wanted to ask what he meant by that comment about pawns, but she was compelled to leave him, her legs pushing her to stand and walk away from the hunter. Reay watched her pass with narrowed eyes but said nothing.

As Carey climbed back under their meagre bedding, Kat whispered, "What did he say?"

Carey, with her eyes on Maël's prone form across the clearing, answered, "We're going back to Monaghan."

*

Their understanding with the bounty hunters meant that their travelling arrangements became far more agreeable. Instead of dangling from the talons of the griffons, they instead rode behind the hunters, bound by Maël's Persuasion to "Sit there and look pretty". Rupert rode behind the diminutive Emilia, Kat with the surly Kaleb, and Kyna was propped up behind the towering Niko, who looked thoroughly put-out with the arrangement, mumbling something about a "nanny".

Carey had started towards Reay, assuming she was to saddle-up with her given the choices, but Maël had called her over to him instead. She'd hesitated, wondering why he would have her ride with him when he clearly despised her, but perhaps that was why he wanted her close. Keep your friends close and your enemies closer and all.

They soared over snow-covered lands, passing quaint towns and sprawling cities. Carey wondered whether Commoners below could see them, or whether they simply resembled great birds, far, far away. She looked around at the others – Kat was scowling, holding onto the fabric at Kaleb's waist reluctantly. Rupert appeared to be deep in thought, his gaze set somewhere in the distance as they sped through the air. And Kyna had her head buried in Niko's back, an action which had the great bearded man arching away from her, though to no effect. Carey saw Reay watching her and Carey turned her gaze from the hunter's glare.

"Does your sister always look like that when she's not seducing unwitting men?" she shouted to Maël over the rush of the wind.

Maël glanced at his sister before offering a shrug. "I'd say she hates you about the same amount as I, but has a harder time hiding that particular emotion."

Carey scowled as his reply played over and over in her head. She couldn't say why it bothered her so much that this man and his friends seemed to hate them, but it did. Their indifference was irksome, and she also couldn't shake his pawn comment from the night before.

They landed sometime around midday to rest and eat before carrying on towards Paris, where they were to stay the night. The hunters apparently had business in the city, about which they were vague enough to discourage Carey and Kat from asking more. They sat in one big circle, sharing a bag of food around as they warmed their hands at a fire.

Maël sat opposite Carey, his bored gaze flitting to her from time to time as they ate. Reay continued to glare, something that seemed to be bothering Kat as much as her, and as the white-haired woman whispered something to Kaleb, her eyes on Carey, Kat sat up straight, her eyes flashing.

"All right. What? What is your problem with us?" she said loudly, gesturing at Reay with a jerk of her chin.

Reay's lips turned up in a challenging smile as she leant forwards, her elbows resting on her knees. "You want to know what my problem is?"

Kat glared in reply and the hunter sauntered over to them.

Carey tensed.

"I'll tell you gladly. You're Seekers. You see everything in black and white – supporter or Imperial. If you're a supporter, you're expected to just drop everything to help the Order, your own life be damned. And if you're an Imperial, well…" Reay shrugged. "You don't care about anyone else's life but your own. You think that if we're not fighting your bloody war, then what are we doing? Some of us don't want to play your game, despite what you might think."

Carey spoke up before Kat could fire a retort.

"You speak of a game," she said to Reay, then turned to Maël, "and you of pawns. What did you mean by that, exactly? What game do you think we're playing here?"

Reay didn't reply, instead deferring to her brother, who looked across at Carey and the others. His hands were clasped in front of him as though in prayer, his lips resting against his steepled fingers.

"You're the Seekers of the Order of the Rose, the elite, the ones pulling the strings. You are the generals, the ones who sit back and order others ahead of them so that they may die in your place, sacrifice themselves so that you might advance. The pawns. Other people – *better* people – thrown in danger's way for the advancement of the king. You say you don't know what game we speak of, but I can bet that you play it better than most. How many people have laid down their lives for you and your war? Do you even know?"

His words were a kick to the chest, a knife between the ribs. They burned into Carey and she couldn't reply, knowing that even though she'd never ordered anyone to die for her, they'd died anyway. Marjen had told her that to blame herself would be to dishonour their sacrifice, but Maël's words had brought back the guilt and pain of each and every one.

Rupert scoffed. "Yer can't seriously believe that, can you?"

Maël's eyes snapped to Rupert. "What? It's true though, isn't it? Don't tell me you weren't expecting us to fall in line the instant you found out we weren't Imperials."

He carried on, not giving them a chance to refute his accusation. "Your presence here brings nothing but a black cloud. Wherever you go, good people fall underfoot, and you don't even stop to look back."

Carey's guilt was shifting to anger, but before either she, Kat, or Rupert could say anything, Kyna got to her feet. Her hands were clenched at her side and her hair flew wild around her face as she shouted at Maël with absolute rage.

"That's not true!" she spat. "That's not true at all! Carey an' Kat have never done anythin' but try an' protect those around them. An' my brother is a Healer – a *Healer*! He doesn't even like weapons an' his biggest fear is not bein' able ter save those who need savin'! Right now, we're tryin' ter save my best friend from a horrible man an' stop him before he does anythin' else ter anyone else, includin' you! So, don't you *dare* say that we don't care! Don't. You. *Dare!*"

Carey, Kat, and Rupert stared speechlessly at Kyna as she stood huffing and puffing from her outburst. Niko had his eyebrows raised, while Kaleb and Emilia looked rather amused by the spectacle. Maël and Reay, on the other hand, looked wholly bored and unmoved by Kyna's speech.

"Regardless," Maël said coolly. "Black and white. You'll never see it any other way."

He turned from the Seekers and began talking to Kaleb.

Kyna looked as though she was about to start crying, and Rupert tugged her back down beside him.

"That was… impressive," Kat said, giving Kyna a nudge on the shoulder, but Kyna looked dejected.

"He didn't even listen ter me," she said in a small voice, so different to that of a moment ago.

Carey glanced over at Maël again, but he was deep in conversation with Kaleb. Reay, however, was still watching them closely, her face a mask of indifference.

"I have a feeling that no matter what we say, we won't be able to change their minds," Carey said, her stomach churning.

It shouldn't have bothered her so much, but his words, his apathy, his general hatred for the Order… it just wasn't what she was used to, and she understood Kyna's desire to make them feel otherwise.

"Don't worry," Rupert said as he tried to comfort Kyna. "We don't have ter put up with them fer long."

"Speaking of which," Kat said, gaze flitting over to the hunters to make sure they weren't eavesdropping. "If it is Saar in Monaghan, how are we going to approach that?"

Looking down at her hands and flexing her fingers, Carey said, "Head on. We have the advantage this time. He won't be expecting us to have made a truce with our bounty hunters, so…."

Rupert's eyes widened as Kat gave an approving nod.

Kyna narrowed her eyes, still glaring at Maël, and whispered in a hard voice, "And we're goin' ter get Seramina back."

~Chapter Twenty-Five~

The Exposition Universelle

The lights of Paris came into view long before they reached the outskirts of the city. Carey marvelled at its beauty, the buildings at its centre glowing brightly against the night sky. The bounty hunters brought their beasts down in a copse of trees on the very edge of the city. Carey slid from her griffon's back, stepping out of the way hastily as Maël leapt down, not caring that he'd almost landed right on top of her. Niko, hulking mountain of a man that he was, helped Kyna down, making sure she landed gently before releasing her hastily and walking away. No sooner had their boots touched the ground than Maël gave Kaleb a nod and the hunter and all five griffons took off.

"If we need a quick escape," Emilia said in answer to Carey's look of confusion. "The dark sky will hide them, and they will fetch us should we need them to."

Emilia had been quiet up until that moment, and Carey felt considerably less hostility from her than the others. She gave Carey a nod before ushering her towards the others.

"We have business to attend to here in the city," Maël said. "You will not try to escape. You will not alert anyone to your situation."

He stared hard at Carey before turning to lead them on, but Carey didn't move.

"Don't you think we'll attract attention," she said loudly, indicating her clothes and the sword that still hung at her back.

Emilia shook her head. "No. You won't."

"You'll see," Maël added. "Now *come*."

Carey had no option but to obey him and they began walking towards the city. A large closed carriage was waiting and a driver leapt down from the front as they approached.

"Monsieur Maël," the older man said with a thick accent and a low bow. He showed a great deal of greying hair and a shiny bald patch on top of his head as he swept the top hat from his brow. "It is good to see you again. To the city?"

As Maël made to step up into the carriage, he replied, "Le Pont Alexandre trois, if you don't mind, Baylac."

The man bowed once more, then waited until they were all crammed inside before shutting the door with a snap and climbing up into the driver's seat.

"How did he know we were coming?" Kat asked, squished between Rupert and Niko, who looked thoroughly too large for such a small space.

Maël gave her a scathing look. "We have people everywhere. How do you think we found *you*?"

There came a command in French from above and the carriage jerked forwards. The curtains on the window were drawn back so Carey was able to see the city pass as they were jostled along. The roads were narrow, paved with cobblestones, and tall, flat-faced buildings rose up on either side. Narrow wrought-iron balconies jutted out overhead, their curtains fluttering in open windows. Light shone from within, a gentle orange glow.

Men and women strolled the streets and gathered in cafes on corners. Music floated on the night breeze, mixing with the laughter echoing off the tall apartments around them. On they drove, travelling farther into the centre of Paris, the buildings becoming grander and halls of white stone looming over them. The roads widened and the traffic increased, horse-drawn buggies and bicycles vying for space.

The carriage turned onto a wide thoroughfare; tall iron lamp posts topped with a triplet of glowing bulbs illuminated the boulevard, and Carey and the others stared in awe at the building on their right. White stone columns rose up from behind a thicket of lush green trees, their scrolled tops supporting a long, low balcony. The roof was dome-shaped at the far end, a striking extension of steel and glittering glass. Green cast-iron statues of warriors in horse-drawn carriages stood atop the corners of the building, racing towards some unknown battle.

They pulled up just beyond this, stepping out to find themselves at the end of a long concourse filled with people. The magnificent building faced another on the opposite side of this walkway, and although it was smaller, it was just as elaborate. Men with black top hats and dinner jackets walked alongside women in long, elegant evening dresses and fur-collared coats. All were clearly out for an evening of entertainment and socialising.

Carey looked down at her own attire and grimaced. "How, exactly, are we meant to go unnoticed?" she asked again, wondering if Maël and his cohort were delusional or simply overly optimistic.

Maël motioned for them to follow and the group began to walk down the centre of the boulevard between the two grand buildings.

"This," he said with a wave of his arms, gesturing to all that surrounded them, "is the Exposition Universelle. An exhibition of everything French and not so French. There are buildings here dedicated to parts of the world as far flung as my ancestral home of Siam, and therefore there are many here, mostly performers, who we should easily pass as. If anything, most of these Commoners will simply view us as roving entertainment. So please, Princess, don't worry your head too much. You'll fit in just fine."

He said these last few words with such condescension that Carey would have gladly slapped him had she been able to. Kat walked alongside her, eyes combing the crowd, while Kyna and Rupert followed close behind. Kyna was torn between fascination and fear, her voice rising over the noise of the crowd in excited bursts.

Passing the end of the glass-roofed building, they encountered dense parkland on either side. The trees lined the slow-moving waters of a wide river, and two square columns rose on either side of a bridge that stretched out before them. Atop these columns perched towering figures of winged beasts, gilded and glowing in the soft light of the streetlamps. People strolled by the river's edge, watching the low boats drifting past.

"Keep them here," Maël told Kaleb and Emilie. "We'll be back soon with more supplies."

Then he turned to Carey, Kat, Rupert, and Kyna. "Once more – you will not fight, or use your magic to escape or attract attention. You will stay with Emilia and Kaleb," he commanded, glaring at each of them in turn.

Carey ground her teeth, fighting against the urge to say something snide in return, and she could feel Kat shifting in frustration at her side.

"You do realise we want you ter take us ter Monaghan? Why would we try ter run now?" Rupert pointed out.

Maël shrugged. "One can never be too careful."

He headed for the bridge and his group was soon swallowed by the crowd, Niko's head bobbing visibly above the sea of top hats.

"This way," Emilia said in her small voice, her short hair swinging around her face as she turned for the trees to their right.

What Carey had thought was parkland was actually more of a riverside walkway covered in foliage. Lamps illuminated the pathways between lines of trees. The spaces between the lamps were thrown into an eerie half-light of shadows and moonbeams. Laughter and disembodied voices came from within, and Kat narrowed her eyes in suspicion.

"Where are we going?" she demanded of Kaleb, who was walking behind them.

He nodded his dark-curled head towards the trees. "To find somewhere to wait. As much as Maël thinks we can blend in, we'd rather not be harassed by Commoners wanting us to perform."

As they moved from the bright boulevard to the shadows of the trees, Carey thought she would rather be harassed by Commoners than hide in here, a sentiment Rupert voiced in a low murmur.

"I don't know. I'm actually not half bad at singin'."

Couples wandered amongst the trees, some talking and giggling, others engaging in more intimate activities. Kyna snorted with laughter, causing one couple who were kissing in the half-shadows to break apart and scowl at the group as they passed.

As they moved away from the riverside, they came across fewer and fewer people until it seemed they were the only ones ensconced in the darkness. They took shelter amongst trees close to a white stone building, where they at least had the light from windows above, the shadows lightened by their soft glow.

Kat crossed her arms and leant against a nearby trunk, frowning as she looked around.

"Expecting someone?" Kaleb asked.

"No. But we've been surprised before," Kat replied.

The noises of the crowd were faint under the rustling of the leaves in the night breeze.

"How long will they be?" Carey asked, trying to ignore a creeping sensation on the back of her neck.

"Not long," Emilia replied as she retrieved a small blade from a coat pocket and began sharpening it on a thin steel.

There was another long stretch of silence.

Kat seemed wholly uninterested in their kidnappers, and Kyna kept shifting nervously. Rupert was the only one watching the bounty hunters with any interest.

Carey cleared her throat. "Why does he hate us so much?"

Carey was still unable to shake how Maël could dismiss them and what they fought for.

Kaleb gave her a look of contempt. "For someone so very *important*, you seem rather clueless." His voice dripped with disdain, but when Carey held his gaze, he gave an irritated huff and said, "Magic wielders have never treated dhampirs with much respect–"

"Zero, actually," Emilia cut in without even looking up from her knife-sharpening.

Kaleb grimaced. "You would think that being part magic, that would afford us some recognition or regard, but we found out early in this war of yours that we were nothing but expendable assets. Once we realised that our lives were not truly our own, we decided to become what we are today. Dhampirs have always been a connection between the Commoners and magic, keeping the balance. We actually care what happens to the people of this realm, even if they don't possess magic of their own. So, when we found out there was a bounty on some Seekers, we decided to take the job. Seekers mean nothing but trouble, and we weren't about to let you just roam about as you like."

"But we're not trying to cause trouble," Carey said loudly, standing up straight, but Kat stopped her with a hand on her arm.

"Don't," she said.

Carey was about to retort when a rush of cold wind raced through the trees, making her shiver.

Kaleb and Emilia whipped around, peering into the darkness towards the river.

Kyna froze, her eyes wide with fear as the hunters pulled weapons, Emilia with her daggers, Kaleb a short stake from beneath his coat.

"Danger," Kyna whispered hoarsely.

A figure flew from the darkness, straight at the two hunters. With an easy grace, Kaleb spun, hitting the man squarely in the chest with his stake. The attacker let out an ear-piercing shriek as he fell with a thud at Rupert's feet.

"What the–" Kat started, but Kaleb bellowed, "Run!"

Deciding not to wait around to ask questions, Carey sprinted after Emilia and the others. She didn't know what they were running from, but it was doubtful that the man Kaleb had just slain was a Commoner. She also wasn't about to doubt these hunters, not when they seemed to know exactly what was coming for them.

Another gust of cold air prickled her skin, and Carey knew it wasn't because of the weather. They burst from the tree line to find themselves amongst the evening crowd once more. A narrow bridge to their left spanned the river. Across the road was an extravagant spire-topped mansion, flags fluttering from poles positioned around the edge of its steep roof. Emilia peeled off to the left of it and disappeared down a set of narrow stairs hidden between the enormous villa and the side of the bridge. Commoners cried out as the group raced past, knocking some aside as they went. Kaleb urged them on as they sped down the stairs and along the river bank, away from the bridge. A low, white stone guardrail was all that separated them from the river below, and dark archways led in under the building to their right. There were very few people on this level. Carey could hear the others panting as they sprinted along the narrow walkway.

"Emilia!"

Kaleb's cry cut through the night air, followed by a loud curse.

Carey skidded to a stop, catching herself on Rupert as he almost barrelled into her.

A dapper young gentleman was fighting Kaleb, ducking and weaving elegantly. Kaleb's arms flew, trying to strike him down as he'd done with the other, but his adversary was too quick. Stepping nimbly to the side, the gentleman caught Kaleb around the back of the neck and deftly flipped him onto his stomach. Kaleb landed with a sickening thud on the pavement.

Dusting unseen dirt from the shiny lapels of his tailcoat, Kaleb's assailant straightened his top hat and stepped over Kaleb. Kaleb groaned, trying to pull himself up from the ground, but the gentleman pushed down between his shoulder blades with the end of a polished black walking stick. The hunter roared. Blood trickled from where the tip of the cane made contact, no doubt sharpened at the point. Fists balled in pain and fury, Kaleb lay where he'd fallen, his black curls a mess across his face.

"Don't even think–" Emilia made to run to Kaleb's aid, but before she'd taken even a single step, a woman in a long beaded evening dress appeared behind her.

Emilia spun, letting two shiny daggers fly, but she wasn't fast enough. The woman side-stepped the missiles easily, bringing her own long, thin dagger to Emilia's throat.

"Don't… move…" the woman said, wrapping her free arm around Emilia's chest and pinning her in place.

The woman and gentleman were not much older than Carey, but there was something about them that reminded her of Maël. Young, but old at the same time. Carey backed closer to Kat, Kyna, and Rupert, and she felt them crowd in behind her. Kyna's breathing was loud and ragged.

"Easy, Lucienne," came a voice from one of the darkened archways. "We do not need the Black Wings after us for killing one of their own."

Another gentleman clothed in evening attire stepped from the shadows. He wore much the same as the other, except for a silver bowtie with a diamond pin at its centre. His voice was thick with a French accent, and he eyed Carey and the others with dark, almost black, eyes. His wavy hair was shoulder-length, a deep caramel brown.

The woman, Lucienne, scowled, her pretty face contorting as she sneered back at him.

"Henri is no better," she spat, nodding her head of elaborately curled blonde hair towards the man with the cane. "At least I 'ave not made this one bleed."

Henri gave a nonchalant shrug, his chiselled features and dark skin highlighted by the light reflecting off the river. "He was making it 'ard, Victor. What do you expect?"

Victor grinned and Kat swore.

"I'm with Kat on this one," Rupert whispered, staring at Victor and swallowing hard.

"What?" Carey asked out of the corner of her mouth, not turning her gaze from the two gentlemen who were clearly anything but.

"Vampires, my dear," Victor answered for Rupert, and his dark eyes snapped back to her. "I believe that is what you were about to say, no?"

Rupert didn't move. Kat cursed softly again, and Carey was inclined to agree. Maël had forbidden them to fight or to escape, and try as she may, Carey couldn't move. Victor grinned again and Carey saw what the others must have: fangs, long and sharp.

"Which one is it, Victor?" Lucienne asked, her own obsidian gaze turning to the Seekers.

Victor moved towards Carey and the others, his movements fluid like a dancer's. Or a snake's. He lifted his nose to the air and took a deep breath as he drew closer. Then, he froze, eyes locking on Carey.

"This one," he said on an exhale, hunger suddenly blazing across his handsome features.

Carey's body fought to flee but Maël's enchantment held tight as dread washed over her. Her fear seemed to excite the vampire. He stalked nearer and lifted a white-gloved hand to brush her hair from her neck. Carey flinched and Victor chuckled low in his throat.

"Normally I don't approach magic wielders – too much trouble, honestly – but you…" He breathed in again, this time lowering his face to Carey's throat.

"You were too much to resist, mon chérie."

Carey felt Kat tense beside her, but knew she couldn't do anything to help.

"What… what was too hard to resist?" she stammered as Victor ran a gloved hand up and down the side of her neck.

"Your blood. It 'as such an… *alluring* scent. Witches and wizards generally do, what with all that magic running through their veins, but you…" He took another breath, and this time Carey could feel it on her skin. She shuddered. "There is magic in you that I must taste."

Without further ado, he plunged his fangs into Carey's neck. Kat and Rupert called out in surprise. Kyna gave a blood-curdling shriek. White-hot pain shot through Carey's body. Victor's arms snaked around her waist as her knees buckled from the agony, and his lips closed on her skin and blood oozed from his bite.

This was it. This was how she died. In the arms of a vampire on a French riverbank. No one to fight for her, to save her. She wouldn't even be able to save herself. Carey closed her eyes and let her mind drift to thoughts of Ji. She thought of how he'd asked her to keep fighting, and of how, now, she'd never get to see him again.

Victor's body went rigid against hers. His arms withdrew from around her waist and Carey fell from his grip. Grasping at his chest, his eyes went wide as he stumbled backwards. Carey's blood trickled down his chin, but he made no move to wipe it away as he gasped for breath, the muscles in his neck taut as he struggled.

"Victor!" Henri leapt over Kaleb and dashed for his companion.

The vampire slumped to the ground and began to spasm. Lucienne threw Emilia to the side and advanced on Carey, her dagger outstretched, her face feral with rage.

"What 'ave you done to 'im, you wretch," she shrieked.

Victor was clawing at his throat as Henri held him helplessly. No one moved – they simply stared in horror as the vampire fought to breathe. Then, eyes bulging, Victor let out a rasping breath before slumping in Henri's arms.

He was dead.

Lucienne screamed and lunged at Carey, who could do nothing but stand there. Just as the vampire was about to stab Carey with her dagger, a quarrel caught Lucienne in the shoulder and she staggered sideways. She roared as she spun around in the direction the crossbow bolt had come from, only to be hit by another in the chest. The woman collapsed, dead before she even hit the pavers.

Henri leapt to his feet, his expression wild. Before he could move, however, Kaleb was in front of him, a sharp wooden stake in hand.

"Die, you bastard," he shouted as he drove the stake through Henri's heart.

Carey spun around to find Maël, Reay, and Niko on their griffons, Reay with a crossbow raised in front of her. The other two griffons circled high above, awaiting their charges.

"What are you waiting for?" Maël bellowed. "They won't be the only ones around here!"

Emilia was at Carey's side, pushing her and the others towards the edge of the riverbank. "Go," she shouted, just as Carey noticed two more figures sprinting towards them from the bridge. They were moving fast, and Carey's heart leapt into her throat.

Niko flew in close, reached down and hauled Kyna up behind him. Rupert scrambled up behind Reay, almost losing his footing on the guardrail as he went. Balancing on the railing, Carey resisted the urge to look back over her shoulder. Maël swooped down and she jumped, Maël catching her by the forearm and pulling her up behind him. Turning back, she could see that the vampires were almost upon Kat, Kaleb, and Emilia.

"Kat! Jump," Carey screamed as the vampires threw aside their top hats and canes and dived for the remaining three, arms outstretched.

Kat, Emilia, and Kaleb took a running leap off the side as their griffons tore past Carey in a blur of wings and talons. With barely a foot between them and the murky waters below, the great beasts snatched them out of the air before shooting straight back up towards the heavens. The vampires hurled curses and cries of fury as the hunters took to the Parisian sky with the Seekers in tow, the dark night shrouding them from the eyes below.

~Chapter Twenty-Six~

The Magic that Surrounds

The half moon shone serenely, at odds with Carey's mess of emotions. She clung to Maël without even thinking, one arm around his waist, the other clutching her wounded neck.

Maël shouted back to her, "You're bleeding!"

Carey rolled her eyes. "No. This is just how my neck usually is."

He grunted in reply.

She wondered when the wound would stop bleeding, or if vampire bites even did. Maël whistled loudly and made a looping motion over his head before gripping his griffon with both hands and steering them into a steep dive. They were far beyond Paris, once more surrounded by wilderness. There was less snow here, though Carey doubted that situation would last long. She could feel the chill of unfallen snow in the air. She gripped Maël tighter as they descended, and as they hit the ground, Carey reeled, light-headed.

Maël slid down from his mount and Carey followed, stumbling. A steady hand caught her by the elbow and for one wild moment she thought it was Maël. But it was Rupert holding her up.

"Whoa there," he said softly, leading her away. "I think the blood loss might be gettin' to yer."

Kat took a bed roll from Niko and spread it out on the cold ground for Rupert to sit Carey down upon.

"Here. Let me have a look at that." Rupert gently pried Carey's fingers away from her neck.

Niko was standing a few feet away, watching with curiosity; Maël and Kaleb were talking in hushed voices a little farther away, glancing over at Carey every so often; Emilia was still over by her griffon; and Reay was leaning against the side of her own mount, arms crossed and surveying the scene with a guarded expression.

Rupert let out a low sigh as he looked at Carey's wound. It still ached and stung with the memory of Victor's bite, but other than that, Carey felt nothing but a curious urge to go to sleep.

"I can heal this," he said, wiping away blood with a cloth from his bag. "He only bit you, an' from what I saw, he barely drank any of yer blood before..."

Rupert let his sentence trail away. Carey didn't blame him. *She* barely knew what had happened.

Rupert turned to Maël. "I need my magic. I can't heal her without it."

Maël and Kaleb walked over to where Carey sat.

"First of all," Maël said, standing over them and crossing his arms, "I want to know what happened. Kaleb says that vampire took one bite before spitting you back out, falling over, and dying. Now, I've been at this a long time, but I've never heard of anything like this before. If you tell me what you did, I'll let your friend heal you."

Carey stared up at him, her mouth hanging open. "What?"

"You heard me," Maël said. "What happened back there?"

Kat stood up slowly to face him. "We don't know what happened. We were waiting for you, then, all of a sudden, your two had us running away from what I can only assume were those vampires. They caught up to us. The main one – Victor – said something about being able to smell Carey, that her magic lured him there. You're the ones who are supposed to be half-vampire. You tell us – what did he mean by that?"

She cocked an eyebrow at Maël, hands on her hips as she waited for him to reply. Maël looked from Kat to Carey.

"Magic wielders... smell," he said. "You lot–" he waved a hand to indicate the four of them "–smell because of your magic." He pointed at Carey. "I can understand what that vampire must have sensed. *Your* magic is much more *distinct.*"

Carey vaguely wondered if it had something to do with that strange magic of hers. But her dizziness was intensifying, and she leant against Rupert, unable to reply. Kyna appeared at her other side to help Rupert lay her down.

"Look, we don't know what happened," Rupert said, brushing Carey's hair away from her face. "Perhaps that vampire couldn't handle Carey's magic. Right now, that doesn't matter. I need ter be able ter help her or she's not goin' ter be any use ter anyone. I imagine yer payment for delivering us would be based on whether we were, in fact, alive?"

Rupert said this last part with such vehemence that if Carey hadn't been so drowsy, she'd have commended him on it.

"Fine. You can use your magic, but *only* to heal her. Nothing else."

There was a rustling of movement around her and Carey felt Rupert's hand on her neck once more. She could hear him murmuring his healing enchantments, and she felt the warmth of his magic as it flowed into her. Kyna was gently stroking her forehead as her brother worked, and soon the dull pain in her throat began to recede. Carey blinked, her eyelids heavy, the dizziness a little less. Then, in a soothing voice, Rupert said, "There. All good. Now sleep, Carey. We'll be here when you wake."

And sleep she did.

*

Carey woke as the morning sun crept over the horizon, her face numb from the cold. She was wedged between Kyna and Kat, who were fast asleep, Kat snoring quietly. Rupert, ever the professional, was still awake, dark circles beneath his eyes but watchful all the same. Sitting by their heads, wrapped in the other sleeping roll, he smiled widely when he saw Carey was awake.

"Feelin' better?" he asked, gently touching where the wound had been.

She felt the smooth, blood-free skin on her neck. There was the slightest of phantom twinges but otherwise felt immensely better.

"Much, thank you," she replied. "Did it take much out of you?"

"No, but I did have ter heal that hunter Kaleb as well, so." He let out a long, exhausted yawn. "I might be a little tired."

"Just one more thing I bet you weren't expecting to deal with?" she croaked.

Rupert rubbed the heels of his palms against his eyes. "No, but I have a feelin' you weren't exactly expectin' it either. Good thing I did come along now, isn't it?"

Carey gave him a sheepish smile, but his words gave her pause. If he hadn't come along, just how far would they have actually got?

She took Rupert's hand in hers. "I'm glad you did come. Honestly, I think we'd be a lot worse off if you hadn't."

Rupert shrugged. "You an' Kat fight. I heal. I've never really been one fer swords and fightin' anyway."

Carey gave his hand a squeeze. "If we'd been able to fight last night, this might never have happened." She grimaced. "Lucky we make a decent team."

Rupert's smile widened, his eyes twinkling. Carey released his hand and tried sitting up without waking Kat and Kyna. Kyna stirred, but Kat's eyes flew open at the sudden exposure of her back to the elements.

"You do realise that is possibly *the* worst way to be woken up?" she said with a scratchy voice, trying to pull the blanket back around her.

Carey gave a chuckle as she climbed out, letting Kat have the blanket.

Kat glanced over at the hunters' camp. Maël was already awake, talking to his sister as the other three slept by a low-burning campfire.

Carey followed her gaze and she felt her stomach clench.

"Kat…" she said. "I think we need to tell them what we have planned."

Kat's gaze flicked back to her, silent.

"Maël might be a piece of work, but they did save us," Carey continued. "If Saar is waiting for us in Monaghan, we can't just lead them into a trap. They need to know what might be coming."

For a moment Kat was still, Rupert watching as Carey waited for her to say something.

She nodded. "You're right. They need to know, and as much as I don't particularly like them, they could've left us for dead last night. But they didn't."

"I don't want ter state the obvious or anythin', but they probably just didn't want ter lose their bounty," Rupert said.

"Doesn't matter," Carey said. "It'd be wrong. Ji wouldn't do it. He'd tell them."

That was the truth. Ji would've told them what their plans were by now. To not tell them would be leading them straight into danger without them even knowing, and that would make the Seekers everything Maël accused them of being.

Kat crawled out from under the blanket and straightened her coat. "Well, no better time than the present."

"We'll be back," Carey said to Rupert.

"Good luck."

The feeling in Carey's stomach twisted tighter at the sentiment. Maël already despised them, and they were possibly about to make things even worse. Maël and Reay looked up as the pair approached.

"Glad to see your friend was able to stop you expiring on us," Maël said in greeting, and Carey grimaced, feeling the contempt in his voice like a physical hit.

"Well, he is the best at what he does," she said.

There was an awkward pause, where Carey stood numbly before the two dhampirs and Maël waited with one eyebrow raised.

Reay coughed impatiently. "You want something?"

"What happened last night," Carey started, figuring that if she were to ask this one thing of Maël, it was before she told him what Saar really was. "We would've never been in such a situation if we'd been able to use our magic. If something like that happens again, we want to be able to defend ourselves."

Maël cocked his head to one side, considering. "You think I'd give you free rein of your magic because of one little vampire encounter?" he scoffed as Reay laughed scornfully.

Grinding her teeth, Carey forced herself to remain civil. "No. Just the ability to use it when required. Not to *attack* you or try to *escape*. We just need to know that if something like that happens again, we're not sitting ducks."

Maël's gaze turned from Carey to Kat, then briefly to his sister. "I suppose it would've made things much simpler last night if Emilia and Kaleb weren't the only ones fighting. Fine. You are not to use your magic to escape, or to attack us. *Nor* are you to alert anyone of your whereabouts," he tacked on, and Carey felt a jolt of relief in her chest. "Other than those stipulations, you may use your magic."

When Carey and Kat didn't turn to leave, he narrowed his eyes.

"Anything else, Princess?"

This part was less easy to navigate. Negotiating their magic was simple compared to telling Maël about what Saar might actually have in store for them, considering it could completely ruin this tenuous alliance.

Sensing Carey's hesitation, Kat stepped forwards.

"There's something you need to be aware of," she said. "The man who we think is waiting for us at Monaghan, the one who put out the bounty on us, is a dangerous man. Not only is he an Imperial, but he basically created Malevolence, and if history is anything to go by, he'd be less likely to pay you your bounty than he would to slaughter you where you stand."

Carey winced. Kat's diplomacy was not going to do them any favours, but if she was being honest with herself, she doubted she'd have been able to do much better. Maël stared at them. Reay's cold gaze turned practically murderous. Slowly, Maël got to his feet.

"Let me get this straight. The man we are to deliver you to is a murderous Imperial."

Neither Kat nor Carey said anything as Maël continued.

"And instead of telling us this when you first came to us with your proposal, you decided to keep this information from us. For all intents and purposes, we could be walking straight into a trap." He released a bark of wry laughter. "I owe you ten, sister."

Upon seeing Carey's look of confusion, Maël added with a sneer, "My dear sister here bet me that there was more to this situation, something you weren't telling us, and here we are. What changed? I'm guessing it was last night, realising you'd need your magic if he's there? Or did you think we'd help you if we knew?"

"No," Carey said, finally finding her voice. "You saved us last night. Whether it was just because of the money or something else, we knew we couldn't keep this from you. It'd be wrong for us to do so."

It was Reay's turn to laugh. "Seriously? You just don't want to feel bad if we end up dead. This is *you* keeping a clear conscience."

"So, what do you suggest, then?" Maël said, interrupting Carey before she could snap a retort. "If this really is about you trying to do good by us bounty hunters?"

"We fly to Monaghan," Kat said. "We leave you at the town's edge. If it turns out it is Saar, then you'll be out of harm's way. If, somehow, it's not him, then we tell your employer where to find you so you can get paid. Now, I know you trust us about as far as you can throw us, so use your *Persuasion* on us if that will give you some piece of mind."

Maël folded his arms, considering Kat's proposal.

"Oh, and we will most certainly need to be able to use our magic," she added.

It was a showdown, Maël and Kat, staring, waiting to see who would crack first. Maël licked his lips, then gave a jerk of his head.

"Fine. You're lucky the bounty's so big. Otherwise I'd have happily left you here." He looked over at his sister, who gave him an approving nod, her face set in a deep scowl. "We'll take you to Monaghan. We'll give you use of your magic. *And*, since this whole thing does nothing to bolster any trust, I'll be ensuring you come back. Make no mistake, Princess – this is *all* business."

He retook his place at his sister's side, dismissing Kat and Carey. They didn't need telling twice, regardless of everything Carey wanted to say to this infuriating man. When they were out of earshot, she cursed under her breath, drawing a look of surprise from Kat.

"Sorry," Carey muttered as they sat back down next to Rupert. "I just… that *man!*"

Kat gave her a consoling pat on the arm. "Don't let him get to you. That was probably the best outcome we could've hoped for."

"But doesn't the whole thing infuriate you?" Carey continued. "How he can dismiss everything we're trying to do, turn our words against us to make us look like the enemy?"

Rupert, who was stretched out on top of the blanket alongside the sleeping Kyna, gave Carey a tight smile. "Yer can't win 'em all, Carey. There are always goin' ter be people like Maël and his men. Like Kat said, don't let it get ter you."

Carey snorted, grumbling, "Easier said than done."

*

A soft FLUMP was all that alerted Carey to her visitor's arrival. She'd been thinking of him the past few nights, and now she'd purposefully reached out in the hope that he would come to her again. Carey had wondered about the Ancient since he'd first summoned her, wrestled with what his intentions might be. She wanted to know why he was helping them and whether he truly was as benevolent as he appeared.

Schooling her features, Carey turned to the Ancient standing before her, his wings folding against his back as he straightened from landing. He was just as impressive as before – dark skin and ivory hair, his icy gaze focused upon her.

"Carey Lee."

His cadence was deep and soothing, like a balm on Carey's soul.

"You came," she managed, resisting the urge to shiver as she took in his awe-inspiring presence.

His expression was a blank slate, giving nothing away as he cast his gaze upon her. "It was time."

"Time?" Carey repeated.

He stayed silent.

"Who are you?"

A beat.

"You know what I am."

Carey cocked her head. "I didn't say what. I said who."

This time his answer was swifter, as though he couldn't get the words out fast enough.

"My name is Anthriel, though my name is inconsequential."

What an odd way to introduce yourself, *Carey thought.*

"Wait. What did you mean by 'You know what I am'? How do you know that?"

Something like impatience flickered across Anthriel's smooth features. "I am an Ancient. I see all that is, all that was, and all that might be. I see the intricate web of choices, actions and consequences, and all that may come of them. I watch, observe. I ensure the balance of all is kept."

The silence that followed this statement was profound. Carey stared at the Ancient. How would it be to have so much power?

"Was it you who helped us escape the Arena?"

It'd been something she'd considered since the first time Carey had encountered him. Something more powerful than any of them had saved them that day. His wings rustled the way she'd heard them in her dreams, though it wasn't until he'd appeared to her that first time that she realised that's what she'd been hearing.

He lifted his chin, an arrogance showing in this slight movement.

"Yes."

Carey chewed on the inside of her cheek, mind racing. It didn't make sense – why was he helping them?

"So, do you help people often?" Carey asked, keeping her tone light.

She couldn't understand the motivations behind his actions. Considering what he was, his interest in them was unnerving.

"No," he rumbled, giving his head a slight shake. "We do not."

"Then why are you helping us?"

"You," he said.

"What?"

"I am helping you. *No one else."*

Crossing her arms in front of her, Carey considered the Ancient for a moment. "Fine. Why are you helping me, *then?"*

"The balance must be kept."

Balance?

Carey frowned. Was he being purposely vague or was this just how Ancients were? She waited, feeling that he was on the cusp of revealing more. After all, he had said it was time. It was just a matter of waiting for him to elaborate.

"There is always a balance – good and evil, dark and light. There is white magic and there is black magic. One cannot exist without the other, and even though one may hold dominion over the other from time to time, it is never for long."

His eyes never left hers, the intensity of his gaze rooting her to the spot.

"Those who can wield magic are born to it. You each possess your own internal magic, both dark and light, separate to the magic that surrounds all of us. You cannot draw upon that which flows through the realms."

Carey's frown deepened. She'd never given much thought to where her magic came from – she'd simply taken it for granted. Yet now Anthriel spoke of it, she wondered why she'd never thought of it before. The Ancient continued, and Carey turned her mind from this oversight.

"There was, however, one with the power to do so. Centuries ago, a witch was born with the unique ability to use the magic around her. It flowed through her, the light and the dark, and she could wield it as she saw fit."

Anthriel blinked calmly. He might as well have been telling her about the weather for all the enthusiasm he showed.

"She was able to wield the magic, dark and light, though gradually her intentions became more nefarious than virtuous. A wizard came to know of the power she possessed and sought to steal it from her. For him to take her power into himself, he separated the magic from the wielder, then killed the one it was bound to. Dispatching the witch, the wizard was able to take into himself the ability to wield the magic around him."

Carey's heart was racing. This had to be the witch she'd seen in her vision, the one from the Stronghold. So, she'd possessed a unique ability like her own Twilight Travelling, only far more powerful. She gulped.

"But... how? How could he take her magic?"

Without something like a Dragon's Heart, Carey couldn't see how it was possible. Anthriel seemed to know what she was thinking.

"Magic can be separated from one's body – extinguishing it will kill the user. However, if one wishes to steal another's magic for themselves, they need only to separate it from their victim, then execute them. The magic will continue to exist, and, therefore, with the right intent, another may take control of it."

"So..."

Carey didn't know what to say. This witch from the Stronghold – her ability had been so much like the magic Carey possessed, yet Carey couldn't understand how she'd now come to possess it. If murder was how it was passed from one to another...

Anthriel spoke through her silence, his voice still low and calm despite the calamity of which he spoke. "Her ability has been stolen again and again over the centuries, leaving a trail of blood in its wake. At times it has been simply captured, kept dormant and unused in what you call a Tear Globe, but it has always been possessed in the end. Last time it was the Council of the Centre City that held it in its protection. It would have been more prudent to simply extinguish it, let it be possessed by none, but they held it with the idea of using it should they need to defend themselves."

"The orb within the Stronghold..." Carey whispered, the puzzle pieces slowly

falling into place. "The one Malevolence ended up stealing."

Anthriel paused, blinking slowly. Carey's thoughts were a mess as she tried to keep up with him, and an empty feeling in the pit of her stomach told her she wasn't going to like what she heard.

"Malevolence attempted to do what none had done before – split it. Or, to put it another way, she wanted the ability to wield only the darkness. She believed any connection to the light would weaken her. She thought it would make her stronger, uninhibited by the balance that exists within everything. But she hadn't intended on her sister trying to stop her." *Anthriel lifted his chin again, looking down his nose at Carey in an appraising manner.* "Fianna Parnell was there the night Malevolence attempted this. But magic desires balance. Even if the wielder chose darkness over light, the light would always be there, it would always eventually create balance. So, when Malevolence tore it asunder, seeking to dispose of that which she did not wish to possess, it sought out another. It took to one who had a connection to Malevolence."

"My grandmother," *Carey said, her heart in her throat.* "That was why she was the only match for her, wasn't it?"

"It was. And for years they fought. Then, upon Fianna Parnell's death, it passed to another. It required another host as it could not die with her. It is one half of a whole after all, always has been and always will, and with Malevolence still in possession of the other, it came to possess the closest being that held a connection to Fianna Parnell," *Anthriel said, his eyes intense as he stared straight into her own.*

Carey felt a weight drop inside of her.

"Me," *she said, slowly bringing her hand to her chest, feeling her heart beating wildly beneath it.* "That's what this is?"

She remembered the day her grandmother had been murdered. She'd felt something knock her down, though she hadn't seen what it was. Now she knew. It had always felt foreign, like it did not truly exist as part of her. And the sheer magnitude of what she'd accomplished with it... Carey looked back up at Anthriel, eyes wide.

"But I've killed with that magic," *she said, tasting bile.* "How is that good?"

"It has protected you in dark times," *Anthriel said.* "As I said, it protects those who possess it. Therefore, it protected you."

Heat flushed Carey's neck and cheeks. This was all so much.

"Why are you telling me all this?" she asked as she balled up her hands in an attempt to hide their shaking. "If you truly are an Ancient, what do you get from telling me this? Why are you helping me?"

"As I said," he replied, sounding almost bored. "Balance. I see the choices and the actions of all. For most, they are unimportant. They have no bearing on the course of the future. But then there are those few, like Malevolence, and like you." He paused, as though waiting for his words to make their mark on her. "You have a choice to make, Carey Lee. And the time is coming soon. If you choose wrongly, the balance will cease to exist. Darkness will fall eternally and there will be no restoring it. I tell you all this, about the ability you possess, in the hopes that when the time comes, you will know what to do."

Carey stood frozen, absolute dread spreading through her body. Darkness eternal. The magic surrounding them. The power to wield it. She'd never felt more overwhelmed in her life. This man stood there as though he truly didn't understand the bombshell he'd just dropped on her. He watched her with cold detachment, waiting for her to react. She wanted to scream, wanted the earth to swallow her whole. She wanted to run.

Instead, she swallowed hard, forcing the next few words from her lips.

"What is this choice?"

Anthriel blinked, then turned his head, finally breaking eye contact with her.

"It is not yet time," he said, and before Carey could say another word, he spread his wings and was gone.

~Chapter Twenty-Seven~

Matters of the Heart

Carey blinked, the sky a swirling blanket of stars and clouds above her.

It had worked.

Despite his stipulations, Maël hadn't said she couldn't Twilight Travel. Nor had he said she couldn't meet with anyone. She might've felt more triumphant about all of this had Anthriel not upended her entire world. Her mouth was dry and her ribs ached from the thrashing of her heart. Every breath was shaky, and she closed her eyes in a bid to calm herself.

"Carey?"

Kat, Rupert, and Kyna looked down at her. Kyna's eyes were as round as dinner plates, her mouth hanging open in surprise. Rupert ran a hand distractedly through his unnaturally coloured hair. And Kat stared with a glint of intrigue in her green eyes.

"So, that was Twilight Travellin', then?" Rupert said with a hint of wonder in his voice.

It'd been an experiment, really. Carey had been toying with the idea for of bringing them along with her some time now, and her meeting with Anthriel had provided the perfect situation to attempt it. By broadening her focus to include not just a single person or place, she had enabled Kat, Rupert, and Kyna to sit at the periphery of her meeting with Anthriel. She knew he'd probably been very much aware of their presence, yet that hadn't stopped him from divulging all he knew of Carey's powers.

Her stomach lurched.

Kat tilted her head to one side, glancing at the hunters' campfire to ensure they weren't in danger of being overheard. "Are you…?"

"All right?" Carey supplied.

She stared up at the stars once more. No, she wasn't all right. Her mind was reeling from what the Ancient had told her, and she felt the weight of the implications like a physical burden. She heaved a sigh and slowly sat up.

"I don't know. I'd always thought it was something different." Carey looked down at her hands, flexing her fingers. "But this?"

Rupert chewed on his lip. "What does it all mean, though? And what is this choice of yers?"

Dread trickled down Carey's spine, and she wrapped her arms around her body as though to protect herself from any untoward thoughts, but they took seed regardless.

"I don't know. But if he's helping us find Saar, then I can only assume it has something to do with him. Or Malevolence."

"We need ter find Seramina," Kyna said. "That means it will have somethin' to do with her too, yes?"

"This ability of yours, though," Kat interjected. "We could use that against him. If it's as strong as Anthriel said."

Carey pursed her lips, thinking hard. Saar was strong, that much was certain, and their plan of going into Monaghan with no pretence and meeting him head on would be the last thing he'd expect. But she knew, deep in her gut, that she might indeed be stronger. At least, that's what Anthriel had inferred. Kat waved a hand in front of her face.

"Uh, Carey?"

Carey blinked, knowing that it was time she let her friends know exactly how strong this ability of hers was, now she knew the truth.

"There's something I need to tell you all," she began, and then recounted each time she'd used her ability, up to and including the moment she'd destroyed an entire Imperial army on magically barren land. By the end, Rupert, Kat, and Kyna were all staring at her, dumbstruck.

"You managed that, and you're only just telling us now?" Kat said.

"That's supposed ter be impossible, though. Seramina said so," Kyna squeaked.

Carey grimaced. "It was. The thing is, though, I might be strong enough to beat Saar, but when I call on that ability, and when I try to control it, it… hurts."

"Hurts?" Kat asked.

Carey lifted a finger to her temple. "Headaches, and pretty bad ones at that."

"And if you don't control it?" Kat said.

"What?"

"What if you didn't control it? What might happen?"

Carey thought back over all the times the magic had manifested, the lives she'd taken without meaning to. She swallowed thickly. "I wouldn't end well. That army – that was my ability protecting me, just like Anthriel said it would. I wasn't controlling it – I was just *there*. If I just let it go and don't try to control it, I might end up hurting someone I don't mean to."

A flicker of panic crossed over Kyna's face. "You mean you might hurt Seramina, because she's with him."

Carey hesitated before nodding, and Kyna's eyes widened with sheer terror at the thought.

"Which is why I've been trying to control it," Carey added hastily. "Like when we went through the gateway to the Third Realm, and at the Arena. Both times I managed to use it without fully unleashing it." She fidgeted with the hem of her cuff. "When I summon it, I can feel it trying to force itself free, as though it wants me to use more. I think that's why it hurts to control it, because I'm holding it back. Or maybe I'm just not strong enough to control it without it hurting." She shook her head. "Sorry. I know this doesn't make any sense."

"But you do think you might be strong enough to stop Saar?" Kat asked.

Carey locked eyes with Kat, who was staring at her so intently, and scrunched her nose up as she considered it. "I want to say yes, but Saar has never really displayed his true abilities. I mean, he *created* Malevolence. Does that mean he's more powerful than her, or that he just knew what to say and do to manipulate her?"

They fell silent, no doubt wondering which one it was and which was the greater evil. In either case, Carey knew that when they finally arrived in

Monaghan, they'd undoubtedly find out.

*

It would take another two days of flying to reach the shores of Ireland and another to reach Monaghan. If all went smoothly, they'd be there before the end of the week, and Carey and the others would know once and for all who they were dealing with. If it was Saar, at least they'd be prepared.

Flying over the waters between the mainland of Europe and England, Carey let her thoughts wander. Not for the first time did she feel a knot of anxiety curl in her chest as her mind turned to Ji. Whenever they weren't fighting for their lives, talking of Saar and his plans, or theorising over Seramina and her powers, thoughts of Ji often surfaced. His voice floated to her on the wind, whispered in her ear at night, and the inexplicable pull she felt never left, like a string stretched across the space between them. But ever since she'd been unable to reach him, Carey couldn't ignore the unsettled feeling that pooled in her stomach. She'd always assumed that he meant for her to find him, that he'd make it possible for her to do so. But what if by hiding from those who would do him harm, Ji had made it impossible for Carey too? She shook her head; these thoughts were of no use to her right now. Or ever. He would find her. He'd promised.

Blinking back to the present, Carey peered around Maël to see tall cliffs ahead of them, waves crashing onto a wide shore at their foot. To their right stood a small town on the cliff's edge, far enough away to not be of any concern, and to their left, jutting from the waters, were the oddest rock formations Carey had ever seen. The rock was stark white and plunged straight down into the water. With winter well underway, the flat tops were coated in a layer of blinding snow, looking like great white pegs protruding out of the ocean. As they flew over the beach, the view below turned from restless blue waves to endless white. Their shadows flitted over the land, looking like those of large birds at that distance. Flat fields stretched out in all directions, the snow interrupted by thickets of trees from time to time.

After a short rest, they were off again, headed for the west coast of England. The snow-covered fields and towns created an eerie sort of calm as they flew, and Carey was infinitely glad her coat protected her from the worst of the cold. Her face was a different matter.

That night as she sat by the fire, trying to bring feeling back to her numb features, Carey listened to Kat and Rupert exchange good-natured barbs.

"I'm tellin' you, Kat, I've never been one fer swordfightin'. I can hold my own with a curse or two, but you can keep yer pointy metal weapons to yerself."

Kat pouted mockingly. "Aww. You won't even give it a try for me? I mean, I'll surely land you on your backside, but at least give it a try. You never know when it might come in handy."

Rupert narrowed his eyes at Kat, and Kyna gave him a playful shove. "Come on, Rupert. Give it a go! I want ter see Kat beat you!"

"Yes, well, now I really want ter try," Rupert replied sarcastically, but he stood, laying his bag on the ground and holding a hand out to Kat. "All right. Show me a few moves an' we'll see how it goes."

With a triumphant grin, Kat slapped her hand into his and Rupert pulled her to her feet.

"Carey? Do you mind if Rupert borrows your sword?" Kat asked.

With a small laugh, Carey drew the Vuletian sword, the dragon on the hilt illuminated by the flames of the campfire. "Try not to cut yourself," she warned with a grin as Rupert grasped the handle.

Rupert huffed. "Thank you fer yer vote of confidence."

"What are you worried about?" Kyna said. "It's not like you can't just heal yerself."

Throwing his arms up in surrender, he strode over to where Kat stood, sai drawn. The bounty hunters were watching from their campsite, clearly interested by the show of weaponry. Kaleb was on watch, as always, but he leant against a tree, eyes following the pair with intrigue.

"Right," Kat said, spinning her sai. "First, you want to stand like this."

Kat gave Rupert a lesson in the basics, and Carey had to admit that despite his initial protestations, Rupert wasn't half bad. Of course, he still ended up flat on his back with Kat's sai at his chest when they finally began sparring. Kyna laughed excitedly, and Carey joined her as Kat and Rupert threw insults, every one of them as ridiculous as the last.

"Again?" Kat asked. "Since you like lying in the snow so much, I'll make this one quick for you."

Rupert laughed. "Is it your skill that has me fallin' over myself or yer hilarious sense of humour?"

Kyna gave a whoop of excitement as Kat swiftly took Rupert down. His head fell at her feet, but before Kat could bring her sai around to his chest once more, he dropped the sword, grabbed hold of Kat's ankles and whipped them out from under her. Kat's eyes widened in shock as she fell, sai flying back over her head as she tumbled down beside Rupert. The weapons landed point down in the snow. Rupert was instantly atop her, attempting to pin her hands above her head, but Kat was having none of that. She brought her knees up, heels to his chest, and kicked. Rupert was thrown off her with a grunt. In a flurry of snow, their roles were quickly reversed. Kat pinned him to the ground, one knee on his chest and his hands by his head. Her chest was heaving, his eyes were on hers, and for a moment they just stared at each other, out of breath, stilled by this impasse.

Then, with a smile tugging at his lips, Rupert said, "I know yer like ter see me flat on my arse, but would you mind helpin' me up at some point? The snow is startin' to seep into my coat."

Releasing Rupert's hands as though she'd just realised what she was doing, Kat jumped to her feet, reached out and pulled Rupert up.

"Sorry," she said, turning to retrieve her sai. "I got carried away. I didn't hurt you, did I?"

Rupert laughed as though her question was ridiculous. "I think I'd be a little more vocal if that were the case, Kat. Perhaps that's enough fer the night, though?"

Kyna groaned. "Oh, but it was just gettin' good!"

Kat and Rupert laughed as they re-joined Carey and Kyna by the fire, Kyna ruffling her brother's hair. Carey sat quietly as she observed her best friend and the boy sitting next to her.

The night crept on, and the hunters and Seekers fell asleep one by one until only Carey sat awake by their fire, Emilia by hers. The hunter was reading, only glancing up at Carey from time to time. Even with Maël's Persuasion stopping them from escaping, and their willingness to let themselves be taken to Monaghan, the hunters still didn't trust the Seekers not to flee. The thought irked Carey more than she cared to admit, and she couldn't let it go, no matter how many times Kat and Rupert urged her to.

Closing her eyes, she thought of her only refuge. She recalled the blue of his eyes, even as they'd dimmed, his ruffled hair and smiling mouth. The sound of his laugh, her name on his lips…

She reached out into the darkness, searching for him. Carey felt for his presence, urged herself onwards when nothing presented. She hit a wall. She pushed as hard as she could. No light slipped from beyond it, or any sound. Carey forced her mind not to panic, held her focus on her memories of Ji. His humour, his stubbornness, his warmth… and she felt the slightest of tugs. Carey grabbed hold of it and followed the pull, but the wall remained, unyielding.

"No," Carey whispered into the dark as she pushed with all her might. "No."

But nothing changed. Her focus slipped, and Carey was flung back to reality, the fire still crackling at her feet and the stars flickering in the ink-black sky. She swore under her breath, balling her fists up in her lap as she tried to calm the rage she felt at her failure. There was definitely something keeping her from him. She assumed it was how he was staying hidden. But how was she supposed to get past that?

Carey withdrew from her pocket the glass box that held the star. The star was constantly moving, a tiny ball of white fire shifting and rolling within its confines. She had no idea how Ji had managed it, but it was a small piece of him, a reminder of the night he'd come to find her.

They are simply stars, and nothing more. But you, Carey – you did something worthy of admiration.'

Her heart ached at the memory, and her knuckles whitened as she gripped the star tightly in her lap.

There came a groan and Carey glanced up to see Kyna stirring. She'd been curled up against Rupert's back, but now she sat up, rubbing her eyes of sleep. She noticed Carey still wide awake and frowned.

"Carey? Aren't yer sleepin'?"

Carey shook her head, then motioned for Kyna to join her. Kyna crawled carefully out from under the blanket and stretched her hands out towards the fire. They sat in silence for a few moments before Carey asked, "Couldn't sleep?"

Kyna scrunched up her nose. "Bad dream."

"Anything I can help with?"

Kyna's eyes flitted to Carey's, then down to the star in her hands, then away once more.

"It's just…" She stared hard into the flames. "I'm sorry."

"What are you sorry for?"

Kyna bit her lip. "I guess… I've not been of much use so far. You an' Kat, yer so good at fightin'. And Rupert, of course, he's been great at bein' a Healer, like he always has. But I…"

Carey placed a hand on Kyna's shoulder. "Look, I won't lie and say that I planned for you to come along, but I understand why you did. Rupert is your only family, and I know I'd have gone mad if I'd been left behind to wait. And as for being useful? You saved me on the mountain, you've helped Rupert, and that ability of yours to sense danger? I have a feeling that that will come in very handy very soon."

Kyna gave her a small smile that faded almost immediately. "That's all very nice of you ter say, thank you."

Carey cocked an eyebrow. "But?"

Kyna shook her head. "But Rupert is only a small part of why I wanted ter come. Actually, he was more of an excuse."

"An excuse? How so?" Carey asked.

Kyna looked down at the star in Carey's lap again. "How did you know Ji was yer Other?"

This sudden change in topic was so abrupt that Carey stumbled over her words. "Oh… um…" She looked down at the star, turning it over in her hands. "It wasn't easy, at least, not for me. Apparently, Ji knew a long time back, but I took a while to realise it was actually him."

"How did it feel?"

"It *feels*… right. I want to be near him all the time, to hear his voice, to know he's there for me, too. And when we're apart, like right now, it's like everything is just slightly wrong, like the world is just off centre. There's a connection, a kind of pull that's constantly trying to draw us back together. Why do you ask?"

Shifting in her spot, Kyna looked into the flames, seeming to steel herself for what she was about to say.

"I think… I think that's how I feel about… Seramina."

Carey blinked. "Oh."

Kyna's eyes flicked up to hers, wide and almost afraid. "Do you think that's possible? I mean, I'm still kind of young, only fourteen. But I don't know anyone else I could ask except you, because you have Ji, an'… you know."

"I don't know," Carey said. "I mean, Ji was sixteen when he realised, but that doesn't mean it's impossible. I lived with girls in the orphanage who, at fourteen, seemed very adamant that they were in love with some boy or other in the village, so–"

"But they were Commoners," Kyna pointed out. "It's not the same."

Carey shook her head. "You're right, it's not." She hesitated. "Does Seramina feel the same way?"

Kyna dropped her gaze to her hands and shook her head. "I don't think so. Or rather, she's not said anythin'."

Rubbing Kyna's arm consolingly, Carey tried to remember what Kat had said when Carey had first confessed to feeling something for Ji.

"Then, unfortunately, you'll just have to wait," she said. "If you feel that way about her, then surely, she'll feel that way too, but you can't force it. It doesn't work that way. It might be tomorrow, or it might be six years from now, but it'll work out. A moment will present itself, you'll see."

Pouting, Kyna gave a heavy sigh. "I suppose. I just… I'm just so afraid that we won't get ter her in time, that somethin' bad will happen to her and I'll just be stuck feelin' this way forever without her."

Carey pulled Kyna into a hug and Kyna, wrapping her arms tightly around Carey's middle, began to sob.

"Don't think like that. I don't intend on letting anything bad happen to Seramina. We'll get her back, I promise," Carey said.

It was unusual, talking of Seramina being Kyna's Other. It wasn't like Carey had never heard of two women being companions before, but with Commoners it had always been something strange, even shameful. A topic of gossip. Kyna, however, seemed wholly unfazed by the notion. Carey thought of how it truly felt when she was around Ji. Despite the misgivings she'd had in the beginning, she couldn't deny or ignore the power that drew her to him. It was beyond anything she could describe or control, and suddenly the idea of Kyna feeling that same thing for Seramina wasn't so odd. It wasn't something Kyna chose – it was magic, inevitable and strong, and who was Carey to say whether it was possible or not? If that was how Kyna felt, then Carey wasn't about to doubt her.

Kyna took a sharp breath and pulled away from Carey, wiping at her face.

"Thank you," she whispered, tucking her hair back away from her face and composing herself. "I've not really said that out loud before, yer know. It's rather dauntin'."

Nodding in understanding, Carey smiled. "Absolutely. And it will happen, just like with me and Ji. Even if it did take some time. It happened, and that's all that matters."

As Kyna curled back under her blanket, Carey looked up at the stars and hoped that Ji was watching them along with her.

~Chapter Twenty-Eight~

Shatter

They crossed the Irish Sea the next day. The journey was long and tiring, and Carey couldn't help but admire the bounty hunters for their endurance and focus as they flew. Rupert kept nodding off behind Emilia. Kyna was leaning against Niko's back, fast asleep with her arms clutched tightly at his waist. The big man was no longer attempting to pull away from her, instead shifting so that she wouldn't slide off into the waves below.

The following night was much the same as the previous: they found a place to camp in the Irish countryside that was hidden from view, this time amongst the dense tree cover of a small wood, and sat either side of the camp, each group avoiding the other.

Maël ignored them for the most part, while Reay continued to glare at them. Emilia alternated between reading her books and sharpening her daggers, happy to go about her own business, while Kaleb spent his rest time either watching the Seekers or hurling wooden stakes at trees. Niko, it seemed, was a man of few words and sat mostly in quiet contemplation. He did, however, give an exhibition of his strength when Kaleb challenged him to a duel; he had Kaleb flat on his back in a matter of seconds, using just one arm to knock him down. Maël had laughed at this, clapping the big man on the back before pulling Kaleb back to his feet.

All of this, however, couldn't distract Carey from the growing feeling of dread bubbling in the pit of her stomach. Come tomorrow, they'd finally arrive at Monaghan, and if their suspicions were true, they'd come face-to-face with Saar. She'd dealt with him before, but most of their previous encounters had been spontaneous. Carey had never had time to contemplate what might or might not happen. This slow approach was a special kind of torture and she wasn't keen on it one bit. All of this was simultaneously compounded by everything Anthriel had told her. She thought she'd faced her fears back in the Corigliphs, but that was before she knew exactly what her power was. She wanted to be able to manipulate it, use the magic that surrounded her as she'd seen the witch from her vision do, but there was still the fact that each time she'd tried to control it, it'd caused her pain. She was tired of feeling lost and inadequate. If it was Saar they faced tomorrow, she wanted to be sure of herself. Carey glanced over at her friends as they sat talking and joking. At least this time, she wasn't facing him alone.

*

Carey stood on the outskirts of Monaghan in the dying light of day, staring down the road that led to the small town. A low stone wall was overshadowed by tall trees that were still green despite the snow at her feet. The dirt lane was a brown slush courtesy of travellers. She shivered, but not from the cold.

Kat came to stand beside her, placing a fortifying hand on her shoulder.

"You all right?" she asked, gazing down the road.

Carey swallowed back a wave of panic. "No. But it doesn't really matter, does it?"

Kat said nothing, and Carey looked for Kyna and Rupert. Fixing his bag on his shoulder, Rupert was waiting alongside Niko's griffon as the big man helped Kyna down. The hunter gave Kyna a warm smile before gesturing for her to join Kat and Carey. It was a small thing, but perhaps one of the hunters didn't hate them as much as Maël would have them believe.

There came a rough clearing of a throat, and she turned to find Maël standing before them, arms crossed. Reay was by his side, mimicking his stance.

"You can use your magic once you enter Monaghan, but not against me or any member of my team," he said almost begrudgingly. "You can use your weapons, but again, not against me or any member of my team. You are to find the person who put out the bounty on you, and if it's *not* the man you assume it to be, then you're to bring the bounty back to us when it's safe to do so. We'll be waiting here until then."

Kat interjected with a cough and Maël raised an eyebrow. "Yes?"

"If it is the man we assume it to be, how will we get word to you?" Kat asked. "I doubt you'll wait here indefinitely."

Maël narrowed his gaze at Kat, then gave a jerk of his head towards his sister. "Reay will follow you at a distance. She has a way of blending in. She'll know."

Kat was about to argue when Rupert spoke up. "Uh, sorry, but how do you manage to blend in? I mean, yer hair, fer one, stands out about as much as mine, I hate ter say." He indicated his own bright locks.

Reay pursed her lips. "If I remember rightly, you had no memory of our encounter. Should someone cross paths with me, I'll be able to make them forget just as easily."

Lifting her chin defiantly, she waited for him to rebuff her claim, but none came.

"If you're done, you might want to get going." Maël handed Carey a piece of paper. "Here's where we were told to meet. Apparently, they'll know when you arrive."

Maël pushed past her to join the rest of his crew.

Carey read the address.

"Do you know where that is?" Kat asked, reading over her shoulder.

"No, only that this street is on the far side of town. We're north – this is past the south side. Kyna – can you sense any danger?"

Kyna's eyes widened momentarily, but then she turned her head and stared hard towards the town, brows knitted in concentration.

"No. Not that I can tell," she said.

Kat clicked her tongue impatiently. "Shall we, then?"

With a final glance at the hunters, Carey turned towards Monaghan, the others at her side. Soon they were passing brown brick houses with white cornerstones and white-powdered gardens. A few people walked by them, some staring, others ignoring them completely.

Monaghan was tiny compared to the sprawling metropolis of Paris. A soft glow shone from behind drawn curtains, and most of the townspeople were already inside on this cold winter's evening. They came to the town square. A series of brick buildings surrounded it, crowded together with no space between. Their rectangular windows stared out at them, blank and lifeless. In the centre of the square was a tall monument. Its circular base was a series of pillars that formed a set of narrow archways. Above these was a section of smaller steepled arches with ornate crosses set atop each point. At the very top of the structure was a second set of pillars, smaller than the first, and all reaching to a point that stretched towards the heavens. The first of the evening stars were blinking into view above, and a few townspeople were milling about the darkening square. Carey wondered if any of them would recognise her. This was where the markets were held each morning, the ones she'd frequented so often during her time in the orphanage. She didn't know what she'd do if they did.

Carey was infinitely glad they were heading south – the orphanage wasn't far from the square, but it was to the west and out of their way. She'd never thought she'd be back here, let alone so close to where she'd effectively been held captive for much of her childhood. She remembered how she'd wanted nothing more than to escape, build a life for herself, perhaps find a place of her own to live. A cottage somewhere far from here. She couldn't help but smile at how naïve she'd been, how simple she'd imagined her life would be. And now she'd returned, no longer an orphan but a witch with a sword on her back.

How times had changed.

"Kyna?" she whispered as they passed an elderly couple shuffling their way home.

Kyna looked around, turning on the spot. "Nothin'."

"Then let's keep going," Kat said. "Any sign of our shadow?"

Rupert nodded over his shoulder. "By th' pub there."

Kat huffed, then continued walking.

Night had fallen by the time they reached the south side of Monaghan. They passed a cathedral, its tall spire lit only by the light of the moon. A high snow-dusted hedge separated them from the mammoth stone structure.

"How much farther?" Kat inquired, indicating the crumpled piece of paper in Carey's hand.

"Not much. I remember there being a farm this way that I'd visit every so often. This address isn't far from that."

Clouds drifted across the moon and they found themselves wandering along the muddy road in almost complete darkness. They reached a gate in a wrought-iron fence. Squinting, Carey tried to make out the inscription on the plaque – the number matched that of Maël's address.

"This is it," she said, her heart in her throat as she placed a hand on the gate to push.

Only then did she look up to see where they were.

"A cemetery?" Kat said, gazing warily about the stone effigies and headstones that jutted from the snowy landscape.

There was a narrow pathway up the centre of the boneyard, leading towards the top of a hill. It was barely more than a narrow track of beaten-down snow, but there appeared to be no other evidence that anyone was there. Cautiously, Carey pushed open the gate. It squealed in the silence, and she grimaced, the sound grating on her already raw nerves. Kat cursed under her breath, and Rupert muttered, "Charmin'."

Kyna stepped in carefully after Carey, her head twisting and turning as though trying to catch a glimpse of something illusive.

"Still nothin'," she confirmed. "But I don't like it here all th' same."

Carey had to agree. In the absence of moonlight, the shadows melded together, the tall stone angels and the squat domed tombstones playing tricks on her eyes. She couldn't help feeling that they were being watched. The spark of magic tingled at her fingers in response to her fear. Carey clenched her fists, holding it back as she walked up the path, flanked by row after row of graves. The dead surrounded them, and it did nothing for Carey's nerves to imagine the ghosts that roamed this land.

As they crested the hill, the clouds shifted and the moon reappeared, gracing them with its light.

"Now what?" Rupert asked nervously.

Carey tried to shrug nonchalantly, but she was shaking too much to be convincing. "We wait."

She looked up at the millions of stars shimmering overhead.

A voice spoke through the silence, loud and clear.

"It's the kind of weather that's perfect for star-gazing, don't you think?"

Carey whirled around, those words lighting a fire in her chest.

Ji?

But it wasn't him. It was a woman, short and slight, standing nearby in the snow. A light flared, a lantern was lit, and Carey recognised her almost immediately.

Kat jumped, her voice sounding higher than usual as she said, "Madame Guise?"

It was their old friend; at least, it appeared to be. She wore a light-grey fur hat pulled low over her ears, her long blonde braids falling out from beneath it. The coat she wore resembled the skirt Carey had last seen her wearing – a patchwork of mismatched wool that created a kaleidoscope of colour in the dim light of her lantern. Boots lined with fur sunk into the snow, and she smiled warmly from behind her large square glasses.

"You finally made it."

Rupert frowned in consternation.

Her words struck Carey as odd, as did her presence here.

"Kyna?" Carey whispered. She took her eyes off Madame Guise momentarily to see Kyna watching the woman with interest rather than alarm.

"Let me," Kat said. She closed her eyes, and her eyelids flitted and flickered.

Madame Guise frowned. "Katrina Lawrence. Are you sifting through my memories?"

Kat's eyes snapped open.

"What did you find?" Carey muttered.

A smile crept cross Kat's face. "It's her."

Madame Guise huffed. "Of course it's me."

Carey gave her an apologetic grimace. "Sorry, but we don't have the luxury of just believing you."

The woman's face softened and she nodded in understanding, her lantern clinking as her head bobbed. "Of course."

The smile on Kat's face slipped straight back off as she looked around the cemetery. "Are you the one who put the bounty out on us?"

"Yes. Sorry about that," Madame Guise answered, wincing. "I do hope they weren't rough with you."

"I'm sorry," Rupert said. "But who are you exactly?"

"This is Madame Guise, an old family friend," Kat said, not taking her eyes from the woman. "Madame Guise – Rupert and Kyna Tagore."

Madame Guise dipped her head in their direction. Ignoring the pleasantries, Carey watched Madame Guise with ill ease. Despite Kat's conviction, she couldn't bring herself to be glad of the woman's presence here. Something still didn't feel right, and she wasn't about to ignore that twinge of uncertainty.

Turning her back to Madame Guise, she said in a low voice, "Kat, are you absolutely sure?"

"I went back into her memories, Carey, back to when we were children. She didn't try blocking me or forcing me out. She knows she needed me to see those memories," Kat replied.

Rupert frowned. "But how did she know that?"

Carey tried to gather her thoughts as she looked from Rupert, to Kat, to Kyna, who was still watching Madame Guise with interest. She faced their old friend once more.

"Why did you put that bounty out on us? You have magic, so why not send us a message like you've done in the past? Wouldn't that have been easier?"

Madame Guise pulled her gaze from Carey.

"We couldn't risk using magic here, not when there are people out there looking for it. We thought it would be safer this way."

"'We'?" Kat said. "Who else is here?"

Knuckles tightening on the lantern's handle, Madame Guise took a steadying breath. "We, as in Ji and I."

Her words almost knocked Carey to the ground. Kat gripped her painfully around her wrist, and there came a sharp intake of breath from Rupert.

"Where is he?" Carey croaked, her concerns wiped away. She marched straight up to Madame Guise. "If he's with you, you need to take me to him. Right this second."

Madame Guise stared back at her, unruffled by Carey's demand. Her expression revealed neither emotion nor intention. After a long moment, she gave a jerk of her head.

"Come. I'll take you to him."

Carey didn't look to see if her friends were following; the crunch of fresh snow told her they weren't far behind. They moved through the rows of graves, the only sound the shuffling of their feet and rustling of their clothes. Carey searched the headstones, waiting for the moment Ji would come into view. Her heart was pounding with anticipation, her body a mess of nerves and excitement. She'd imagined what she might say to him when she finally saw him again, how it would be upon their reunion. She still hadn't decided whether to reprimand him for how he'd left or throw herself upon him. The latter sounded much more appealing in that moment, so much so that Carey didn't notice Madame Guise come to a halt and almost ran into her.

She looked about the trees and tombstones, her heart in her throat. "Where is he?"

She sounded manic, but she couldn't help it. Where was he?

"Carey."

Kat's voice cut through the silence, but Carey wasn't paying any attention. Madame Guise knew where Ji was, so why wasn't she taking them to him?

"Carey!"

Something about Kat's tone broke through to her.

"What?" Carey barked, unable to restrain the desperation, but Kat wasn't looking at her. Her eyes were set on a point beyond where Carey stood. Her body was rigid, her face deathly pale in the lantern light. Rupert and Kyna were watching Carey, their eyes wide with… what was that? Fear?

Slowly she followed Kat's gaze, suddenly afraid. Her eyes landed upon the headstone by Madame Guise's feet. The lantern light swung over it, illuminating the words etched on the granite.

Carey's heart slammed in her chest, stilled, and then shattered. Her knees gave way and she fell, clutching the grey monument as pain untold ripped through her soul.

Upon the stone she saw four words.

Here lies Ji Binx.

~Chapter Twenty-Nine~

Promises

Carey read the words over and over.

Here lies Ji Binx.

Here lies...

Ji...

Binx...

"No," she said with a shuddering breath, still holding onto the grey stone. "This isn't true."

This had to be a ploy. It was Ji's way of staying hidden. But then, why was Madame Guise playing along with it? This was absurd.

Carey looked up at the woman, whose expression was a mix of pity and sorrow.

"Where is he?" she asked, her voice like steel. "This is just some sort of trick to keep the Empire away from him. A ruse. So, where is he, and why won't you take me to him?"

Madame Guise made no move to walk from the accursed headstone. She gave a small shake of her head and said, "I'm sorry, Carey. This is no trick. Ji passed away just over a week ago."

Carey stared at her, her heart in her throat and the world crumbling around her. "How?"

"The dragon's bite. The venom took him, despite my ministrations," she said.

Dragon bite?

Slowly, Carey turned to Rupert, who was avoiding looking at her, his expression one of anguish and guilt.

"You said he was *fine*," Carey said. "You said he was going to recover."

They were all watching Rupert, who shifted uncomfortably beneath their collective gaze.

"He was in bad shape when he got back ter the Centre City. The dragon's venom was already workin' its way around his body. I told him I could extend his life as best I could, but it was only a matter of time," Rupert said. "He made me promise not ter tell you, Carey, I swear. He made me promise. I'd just hoped we'd get ter him before…"

Rupert wavered under Carey's piercing glare. She pulled herself back to her feet. Pain and grief curled into a wave of fiery rage, and Rupert's words had shocked something awake. Her chest was burning, an agony that was only growing, and the disbelief at his confession only made it burn brighter and hotter.

"You *knew?*" she shouted at Rupert, flinging her words at him. "You knew all this time that he was… and you said *nothing?*"

She couldn't say it. Couldn't say that word out loud. It felt like an impossible thing, an admission to something she wasn't ready to accept. That she was *unable* to accept.

He clenched his jaw against her fury.

"I didn't know he was dead, Carey. I told him I didn't know how long he had, and I tried ter get him ter stay but–"

"Oh, you *tried*, did you?" Carey snapped. "You *tried*? Oh, well, I'm so glad you *tried*, Rupert, because look how well that worked out!"

"Carey…" Kat said, approaching with her hands outstretched. Glittering tears streaked her face, but Carey barely noticed them, so fierce was her attention on Rupert.

"You lied to me, Rupert, to everyone," she screamed. "Ji left, and you said nothing, even when I was trying to find him! You knew! You. Knew!"

Without even thinking about what she was doing, Carey flung her hands up, summoning magic faster than she'd ever done before. She wanted to hurt him for this, wanted him to feel a modicum of the agony that was tearing through her. A flash of red flew from her fingertips. Kat lunged, knocking her arms sideways, sending the curse flying over Rupert's head. Kyna screamed and Rupert ducked, flinging his hands over his head. The magic hit a tree, the cracking of the wood splitting the night air. The sound shocked Carey from her rage-filled tirade. Instantly she felt her fury and her rage leave her, and she slumped in Kat's arms.

"Oh my… Rupert. No. No…"

She wept, clutching at Kat's coat. Her friend's arms tightened around her as her body quivered. The grief seeped into her bones, settled on her heart and began slowly tearing it to shreds. The fight went out of her like a fire being snuffed out, and Carey and Kat sunk to the ground, tears falling with abandon.

Carey sobbed into Kat's shoulder. "All this time I'd been trying to reach him and couldn't and it wasn't because he was hiding himself. It was because he was… he wasn't even… he…"

She couldn't breathe. Her chest was constricting – it felt like something was lodged in her throat, depriving her of air. Carey pushed away from Kat, clawing at the front of her coat as she gasped for breath.

"He's… Ji's g… Ji's not…" It was impossible to get the words out.

Panic spiked through her, spurring on the grief and terror. Black spots dotted her eyesight as she struggled for air. She saw Rupert and Kyna dive for her as she spluttered wordlessly, the same devastating thought pounding in her head, piercing her heart.

Ji.

Ji was gone.

Ji was dead.

*

She wasn't sure where she was but assumed it'd been Rupert who'd carried her there. She was bundled beneath layers of blankets beside a dwindling fire. The flames were the first thing she saw when she woke. She'd dreamt of blue eyes and messy hair, of laughter and a warm embrace. Hot tears burned in her eyes and she didn't move to wipe them away as they trickled down her face. Her chest felt as though someone had punched their way through her ribs and pried her heart from her chest. She didn't know how she was still alive, how she was still breathing, when a part of her was no longer there.

Ji.

How hadn't she felt his passing? Wasn't she supposed to be able to feel something like that? They were still connected, she could feel it. But how? How was it that she could still feel a connection to someone who was… Carey gripped her hair, tugging at it, a hoarse sob wracking her body as she curled in on herself, as though by doing so she might protect herself from the pain of it all. But it was too late. She was saturated in heartache, every part of her body burning with the agony of it. Her body shuddered. She just wanted him back, wanted his arms about her, his voice in her ear. The more she thought of him, though, the more it hurt, and she was taken over again by devastating hopelessness.

Yet as she lay there staring into the fire in the grate, she found herself overcome by a strange frenetic energy. She tried to ignore it, tried to huddle deeper within her cocoon, but it wouldn't allow it. It was pulling at her, restlessness coaxing her to action. Huffing, Carey sat up, throwing the blankets off impatiently. Everyone else was asleep, their heavy breathing filling the quiet of the small cottage. Kat lay huddled under her own covers with her back to Carey. Rupert was in an armchair, his head lolling on his shoulder, and Kyna was stretched out on a tattered lounge chair. An archway revealed the kitchen, and a door was ajar enough for her to guess it was Madame Guise's bedroom. Cloaks hanging from pegs indicated the front door.

She had to get out.

It was still dark outside. Wrapped in a woollen blanket and armed with Madame Guise's lantern, Carey made for the front door. Her chest aching, her mind a mess, she flicked open the latch and slipped out into the night.

Letting her eyes grow accustomed to the dark, Carey saw that the cottage was on the edge of the cemetery. There was a small gate nearby, similar to the one they'd entered the cemetery through, and Carey could make out the path they'd created through the graveyard. A thought punctuated the haze of grief. Had Ji and Madame Guise been here all along? Had they been waiting here, waiting for Ji to die?

Carey shook her head, a sob threatening to escape her lips.

She lit the lantern and, clutching the blanket around her shoulders, made her way slowly through the cemetery. Dark, heavy clouds hung low in the sky, threatening more snow, and a biting wind whistled through the lines of grey stone, rustling the leaves of the trees.

The inexplicable pull she'd always felt for Ji steered her towards the headstone bearing his name. It was unremarkable, a simple slab of granite with a rounded top. The words were etched in large letters, as though daring her to defy their truth. Slowly, Carey approached, fear urging her to stop, to flee, but she forced her feet to keep moving. Dropping to her knees before the stone, she placed the lantern at its base. With shaking fingers, Carey lifted her hand to the inscription. She hadn't seen it before, having been unable to read past Ji's name. Running a finger over the letters, Carey whispered the words to the wind.

"Fear not death,
but fear a life without light."

Hot tears splashed down on the snow as Carey flattened her hand against the cold stone, wishing with all her might for this nightmare to end, for Ji to appear and tell her there had been some terrible mistake. This was not how it was meant to be. It was not how they were supposed to meet again. He'd promised her they'd find each other, that they'd be together again. She leant her forehead against Ji's name, feeling her heart break over and over again. Each memory was a painful reminder that there would be no more.

No more firsts, only lasts.

She had no idea how long she sat there in the cold, pressed against the frigid memorial, but her grief seemed endless, unwilling to let her rest or permit her a reprieve. Ji's face held in her mind's eye, his words both a soothing balm and searing knife for her already bleeding soul…

The blue velvet of the night sky stretched above her, a million stars dotting the expanse. The dark clouds that had lain so threateningly were gone, though no wind blew that may have spirited them away. Carey was lying on her back, surrounded by soft, green grass. She let her head fall to her left to look at Ji, who lay at her side, gazing back at her as though he'd been there watching her all along.

"Ji?"

This was a dream.

Carey's heart fell in her chest and her stomach lurched. Why did her sleeping mind have to be so cruel? Was grieving during her waking hours not enough that it sought to torment her further?

Ji lifted his hand to her cheek, brushing his fingertips along her jaw line. It feels so real, Carey thought as she let her eyes flutter closed. She could feel his hand brush her hair from her face and gently tuck it behind her ear.

"Carey," he said gently. "Open your eyes."

Reluctantly, Carey lifted her gaze to his. His eyes had returned to their original piercing blue. This was definitely a dream.

As though he guessed what she was thinking, Ji smiled.

"This isn't a dream, Carey."

Carey's eyebrows pinched in consternation. "Yes it is. You're..." She couldn't bring herself to say it.

"I know," Ji replied. "But you can feel it, can't you?"

Carey let herself feel her surroundings: the stillness in the air, the grass beneath her. She always knew when it wasn't a dream, when she was Twilight Travelling. But how? How was this possible?

Shaking, she reached out to him. She hesitated, her eyes on his, then drew her fingers across his forehead, sweeping aside the flop of brown hair that had fallen towards his eyes. As she lingered, heart pounding, he took her hand. Slowly, deliberately, he pressed a kiss to her palm, his eyes never leaving hers. It was soft and real.

He was real.

"Oh, Ji."

Carey pulled him to her as his hand slipped behind her neck, twisting in her hair. He tipped her head back ever so slightly, and he whispered her name with a longing that almost made her heart break all over again before pressing his lips to hers.

This was where she was meant to be, Carey thought as she ran her fingers through Ji's hair, a tremble of euphoria running through her body. She could feel his heart beating strong against her chest as his lips moved against hers, the desire that had grown during their time apart crashing down upon them. There was nothing that mattered in that moment, nothing that Carey cared more about than the sensation of Ji's hands at her waist, his warmth as he pulled her closer, or the way he spoke her name in whispered tones.

Pulling away, the tip of his nose grazing hers, Ji cupped her face with his hand. His eyes were glistening with unshed tears that surely reflected her own as he looked upon her with a hint of sadness.

"I missed you. So much," he said in a hushed voice. "I was afraid you wouldn't make it in time, that I'd miss my chance."

"Your chance?" Carey said as she ran her fingertips down the side of his face.

"I knew I didn't have long, that my life was drawing to a close. And I had to see you..."

The light in Ji's eyes had turned dark, the pain of the past reflecting in them like a rolling storm. Carey fell still, her hands fisted in the front of his shirt as she listened, not daring to move.

"This place," he continued, not looking away from her face, "is the In-between. I've waited here, hoping you'd find me before I had to go. It calls me onwards, Carey, what comes next, and if I don't heed its call, I'll be doomed to roam this plane forever. I'll never be at rest. I'll never find peace."

Ji's voice was low and calm though Carey couldn't understand how. What he said made no sense. He spoke as though he truly was dead. But he was here, warm against her touch, his breath prickling her skin.

"I don't understand," she managed, unable to keep the pleading from her voice, willing him back to a place of rationality. "You're here. You're real."

"And so are you," he said as he ran his hand through her hair.

"But..." Carey wrenched her gaze away from his to look up at the sky.

She heard Ji shift beside her, and he sat up, leaning on one arm as he looked down upon her, his eyes roaming all over, taking her in.

"You're a Fiorilusa. Your Twilight Travelling isn't bound to just the plane of the living. You can visit the In-between – but not for long."

Carey frowned at him; she reached out to the arm he leant upon, feeling the strength of his forearm, the muscle taut beneath his skin.

"How do you know this?"

Letting out a sigh, Ji leant over her, hand on either side of her, his body blocking out the sky.

"When you were taken by Saar, I had Lady Marksis find everything she could about Fiorilusa and Twilight Travelling just in case there was a way I could find you. It was then that I discovered that you could travel to the plane in between life and death and seek out those who were yet to pass on. It's how I knew to wait here just in case you came. Lucky for me that you came when you did."

"But then..." Carey said as his words sunk in. "That means... does that really mean that... you're..."

The word and all its implications hung between them.

Ji gave a tiny grimace.

"Yes."

His confirmation made Carey's skin prickle and any hope that had manifested in the past few minutes shattered.

"Ji," was all Carey could say, pulling herself up and wrapping her arms around Ji's neck, burying herself against him.

She felt his arms envelop her, his face as he nuzzled into the hair by her neck, and for a good long moment they stayed that way, unwilling to pull away. She hadn't realised how deeply she'd missed him and how lonely she'd felt until this moment. Ji's absence had left her adrift with no mooring. She didn't think she could stand losing him so completely. They were together here, in this strange place, and she didn't want to release him. Carey let out a loud sob. Tears pricked at the corners of her eyes and she scrunched up her face in a vain attempt to hold them back.

"It's not fair," she said, and although she knew she sounded like a petulant child, it didn't make it any less true. "If Rupert had only told me the truth..."

"Carey, look at me."

Carey pulled away and Ji smiled sadly.

"After he told me my prospects, I knew I couldn't tell you. I couldn't leave you without any hope. I left knowing that I might never get to see you again." Ji swallowed hard, his voice cracking. "And if my pain was anything to go by, I wasn't about to inflict that upon you by telling you the truth. Saying goodbye was hard enough."

"But that wasn't your choice to make," Carey cried, her hands tightening around

him. "If I'd known—"

"I still would've gone," he said. "Like I said in my letter, you have a destiny far greater than my own. If I'd stayed, I wouldn't have been able to go with you. And you'd have stayed with me, I know it – it's what I would've done – and the realms would've been the lesser for it. I couldn't be responsible for that. I just couldn't."

Carey huffed in frustration. "Damn you and your stubbornness, Ji Binx," she said, shifting closer to him.

His presence was distracting. She'd forgotten how just being close to him made her heart flutter in her chest with anticipation. She couldn't believe she'd ever questioned these emotions, pushed back against them and refused to see the truth of them for so long. Now, however, she felt a keen sense of desperation crackle between them; the realisation that the end was upon them made them determined to take full advantage of these last moments.

Carey raked her fingers through Ji's hair, taking in every bit of him she could – his strong jaw line, the way his lips tweaked into that mischievous smile she adored, his keen blue eyes the colour of a clear midsummer's sky...

"You're ridiculous," she said, not meaning it in the slightest, and his mouth stretched into a heart-warming grin.

"I'll take that as a compliment," he said as he leant back into her, and this time it wasn't just a kiss. It was desperation and longing, a furious desire to do everything they never got to do, say all the things they never got to say. Carey was lost and then found as Ji kissed her long and hard, one hand wrapped around her waist, pulling her in, the other gathered in her hair. Carey pulled at his shirt, holding so tightly as to never let go, determined to remain here forever, Ji's lips on hers, his body warm in their embrace.

She couldn't do it anymore. The course that had been laid out for her, this destiny, whatever it was, seemed too much. It felt too hard to go on, sacrificing everything and everyone. The thought of not having this, not having Ji with her, was sheer torture and she jerked away, eyes closed against the torment.

"I can't! I can't do this, not without you. Not without you with me."

Tears streamed down her face and, bleary-eyed and hopeless, she looked up at him.

Ji was calm, his face holding a look of sincere admiration.

"Yes, you can," he said, bringing her in to rest on his shoulder. He stroked her hair. "You must."

"But what if I can't?" Carey sobbed, taking hold of his other hand and holding it tightly in both of hers.

"Carey, no. You can't think that way," Ji said, leaning his head against hers. "You..." He let out a long sigh that ruffled her hair. "You have the capacity for great strength and even greater courage. I've seen it in you, time and again, but you don't seem to see it in yourself. You will carry on, even without me. I know you can." He smiled. "I feel the call to go on, to move on from this plane. It's getting stronger, Carey, and when I do, wherever I end up, I will wait for you, just like I promised."

Ji put a finger under Carey's chin and raised her face to his. Letting go of his hand, Carey reached up and traced his features with the tips of her fingers.

"I miss this," she whispered, choking on the words, but she needed to say it before it was too late. "Your eyes... the way they would light up when you were up to no good. Your smile, whenever you saw me." She traced his lips, his breath warm and steady as she touched them. "And this," she said finally, pressing her hand flat against his chest. "Your love, your selflessness, and your stubborn sense of nobility."

Ji chuckled and she smiled.

"That is what I'll miss the most," she said.

He covered her hand with his and pulled her back onto the grass so that they lay side-by-side, Carey's head resting on Ji's shoulder, his arm curled around her. Together they watched as a single star streaked across the night sky.

"You know what?" Ji said with a squeeze of Carey's hand. "You are a star. You're the brightest one, blazing through the darkness. You are fire and light, Carey Lee, and I love you. Always have, always will."

Carey turned her face to his to find him looking down at her, all the wonder of the world apparent in his eyes.

"And I love you, Ji Binx," she replied, and their lips met once more, each kiss becoming softer and lighter until she opened her eyes to find him gone.

~Chapter Thirty~

Time

"Carey."

Carey shifted at the sound of her name, but she didn't open her eyes. Someone gave her a gentle shake.

"Come on, Carey. Wake up."

It was Kat, her voice soft in Carey's ear. Slowly, she forced herself to open her eyes.

She'd fallen asleep propped up against Ji's headstone, curled up in the thick woollen blanket she'd taken from the cottage. Her face was cold and raw from the wind, and she wondered how she'd managed to sleep at all given her uncomfortable position. Kat was crouched beside her, giving her a wan smile. It must've been just on dawn – there was a faint pink hue to the sky as it changed from black to pale blue.

"How long have you been out here?" Kat asked, her eyes flicking to Ji's name by Carey's head.

The events of the night before came floating back to Carey on the morning breeze, and despite the intense ache in her chest, she felt a little lighter, as though seeing Ji that one last time had given her just that smallest bit of hope.

"I saw Ji," Carey said as she straightened up, her voice rough from sleep.

"What do you mean? Like in a dream?"

Carey took Kat's hand. "No. I Twilight Travelled. I didn't mean to – I hadn't realised I could. It was accidental, but I managed it. He was in a place called the In-between, somewhere between the living and... what comes next." Carey looked down at Kat's hand. "It's hard to explain, but I swear, he was real."

She wanted to share this with Kat, show her the miracle that had been last night. And then she remembered that she could.

"You could see it," Carey said eagerly. "You could look back into my memories."

Kat's eyes went wide. "Carey…"

"It's all right. You should see it." Carey squeezed Kat's hands in encouragement.

Kat swallowed hard, hesitating, then, slowly, she closed her eyes. Her face was a mask of concentration. A small gasp escaped her lips as she alighted on Carey's memory. Kat's hand tightened on Carey's as a lone tear slipped from beneath her lashes. Carey squeezed back, letting Kat know it was all right. After another long moment, Kat came back to her with a shuddering breath, her eyes glassy with unshed tears.

"Oh, Carey," she said in barely a whisper, and they flung their arms about each other, holding on as though they'd never let go.

Ji had been more than a friend to Kat. Kat and Ji had grown up together, just the two of them, surviving with only each other to depend on. To Kat, Ji was her family, her brother, and his loss… Kat would undoubtedly be feeling it just as keenly as Carey was.

They still had each other, though – they weren't alone in their grief. It may have felt insurmountable in that moment, a constant barrage of lost moments and never-will-bes, but that didn't mean it would always be so. And if Carey knew anything, it was that they couldn't let it take them over, not right now. Ji wouldn't have wanted that. He'd taken himself away so that they might carry on, do what needed to be done. Carey thought of the letter still tucked in her coat pocket and of the words he'd spoken to her last night. How he'd spoken of courage. He'd always believed she was courageous, that she had the ability to be stronger. Perhaps it was time she started believing it, too. Perhaps it was time she started believing in herself.

Carey drew back from Kat and forced a smile onto her face. "I didn't mean to fall apart on you," she said. "I know what Ji meant to you, too."

Referring to Ji in the past tense caught in her throat, but she forced herself past it, holding herself strong.

Courage.

Kat squeezed Carey's arms. "You don't need to apologise. He meant a lot to both of us."

Her eyes lingered on his name over Carey's shoulder and her bottom lip trembled.

"He was the only person I had for the longest time," she finally said, a crack forming in her façade. "I'd said goodbye to my mother a long time ago, long before her death, so losing her wasn't... I'd already lost her. But Ji..."

Kat squeezed her eyes shut then looked to the sky.

"He got me through so much. Fought alongside me. Made me... better."

Tears streaked Kat's cheeks, breaking Carey's heart. She'd hardly ever seen Kat cry. Her stoic personality was a testament to her strength, something born from years fighting and dealing with the absolute worst. So, the fact that she sat there, tears streaming, her face a storm of emotions... this was her breaking point.

"Kat," she said gently. "Look at me."

Slowly, Kat brought her gaze back to Carey's.

"This is not where we break," Carey said fervently, holding Kat's hands in hers once more. "You hear me? If there was anything Ji taught me it was to keep going, despite it all. He never let anything stop him, so we are not about to let this stop us from doing what needs to be done."

Slowly, the tears dried, and Kat's stolid veneer slid back into place.

"You're right," she said. "He was a stubborn piece of work."

Carey chuckled before quickly sobering. "But we have to keep going. If not for Ji, for Seramina."

Kat looked towards the cottage. "Indeed. For Seramina."

They got to their feet, staring down at Ji's headstone again.

"You know what," Kat said, a small smile lifting her mouth. "I'd always imagined Ji going out in a blaze of glory, most possibly with me at his side." She sighed. "Bet he really hated the fact that what got him in the end was a lousy dragon bite."

They chuckled, and Carey pulled the blanket tighter around her shoulders as they began to walk back down to Madame Guise's cottage. The pain was still there and she doubted it would dull any time soon. But her heart would endure.

They both would.

*

They decided to stay one more night with Madame Guise to rest and regather their strength. Despite her initial nervousness about being back in this town, Carey knew she'd find it hard to leave Monaghan now that a part of her was buried there. The connection she felt with Ji was as strong as it had ever been but, now she knew the truth, the feeling would be forever linked with a deep sense of sadness.

There was also the small issue of their bounty hunters. Shortly after breakfast, Carey and Kat, laden with a large purse filled with clinking gold coins, waited outside Madame Guise's cottage.

Reay soon appeared.

"Got our payment?" she said, holding out her hand. "I see you're all still in one piece."

Carey held back a retort – and the purse. "I'd like to give the payment to your brother, if it's all the same to you."

The white-haired dhampir narrowed her eyes at them before turning with a swish of her long coat. "Fine. Come along, then."

They walked in silence, trailing the hunter to the far side of town where the rest were camped.

Maël stood from his spot by the campfire when he saw them approach.

"I see they're still in one piece," he said, echoing his sister and earning a derisive snort from Kat.

Stepping right up to the dhampir, Carey thrust the coin purse into Maël's chest.

"Here. Your payment," she snarled. "Now leave. We're done here."

Not bothering to count the coins, Maël tucked the purse into his belt and stared hard at Carey. "Really, now?"

Ji's death had afforded Carey some clarity regarding the bounty hunters and their indifference. She couldn't help what had happened to them in the past, nor did she want to waste her energy trying to change their minds. Saar was still out there and Seramina was still in danger. Worrying about what these bounty hunters thought was not going to help her with either.

"Yes, really," Carey replied, lifting her chin. "We. Are. Done."

Maël stepped up to her. "Still think you're better than us?"

Carey's lip curled. "I don't think I am. I *know* I am. I'm better because I'm willing to die fighting for what I believe in, die fighting for those I love. And you know what? I will *keep* fighting despite losing more than you could possibly imagine. You, however? You only fight for yourself and look down your nose at those who might do otherwise. Oh, and I fight my own battles, thank you very much. If you knew us, you'd have never accused us of sitting back and sending others in our stead. But since you'd never believe me, here's something for you – I *never* want to see you again. And if I do, you better stay out of my way, because if you're not with us, you're against us. There is no neutral ground as far as we're concerned."

Without waiting for a reply, Carey turned on her heel and walked away, Kat shooting the bounty hunters a satisfied smirk as she joined her.

*

Carey and Kat returned to find Rupert, Kyna, and Madame Guise deep in conversation. Something had happened. The air within the cottage was tense, the ominous feeling driven home by the look on Rupert's face as he lifted his head in greeting.

"What is it?" Carey asked, the deep throb of pain she now carried clenching tightly in her chest.

"We think we know why Saar hasn't acted yet," Rupert replied with a tight voice, looking over at his sister who sat quietly wringing her hands in her lap. "Why he hasn't attempted ter bring back Malevolence."

Kat was frozen in the act of hanging her coat. "What?"

Madame Guise summoned them to sit.

"I was saying how I wished I had more herbs for Rupert to take with you, but that my stores were almost empty and I was going to have to wait for the full moon to gather more. Because at full moon, magic is at its most potent. Picking herbs, performing enchantments – the benefits are, shall we say, far more than at any other time."

"Wait," Carey said slowly, her mind whirring. "Are you saying–"

"He's waiting for the full moon?" Kat finished, turning her head to the window as though she might glimpse it from where she sat.

When Rupert nodded in affirmation, Kat said, "When is that supposed to be?"

"Six nights from now," Madame Guise confirmed.

Carey looked over at Kyna, who sat silent, hands working the edge of her tunic. Carey reached over and placed a hand on hers, forcing Kyna to look up at her.

"We'll get her back. I promised, remember?"

Kyna bit her lip, her face drawn and worried. If Carey's own pain and grief were anything to go by, she knew exactly how Kyna was feeling, and until Seramina was safely back with them, nothing she said would ease Kyna's fear.

"Do yer think we should be headin' north-west still?" Rupert asked, watching Carey and Kyna's exchange with curiosity.

Carey pulled back, an idea coming to mind.

"I think it might be time I had another chat with our friend."

*

Carey stood by Ji's grave, the stars emerging as she waited, her coat fluttering in the breeze. She went over what they'd planned in her head, what she would ask of the Ancient should she get the chance. For that was who she waited for now, ankle deep in fresh snow surrounded by the dead.

"This is certainly not where we were expecting to be, is it?" she said to Ji's grave as though he might hear. What did she know? He may very well be listening to everything she said.

"Who knew?" she continued. "Who knew that when you and Kat rescued me from those highwaymen that this is where we'd end up? Me, waiting for an Ancient, and you..." Carey clutched at her chest as regret for all they'd never have welled up inside of her. "I always thought we'd have more time."

Suddenly, a fierce wind whipped up around her, and within the swirling of the snow appeared the looming silhouette of Anthriel, his wings outspread, the very tips trailing in the snow.

"You summoned me?"

His voice was the familiar soulful timbre, though there was a slight edge to it, as though he didn't appreciate being called.

Carey was not about to cower under his steely glare. "Yes. You wish to help. We need to know where Saar is headed."

Anthriel seemed unperturbed by the winter weather swirling about him, his bare chest rising and falling in a steady rhythm. He stopped before her, his wings still spread wide. He blinked, considering her with his usual cool countenance.

"It is time," he replied in his vague, irritating way.

"What?"

He was staring at her in that intent manner of his, and it made Carey want to fidget with discomfort.

"It is time you knew the choice you have to make."

She froze. Carey had almost forgotten about that.

Anthriel spoke over her silence. "The prophecy concerning you and the fall of Malevolence," he said. "You know of it, but you do not know the manner of your victory, nor why it must be as such."

"My victory?" Carey asked, her throat dry. "I've defeated Malevolence already. That prophecy is no longer relevant."

"You're wrong," he said. "As an Ancient, I see every choice that is ever made and the consequences wrought by them. For the most part, they are small. Inconsequential. One individual is rarely the cause of any great change. But there is coming a time where a choice will be made that will bring either light to the realms or plunge them all into an everlasting darkness. That choice is yours, Carey Lee."

"You've told me this already." Carey worked to still her wildly beating heart. "What has this got to do with my prophecy?"

Anthriel's narrowed his eyes, clearly not used to being interrupted. "It has *everything* to do with it. Your prophecy is yet to be realised. You halted her progress but you never truly defeated Malevolence. It is a mermaid prophecy, and they are unique. If you had truly fulfilled your prophecy, you would not be standing here before me today."

Her heart in her throat, Carey barely managed the next few words. "What do you mean?"

The Ancient lowered his ice-blue gaze to hers. "For such a prophecy to be fulfilled, the person of whom it was made must die."

Carey felt as though the air had been punched from her lungs. She stumbled a little, shaking her head, uncomprehending.

Die?

That couldn't be right. This had to be some sort of mistake.

"No," Carey stammered, backing away from the Ancient as though his words might physically hurt her. "No. That can't be true."

"It is," Anthriel replied coldly. "Balance must be kept. Good does not exist without evil, darkness without light. The wizard Saar will revive Malevolence, using the magic of an Innocent. This will make her powerful beyond belief. You, even with your ability to wield the magic around you, will be unable to defeat her. The ability you both possess is two halves of one whole. You know this – you have felt its pull when it is near."

Carey knew exactly what he meant. How could she forget how Malevolence's magic had called to her in the Stronghold. Now it made sense why.

"One half cannot die while the other lives on. Either you both live, or you both die, and you must do so at the exact same moment. Only then will that magic be extinguished for good. I have seen what is to come, Carey Lee." Anthriel bore down on her, his eyes aflame. "There will be no other who can destroy her should you fail."

The world swayed beneath Carey's feet and she stumbled over to clutch a tree for support. Anthriel made no move to assist her, but simply waited. What could she say, though? What did he want her to say? First Ji and now this?

"No," she said, trying to keep her voice steady. "No, you're wrong. You said there was a choice. Tell me what it is."

Carey couldn't help the pleading in her voice but she wasn't about to simply accept this, not after everything she'd been through. Magic was enduring, wonderful, terrifying. Never ending. She would find a way to defeat Malevolence and restore balance to the realms without dying. There just had to be another way.

"I said you *must* die in order to fulfil the prophecy, meaning, in order to defeat Malevolence, you *must* choose death. If you do not, then it will not be fulfilled and she will not be defeated. There is no other way," Anthriel said.

Carey set him a steely glare. "Then I choose to live. I am not the only one who can fight her, regardless of what you might say. You might be an Ancient, but that doesn't mean I have to take your word as gospel. The only thing I need you to tell me is which way Saar is heading."

Anthriel took a deep breath, looking to the stars. After a long moment, he said, "North-west."

Then, with a swoop of his wings and a flurry of snow, he disappeared, leaving Carey gasping and her head spinning.

*

Carey paused outside the cottage. Through the window, she could see Kat, Rupert, Kyna, and Madame Guise sitting in front of the fire. They'd wanted to join her, but Carey had convinced them to stay, luckily. She was still in shock from what Anthriel had told her. She wasn't sure how she would've dealt with the others hearing that too.

Carey shook her head. He was wrong. There had to be another way. She didn't care that he claimed to have seen the future – she wasn't about to just take his word for it. Besides, stranger things had happened. Why did she have to believe anything he said? He appeared out of nowhere, pretentious attitude and all, and he expected her to just trust him on this? Carey felt a flush of heat burn through her as she considered what he'd said. Ji had encouraged her to carry on, to live up to the destiny he'd somehow envisioned her having. Had he envisioned this?

She went inside, closing the door quietly and hanging up her coat, aware of Kat looking up at her. How would Kat cope if Anthriel was right? Would she even understand? Ji had been the final straw, the one thing that had finally breached her walls, and Carey couldn't help but think that if something happened to her, it might destroy Kat completely.

And then there were her parents. They'd already lost her sisters.

Carey thought of how her parents had reacted to her leaving and how she'd thought it so strange at the time. Had they known? Had they seen something like this coming?

"Carey? Which way?"

Kat cut across her musings and she gathered herself quickly, schooling her features. She didn't know why, but Carey felt incapable of telling them about what had just happened. Not because of how terrible it was – that in itself should've been enough – but because by saying it aloud, Carey felt she'd be acknowledging it as something to be considered. She didn't want to consider it, though, and she didn't want her friends to either.

So, Carey pushed it away. Ji had wanted her to have courage. Her heart would be as his was and his words would be her armour. And she was determined to prove Anthriel wrong.

"North-west."

~Chapter Thirty-One~

Directions

Madame Guise farewelled them early the next morning, having filled their bags with food and medicines for the journey ahead. She spoke with each of them in turn, an encouraging smile upon her thin face. When she reached Carey, she pulled her in for a tight hug, pressing something into her hand as she did so.

"He wanted you to have it," Madame Guise whispered in her ear before pulling away. "Be safe, my dear girl. And if you can't be safe, be strong."

Carey looked down at her hand to find Ji's Seeker pendant, the runes surrounding his name flashing in the early-morning light. She felt a lump rise in her throat, the now all-too-familiar ache in her chest tightening. Closing her fist around it, she offered Madame Guise a grateful smile in return, unwilling to speak for fear her emotions would get the better of her once more.

"Good luck, my darlings," she said to them, shooing them out the gate. "I look forwards to hearing of your victory."

Kat gave a laugh in reply. "No pressure, then."

With a wink, Madame Guise snapped the gate shut and waved them off down the road. Carey gave one last glance at the cemetery as they passed, her hand tightening on the necklace in her hand and her heart pulling her back, urging her to stay. A winter breeze swirled about her, whispering in her ear.

Have courage.

Carey fastened the necklace around her neck where it clinked against her own, two halves of a whole, and she rested her hand over both. Heaving a great sigh, she finally pulled her eyes from the graves, vowing silently that this was not the end.

This was not goodbye.

"Ready?" Kat said, coming to walk beside her.

Shifting the weight of her sword between her shoulders, Carey gave a grim smile.

"As ready as I'll ever be."

"So, where is it we'll be headin' first?" Rupert inquired, his bag bulging with newly acquired supplies.

Kat led the way, her past wanderings of this countryside making her the perfect compass. They walked along narrow lanes, staying away from towns and villages. Kyna became more relaxed the farther they got from Monaghan, aiming playful jabs at her brother and managing to turn his hair a deep shade of violet. Kat ruffled it teasingly, saying it might be her favourite colour yet.

As nightfall neared, Carey put voice to something she'd been thinking about since they'd started out that morning.

"Why do you think he's going this way?"

Kat, the snow crunching beneath her boots, said, "Honestly, I've been wondering the same thing. It's almost like he's heading back to the gateway, but that doesn't make any sense."

"It doesn't," Rupert said, walking backwards to face them. "If he just wanted ter take her back, then why the roundabout way? Why go ter all the trouble of opening up all th' gateways, only ter end up back in the realm he began in?"

"And why take Seramina ter begin with?" Kyna added.

Rupert was right – it made absolutely no sense. Saar had done so much since opening the Third Realm that to go back seemed almost redundant. He'd opened two gateways, kidnapped Seramina and formed alliances with warlords, and that was just what they knew of. Who knew what else he'd done in that time.

They came to the end of the laneway, a gate separating them from the snowy field beyond. As they hauled themselves over, Carey stopped, mid-climb.

"The gateways."

Landing on the other side of the gate, Kat turned back. "What?"

Gaze caught somewhere in the distance, Carey repeated, "The gateways."

Rupert and Kyna stopped walking, only just realising that Kat and Carey were still back at the gate.

Kat frowned. "What about them?"

"All three of them are open."

Rupert stopped at Kat's side. "And?"

"All three realms are open now. He's made sure of it. Even if it was the long way around, Saar has always played the long game. Think about it – Malevolence can draw power from the dark magic that surrounds her. We know that Saar wants to use the magic of an Innocent to bring her back, making her even more powerful. If he'd done that without opening up all three realms, then Malevolence would have dominion over only what she'd had before. But now he has set it all up. Allies, gateways… everything is ready for her. She's going to be able to spread her darkness through all three realms without *any* resistance."

Carey gasped for breath as though the words had stolen it from her lungs. The other three gaped at her, stunned into silence by this pronouncement. It was like puzzle pieces sliding into place. Anthriel's proclamation from the night before of how Malevolence would bring about a never-ending darkness suddenly seemed very believable. And that she would prove unstoppable. But that would also mean that everything else he'd said was true, too…

No. She shook her head of the notion. No – *that* she was determined to change.

"Well, then," Rupert said, clearing the silence. "If that's the case, shall we?"

He offered a hand to Carey and she took it, hopping down from the gate before straightening her bag. As if they needed more reason to catch Saar, this just solidified their need to succeed. And the full moon was barely a week away.

"That man…" Kat growled through gritted teeth as they made for a woods on the other side of the field. "When I see him…"

She didn't need to finish her sentence. Each of them were only too happy to imagine their own personal kinds of retribution.

As they entered the woods, the afternoon sunlight dimmed almost instantly. The trees created a heavy canopy, casting half shadows on the thin snow at their feet. Kyna trailed a hand lightly across a moss-dappled tree trunk. She paused, leaning in to study something, then jumped back with a squeal. Carey and Kat had their weapons drawn before they could see what had startled her, but relaxed their grips when they saw what it was.

A thin, pixie-like creature broke away from the trunk, seemingly made from the wood itself. Gossamer wings fluttered at its back and its small black eyes blinked as it surveyed them. It made chirruping noises as it turned its head the way a bird would, quick and curious.

"It's a kiyosei," Carey said, sheathing her sword.

"Wood spirits?" Rupert added in wonder.

Carey nodded, watching it closely.

"What does it want?" Kat asked, lowering her sai as the kiyosei darted about them.

"They aid travellers," Rupert whispered back, following the sprite's movements with excitement in his eyes. "But I don't think I've ever seen one before."

"I have," Carey said. "When I was trying to get back to the Centre City."

The kiyosei hovered so its eyes were level with Carey's. The sprite tipped its head to one side, its slim features difficult to read as it considered her.

Not daring to move or even blink, Carey stared back, wondering what it was thinking.

Then, lifting its brittle hand, it stretched open its fingers and a drop of pearlescent light lifted from its fingertips. It was the same light, bright and ethereal, they had used when defending her from the daeva.

"Oh, look!" Kyna said.

More sprites appeared, holding out their hands to the Seekers. One by one, more tiny droplets of light lifted into the dark woodland air, shimmering around the four travellers. The sprites drifted lazily up into the canopy, then down again, rising and dipping, over and over in a way that made it look like they were dancing. They lit up the woods surrounding them with breathtaking beauty. The first sprite raised a stick-thin arm, gesturing for the Seekers to continue through the woods, and as they began to walk, the kiyosei faded back into their trees until only the four Seekers remained, a cloud of starlight droplets accompanying them.

"Wow," Kyna breathed, turning on the spot as she took it all in.

It was indeed a spectacular sight, the light providing a comforting warmth as they moved deeper into the woods.

"Is that normal?" Kat enquired, looking to Rupert, who was smiling serenely.

"Like I said, they aid travellers. They're generally not malevolent creatures," he said, giving his sister a look. "Do you sense anythin'?"

Kyna dropped her gaze from the lights and looked out into the darkness beyond them. "No. No danger here."

With pursed lips, Kat sheathed her sai, continuing to watch the shadows suspiciously despite Kyna's reassurances. Carey also kept a wary eye out.

When the sun set, the woods plunged into an almost impenetrable darkness. There were no stars to be seen through the treetops, and after some time the Seekers decided to stop and set up camp for the evening. They rolled out the blankets and sleeping rolls Madame Guise had given them and conjured a fire, their luminescent escorts settling overhead. As Rupert passed food around, Carey lay back against a tree trunk and pulled the star Ji had given her from her pocket. She imagined him there with them, the jokes and stories he'd share with Rupert. She could see his eyes, alight with humour, and hear his laughter echoing around them, wrapping her in its warmth. Carey ran a finger around the edges of the casing, watching the star tumble and swirl, and the chasm within her crumbled a little more with every thought of him.

Half-listening to the conversation around her, Carey's mind wandered to her parents. Again, she conjured the memory of their departure and how her parents' words and actions had concerned her. She wanted to know if they had actually known something or if they'd simply desired for her not to go. As the others slowly drifted off to sleep, Carey offering them half-hearted goodnights, she settled herself a little more comfortably against the tree. She was meant to be keeping watch, but she needed only a few minutes.

She had to know for sure.

As she let her eyes drift closed, the beads of fairy light faded from sight and she imagined her parents. Her mother and her kind face. Her father's tall frame and commanding presence.

There was a tug and she blinked.

She was in their quarters, lit by a few candles and a roaring fire in the grate of a grand fireplace. By the fire two figures sat talking in low voices.

"Mother? Father?"

They whipped around, standing at the sound her voice. They rushed to her, Carey's mother pulling her into a tight embrace. Her father stood near, wearing a worried expression.

"Is something wrong? Do you need our help?" Jenny asked, pulling back and smoothing Carey's hair.

Carey wasn't sure where to begin – whether to tell them about Ji or ask about the prophecy. She took a deep breath, bracing herself.

"We're in Ireland again, and... we found Ji," she began, willing her voice not to shake.

Her mother and father began to say something, but she cut them off, knowing that whatever their reaction, it would make it that much harder to keep going if she stopped to listen.

"He's dead."

Their words died on their lips. Robert shook his head, his brow furrowing. "Dead? How?"

"The dragon. Apparently, his wound was fatal, only, he didn't want anyone to know. He... he..." Carey's throat caught, and her mother pulled her in again, holding her tightly, and Carey let out a wracking sob.

She hadn't realised how much she'd needed this – a mother's embrace and the comfort it brought. She'd gone without it for so long that she hadn't realised she'd been missing it all this time. Her father wrapped his arms around both of them, resting his head on the top of Carey's, and for the longest moment they just stood there, wrapped in each other's love, Carey's pain easing just that little bit.

The fire crackled behind her and Carey sighed deeply, pulling slowly away from her parents. She wished she didn't have to say what came next, wished she could just leave now with the knowledge that they were there for her.

But she had to know.

"There's something else," Carey said, stepping back out of their reach. She wanted

to see their faces when she asked them. "The prophecy that was made about me and Malevolence. Did you know that it was a mermaid prophecy?"

There was a pause. Then Jenny nodded.

"Do you know how mermaid prophecies work?" Carey asked.

This time neither of them moved to acknowledge or deny, and Carey's stomach dipped unpleasantly.

"When we left to find Seramina, did you know that there was a possibility that I wouldn't come back?" she continued, her voice tight in her throat.

The firelight swayed about them, casting deep shadows on her parents' still faces. Then, Jenny spoke.

"We knew."

Carey didn't know what was worse – her parents knowing the truth about the prophecy or that they hadn't told her.

Her mother moved to comfort her but Carey stepped back out of her reach.

"Why didn't you say anything?" Carey said, her eyes burning.

Jenny let her arm drop as Robert answered. "Self-preservation, my darling."

Carey's lips quivered, forcing herself to face her father.

He sighed, regret shining in his eyes.

"We'd already lost your sisters. When we found out about the true nature of your prophecy, we knew that we would lose you too. Every day that passed, every day we enjoyed with you here in the castle felt like both a blessing and a curse. We got to know more of you and with that, we had more to lose."

"But we knew, deep in our hearts, that we couldn't be selfish with this," Carey's mother said. She moved towards Carey, her hands outstretched. "If we tried to hold you back, to stop it from happening, more would suffer, and then what kind of leaders would we be? But if we told you, the pain and confusion and fear it would instil in you, knowing of your death in that manner... what kind of parents would we then be?"

"But I could've done something, could've planned, or prepared, or – or anything," Carey cried, running her hands distractedly through her hair. "You could've given me that at least!"

"But we didn't, and we're sorry," Robert said in a low, sorrowful voice, and Carey suddenly saw them not as the great leaders they were, or the fearless warriors, but *her parents, afraid of losing their child.*

She rushed back into their arms, wishing for nothing more than to be rid of the nightmare she was living and to return to the Centre City at once. But she knew it couldn't happen. She had Seramina to save, and Saar to stop. And Malevolence to defeat. She didn't know how she was going to achieve that just yet, but she was determined to prove the prophecy wrong.

"I'm going to figure something out," she said. "You'll see. This prophecy is not going to mean my death."

Judging by the looks on Jenny and Robert Lee's faces, it was clear they didn't believe her, but they didn't rebuke her either.

"I'll see you again soon," she promised. "You'll see." And she let go.

The cold of the woods assaulted her senses immediately, and Carey opened her eyes once more to the darkness surrounding them. The lights from the kiyosei still hung overhead, tiny drops of luminescence in the dark to light their way. As she gazed up at them, Carey held her hands to her chest, breathing past the weight that had settled there these past few days. So much had happened, altering any reality she'd imagined for herself, and Carey squeezed her eyes shut for a moment, wishing it would all go back to the way it'd been before. Before Seramina had been taken, before Saar had tried to steal her magic, before she'd even known about Malevolence.

Something inside of her clicked, like a lens shifting the focus in a telescope, and Carey opened her eyes. Her hand drifted to the small golden triangles hanging about her neck and she closed her hand about them. That was the thing, though. It was like Zacharia had said – it was the nature of their existence to expect and endure the worst. They'd been born to this, named Seekers at birth, and even though it might seem like a harsh life, Carey honestly couldn't imagine being anything else. Seramina's kidnapping, the truth about her magic, Ji's death, the revelation of the prophecy, and her parents' knowledge of it – this was all, simply, par for the course. She couldn't expect to fight a war and come out the other side unscathed. That wasn't how wars worked, unfortunately. But she didn't have to let it crush her, either. She had to refocus, look to what mattered the most and what they'd been trying to do all this time – destroy Malevolence. Maybe then, and only then,

would Carey be able to have what she'd always wanted.
Peace.

321

~Chapter Thirty-Two~

The Next War

Carey woke the next morning to snow drifting through the overgrowth to the forest floor. The kiyoseis' lights still bobbed overhead, the campfire just glowing embers. There was little sound other than the breathing and shifting of the others, and Carey sat up slowly, rubbing her eyes free of sleep. Kat had taken over her watch shortly after midnight and Carey had gone on to have the best sleep she'd had in a while because now, despite all the setbacks, she felt a sense of certainty. Of purpose. She still hadn't told Kat, Rupert, or Kyna about the prophecy, but not because she wanted to keep it a secret. She knew she would have to tell them eventually – besides, they might know something she didn't that could help. She just had to wait for the right time, and, right now, Carey was enjoying the clarity of mind that her epiphany of last night afforded her. There was no need to muddy that just yet.

Kat bade her a good morning before leaning over and giving Rupert a poke in the side to wake him. He grunted and rolled over, ignoring her. Kat huffed impatiently before giving him another, harder poke in the back.

"Hey," he yelped, flailing about in his blanket, entangling himself.

Chuckling mischievously, Kat pulled it off him, revealing tousled purple hair and wide, alarmed eyes.

"What's goin' on?"

"Morning," Kat replied brightly. "Sleep well?"

Rupert glared at her. "Was until just now."

They ate and packed, and tried to cover their tracks as they continued on under the glow of the lights. It wasn't until midday that they finally saw the glint of sunlight up ahead.

"Oh, thank goodness." Kat took a swig from a canteen before handing it to Carey. "I was starting to think these woods would never end."

As they drew closer, the sound of voices and horses nickering filtered in through the trees. They slowed, keeping to cover. As though sensing danger, or their charges' need to stay hidden, the droplets of light faded into the darkness, leaving them alone once more. The Seekers inched forwards until they were just a few trees away from the source of the noise.

Gathered in a circle in the shade at the edge of the woods were a number of brightly coloured wagons. Horses stood tethered to trees, and people moved about, talking and laughing. A fire was lit in the centre of the gathering and the smell of cooking food wafted through the air. A young woman dressed in a bright-red woollen coat trimmed with fur caught Carey's attention. Dark hair spilled from beneath a green knitted hat pulled down over her ears. There was something familiar about her, and when she turned, Carey received a nudge to the ribs.

"It's Diira!" Kat whispered.

It was, indeed, the noma-witch who had helped them in Burtonport when they'd saved Seramina from Saar the first time. She was laughing and calling to someone when she turned suddenly and looked straight at where the four stood hidden.

"What do we do?" Carey whispered back.

"She a friend of yers?" Rupert asked in a low voice.

"Yes," Kat replied, ducking down behind the bush so Diira couldn't see.

"Then why are we hidin'?" Rupert shot back.

That was a very good question. Probably because, despite everything Diira may have done for them in the past, Carey had learnt the hard way not to trust easily. She wasn't about to go striding out of the woods, arms wide, in the hope that Diira would receive her likewise. She also couldn't trust that that actually was Diira.

As Carey struggled to decide what to do, Kyna spoke up. "Ah, Carey? Where did she go?"

Carey peered back at the camp and felt a jolt of panic. Diira was no longer standing by the wagons. In fact, she wasn't anywhere. Carey scanned the others milling about the campsite, but Diira's red coat was nowhere to be seen.

Kat swore.

"Charmin'," Rupert replied absentmindedly.

Carey lifted herself up a little, trying to get a better look, but still she couldn't see where Diira had disappeared to.

"I'm going for a better look," she told Kat, and as she turned to move, there was a flash of silver and red.

A dagger pressed against her throat and Carey froze. Diira stood before her, arm outstretched. Her expression was furious, but as her eyes met Carey's, her expression gave way to surprise. She stumbled back, and Carey's hand flew to her throat instinctively as Diira's eyes roamed from her to Kat, then Rupert and Kyna.

"What?" Diira stammered.

Kat moved to Carey's side and murmured, "It's her."

Carey let out a sigh of relief, her muscles relaxing.

"Are you really here?" Diira said, slowly moving towards them.

She stopped, almost toe-to-toe with Carey, taking her in with wide eyes.

Carey swallowed. "Diira."

The woman's smile stretched across her face and she threw her arms around Carey's neck.

"This is amazing," Diira cried, releasing Carey and hugging Kat with equal enthusiasm. "This is just so wonderful! Wait 'til my mother finds out!"

Carey chuckled at Diira's glee and Kat couldn't help but smile.

As she released Kat, Diira turned to Rupert and Kyna. "Sorry, I don't think we've met before."

"Rupert," he supplied, "and this is my sister, Kyna."

Diira gave them both big hugs, surprising Rupert and making Kyna smile widely.

"Come," she cried, gesturing for them to follow her towards the caravans. "We're just about to serve lunch."

Carey, Kat, Rupert, and Kyna followed Diira into the camp. Bright colours surrounded them on all sides, beautiful patterns and murals covering every surface. Fluttering silk pennants were strung along the caravans' sides, and brilliant curtains hung in the windows. The other Travellers watched with interest as Diira led them to a wagon with a bright-blue door. She gave it a short, sharp knock before poking her head inside and calling to someone. Moments later, an older woman emerged, fixing a blue coat about her shoulders. She stopped the moment she saw Carey and Kat, then rushed down to greet them in very much the same manner Diira had.

Anoueshka Farro embraced them tightly, then held Carey and Kat at arm's length to inspect them in turn.

"Carey Lee and Katrina Lawrence. You've both changed so much," she said with a broad grin. "It's such a wonderful surprise to see you both."

Kat introduced Rupert and Kyna, who Anoueshka welcomed warmly, and with a swish of her many skirts and long dark hair, she motioned for them to join her inside her wagon. The bright motifs of the wagons continued inside, with silk cushions and knit blankets covering most surfaces. A table was covered in plants and bottles, and more plants hung from the ceiling, drying. The air inside was warm and scented with the smells of the florae.

Anoueshka brewed a pot of herbal tea and, as she handed the cups around, she asked, "It's wonderful to see you again, but what brings you back to this realm, my dears? We'd heard a few rumours but couldn't be sure of their truth."

Carey took a sip of the hot liquid before placing it down on a table beside her. She glanced at Kat and Rupert, the former giving her an almost imperceptible nod.

"We're trying to find an Imperial – a very dangerous Imperial. His name is Saar. He kidnapped Seramina and took her through to the Third World."

Anoueshka and Diira stared at her.

"So, is that why the gateway to the Mystic Realm was closed?" Diira said in a hushed tone. "I always thought the Third World was just a story. A myth of sorts."

She looked to her mother for confirmation.

Anoueshka gripped her cup tightly. "That's what we were always taught.

But when they closed the gateway I thought perhaps it might not be."

"But, didn't Cassien Heronstairs say that it was open again?" Diira asked her mother before turning to the Seekers. "The weather went absolutely mad there for a bit, and then Cassien passed through a few days later saying he'd heard the gate had been opened again."

"That's true." Kat told Diira and Anoueshka all that had happened from the moment Saar had opened the gateway to the Third World to the opening of all three.

Anoueshka sat with raised eyebrows, her tea forgotten.

Diira gave an incredulous laugh. "That is…" She floundered, unable to find the words.

"And you think this man has come this way with Seramina?" Anoueshka asked, finally taking a sip of her drink.

Anoueshka and her people had taken care of Seramina after the fall of the Empire, and Carey knew she'd be just as invested in finding her as they were.

"We have it on good authority," she replied.

"Why are you all the way out here?" Kat asked. "And where is Crissto?"

"You mean my *husband*?" Diira said with a smirk.

"Really?" Carey exclaimed. "You're married?"

"As of this past summer. But he's not here."

"Oh? Why not?" Carey asked.

Diira and Anoueshka exchanged worried glances.

"You haven't heard?" Diira said.

"Heard what?" Rupert asked, drawing out the words warily.

"Imperials," Anoueshka said. "For a while there they disappeared, but recently there have been more and more coming out of the woodwork, heading west. We heard whispers of another war. We think that's where they're assembling."

Carey, Rupert, Kat, and Kyna looked from one to another, stricken.

"War?" Kat said.

"Crissto is off rallying those who might fight," Diira said. "I thought, when I realised it was you in the woods, that that's why you were here."

Carey swallowed, a burning anxiety creeping up her neck. "We had no idea,

Diira. This is news to us."

"Where exactly are they all headin'? Do yer know?" Rupert leant forwards, worry lines creasing his forehead.

Diira nodded. "That we do know."

She pulled a weathered map from a cupboard overhead and unfolded it across her knees. It was a map of Ireland, and for a moment her finger hovered as she searched before she brought the tip down on the paper.

"Here. There's a forest there, perhaps more woods than forest. No villages nearby. Apparently, the Commoners aren't too keen on that area – something about hauntings or curses. We think it's a rumour or enchantment set in motion by Imperials so they can gather without trouble."

Kat pulled the map towards her and the other three leant over it, looking at where Diira had pointed. Carey was wondering how much of a hand Saar had in all of this when Kat muttered something.

"What?"

She cleared her throat and repeated herself. "I know where this is." She pointed to the woods. "This is where we first came across Seramina and her family's wagon. Remember?"

Carey nodded. How could she forget? The mangled caravan and the vision of the assault on Seramina's family was something that would haunt her until the end of her days. But why would the Imperials be gathering there?

"Wait a second," Rupert said, raising a finger. "Ilvisar. What he said about how Innocents are made."

Kat lifted her gaze from the map. "Yes?"

"Well, didn't he say that it was trauma that made an Innocent?" Rupert continued, his forehead creased in concentration. "Seramina lost her family in a horrific way, leavin' her behind. Then, after you lot rescued her, she began exhibitin' these new abilities. That would have ter mean that whatever made her what she is now, it started with that attack on her family."

Carey worried her bottom lip between her teeth as she looked down at the map. "What are you getting at exactly?"

Rupert swallowed. "Maybe this place holds some magic still. What if that is where Saar is takin' Seramina and that's where he plans on bringin' back

Malevolence?"

It made sense. More sense than him going back to the Mystic Realm, in any case.

"And this war?" Kyna said in a quiet, hesitant voice.

"A distraction. A new start. A way of making sure we don't get to him on time," Kat listed off. "It could be any of those. You know Saar – he doesn't care how many people have to die or what he has to do in order to achieve his goals. He'll do whatever he has to." She turned to Rupert. "And you're right That place is significant to Seramina. Perhaps that's where it all began for her. And if that's the case, then it may very well be why Saar has taken her there. Whether it's symbolic or magically motivated, though…"

Kyna let out a terrified squeak and Rupert ran his hands through his hair, still staring down at the map. Carey felt that familiar feeling of dread seeping through her and she looked over at Diira and Anoueshka, who'd been listening intently. Although she appeared composed, Diira's knuckles were white as she clutched her teacup.

"Is this where you're heading?" Carey asked them.

Anoueshka nodded. "For the first time in a long time, we've tasted freedom from the Empire. When we heard of these loyalists, we knew we had to fight." She took a fortifying sip of tea, swallowing hard. "Do you think this man Saar is truly inciting war for no other reason than for his own gains?"

Carey wished she could say no, but she knew Saar better than that. "I hate to say it, but Saar would raze entire countries if it meant bringing Malevolence back. He made her. He's not about to let his hard work go to waste."

Folding the map away, Kat passed it back to Diira with an apology. "This isn't your fight. As long as we save Seramina and stop him from bringing Malevolence back, there shouldn't be a war."

"But it's already started," Diira said, getting to her feet. "Did you really think these Imperials were just making their way quietly to this place? These are *Imperials* we're talking about. They've been causing as much trouble as they possibly can without catching the attention of the Commoners. They've already attacked some of our people to the south. We've fought them our entire lives. You might think this isn't our war, but my husband is out there right now, already fighting it."

Diira's voice had risen as she spoke, and Carey felt herself recoil.

Anoueshka placed a calming hand on her daughter's arm, pulling her back into her seat.

"It's not their fault, dearest, they're here to help. You can't blame them for the actions of a madman." Anoueshka turned to Carey and the others. "We are willing to do what needs to be done, if it means we'll finally be rid of the Empire. You can travel with us, if you like. We'll be heading out in the morning."

Carey couldn't deny how tempting her invitation sounded. She looked around at Kat and Rupert, and finally Kyna, who'd drawn into herself again, knees tucked up under her chin, hugging them tightly.

"We could do this," Carey murmured to Kat and Rupert. "Perhaps… perhaps it's time we stopped trying to do everything ourselves."

Kat chewed her lip for a moment, no doubt contemplating the pros and cons. Rupert leant over to Kat and whispered in her ear. Carey couldn't hear him but when he pulled away, Kat looked to him, her face searching his. He gave her a small nod, which she returned, and Carey wondered what he'd said.

"You're right," Kat finally said. "We can't do this alone." She turned to Anoueshka and Diira. "We'd be grateful if we could travel with you. There's just one thing. Can we get there before the full moon?"

"The full moon?" Anoueshka consulted a chart on her wall. "That's less than a week away." She paused, gazing up at the depiction of moon phases that had been marked with dates and calculations. "We should be able to."

"Diira, is this all right with you?" Carey asked.

Diira smiled. "Yes, of course. I'm sorry. Just, having Crissto away right now is…"

As her sentence trailed off, Carey's throat constricted. She knew exactly how Diira felt and the very thought brought a rush of emotion to the surface. She gripped the hem of her coat tightly, turning from Diira's face as she fought to hold it back. She couldn't lose control, not in front of everyone.

"Good. Well, if no one objects, I'm just going to go get some fresh air."

Carey got to her feet and Kat snatched at her hand. She gave Carey a questioning look, but on seeing Carey's pinched expression, she let her go. Carey raced from the caravan as quickly as she could without appearing rude and strode to the edge of the camp. She leant against the cold timber of a wagon. She relaxed the knot of tension in her chest, allowing the pain that Diira's words had summoned to take her. She had to give in, if only for a minute. If she didn't, it would consume her whole.

Tears fell from her eyes. They were warm against the cold air as they streamed down her face. Carey let herself feel the ache within, the many pieces of her broken soul she knew would never mend. They were shards of ice that would never thaw, sharp and lethal, slicing at her from within. For a brief moment, she let them overwhelm her.

Bit by bit, she came back to her senses, gathering the shattered pieces of her heart and locking them away. Her heartbeat slowly returned to its usual steady rhythm and she focused on it, counting each beat. Wiping the moisture from her cheeks, she straightened her back and smoothed out her coat. She promised herself that this was the last time. She had to focus on finding Seramina and stopping Saar. Once this was all over, she'd allow herself to feel it all. But, for now…

Carey touched a finger to the pendant resting at her throat.

"Courage."

Chapter Thirty-Three

Final Offer

The next morning brought wind and heavy snow, and Carey was torn between being immensely grateful for the inside of a warm wagon and anxious at the fact that they weren't able to move. Kyna was playing a card game with Diira, one that elicited frequent squeals of excitement and indignation. Rupert was talking with Kat about some remedy he'd invented as Kat, nodding along to his words, sharpened and polished her sai.

"Honestly, it'll help with the muscle strain you lot get after all that practice yer do," he said, flicking the handle of Kat's sai. "Yer know, yer wouldn't have ter deal with that kind of thing if yer didn't do it at all. I'm just sayin'."

Kat bumped her shoulder against his. "But then who'd save your sorry behind?"

"You do realise I'm more than just healin' elixirs an' a pretty face now, right?"

Carey listened to their banter with a smile, reminded of how Kat would parry with Ji in much the same way. The thought that Kat still had someone to verbally spar with gave her warmth rather than pain.

Anoueshka sat nearby, quietly observing. Carey caught her watching her more than once, until the woman finally moved to sit at her side.

"I'm sorry," Anoueshka whispered tentatively. "I should've said something earlier, but I didn't know how. That's why he isn't here, isn't it?"

Carey had almost forgotten about Anoueshka's ability to read auras. No doubt she'd seen something about Carey's to elicit her sympathy. What shade was grief, she wondered.

Ignoring the swooping sensation in her stomach, Carey nodded.

Anoueshka took her hand. "The person we met – was that…?"

"No."

Carey hadn't meant for it to come out so forcefully and she took a deep breath. "No. That was an imposter."

The last time Anoueshka had met Ji it had actually been the shapeshifter, Jeremy Shultz. Even though Carey had long ago come to terms with what he'd done and how she felt about him, the memory of him still turned her stomach.

"But you did find him?" Anoueshka asked with a smile, and Carey couldn't help but return it.

"Yes, we did. But then we lost him again."

There was a moment where Carey wasn't sure if she should say more or leave it at that, but her mouth had other plans. All of a sudden, she was telling Anoueshka everything. About how Ji and Kat would spar in the training hall for hours on end, how he was always the voice of reason, calm when she wasn't. She told Anoueshka how, even after he'd lost his eyesight, he was determined to keep going and that he wouldn't accept anyone's pity.

Kat joined in, followed by Rupert and Kyna, each adding their own stories. Mischief and training and daring escapes. There was laughter, and there were tears, and Carey felt fortified and warmed by their words and remembrances. For the rest of the day, they lost themselves in memories of Ji, allowing themselves to forget what was on the horizon. Carey had thought it would be hard reliving the moments she'd shared with him but it turned out to be quite the opposite. In her grief, she found pain and despair, yet in those quiet moments of shared smiles and laughter, there was joy. There was light. And with it, Carey banished the darkness that had welled up inside her.

It gave her strength and she held onto it tightly.

Their reminiscences were interrupted by the arrival of a note from Crissto. Diira relayed it to them.

"They've set up camp. Not far from that forest. A place called Lough Chrathai, on its eastern banks."

"It's a lake," Anoueshka said. "We should be able to get there in time."

"What if this storm keeps up, though?" Carey asked.

Anoueshka looked at Diira, brows furrowed. "We were discussing that earlier. The plan is to take the horses and travel light. Leave the wagons behind."

Diira moved to her mother's side and took her hands in hers. "We'll come back for them."

"What about yer people?" Rupert asked. "Will travellin' by horse and foot be a problem?"

"No," Diira said. "They've trained for this. Each of them is a volunteer but are warriors just the same. Jem, Emily, and Faye are skilled in the bow and arrow; Jayse, Riley, Fletcher, and Star are equally matched in their magical abilities; and William, Ash, Chiara, and Brie are not only fighters but healers too." Diira raised her chin proudly. "Our families were forced to become nomads when the Empire ruled, but now that we're free, we're ready to fight to protect this life we've built."

There was fire in Diira's words and Carey felt the pride with which she spoke.

"Then we'll be glad to fight alongside you," Kat replied.

Shortly before sunset the blizzard finally died down, and they found themselves surrounded by snow that reached almost to their waists. It was easy enough to melt the snow around the camp using magic, but it was soon apparent that the wagons would be going no farther. As a few of Anoueshka's troop set up the fire for dinner, the rest took to training, Carey and the others joining them as the sun sank low. Kat relished the opportunity to help Rupert and Kyna with their defensive work. Carey could tell that Rupert was more inclined to watch from the sidelines, but even he knew that when push came to shove, there was every possibility that he'd be fighting right alongside them.

Diira wasn't wrong when she'd said her people were skilled. Jem, a tall red-haired woman, failed to miss a single bullseye with her bow and arrow, and the short, bespectacled fellow, Riley, was so quick with his spell work that he almost caught Kat unawares. Faye, a lithe brunette who moved as though she was floating, could throw a curse with scary accuracy, and the tall, broad-chested Jayse was particularly skilled at defence, able to ward off any and every spell or curse aimed in his direction.

Later, lured by the tantalising aroma of roasting meat, Carey, Kat, and Rupert sat by the campfire, stiff but exhilarated from their training session. Kyna wandered to where a tall woman with white hair and dark clothing turned a spit over the flames.

"That smells…" Carey groaned.

"It's almost done," Kyna proclaimed with a wide grin as she watched the meat turning.

"Good," Carey said, leaning back on her hands and staring up at the star-spangled sky.

It really was beautiful out there in the wilderness. She wished they were there for other reasons.

"Carey. Rupert and I were thinking…" Kat started, leaning across Rupert to speak to her.

"Yes?"

There was slight annoyance and discomfort splashed across Kat's pinched expression, but with a quick glance at Rupert, she carried on. "We didn't want to ask you this, but… could you try finding Saar again? I mean, for all the time we're spending travelling across this country, I think we should be absolutely sure that that's where he's heading."

"We're not sayin' that we think we're wrong," Rupert interjected before Carey could argue. "We're sayin' that Saar has a way of pullin' one over on us, an' I don't think we can afford ter let that happen again."

"You really think he'll have lowered his guard, though?" Carey asked, crossing her arms. "He hasn't yet."

Kat shrugged. "It's worth a try, though, right? You can take us with you again, if that'll make it easier?"

Shaking her head vigorously, Carey stared into the flames before her. "No. If you come, there's no telling what he'd do. I'm pretty sure I'm strong enough to fight him now if he tries to keep me there, but I can't guarantee your safety, too."

She looked around, taking stock of what the rest of the camp were doing. Diira was helping her mother with something by their wagon, and the rest were either settled around the campfire, conversing in their own small groups, or flitting about the campsite, performing their evening tasks. Carey turned back to Kat and Rupert.

"Fine. I'll give it a try. But I'm honestly not expecting much."

Rupert moved to Carey's left, while Kat scooted over to sit close on her right. They held out a hand each. Staring, Carey asked, "What are you doing?"

Kat gave her a strained smile. "We're in this together, remember? You don't have to take us with you, but we're not about to let you do this alone."

A rush of gratitude flooded Carey, and with the prick of a tear in her eye, she grasped their hands. Giving them a nod, she said, "All right. See you on the other side."

Taking a deep breath, Carey closed her eyes. She let her mind wander for a moment before settling on Saar. She reached out as she'd done countless times before, searching for him in the dark. Expecting to find nothing, she was surprised when she felt her stomach clench and she was pulled forwards by an invisible force.

There was no longer the chill of the wind around her, nor the warmth of the campfire. She was standing in an eerily familiar clearing, her eyes coming to focus on a burnt-out wagon, which had long been overtaken by nature. Vines and weeds crawled up the sides and sprouted from the blackened windows that stared at her like dead, unseeing eyes.

Words whispered in her ear.

"Good evening, Princess. What a pleasure to see you here tonight."

Chills ran down her spine at the sound of that low, slick voice. Carefully schooling her features, Carey turned slowly to face Saar. He looked as he always did – tall and dark, his ink-black hair tied back from his face, his burning silver eyes watching her with faint amusement.

"Saar," she replied, holding her voice steady, deathly aware of how close he was. She had to remind herself that she was in control here – he couldn't hurt her in this form.

Carey moved her eyes slowly around the clearing, passing over the wagon that had once been Seramina's family's, to the dancing flames of a small campfire. At its side lay a small figure bundled inside blankets, her bright-red hair spilling out from the layers. Seramina was asleep, her chest rising and falling slowly, and Carey resisted the urge to run to her. She was safe at least.

For now.

Carey wrenched her eyes from her young friend and forced them back to the man before her who was patiently watching her every move.

"Why don't you have her Bound or something?" Carey asked, jerking her head towards Seramina.

"I've made sure she's been kept in a dreamless sleep ever since that unfortunate incident back in the Third Realm," he said, his eyes never leaving Carey's face. "I'm sure we both know by now how truly powerful our young friend here is."

"Yes, and we know exactly what you have planned, too." Carey glared at him defiantly, daring him to deny it.

A sneer spread across Saar's face. "I was wondering how long it would take you."

Carey's heart skipped a beat. Confirmation.

Saar circled her like a deadly predator.

"The game is up, Princess. I'm sure you're aware of the legions flocking to my side at this very moment. That when I sacrifice dear Seramina, the Empress will return and her reign will begin once more."

"If you're so hell-bent on bringing Malevolence back, why, all those months ago, did you approach me instead? You were so sure she was gone. What ever happened to those aspirations?" Carey said.

Saar waved a hand dismissively. "I was impatient. I thought I could sway you, much like I did Elara when she was your age. But you didn't grow up in the shadow of a beloved sister. You didn't have the spite and the envy she possessed, spurring her on to greater, more desperate lengths." He continued to circle, and Carey felt his eyes boring into her. "When I realised you were a lost cause, I looked elsewhere."

Carey's gaze flicked back to where Seramina lay, and she remembered the night Saar had returned to the castle as Lord Acheron. It'd been the same time Seramina had arrived.

"How could you have known Seramina was the one you needed?" Carey asked, unable to help herself. She had to know.

Saar gave the smallest of shrugs. "I hedged my bets. I've always been good at spotting real power. When my attempt to use the Dragon's Heart failed..."

Suddenly, Carey regretted having brought Seramina to the castle. If she'd never come, Saar would never have made her a target. She wanted to snap at him, rage, hurt him, but in this form there was little she could do, and so she stood, fuming. He stepped behind her, leaning in as he spoke.

"It's not too late," he whispered silkily into her ear, and Carey couldn't help a shudder. "Join me. Join us. You and the Empress are blood. Together, think of what you might achieve. How you might shape the worlds."

The reminder of her connection to Malevolence made her physically ill, but she balled her hands into fists and took a single step away from Saar, turning on him and glowering.

"You cannot seriously think I would still join you after everything you've done," she said through gritted teeth. "You've tried to force me to work with you, stolen my magic, killed people I cared for, and kidnapped my friend in order to use her as a sacrifice. Not to mention that you started all of this, and you think I might still be swayed into accepting a proposal from you? You might have come across some powerful people in your time, corrupted enough by their past that you've been able to manipulate them and use them, but know this – I am not, nor will I ever be, one of your puppets. I am not Elara Parnell, and I am not my sisters. I am not Jody and Laurel." Carey took a step towards him, crowding his space. "I am a Seeker of the Order of the Rose. The only desire I have when it comes to you is to see you burn."

She'd hoped her declaration would have more effect on Saar, but he simply laughed, a low, mocking chuckle. "Your sisters? Oh, my dear Princess. If only."

He gave a great theatrical sigh, then stepped back, straightening his features so that only a pleasant, albeit slightly terrifying, smile played on his face. "If that is your absolute final answer, then this is where we say good night."

And with a swipe of his arm, Carey felt herself falter and then fall, the scene around her fading to black before she could resist his dismissal.

Carey gasped, lurching forwards as the campsite materialised around her. She was still holding Kat and Rupert's hands, but released them quickly when she realised she was crushing more than holding.

"Sorry. Sorry," she said.

Her heart was thundering and she was gasping for breath as though she'd just run a mile.

"He's there already," she managed to say, dropping her head in her hands in an attempt to steady herself. "He's there with Seramina and he pretty much confirmed everything. He's going to bring back Malevolence, and he's going to sacrifice Seramina to do it."

Kyna, who had joined them during Carey's absence, paled, and Rupert's mouth pinched at the corners.

Kat nodded. "Then at least we have a way forwards now."

Kat went to find Anoueshka as Rupert made to comfort his sister.

Carey stared into the flames of the campfire, her exchange with Saar running through her head. Out of everything he'd said or implied, there was one thing she couldn't shake. One thing she couldn't ignore.

Your sisters? Oh, my dear Princess. If only.

~Chapter Thirty-Four~

Plans

Thoughts of her sisters, of Jody and Laurel, were pushed from Carey's mind as the group set off the next day. They left the wagons behind, travelling by foot and horseback. Carey and Kat rode a grey mare, while Rupert and Kyna were mounted on a chestnut steed with small white spots highlighting its flank. Their progress was made difficult by the snow and their need to use rough back roads. Carey's anxiety rose as the day went on, and mid afternoon she brought her horse up to Rupert's, speaking in a low voice so they wouldn't be overheard.

"I feel like we're not going to make it in time," she said as she watched Diira's back, her black stallion just ahead of theirs. "We're not making enough distance. And this weather – what if it starts snowing again? This isn't helping us."

Kat shifted behind her. "I was thinking the same. If we can't get there in time, then perhaps we need to use that last medallion of Efren's."

"You still have it, right, Rupert?"

Rupert patted a front pocket of the satchel at his hip. "Been there all along."

"How many people do you think it would work with?" Carey asked.

Kat shrugged. "Can't know until we try. Speaking of time – do you think your parents' troops will be there when we arrive?"

On their first night with Diira and Anoueshka, they'd come to the conclusion that this had all become too big for them to handle alone. If there was to be a war, then they needed troops. Carey had reached out to her parents, relaying everything Anoueshka and Diira had told them about the army of Imperials waiting for them. They had promised to send help, though

Carey wasn't sure how many were coming or of their arrival.

"Hopefully. They gave their word, though with this weather and all…"

"Hopefully?" Kyna asked.

Carey gave her a reassuring smile. "We won't let anything happen to Seramina. I promised, remember?"

"Speaking of which," Kat said. "What's the plan there?"

Carey tightened her grip on the reins. She'd been going over and over every way she might stop Saar carrying out his plan, while still saving herself, and she'd come up with some possibilities.

"Firstly, I think we should try to get Malevolence's magic from Saar. If we can do that, then there's no way he can bring her back," she said, keeping her voice strong and steady.

If they managed get their hands on Malevolence's magic, it would give her more time to work out a way of separating herself and Malevolence from the ability that bound them.

Kat nodded slowly. "Of course, that's if we get there in time. What if we don't and he's already started the ritual?"

Carey swallowed, her gaze flitting to Kyna's still face. "Then we get Seramina away from him."

Rupert frowned, his eyes narrowing in thought. "What's ter say he won't just go an' find another Innocent? Those Eternals didn't seem ter have any trouble findin' some. If we simply steal Seramina back from him, he'll just go an' find another, an' another, an' another."

Carey slumped, feeling herself deflate. "I…" She didn't know what to say. This was the moment she'd been waiting for, the perfect opportunity to tell them about the prophecy, but now she was there, Carey found herself floundering, struggling to find the right words.

Kat must have noticed. "Carey? What is it?"

Heat rose in her cheeks and her head felt oddly light all of a sudden. The three of them were watching her and she suddenly wanted to tell them all to leave her alone.

But that would solve nothing.

Instead, she took a fortifying breath.

"Remember the prophecy that was made about me?"

They all nodded cautiously.

Carey took another shaking breath, checking to make sure they wouldn't be overheard. "The day before we left Madame Guise's, Anthriel told me it hadn't been fulfilled yet. He said that for me to truly defeat Malevolence, I had a choice. If I want to succeed in stopping her once and for all, I…" Her voice cracked, and she stopped a moment, trying to calm her beating heart.

Kat gave Carey a reassuring squeeze around the waist. "Carey?"

Carey squeezed her eyes shut and said, "I have to die."

Kat stiffened, Rupert's mouth dropped open in shock, and Kyna gave a frightened squeak, jumping in her seat.

"What?" Kat managed to say finally, her voice hollow.

Carey knew she'd heard, and she wasn't about to repeat herself lest she completely lose her composure. Instead, she forced herself to sit up straight and said, "That's why we can't let him succeed. If Malevolence returns using the full strength of an Innocent, then no one will be able to stop her. Not even me."

Rupert spoke up. "What if Saar didn't use an Innocent? What if Malevolence was brought back usin' th' magic of just some ordinary witch or wizard."

Carey frowned. "How would we even manage that? It's not like we can just switch Seramina out for someone else."

"I'm sorry," Kat said, her voice a little louder. "But you just said you had to *die*. No." She shook her head emphatically. "No. Not going to happen. I'm *not* going to let it."

Carey couldn't help but smile. Even though the news was terrible, telling them was like a weight being lifted from her shoulders. They could figure this out together now.

"That's the thing," she said to her best friend. "Anthriel said that if Malevolence came back using the magic of an Innocent, she would be unstoppable. But–"

"Wait," Rupert said. "Wait wait wait." He pressed a finger against his temple as though trying to recall some long-lost memory. "Ilvisar said somethin'. His daughter." He snapped his fingers, eyes lighting up.

"What about her?" Kat asked.

"He said somethin' to his daughter, remember? An' when she faced the Eternals, she was no longer an Innocent."

Carey remembered now. "Yes. He said something about telling her the truth? Was that it?"

"But what is that?" Kat frowned, looking from Rupert to Carey.

"That she was an Innocent," Kyna said.

The three of them turned to the girl, her voice quiet but determined. "The truth was that she was an Innocent, right? Isn't that what Innocent means – not knowin' the truth?"

Kat laughed in surprise. "You're right. You're absolutely right."

"So, if we tell Seramina the truth…" Rupert said slowly.

"Then she'll no longer be an Innocent," Carey finished. "But we can't just let Saar sacrifice her once we tell her. What would be the point of coming all this way?"

"Does she need to be completely dead for Malevolence to come back?" Kat asked.

Her morbid question covered them with a thick layer of tension, the images it evoked too painful to consider.

"What are you saying?" Carey asked, pushing past the torturous thoughts.

Kat chewed on one of her nails in thought. "If we let Saar think he's done it…"

"You're sayin' we should let him *almost* kill her?" Rupert choked on the words.

Carey blinked.

Kat continued. "Say we let Saar think he's done it, wait until the very last moment–"

"No!"

Kyna's voice rang through the cold winter air. Her face had turned from pale to bright red with apparent rage. "You can't do that!"

"Kyna–" Rupert began.

"No – this is ridiculous!" Kyna said. "I can't even believe that you would think ter do somethin' like that!"

Her outburst momentarily stunned them. Her chest was rising and falling rapidly, and she glared at each of them in turn.

"We have to have a plan, Kyna, in case we don't get there in time to steal Malevolence's magic back from him," Kat reasoned. "If we get there and he's already begun–"

"Then it'll already be too late, won't it?" Kyna countered. "If you get there with time ter tell Seramina she's an Innocent, then clearly you'll have time ter stop Saar, no?"

She was right. If they didn't get there in time, then what was the point of entertaining this idea? They had only one obvious route and that was to get to Saar before he could execute his plan.

Carey ran a hand over her face. "Fine. We get to him before anything happens. That said, we don't want to all go barging in at once, just in case. I say one of us goes ahead to see what the situation is. Agreed?"

Kat and Rupert nodded. Kyna relaxed a little, clearly glad of the direction they'd chosen.

"How do yer suggest we do that, though?" Rupert asked.

Carey bit her lip in thought. Slowly, she lifted her hand to her lapel. "Wait…" Flipping it over, she revealed the tiny S-shaped pin she'd placed there before leaving the Centre City. She'd completely forgotten about it until that very moment.

Kat grinned. "Excellent. All right – timing notwithstanding, we have a plan. We can do this. We're going to save Seramina, and we are not going to let Saar succeed." Kat poked Carey in the back defiantly. "And you are *not* going to die."

That night they made camp on the edge of a small frozen lake. Carey wandered over to the bank, leaving the others by the campfire. Their laughter and conversation followed her but she tuned them out. Staring out over the moonlit ice, Carey lifted a hand in front of her. She thought of the witch from her vision in the Stronghold and imagined herself being able to wield the magic around her in the same way. Carey closed her eyes, holding that desire in her mind. Then, gradually, she summoned the power. She focused on the magic that surrounded her, trying to envision drawing it into herself. That familiar tingling sensation flooded her body in response, and she brought just the tiniest bit of magic forth, forcing the rest back. A sharp pain pierced her forehead at the attempt. Wincing, Carey let it go, feeling the magic slowly recede.

She slumped to the ground, hugging her knees to her chest. She was doing something wrong, she knew it. That'd been barely any magic at all. How had she been able to raze an entire army without hurting herself, and yet this minute action…

Burying her head in her arms, Carey shook the thought away. They hadn't managed to travel very far that day, and the anxiety had built to a low hum that kept her from feeling completely at ease. Trying to distract herself, Carey tried focusing on what they planned to do, going over every step and possibility. The thought of Saar, however, brought their last conversation back to the fore. His cryptic words regarding her sisters set her nerves on edge. There was no point in asking Kat or Rupert – they knew just as much as she when it came to her sisters' betrayal – but perhaps there was one who might know.

"Carey Lee…"

They were once more on the top of a mountain, the one where she'd first encountered the Ancient. She looked up at him as he folded his wings at his back, his long white hair fluttering gently in the wind. His expression was that of detached boredom.

"Anthriel," she replied, clearing her throat. "I have a question."

"Your sisters."

She wasn't surprised he knew – of course he did. He saw everything, apparently, knew everything. Perhaps that explained the arrogance.

"Yes," Carey said. "What did Saar mean by 'if only' when I spoke of their betrayal?"

He stood motionless for a moment, considering her, then he looked up to the stars as though he was searching for something.

Carey pushed on. "You've seen everything that has happened. Surely you know what he's talking about."

A muscle tensed in his jaw and he turned his gaze back to earth. "I have. And I do see. But that does not mean I can simply tell you everything."

Carey narrowed her eyes. "That hasn't really stopped you before though, has it?"

"We Ancients aren't meant to interfere," he said in his deep voice, slow and deliberate. "We only step forth if the consequences of not doing so are too dire."

"Like with me." Carey shifted uncomfortably. "We have a plan, you know. You said I had a choice—"

"I'm well aware of your plan, Carey Lee," Anthriel said, staring down at her with those piercing eyes. "It will not work. One way or another, the only way to stop Malevolence is for you to accept your fate."

Carey stared defiantly up at Anthriel, but he simply looked back down at her with absolute certainty.

"I know you don't care about any of this, but one time, back before I knew I was a witch, before the Order or any of it, I dreamt that one day I'd escape that god-awful orphanage, perhaps find something that would earn me a little money, perhaps enough to live in a cottage by the woods. And it wouldn't be much but it'd be mine. But having this life instead, I've come to realise that it was never truly mine to begin with. That my life was never truly my own. And worse, I don't know how I feel about that."

"You don't have to feel anything, though. You just have to accept it."

"But that's just the thing," Carey said, looking back into the cold blue eyes of the Ancient. "We feel, we have emotions. It's what makes us who we are, dictates our choices. I could be angry, furious, vengeful. I could be caring, loving, or scared, or courageous. These feelings, they determine what we do. Even the most logical feel on some level. If I knew how I felt, then perhaps I'd know how to act. You can't just expect me to accept death and not have me respond to that."

Anthriel tilted his head. "And you're sure you don't know how you feel?"

Carey paused. "If I'd never had this life, then perhaps Ji and I might've had a chance. We could've had a life together, grown old together. Kat and I could've been just friends, although I doubt I could ever imagine Kat as anything but who she is. All of this, all that I'm supposed to do, it just makes me... it's all so... it just makes me feel so sad."

A frown puckered Anthriel's forehead and it was possibly the most expressive Carey had seen him. "Sad? That seems very simple given everything you've just said."

Carey shrugged. "Perhaps it's simple, then. Isn't everything already complicated enough?"

She sighed, feeling the full weight of the expectation that had been placed on her. "That's why we're going ahead with our plan, regardless of what you might think. I've seen the impossible occur just enough to make me believe more in myself than in some prophecy. If I'm to do anything, I'm going to do it my way. I'm done with not being in control of my own life. So please – I just need to know about my sisters. If you're not going to tell me, then I'm all too happy to let you go."

Anthriel glared at her for a moment then stepped closer, reaching out.

"It is better if I show you."

Before Carey could ask what he meant, his hand clasped her shoulder and the scenery around them shimmered, then changed completely. The night sky and the mountainside were wiped away to reveal a brightly lit forest. Warm sunlight filtered through the canopy, casting dappled light on the forest floor, and the trees were filled with the chirping and humming of birds and insects. The rusting of leaves announced the arrival of two teenage girls.

Carey recognised them immediately as Jody and Laurel. Her elder twin sisters were perhaps fifteen or sixteen, their long brown hair pulled back from their faces, gazing about with bright blue eyes. They both wore loose-fitting blouses tucked into fitted pants and boots, and they had empty sacks slung over their shoulders.

"I swear, Jody, they were somewhere around here," Laurel said, searching the leaf-covered ground.

Jody snorted in disbelief. "Yes, well, clearly, they're not. You said we'd find those blasted mushrooms and be home before dark. We're going to end up in so much trouble again because of your memory."

Laurel gave Jody a playful smack on the arm. "Like your memory is so much better! I distinctly remember you misplacing your book and then blaming it on Carey when you couldn't find it. And you'd only just put it down!"

"Ah, see the difference there is that at least we won't be stuck in this forest after dark because of my book," Jody retorted, kicking some leaves to the side in a half-hearted attempt to locate Laurel's mushrooms.

Carey watched her sisters with intrigue and wonder, surrounded by a memory of the past so vivid she had to remind herself that she wasn't really there. Carey and Anthriel stood mere feet from her sisters, but the girls neither saw nor heard them. She was there but not, separated by a lifetime. Watching them joking and shuffling through the undergrowth, Carey realised they hadn't always been the monsters she'd come to imagine them as, selfish and cruel despite their familial ties. They'd once been young and carefree, no different to her.

A shout echoed through the trees and the two girls and Carey whipped their heads towards it. Anthriel simply stood at her side, the same uninterested look upon his face as always.

"Who's that, do you think?" Laurel asked, abandoning her mushroom hunt.

Jody shook her head, craning her neck to see if she could spot whoever had made the sound. "I don't know. Drifters? Highwaymen?"

"But we're nowhere near the road," Laurel pointed out, and Jody huffed in frustration.

"They don't have to actually be near the road to be highwaymen, Laurel," Jody said in a long-suffering voice, but she began creeping towards the disturbance all the same, Laurel close behind her.

Carey followed as they sneaked through the trees, the sounds of what seemed to be a group of people growing louder as they went. Soon, a group of ten or so came into view, all huddled in a circle around a campfire. They wore long cloaks and Carey recognised them immediately for what they really were.

Jody cursed in a whisper. "Essedarian."

"What are they doing here?" Laurel said, watching the deadly group talk loudly, clearly unconcerned about getting caught.

The two sisters fell quiet, listening to the Essedarian. Carey held her breath as though she, too, was in danger of being spotted, then gasped, terrified by what she heard.

Jody and Laurel were wide-eyed, their breathing growing rapid.

"Oh my gosh. We have to go get Mother and Father," Laurel whispered, but Jody shook her head.

"They're here for our families, Lor. They're faster and stronger than we are. We won't have time." Jody stared at the ground, thinking quickly. "We have to stop them."

"How, though?" Laurel said, desperation in her voice. "It's just the two of us!"

Jody looked into her twin's eyes, grasping Laurel's hands in hers. Carey watched as they leant into each other, resting their foreheads together. Jody was whispering something to Laurel that Carey couldn't hear, her lips moving swiftly over words meant only for her twin. When they pulled apart, Laurel gave her a nod, her face set with determination. Then they stood, revealing themselves to the group with their hands raised in surrender.

And as Carey watched from the shadows, tears streaming down her face, she realised just how wrong she'd been about everything.

~Chapter Thirty-Five~

The Beginning

Carey woke the next morning to clear skies and a clearer mind. After everything Anthriel had shown her of her sisters, she'd lain awake long into the night, thinking. What she'd seen had provided her with a level of clarity she'd never experienced before. Her new perspective meant she no longer felt nervous about the impending battle.

Courage.

Ji had asked for it, but her sisters had shown it to her, and now she felt no hesitation in facing Saar again.

In facing Malevolence again.

She'd fought for so long, not just against Imperials, but everything. This magic within her; who she was. She'd tried to control that magic, but never had she accepted it. That was where she'd gone wrong. She'd never accepted anything. She'd always fought. But now, she knew that the only way to defeat Saar and Malevolence was to accept what she was.

And what she was, was powerful.

After a quick breakfast and assurances from Anoueshka that they'd make it in time for the full moon despite the weather, they set off, blue sky stretching towards the horizon. They cantered out front of the troop, Carey enjoying the briskness of the morning air. The countryside stretched before them, a white canvas broken by tufts of trees and low stone walls. The occasional farmhouse came into view, each like an iced cake with a thick layer of snow frosting its gables.

Carey took it all in, relishing the light of the winter sun, the warmth of the horse beneath her, and the way the world carried on around them, oblivious to the war that was being fought just out of sight. She lifted a hand and invoked the magic she'd been so unwittingly given, watching the sparks dance about her fingertips. She could feel it now, the truth of this power within her. It flowed through her, strands of magic pulled from every part of existence, and within her, she could weave whatever spell she wanted. It was as though it'd been waiting for her to surrender to it, to understand who she was in relation to the magic that surrounded them all.

And it was *magical*.

"What are you doing?"

Kat had taken the reins today, Carey sitting behind, and she glanced over her shoulder as Carey let the sparks die on her fingertips.

"Nothing. Just trying something out."

They stopped to rest at midday at the edge of a snow-covered field. Unlike the day before, they had made good time and everyone seemed in high spirits because of it. Carey sat on a stone wall alongside the road, talking cheerfully with Diira about Crissto and feeling more light-hearted than she had in a long time.

Kat peered at her over the top of her drinking flask, eyes narrowed.

"What?" Carey asked, noticing Kat's stare.

"You," she said with a jerk of her head. "You seem… different."

Carey grinned. "And that's bad because?"

Kat raised her eyebrow into a perfect arch. "It's not. It's just that you seem almost … happy?" She pouted, apparently not convinced by her choice of words. "Elated?"

Diira looked between the two, confused. "Um, I'm just going to go see if my mother needs anything." She scurried away, shooting glances over her shoulder at the two of them.

"Oh, look," Carey said in disappointment. "You scared Diira away."

This just made Kat narrow her eyes even further in suspicion. "No, seriously. What's going on?"

Carey looked down at her hands, opening and closing her fists, feeling the magic all around her as she pulled gently at the strands. "Nothing happened," she said finally, looking into Kat's big green eyes. "Last night, I came to the realisation that all this time I've been fighting this power I have when I should've been accepting it instead. Even when I thought I had control, I was still keeping it at arm's length."

Sitting perfectly still, Kat didn't reply, watching Carey with a frown on her face.

Carey sighed. "I can feel it now. *Really* feel it. All the magic surrounding me. The way it flows through me. And you know what?" She smiled. "I don't *think* we can beat Saar. I *know* we can."

Kat's frown was replaced with a mild look of surprise as she processed what Carey was trying to say. "You know? But how?"

"Like I said." Carey waved a hand and felt the magic in the air pull tighter around her in anticipation. "I can feel it."

For a moment Kat sat, blinking at Carey, a million thoughts and questions evident in her expression. "And you only just realised this?"

"Something… shifted. I was just so tired of fighting, so tired of the grief and the worry and the panic, that I just…" She shook her head. "I just gave up. I gave up worrying, and grieving, and *fighting*, and it just happened."

Swallowing hard, Kat nodded. "All right. And you really think we can do this?"

Carey laughed. "What's this? The great Katrina Lawrence doubting herself?"

Kat nudged her hard in the shoulder. "Stop that."

Rupert and Kyna wandered over to them, and Kat turned to greet them, a smile replacing the frown of a moment ago. Carey watched as she spoke, her eyes on Rupert, who was sporting turquoise locks today. Carey felt something warm stir in her chest at the sight of Rupert's beaming face and she grinned a slow, knowing smile.

That night they set up camp in a valley where the ground sank between massive ancient boulders, hiding them from view. Sitting around the campfire, Anoueshka, Fletcher, and Ash struck up a melody, much to the delight of everyone. Brie, an exuberant woman with an abundance of blonde curly hair, produced a tin whistle and lively folk music filled the night air, prompting more than a few to dance. The notes threaded through the camp like magic, the tunes banishing the nerves and anxiety that had gathered during the day. Carey watched as Kat joined in, never one to be left sitting on the side of a dance floor. She swayed and twirled to the music. Star and Emily joined her, their long hair flying about them as they danced, feet moving in time with the beat. Kyna got up too, dancing by herself, her eyes closed as she wove through the others. Carey smiled as she looked on, thinking of Ji and the last time they'd danced together.

Rupert offered his hand. "Care ter dance?"

She hesitated for a moment. Then, lifting her hand to his, Carey gave him a small nod. "I'd love to."

With a firm hand on her waist, he took the lead, weaving through the others with ease. His movements were light and graceful, surprising Carey as he spun her under his arm.

"You're rather good at this!" she said as he twirled them about the campfire.

Rupert chuckled. "No need ter sound so surprised. My mother taught us. She said there was nothin' more wonderful than dancin'."

"She sounds lovely," Carey remarked.

"She was," Rupert said, his eyes sparkling at the memory. "How are you feelin' about Saar?"

She hadn't been expecting this question, but she suspected Kat and he had spoken since that morning. No doubt Kat had told him everything she'd said.

"I have faith in our plan. I think we can do it."

"An' what about that prophecy of yers?"

Carey missed a step and Rupert caught her, slowing their progress.

Composing herself, she looked into Rupert's eyes. "We'll find another way. Like Kat said – I'm not dying here."

Rupert tilted his head, his hand tightening on hers as he searched her face. After a moment, when it seemed he could find nothing to contradict her words, he gave her a wide smile.

"Right. Then how about you show me how ter dance?"

Laughing, her heart flying with the music, they twirled and spun, dipped and swayed about the others without a care of what was to come. When they were almost out of breath, Kat approached them, a twinkle in her eye.

"Mind if I cut in?" she asked Carey, and with a grateful nod, Carey stepped aside.

Kat took Rupert's hand, and together they joined the dance, their eyes locked on each other and no other. Backing to the edge of the dance floor, Carey glanced about – everyone was either dancing or engaged in their own private affairs. No one was paying her any mind. Seizing the opportunity, Carey slipped from the light of the campfire, between the horses where they stood eating their oats, and away from everyone else.

The music, singing, and laughter drifted on the night air as the snow crunched beneath her feet, and Carey pulled the small glass box containing Ji's star from her pocket. Turning it over in her hands, she walked up the slope to the edge of the valley. She stopped when she could only just hear the revelry below and looked up to the heavens. The majesty of the universe was sprawled before her, a million stars suspended in the dark, lighting the way. She knew that magic now. The truth of the balance Anthriel spoke of was as plain as day. Without the stars, there'd be nothing but darkness, but without the dark, the stars would never shine.

Carey lifted the box and stared into the spark within.

"You are the only true light I have ever known," she whispered, speaking Ji's words to the night.

She opened the box.

There was a flash of blinding light and Carey felt the magic around her tremble and shudder. She threw up her hand against it, shielding her eyes as it shot into the night, a flare flying higher and higher. Shouts of surprise erupted from the camp but she concentrated on her star until it became but a pin prick in the sky above, joining its brothers and sisters. Carey stared up at its new-found constellation until it was burned into her memory.

"Carey!"

Kat came running up, breathless and wide eyed. "What just happened?"

Carey held up the empty box.

Kat's eyes widened further. "You let it go?"

Carey placed the box back inside her coat pocket. "It was time."

And it was. She had her memories and she had her courage. She'd kept the star out of fear and uncertainty, and she had vanquished both. It was time to let the star go, as she had let go of her doubts, and set it free amongst the constellations.

Kat pulled Carey into a tight embrace.

"Come," Kat said after a long while. "The night is still young and we're on the cusp of war. What better time is there for a dance?"

*

They rose just before dawn. The weather was clear, giving them a good chance of reaching their destination before nightfall. The full moon was tomorrow, a fact that was painfully obvious in the almost perfect orb that hung low in the pre-dawn sky. Kat greeted Carey by the dying embers of the campfire, Rupert standing bedraggled beside her. Kyna sat huddled by the last warmth of the coals, rubbing her eyes wearily.

The nerves that'd been wiped away by the music of the night before were back, and Carey could feel the ripple of anxiety in the air as everyone moved around them, packing and readying the horses. Few words were spoken and even fewer smiles were seen.

Diira approached them, a wary look on her face.

"I would say good morning, if that indeed were the truth," she said. "We've just received word that there are Imperials nearby, possible Essedarian by the sounds of it."

"How far away?" Kat asked.

"They attacked farmhouses barely half a day away, though we have no idea how fast they are travelling or even how they are moving from site to site," she replied. "All we know is that we need to get moving as soon as possible."

The words had barely left Diira's mouth when two things happened in quick succession – a crackle of malevolent energy rippled through the air, and Kyna jumped to her feet, a single word escaping her lips: "Danger!"

Kat unsheathed her sai and bellowed, "Attack!"

As people ran for cover, an explosion erupted to Carey's right.

"Kyna! Get behind us," Carey called, summoning her magic, and the younger girl scurried to obey.

Kat stood to her right, Rupert on her left, eyes wide as the first of the

Imperial loyalists came into sight. Dressed in worn robes, three Essedarian strode into the camp, curses and spells flying from their outstretched hands. Anoueshka's warriors raced forwards, their own magic meeting the attackers with full force. A shot of magic flew past Carey's head from behind and she spun to find four more. Just as the sunken ground had given them cover the night before, it now provided the perfect place for an ambush.

Kat let out a cry of fury before rushing forth, a blur of magic and weapons. She threw one of her sai, striking an Essedarian in the shoulder, before her curse hit him square in the face. He slumped against a boulder and Kat pulled her sai from him before spinning and taking out another, ducking beneath his curse and slicing his middle.

Rupert threw curse after curse, shielding his sister from the onslaught, beads of sweat rolling down his forehead. Carey took it all in, the seconds stretching to minutes inside her mind as she saw each of the Essedarian. She engaged that trigger within her, summoned the magic that surrounded her, and felt it surge through her at the very thought. It wove and created the perfect magic, spreading down her limbs until it filled her completely. There was so much, though. So much that she felt her head start to ache from trying to control it.

So, she didn't.

She released it.

Magic flew from her, passing over her friends and comrades and knocking the Essedarian from their feet with barely a scream of pain. Collapsing to one knee, Carey gasped; the headache that had started to bloom faded at once. As she looked at the nearest fallen enemy, bile rose in her throat. His hood had fallen back with the force of her magic and his eyes were blank, a small trickle of blood bubbling at the corner of his mouth. She doubted she'd ever get used to seeing death up close. She didn't want to kill, but these Imperials weren't going to stop until each and every one of them were put in their grave, so–

Carey's thoughts were cut short by Kyna's warning, a warning echoed in the swelling of magic around her. "There are more!"

It was as though her words had summoned them. More Essedarian swarmed past the horses, moving fast. Carey pushed to her feet, the magic already heating her fingertips. She raced forwards, throwing curses and spells, ducking and weaving through the attack. Sliding past one Essedarian, she pulled her sword and sliced across his side and back. Blood sprayed and the Essedarian howled in pain before staggering and falling. Carey didn't pause to watch but turned to meet another, her sword deflecting the magic they threw at her.

Diira and Anoueshka were amongst the fray, magic flying furiously from them both, and as Anoueshka felled another loyalist, she cried, "There are too many!"

Carey spun to find the others. She spotted Kat, her raven hair flying wild about her face as she fought a tall, burly Essedarian whose hood had fallen back from his bald head. He was clearly a match for her, and Kat's face contorted as she threw curse after curse, trying to catch him off guard. Rupert and Kyna were in the centre of the campsite, Rupert still protecting his sister who was now standing at his back, joining the fight. Kyna managed to hit the man fighting Kat and he roared in pain. It was the perfect diversion; Kat ducked beneath his defences and made a swiping motion across his chest, vivid red erupting from her hands. The man went crashing to the ground and Kat was off and fighting before he'd even stilled.

Despite their efforts, Carey could see that Anoueshka was right. There were too many of them. Carey blocked another attack as she summoned her magic, but before she could unleash it, something hit her from behind. Her left shoulder blade erupted in agony and she screamed; the magic she'd summoned flew from her. She watched in horror as it not only felled three Essedarian, but Fletcher and Chiara as well.

"No," she cried as she stumbled forwards.

She didn't know if they were dead or alive.

A strong arm gripped her around the waist, preventing her from going to them.

"No, Carey!" It was Rupert. "We have ter get out of here!"

Kat, her bloodied sai slicing through the air, was yelling for Anoueshka and the others to gather.

"We're goin' ter use the medallion," Rupert shouted in Carey's ear. "We have ter get everyone together!"

It wasn't hard. The Essedarian were backing them into the centre of the campsite. Only Anoueshka, Riley, and Faye were stuck on the edge, their backs against one of the massive boulders as they fought.

"Everyone," Kat shouted. "Take hold of those around you!"

Regaining her composure, Carey sliced at an advancing Essedarian.

Rupert grabbed her belt, holding onto her from behind as they backed towards the others.

"Anoueshka," Carey screamed over the chaos. "Get over here!"

In between curses, long hair wild and dark eyes flashing with fury, Anoueshka shouted back: "No! Go!"

Diira sprang forwards, trying to get past Carey to her mother. Carey flung out her free hand, her injured shoulder flaring, and winced as she caught her. "No, Diira! Don't!"

"Mother! No!"

One of the Imperials advanced on Diira as she struggled against Carey's grip. A flare of magic shot past Carey from behind and he stumbled, gripping his chest as he fell.

"Kat!" Carey bellowed as the Essedarian advanced, and she felt the tug of the medallion as it pulled them from the campsite.

Diira screamed her mother's name as it all disappeared, nothing but a swirling mass of colour and wind surrounding them. Then they hit the ground, coming to a jarring stop, and they all stumbled apart. Carey released Diira, catching herself on Rupert as she tried to regain her footing. She glanced about, but none of the Essedarian had managed to follow, and she dropped her sword as her hands began to shake, her heart racing.

To her dismay, barely half of Anoueshka's troop had made it. Brie was tending to Jem, who was nursing a bleeding arm. Emily was clutching her bow, blood spattered across her face. Star was looking around wildly, her coat torn and bloodied, and William and Ash slumped to the ground, Ash holding her head as William tried to steady her.

"Take me back," Diira screamed at Carey, her hair flying about her face, flecks of blood staining her blouse. She grabbed Carey by the shirt and pulled her in close. Diira's face was contorted with fear and desperation. "Take me back! My mother is back there! We have to go back!"

Feeling as though the world was falling away from under her feet, Carey stammered as Diira shook her.

"I… I can't. Diira – we can't go back."

Diira froze, shock registering in her face before rage took over. "What? No! You are going to take me back, Carey Lee! You are going to take me back *right now!*"

Jem was suddenly at Diira's side and she pulled Diira's hands away.

"Diira, darlin'," she said. "Yer mother knew what this was all about. She knew somethin' like this might happen. Even if Carey could take yer back, there'd be a swarm of Imperials waitin' for yer."

"I don't care," Diira screamed, tears streaming down her face. "I don't care!"

She struggled against Jem's grasp, desperation replacing her anger. Jem held tight, though, and she continued to try to placate Diira as she fought to hold her back. Carey could do nothing but stare as a new wave of horror washed over her. The Imperials she'd killed, those who she'd attacked without meaning to, Anoueshka yelling at them to leave her behind…

"I'm sorry," was all she could say, feeble words in the face of Diira's fury.

"Sorry?" Diira spat back. She glared at Carey. "Sorry you brought this down on us? Sorry you left my mother to die? Sorry you didn't do what you were supposed to? You're *Seekers*! Aren't you supposed to *help* us?"

Carey knew her words were born of anger and pain, but it made them no less hurtful. She wasn't going to refute them, however. Diira had a right to feel this. When Carey made no move to answer her accusations, Diira stopped struggling and shook off her restraint. Slowly, she advanced on Carey, Jem trailing her warily. When she was but a foot away from Carey, Diira stopped, fire burning in her deep brown eyes.

"I will never forget what happened today," she snarled. "But Jem is right – my mother knew what this was about. So, I'll fight, to the very end if it comes to that, but only because *she* would've wanted me to."

Before Carey could open her mouth to reply, there came a thundering of hooves and a warning cry from behind them.

"Don't move, or you're dead!"

~Chapter Thirty-Six~

Before the Dawn

Carey spun towards the voice. A group of about twenty riders on horseback stood at the edge of a thicket that stretched out behind them. Their hands were raised, magic poised to attack, along with bows laden with gleaming arrows. The riders wore a mix of riding coats and cloaks lined with fur, and the leader stood a few feet before the rest at the very centre. He was young and rather handsome with his bright green eyes and dark hair pulled back from his face in a ponytail. He looked an awful lot like–

"Crissto!"

Diira ran straight for the man, who lowered his hand at once, leapt from his horse and caught Diira up in his arms. Crissto called to his entourage and the other riders lowered their weapons. Some spotted familiar faces amongst those standing alongside Carey and they dismounted, rushing to help.

A sigh of relief escaped Rupert's mouth.

"What?" Carey asked, still shaken by Diira's words.

"Well, when I used the medallion, I was tryin' real hard to remember the location Crissto had mentioned in his letter." Rupert gave a nervous laugh. "It's a lot harder than yer think when yer in the middle of an attack."

Kat placed a hand on his shoulder. "That was some quick thinking."

After a quick word with Diira, Crissto strode over to them. Carey had always remembered Crissto as tall and strong, but right now she had no problem imagining him riding into battle. His long dark coat, leather riding pants and boots made him look less like the young noma-wizard she'd met all that time ago and more like a fierce warrior.

"Carey Lee. Kat Lawrence." He gave them both a deep bow, accompanied by a wide, friendly grin. He quickly introduced himself to Rupert and Kyna with enthusiastic shakes of their hands before turning back to Carey and Kat. "I would say that it's good to see you, but Diira said there was an attack?"

"Essedarian," Kat said, her bloodied weapons at her side. "They caught us unawares, unfortunately. And we had to leave some behind in order to escape."

Crissto nodded solemnly. "Diira said her mother... Is there truly no other way to get back to her?"

Carey shook her head regretfully. "No. I'm sorry."

"Don't be," Crissto replied in a low voice, taking her hand. "I'm just glad you managed to get at least some of our people out."

"But Anoueshka..." Carey swallowed, closing her eyes. "I could see if she's all right, if she made it out. I'm able to travel using my mind. I can see, at least."

Crissto considered this, then called Diira over. "Carey said that, even though she can't go back for your mother, she can check to see if she escaped."

Her eyes widened, the fury on her face dissipating at once. But as she thought about this offer, Diira's expression turned from one of hope to despair and she shook her head.

"No. I don't want that."

"But–" Carey began.

"Right now, I can imagine that she survived that attack," said Diira. "But if you tell me exactly what happened... I don't want that right now. I couldn't handle knowing if it meant the worst."

There was a tense moment where Diira stared at Carey, almost daring her to contradict her words, but Carey couldn't. She knew what that kind of grief could do and she wasn't about to add to what she'd already done today.

Stepping between them, Crissto broke the tension with a cry.

"Come! We have a camp set up nearby. Let's not loiter out in the open any longer than we need to."

*

Crissto's camp was well hidden in the woods and they had to trek for a good half-hour through the snow and undergrowth before they reached it. Carey saw a few lookouts posted high up in the trees, but only because Crissto pointed them out. Diira kept close to his side; she kept her face turned away from the Seekers. The sight compounded Carey's guilt and it burned in her gut. How had it gone so wrong, so fast? She'd been so confident in her new understanding of her powers only to have it be her downfall. Arrogance. That's what it was, and because of it, people were dead.

She felt Kat's hand press into hers.

"I know what you're doing right now," Kat said in a low voice so no one else could hear. "That attack wasn't your fault. None of it was. It was chaos and you did your best. You can't expect to be perfect in the heat of battle."

Carey looked away from Kat's green eyes. "I know. But still…"

"No – no *but still*," Kat said. "We are this close now. You can't afford to start doubting yourself now."

Carey took in a shuddering breath. She was right. Of course Kat was right. This wasn't the time to start second guessing herself. She couldn't afford doubt and insecurity right now, not when they were so close. It wasn't just she who would suffer if she retreated into herself again – Kat and Rupert and Kyna needed her to be on her game. Seramina's life was depending on it. Carey had to stop treating her failures like a weakness – she needed to take them and learn from them. Make them her strength.

Carey gave Kat's hand a quick squeeze before letting go.

"You're right. Tomorrow is the full moon," she said. "Now isn't the time."

Shortly after, they came to a wide basin filled with tents. People were sharpening and readying weapons, while others trained or tended their mounts. It was an army, and, for the first time that day, Carey's heart lifted. It was encouraging to see so many willing to fight on their side.

"Come," Crissto said, leading the Seekers away from the small band of new arrivals. "We have strategy to discuss."

They followed Crissto to his tent, made from a patchwork of colours and materials. Inside was a single sleeping roll, a bag with clothes spilling out of the top, and a large map, which had been laid out in the centre of the floor. Upon the map were stone markers.

Carey knelt beside it.

A number of markers with blue smudges were grouped near the bottom of the map. To the north and north-west were others smudged with red. At the very centre of them all, highlighted by a large black cross, were the woods where Saar was ensconced with Seramina.

Kat crouched to run a finger over the blue stones.

"How many do you have?" she asked Crissto.

Diira answered, her voice barbed with anger. "Not enough."

Crissto moved to Diira's side and placed a hand on her arm. She looked into his face and for a moment they held each other's gaze, unspoken things passing between them. Slowly, Diira's face softened, and Crissto gave her a small smile before turning to Kat.

"We have a few hundred," he said, striding over to the opposite side of the map. "As for Imperials and loyalists, our runners have confirmed their numbers to be triple ours, if not more."

Carey's stomach turned to ice. "Are you sure?"

Crissto knelt to point to the red markers. "They started gathering a fortnight back. But their numbers have only really grown these past few days, as though they know something we don't."

Diira moved closer, averting her eyes from Carey's. "We know why. Remember Seramina?"

Crissto stood. "Yes."

"Well, tomorrow, at full moon, there is some lunatic wizard who is hell-bent on bringing Malevolence back, and to do that he plans on sacrificing Seramina."

Diira turned her eyes to Carey, and Carey gave her a nod of gratitude. Diira might hate her right now but she knew what was at stake.

"And you think these Imperials are here as, what, a diversion?" Crissto said.

"Most probably to try an' stop us from gettin' too close too early," Rupert said.

"Too early?"

Carey ran a finger over the big X. "He knows we're coming. He showed us where he was a few nights back, or rather, confirmed it. He wouldn't have done so if he didn't want us there. He'll want us to witness his triumph, he's so confident in what he's about to attempt. The Imperials are there to fight us, but they're also there to join Malevolence once she rises again. No doubt Saar put the word out and that's why they've come."

A frisson of fear ran through the tent.

Kyna, who had been standing quietly beside her brother, spoke in a small voice. "Do yer still think we can get ter where he has Seramina in time?"

The doubt was there, plotted on a map in red and blue, but Carey could feel the magic stirring all around them, the pull of each thread, making the numbers irrelevant.

"Yes. I do."

*

They spent much of the day strategising in Crissto's tent, meeting with other members of his legion and preparing themselves for the next day. Rupert saw to Carey's injured shoulder; he wrapped it with some special salve and a bandage from his bag, assuring her that it would be better by the morning. To help keep her mind off Seramina, Rupert sent Kyna out with Jem to help prepare food and the horses. She came back before sunset to tell them excitedly that not only were there horses but griffons too. She'd also found a particularly spectacular creature called a firebird – a great eagle-like creature with burning red feathers and a bright yellow crest – which she'd decided to befriend and call Feidhelm.

As the sun disappeared, a large fire was lit in the centre of the camp, and the warriors gathered around it. Everyone was speaking in hushed tones. As Carey joined them, Kat, Rupert, and Kyna by her side, she felt the air shift. There was an undercurrent in the magic surrounding them; it pulled them together, binding them in this moment. It was as though the universe knew what was to come. It made Carey think of Anthriel and the prophecy about her fate, and neither of these made her uneasy or twisted inside anymore. Instead, as she watched Diira approach the fire and face the troops, Carey felt completely calm. She knew her place now; she knew her magic.

She knew who she was meant to be, and that knowledge was all she needed to face tomorrow.

Diira held up her hands for silence. Closing her eyes, Diira took a deep breath, and from her lips came a haunting melody. The words were in Gadælic, but Carey didn't need an interpreter to tell her what they meant. It spoke of loss and love, of those who would go to war and not return. Diira's voice filled the air and Carey's heart swelled with an unnamed emotion. The song wove heartbreak and hope together as one, and Carey felt a single tear roll down her cheek. She reached out for Kat's hand, and her fingers curled around her friend's, anchoring them together as they listened. As the last lingering note faded into the night, Carey heaved a great sigh. For the longest time, no one spoke.

Then Crissto joined his wife, his face sombre. He lifted his head to speak to them all, his presence commanding.

"Fellow rebels," he began, looking around the camp. "For years we lived in darkness, compelled by fear. For years, that shadow commanded every move we made. Our children were born into it, never knowing anything but a life of subservience and pain. We were forced into hiding – driven to a life that was no life at all, but a pale imitation of one.

"But then we tasted freedom. For so long we'd existed without it that we thought we might never know such a thing again, never know what it was to live without fear. And yet now that we have tasted that freedom, felt its warmth on our skin, that shadow threatens to cloak us in darkness once more!"

His voice was rising, and Carey felt the crowd stir, heads nodding and feet moving restlessly.

"The Empire kept us downtrodden and afraid for decades! And just as we thought it was gone for good, we find it rearing its ugly head once more. Well, you know what I say to that? *Never again!*"

Crissto roared the last two words into the night, one fist raised in the air, and his soldiers erupted with cheers, echoing his cry.

"Tomorrow we ride to war!" He dropped his voice to a low, fervent tone. "Fellow rebels, that shadow looms once more, but we will not go quietly. We will not be silenced without a fight! We will become the light that burns through the darkness. We will show them that the Empire holds power over us *no more*! And if we are to burn, *let them burn with us*!"

The din was deafening and Carey found herself cheering along with the rest, her hand in Kat's raised above their heads.

"For light," Crissto shouted, punching the air.

"For light," the group echoed.

"For freedom!"

"For freedom!"

"And for a new world dawning!"

There was nothing to be heard now but the stomping of feet, the roars and cheers. Carey cheered and stomped along with them, surrounded by her friends, lifted by Crissto's words. The night would be long, yes, but a new world was dawning. And she was going to be there to see it.

*

Dawn arrived much too quickly for Carey's liking. She'd managed some sleep, helped along by a tonic Rupert had given her, but the feeling of restfulness lasted as long as it took her to open her eyes. The moment she was awake, she felt hyper alert. Her body tingled with anticipation, and she couldn't help the way her body fidgeted with restless energy. Kat laughed it off, though her laughter died rather a lot quicker than usual, and Rupert attempted his customary smile, but it fell just that tiny bit short of convincing. Kyna brought them breakfast.

"You know what," Kyna said, looking at Rupert. "This colour really doesn't suit today."

Rupert replied, "Oh, an' what hair does suit ridin' into battle?"

Kyna touched a finger to her lips in thought, then ran her hands through Rupert's hair. Jet black took over the bright turquoise, and red streaks followed her fingertips.

Kyna stood back to admire her handiwork. "There. Much more intimi-datin'."

Carey smiled approvingly, and Kat leant over to flick at one of the red tips.

"Oh yes, *very* intimidating," she laughed, giving Rupert a wink.

He pushed her away, though only half-heartedly, before standing to brush the crumbs from his tunic.

"I'll have yer know, Miss Lawrence, that I can be *very* intimidatin' when I want to," Rupert said, reaching for his coat and bag. "Now, shall we?"

They pulled on their coats and strapped on their weapons. Carey had cleaned her sword the night before, sharpening and polishing it until Arach gleamed in the moonlight. As she sheathed the sword, Carey hoped to be worthy of the weapon Marjen had bestowed on her.

They found Crissto's warriors ready to leave when they finally emerged from their tent. Horses, griffons, and Kyna's brilliantly feathered firebird friend pawed nervously at the ground, their riders bright-eyed and eager to depart. Two horses had been prepared for the four of them. Carey rode behind Kat, and Kyna behind Rupert once more. They cantered up to the front of the legion where Crissto and Diira waited. The couple wore matching dark riding gear with short woollen coats, daggers at their sides. They greeted the four with short nods. As they came up beside them, Diira extended a hand to Carey.

"We are in this together," she said, her eyes determined and jaw set. "And I am ready to fight at your side."

Carey took Diira's hand in hers. "And I at yours."

As Diira released her grasp, Crissto turned to his legion, raising his fist.

"Onwards. Death waits for no one!"

~Chapter Thirty-Seven~

To War

They emerged from the trees surrounding Lough Chrathai to dark skies and glacial winds. The clouds, grey and foreboding, rolled over them as they made their way north-west towards the Imperial army.

Towards Saar.

The sun was nowhere to be seen. Snow whipped around them, biting at exposed skin, and Carey drew her hood over her head in an effort to shield herself. The horses and griffons ducked their heads against the weather.

"Do you think this is him?" Kat shouted over the howling wind.

Carey squinted at the unnaturally fast-moving clouds. "I'd have to say yes." She ducked her head back down as sharp pricks of sleet hit her bare face. "He has a thing for playing with the weather."

She'd experienced Saar's manipulations before. Once on the way to the Aran Island gateway, and again as she'd raced for the Centre City to expose him. The first time she'd assumed it had been Malevolence, but now she saw that it always had been him, clearing the way for her, doing her dirty work.

"Well, let's just hope it doesn't get any worse or we'll never get there," Kat said.

The snowstorm grew steadily worse the closer they drew to their destination, and Carey's horse began to flag as it struggled against the wind. She could barely make out the rest of their party, strung out behind her. The wind was blowing at them sideways, beating down on them, and Carey could only hope that Crissto knew where they were going. The danger of not reaching Seramina in time weighed heavily upon her, growing with the force of the storm as they slogged onwards.

Carey was starting to despair when, suddenly, the magic around her shuddered, then pressed in on her, as though the air was thickening.

Kat must have felt it too, because she gasped in surprise. "What in the…"

It was as if they'd passed through a gateway; the air became eerily still. The sky was still heavy with dark-grey clouds, but neither snow nor sleet fell from them. Behind them, the storm still raged.

"A barrier?" Carey said.

"An arena," Kat replied, pointing ahead.

An undulating expanse of Irish countryside stretched before them, covered in a layer of snow and dotted by grey boulders. Scores of black-clad Imperials waited in battle lines in the open spaces. Behind them stood a dark line of trees, and, as it had in the Stronghold, Carey's magic was drawn to its ilk just beyond the forest.

"Look at 'em all," Rupert muttered.

There were easily five times as many loyalists as there were rebels, and not just wizards but örd as well with their hideous canine-like faces, scabbed and greying, sniffing at the air and the magic they could undoubtedly smell. Many were on horseback or on foot, but some rode magical creatures – griffons, chimeras, and a single dragon, it's long, black scaly body writhing in the air as it hovered above its comrades, its rider waiting for a command.

"What are they waitin' fer?" Rupert said.

"They're waiting for us to move first," Crissto replied.

"I can't see the sun." Carey looked up at the clouds in frustration. "I can't tell what the time is. We need to get to those woods before the sun sets."

Kyna peered out from behind Rupert's back. "But how are we goin' ter get past 'em?"

Kat turned to Carey. "Do what you did at the Dead Plains."

"What?"

Kat was dead serious, her green eyes wide and expectant.

Carey's stomach turned at the thought.

"No."

"Why not?"

"Listen to what you're asking me, Kat," she said, her heart constricting in her chest.

"I'm asking you to give us a way through."

Carey shook her head. "No. What you're asking for is a massacre. I can't do that."

"Yes, you can."

Carey squeezed her eyes shut. How could she explain this to Kat? "I know they're our enemy, Kat, and I know they'd rather kill us than show us mercy, but how many of them are like Jensen? How many of those loyalists are simply fighting because they have no other choice? I'll fight when I need to, Kat. I'll even kill when I have to. But I'm not about to slaughter hundreds simply because they stand in my way. I'm not Malevolence."

Kat's mouth pinched into a thin line. "That's not what I meant."

"But that's what you're asking." Carey looked at the waiting Imperials, still as statues. "No. If I do that, I'm no better than them."

She knew by saying this she was risking the lives of everyone there, but if she did as Kat asked, summon that kind of magic for that purpose… Her hands were already drenched in blood. Carey didn't know what she would become if she allowed herself to do that.

Kat let out a sigh, one that told Carey she wasn't convinced but was also not about to argue. She turned back to face the enemy.

"Fine," she said. "What do you suggest then?"

Carey surveyed the field. The Imperials had left few gaps for them to exploit, and their griffons and scaly dragon-beast left the rebels with no aerial advantage. The magic surrounding her was frenetic, twisting and rippling like a flag in the wind. The energy emanating from their enemy was dark and vicious, curling towards her like searching tendrils. Their horse tossed its head nervously, stamping its feet as though readying to flee. Tension suffocated them like smoke, and Carey knew that if they didn't act soon, the Imperials would.

With a jerk of his reins, Crissto turned his horse to face his people. He glanced at Carey, his expression determined, his jaw set.

She nodded.

"Rebels," he cried into the silence, his words echoing across the plain. "We stand on the precipice. Too long have we borne the darkness brought on by the Empire. Too long have we stood by, idle, watching as others fought in our stead! Today, that changes. Today we pick up our weapons and wield our magic for the good of our people and the good of all! Today, we say *no more!*"

Raising his fist into the air, Crissto turned back to face their enemy.

"For light! For freedom! And for a new world dawning!"

The rebels surged forwards, bellowing battle cries. Those on horseback rode out hard and fast towards the Imperials. Carey pulled at the magic around her, feeling it rush down to alight at her fingertips. She raised a hand, ready to strike or deflect, but nothing came. The Imperials stood still.

Then a swarm of black-furred creatures burst from the front line, spitting and snarling as they raced towards the rebels. They resembled cats, except they were almost big enough for a person to ride.

"Kellas!" Crissto released his reins and raised both hands as he prepared to cast.

Curses and spells flew at the kellas, but they were quick, dodging and weaving through the barrage of magic. One leapt for Crissto's horse, but he felled it before it could reach him. With Kat at the reins, Carey raised both hands. As three of the great cats charged at them, she clenched her hands and threw them downwards. The earth cracked, and snow and dirt flew through the air as her magic slammed the kellas into the ground. Their horse tossed its head as debris showered them.

Magic flew past them, lighting up the landscape. Some rebels managed to ward off the kellas, but others were not so lucky. One of the great black felines lunged at a white stallion, its claws and teeth sinking into its flank. Its rider fell to the snow with a shriek, but their fate was lost amongst the stampede of hooves and feet, snarls and whinnies. Shouts and screams surrounded them and Carey looked for Rupert and Kyna. They were right behind them, Rupert's knuckles white on the reins as Kyna attempted to throw curses from behind.

"Carey," Kat screamed as their horse reared. Carey fell, and hit the snow hard. Pain shot through her injured shoulder but she didn't stop to react.

She rolled onto her feet as their horse trampled the ground around her, and drew her sword. A kellas was swiping viciously at Kat and Carey ran for it. She knocked it aside with a well-aimed curse before slashing at it with her weapon. Dark blood spattered across the snowy ground.

Horses raced past, and griffons and the firebird cried out overhead as they launched their attacks. Kat regained control of their mount and hoisted Carey back up behind her.

"We've got to catch up to Rupert," Kat shouted as she urged their horse onwards.

Carey searched the battlefield, rebels moving in all directions as they fought the kellas.

"There!" She pointed to where Rupert and Kyna were riding towards the line of Imperials.

Horns sounded, low and coarse.

The Imperial soldiers surged forth like a swarm of insects.

"Go," Carey screamed into Kat's ear as they rode hard to catch Rupert and Kyna.

Dodging battling knots of kellas and rebels, Kat raced towards the others as the Imperial army bore down on them. Griffons collided overhead, magic rained down on them, and in the split moment before the two armies collided, Carey felt the magic without and within ripple. She knew the sensation – it was the one she always felt when danger surrounded her. It was trying to protect her.

But Carey didn't need it to protect her anymore. The magic that was flowing through her – she could wield it now. All of it.

And she was no longer afraid.

The threads of magic twisted and formed, and she sent them forth, feeling them surge through her with incredible force. The magic struck down the front line of Imperials. Carey jerked her arm to the side and they were sent crashing into their comrades. The rebels took advantage, throwing all they had at the enemy.

Kat caught up to Rupert and Kyna. Rupert's face relaxed at the sight of them, but his lapse in concentration meant he didn't notice the kellas running at them from the opposite side.

"Duck!" Carey screamed as the beast leapt for Kyna.

Before Carey could raise a defence, the great cat struck, knocking Rupert and Kyna from their horse. Kat flung one of her sai at the beast, the sharp metal point sinking into its side before it landed. Rupert's horse stumbled, narrowly missing its riders, before taking off into the mêlée. Kat cursed loudly before leaping off their horse to pull Rupert and Kyna to their feet.

Carey glanced about the battle. Crissto and Diira were nowhere to be seen, lost to the chaos. The rebels and the Imperials were going head-to-head, the magic almost blinding. A griffon screeched overhead and Carey dived from her horse a moment before the tumbling creature ploughed into the earth and knocked the poor animal aside.

The four Seekers stood surrounded on all sides by the conflict. The Imperials were still coming, ploughing through the rebels at the front, claiming victim after victim. Carey's mind was clear even though her heart was racing.

As magic flew from all sides, Kat called to her friends.

"We need to get around somehow! We can't stay here!"

A gap appeared in the rebel line as the Imperials broke through. Without a moment's hesitation, Carey ran straight at the horde. She heard Kat scream her name, but Carey ignored her, pulling in the magic around her until it burned. The world around her slowed and she stopped right before the river of black, raising her sword high. The magic was a storm inside her, crackling lightning behind her eyes and rolling thunder in her chest. The Imperials shouted their determination, and Carey brought her sword down, driving it into the sodden ground at her feet.

The earth shattered. Shards of rock and earth exploded towards the oncoming Imperials, throwing them back. The swell of power cracked the earth and pushed up mounds of jagged rock, separating the rebels from the loyalists. A hail of dislodged stone and earth rained down upon the Imperial army, but the enemy kept coming. Climbing over their fallen comrades, the loyalists fired curse after curse at the barrier Carey had created.

She wrenched her sword from the ground and ran for the others.

"That should hold them back for a bit," she shouted as they turned and sprinted, parallel to the battle.

"Next time maybe start with that," Kat shouted.

A deafening screech sounded overhead as the Imperial's dragon dived at them. It opened its maw, a rumble of flame licking its snout.

"Dragon!" Rupert bellowed.

He rammed Carey and Kat, knocking them out of the way as the creature plummeted towards them. There came a deafening scream. Somehow Kyna had ended up several yards behind them, and the dragon fixed its black eyes on her.

"No!" Rupert reached for her and Carey moved to defend her, but they were too slow. Kyna flung her hands up over her head.

The dragon roared its victory, talons outstretched.

Heat rolled over them as a ball of fire struck the dragon. The beast veered off course, missing Kyna by a whisper. An ear-splitting cry rent the air, and the red and gold of the massive firebird followed, flying at the black-scaled dragon and its rider. The bird hit the beast as Rupert pulled Kyna towards him. The dragon's rider was thrown from their seat as the flaming bird pinned the thrashing creature to the ground.

"Feidhelm," Kyna whispered, staring as the firebird clung viciously to the dragon's scaly hide, dragging it away from them.

"I'd say it was a good thing yer made friends with that bird," Rupert said.

"Yes, well, let's get moving before something else decides to take a swing at us," Kat said.

Carey glanced at the sky, trying to discern the time. It was so dark, the storm clouds swirling above them, that it could've been midday or sunset for all she knew. Whatever the time, they needed to get to those woods and soon. The Imperials were slowly breaking through the barrier she'd created.

"Look!" Kyna pointed past the barricade of jagged rock and the legions of Imperials. More soldiers were rounding the far right edge of the woods, riding hard and fast, a sea of black and silver.

Carey's stomach dropped. "Not more Imperials…"

"No!" Kat said, dodging another stream of magic. "They're not Imperials!

Carey – up in the sky!"

And there, bright and brilliant against the darkness above, flying towards them at speed, was a pegasus.

"Firefly!"

Carey held up a hand as she flew overhead, winding and twisting as Imperials aimed curses at her. Her wings were spread wide as she circled back towards them.

"Oh no," Rupert said, pulling on Carey and Kat. "We need ter–"

With a roar of triumph, a great chunk of rock flew through the air and the enemy army broke through the barrier.

The four of them ran, Kat throwing curses haphazardly over her shoulder as Imperials gave chase. Crissto's rebels ran to meet them, and they clashed in a cacophony of weapons, screaming, and explosions of magic.

Firefly swooped, clipping the pursuing Imperials with her wings and sending them flying. She landed just ahead of Rupert. He lifted Kyna up before mounting behind her, then reaching out to help Kat.

Carey came skidding to their side.

"We're not all going to fit," she shouted as Kat reached down. "Get to the woods. I'll meet you there!"

Rupert and Kyna began to protest, but then Carey tapped her lapel and Kat grinned.

"Firefly, get us out of here," Kat said.

Carey turned, sword in hand, as Firefly lifted from the ground. Imperials were advancing, having broken through the rebel lines. A towering örd was at the fore, thundering towards her with a bloodthirsty screech. Sword in hand, Carey threw her arms out wide. She closed her eyes, felt the chaos surrounding her, and summoned the magic to her. The power came fast, flooding her entire being with the purest light, setting every nerve buzzing. As the örd bore down on her, its crude weapon of jagged metal raised over its head, Carey clasped both hands to her hilt and thrust her sword at it.

Her magic crackled down the blade, flashing bright as the bolt struck the örd in the chest and burned straight through. The creature dropped to its knees, then fell to the ground dead.

She swung her sword around. Bolts of vivid blue lanced through the air, wrapping themselves around the Imperials. They screamed in agony before collapsing.

Carey ran past the fallen bodies, her sword blinding, the magic hers to command.

It was unlike anything Carey had felt before. Magic wasn't just tingling at her fingertips; it was everywhere at once, lighting her up from the inside. It burned so brightly; it was intoxicating, all-consuming. Imperials fell like marionettes with their strings cut. Spells glanced off her.

Another horn blew in the distance, this one clear and crisp, and the spell was broken.

The cavalry her parents had promised charged at the enemy's rear. Imperials howled in fury and bloodlust. This was no longer a battle between an army and a few rebels. This was now all-out war.

Carey blinked. This was not where she was meant to be.

An Imperial slung a curse at her and Carey flung up her sword to block it. As it glanced off the blade, Carey spun, her mind travelling to the S-shaped pin on her lapel.

She shifted.

Before the Imperials around her could react, she shot into the air, great auburn wings carrying her out of their reach.

Towards Saar.

~Chapter Thirty-Eight~

Vengeance

They had come.

Her parents had done what they'd promised and sent an army. Hundreds of soldiers from the Centre City had appeared at the forest's edge, flags flying out behind them as they rode. A contingent of Vuletians in their impressive armour with their giant vuk were amongst them, their flashing weaponry held high.

Oliver Binx and her father rode out ahead, both of them wearing silver and red armour, a rose emblazoned upon their chests. Efren and Fiika were right behind them with Daaren and Versi. In the form of an eagle, Carey swooped over them as the Imperials turned to engage, now facing rebels on two sides.

But this wasn't where she was meant to be.

With powerful flaps of her wings, Carey wove between the griffons and other flying beasts. A dragon-headed serpent slithered through the sky, accompanied by grey-and-white creatures that were part stag, part eagle. Their riders dodged spells as they ploughed through the Imperial lines.

The armies below swarmed each other as Carey flew after her friends. She could see them far off in the distance, almost at the woods now. Putting on a burst of speed, Carey soared towards them, her heart pounding and the magic within giving a mighty tug. It sensed that its other half was ahead, and Carey was drawn to it as though it was a compass showing her the way. Drawing nearer, she saw Firefly land and Rupert, Kat, and Kyna dismount.

There were no Imperials there, no guards or lookouts.

Carey landed near them and shifted back into herself.

Kat said, "Keep an eye out. He won't let it be so easy."

Carey approached Firefly, who nuzzled into her at once. "Hey girl," Carey whispered. "Saved us again." She gave the pegasus a kiss on her head. "Stay here."

Firefly did as she was told as the four of them stepped into the woods, the sounds of the battle muffled in the distance. Carey immediately felt the magic that lived in the trees. She hadn't noticed it the last time they were there, but then, she hadn't been so in tune with her abilities. It radiated through the trees, the source somewhere ahead. It wasn't hard to guess what was causing it.

Kyna stopped and held out an arm.

"Danger," she whispered, pointing ahead into the darkness.

"Kyna, we–" Kat bit off her retort as trails of light appeared from the shadows, thin as spider webs as they threaded their way across the forest floor.

"What are they?" Rupert said.

"I don't know, but whatever they are don't let them touch–"

Carey's warning was cut short as the slithering lights shot towards them.

One hit Kyna's feet. She froze. Rupert lunged at her, only to solidify at her side. With wide eyes, Kat whipped around to Carey.

"Go," she managed to shout before she, too, froze in place.

With barely a thought, Carey shifted, another of the strange lights barely missing her as she shot up towards the treetops. It didn't follow her, and, as she perched upon a branch, it circled the others. This was Saar. His army had failed to hold them back, so he was employing other tactics to waylay them. Carey took one last look at Kat, Kyna, and Rupert before taking off. She followed the pull in her chest, knowing it would lead her straight to him.

A clearing appeared ahead, and she shifted again, this time to something less conspicuous. She dropped amongst the leaves of the tallest tree as a long, thin lizard, blending in with the greenery as she slithered down the trunk and out onto an overhanging branch.

To one side of the clearing were the ruins of the wagon that had once belonged to Seramina's family, their home as they'd made a new life only to be found by Imperials. Plants climbed through the rotting timbers, and the faded paint was barely visible under a layer of snow.

Saar stood by a pyre on the opposite side of the clearing. He was looking into the flames, as though watching something, completely still despite the turmoil beyond the trees.

And there, right below Carey, lay Seramina, bound and silent.

Keeping her eyes on Saar, Carey scurried down the tree trunk. This would've been the time to enact their plan to try to steal Malevolence's magic – Saar was right there and clearly hadn't begun his ritual. But Carey had another idea.

A riskier one.

And for it to work, she had to let him begin.

As Carey drew closer to Seramina, she felt a wave of something new. It was magic, but bright... pure. It was soft and ethereal and strangely calming. She followed it, intrigued by such magic, and found it was emanating from the flame-haired girl at the bottom of the tree.

Seramina.

It was the magic of an Innocent.

Carey crept towards her, Seramina's power twirling and dancing with the magic that surrounded them. Inching closer, tiny heart thrumming within her reptilian chest, Carey moved within the magic encasing Seramina. Had she been her human self, she would've gasped. The magic Seramina possessed was overwhelming, like stepping into a bright light. Carey reached out to Seramina and felt their minds connect.

"Seramina?"

Carey felt her react. Fear and surprise wrapped around her, and she had to force herself not to pull away.

"Carey? How... how are you here?"

Carey saw thoughts of the magic-dampening collar encircling Seramina's throat and knew she must be wondering how she was able to talk to her despite it.

"Are you here to save me?"

"Yes. We're here. Me, Kat, Rupert, and Kyna."

An overwhelming sense of joy and hope flooded Carey. She'd never felt such a connection, and it was proving difficult to concentrate. She forced her mind to ignore the sensation. She didn't have time to consider it.

"Seramina, listen to me carefully. I have something I need to tell you."

"Yes?"

"There's something you must know about your powers. You don't just have a few special abilities. The reason why you can fight like you do, read forgotten languages you've never studied, and do anything you put your mind to, is because you are a magical being known as an Innocent. Your past trauma caused your magic to expand exponentially, and because of that you can essentially do anything."

Seramina was still, shock and disbelief roiling off her.

"What? Does that mean I can get out of this cuff?"

Before Carey could answer, the magic surrounding Seramina began to fade. Carey's plan was working.

"Seramina, listen to me," Carey said in a rush. *"We're coming for you. You hear me?"*

But Seramina didn't answer. As strong as the power had been only moments before, Carey felt almost nothing surrounding Seramina now. Reaching out once more, Carey could feel magic still, but it was now only that of a normal thirteen-year-old girl. Innocent no more.

There was a crunching of boots, and from where Carey lay in lizard form, she saw the massive form of Saar approaching. She crept closer to Seramina, shifting into something even smaller. She needed to be close to Seramina for this next part. As a small black beetle, she crawled onto the hem of Seramina's coat. Saar's gargantuan form loomed as he stood over Seramina. Carey clung to the wool fibres, hiding herself amongst the embroidery.

"Come, child," Saar said, reaching for Seramina. "It is time."

For a wild moment Carey thought he was offering his hand for Seramina to take, but then she felt Seramina lift from the ground, Saar drawing her to her feet with a slow pulling motion. Seramina was awake now, and a soft sob escaped her lips. He brought her upright, her toes lightly grazing the snowy ground, then, with a flick of his wrist, she began to drift through the air. Saar backed into the centre of the clearing, bringing Seramina to a halt beside him.

"Now, kneel," Saar commanded, and Seramina was lowered into a kneeling position. Her head hung, her eyes downcast.

Carey could feel Seramina's fear. She could feel the darkness surrounding Saar. And she could feel the inexplicable pull of Malevolence's half of the ability they shared, how it was almost a living thing. She was so close…

Saar moved in a circle around Seramina, muttering, his hand trailing at his side. There came a sizzling sound as the snow melted in his wake, a harsh black line burnt into the ground. He came to a halt in front of Seramina, and even in her tiny form, Carey could see his white eyes glitter with malice.

He pulled a dagger the colour of midnight from under his long black cloak. It was impossibly thin, with runic symbols etched on the hilt. He held it up to the sky, the clouds parting to reveal the last vestiges of a blood-red sunset. And there, right overhead, was the pale form of the full moon. Throwing his head back, he began to speak, this time loud enough for Carey to hear.

Pale daughter of the night,
Mistress of the dark,
Giver of divine power,
I ask of thee.
With this obsidian blade,
Take this blood of one as pure,
Draw from within the gift,
And arise the darkness to serve thee.

The magic in the clearing shuddered and shifted. A strange sensation overcame Carey, a feeling of dizzying weightlessness. Seramina remained kneeling, but her sobbing had stopped. Her head tilted back slowly and her hair fluttered gently about her face as she stared up at the moon. Carey felt a surge of panic, wondering if Saar was about to slit Seramina's throat as he had Sirona's. If he did, Carey's plan would be ruined and she would've failed Seramina. But Seramina lifted her right arm up to the sky, imitating Saar's movement.

Silently, Saar clasped Seramina's proffered wrist and pulled back her sleeve, exposing her arm. Then, with painful deliberateness, he pierced her skin with the tip of the blade. Blood trickled down her arm, crimson drops splattering onto the snow as Saar dragged the blade from her wrist to the crook of her arm. Bound by the magic of the enchantment, Seramina remained silent, but Carey could sense her agony, and it was all she could do to stop herself shifting back and striking Saar down where he stood.

He let Seramina's wrist fall back by her side, where the wound began to flow freely. The blood pooled on the ground, the heat of it melting the snow.

Blocking out the gruesome sight, Carey concentrated on Seramina's magic. She had to focus – this moment was crucial.

Blood flowed from Seramina, and with it her life force, drawn out by the enchantment. Carey would've smiled if she'd been able. The magic within Seramina was so similar to the magic surrounding them. A million threads entwined to create her, define who Seramina was.

This was going to work.

Carey harnessed the power around her and reached out. She captured the tiniest thread of Seramina's magic, wrapped herself in it, and broke it off from the whole. Carey then bound it to the light within her young friend's soul.

As the rest of her magic left her body, Seramina slumped to the ground. Carey clung to her sleeve in her insect form, waiting. Seramina was still alive, but only just; the tiny bit of magic Carey had managed to withhold was keeping her from tumbling over the edge, and Saar had yet to notice anything amiss.

As Seramina lay still, the Imperial lowered his hand towards the circle surrounding her, eyes closed in concentration. At first, nothing happened. Then, from the snow, crimson droplets rose into the air.

Seramina's blood.

Carey watched with barely contained fury as Saar held out a sickeningly familiar tear-shaped orb. Beneath the pale light of the moon, Carey felt the magic exuding from that globe, felt it drawing her in just as it was doing with Seramina's magic. The glistening ruby-red beads of blood drifted towards it and sank into it, absorbed by the power within. Saar took a step back, releasing the Tear Globe, leaving it suspended in the air. He watched it expectantly, his entire body tense.

It was now or never.

Carey shifted.

Her sudden appearance before him seemed to momentarily stun Saar. Before he could react, Carey struck at him, focusing on the enchantment he was using to hold Kat, Rupert, and Kyna hostage. Her bolt of magic hit him in the chest, his eyes widening at the contact before he was thrown backwards, arms flailing. Carey felt the spell lift from around the clearing. As it vanished, bright lights popped and flashed in the darkness.

"Princess."

Carey glared unwaveringly at the man before her. He'd wiped the initial shock of her attack from his face, his usual demeanour taking its place.

"You do realise you're too late." He indicated the Tear Globe between them. "Let your friends come. At least you'll be in time for her resurrection."

Darkness poured from the globe in cloud-like plumes. Carey took an involuntary step backwards as it began to draw into itself, forming an outline around the globe – a familiar tall shape. The sound of running feet alerted Carey to her friends' approach, but she didn't move her gaze from the scene before her. The magic dragged at her very core and she couldn't look away as the smoky outline began to solidify. Somewhere to her left, Carey heard Kyna call Seramina's name, but it was from far off. The whole universe melted away and she felt suspended in this moment, just her and the woman standing in front of her.

She was tall and elegant. The darkness that formed her wove around her body, clothing her in long silken waves of material the colour of moonlight. She was facing away from Carey, stepping out of the enchantment encircling Seramina and towards Saar. Her long dark hair fell down her back and over her shoulders, hiding her face from view. Saar dropped to a knee before her.

"Empress."

Carey sensed the others moving, felt the tug of Kat's hand on her wrist, but she didn't move, couldn't move.

Malevolence turned.

When Carey had thought of this moment, she'd imagined Malevolence as she had been – tall and cloaked in darkness. But the woman who stood before her was not what she'd expected at all. Her eyes were the colour of amber, shrewd and calculating. Her silken black hair framed a slim olive face with high cheekbones, and her mouth was crooked into a curious smile. She was nothing short of stunning, and for a moment it threw Carey off.

Then she spoke.

Carey remembered how painful it had been the last time when Malevolence's voice had echoed inside her head, threatening to tear her apart. This time, however… Her lips parted and what came out were silken tones, music that wrapped around her ears like a siren's song.

"Carey Lee."

Kat's insistent tugging stopped as Carey stepped towards the woman. She raised her chin defiantly. "Malevolence."

Malevolence's beautiful face twisted into a sneer. "Have you come to stop me, little Seeker?"

"I did once before, didn't I?" Carey retorted, holding her ground. "Who's to say I won't do it again?"

The magic surrounding Malevolence stirred as she grinned in amusement, the darkness she commanded tightening around her. "An oversight on my part. I did not realise the power you possessed. So much like my own…"

Malevolence looked down at her hands and Carey instinctually felt the magic pull around them as she flexed her fingers. The grin slid from her face and her amber eyes turned dark.

"There is something… wrong…"

Saar came to her side, his head bowed as he spoke. "What is it, Your Majesty?"

Her eyes flicked to his, her gaze venomous. "The magic you used to bring me back… it is that of a child."

She spat the last word as though it was poison, but Saar merely dipped his head. "Yes, but she is no ordinary child. The blood of an Innocent is what resurrected you."

Malevolence shifted her gaze to where Rupert stood in the shadows of the trees, cradling Seramina, Kyna at her side. Her nostrils flared as her eyes moved to Carey's, who merely smiled back at her.

"Perhaps she was, once upon a time," Carey said, watching with satisfaction as Saar's expression turned from confident to ice cold.

Her heart was pounding but she was focused, her muscles tensed, waiting for the moment they would strike.

"I told her the truth. Told Seramina exactly what she was, which, as it turns out, is the *only* way to purge an Innocent of everything that makes them one. Once she knew what she was, her magic dissipated, innocent no more." Carey allowed herself a small smirk. "You were just resurrected using the magic of a thirteen-year-old girl."

Malevolence's eyes flashed murderously but she made no move to strike Carey. Instead, the Empress spoke to Saar, her gaze never shifting from Carey's.

"Deal with her."

Carey could feel his fury as he turned to her. She had just foiled his plans for an all-powerful Empress and now he was going to exact his revenge. Carey drew her sword and Saar sneered, the amusement not quite reaching his eyes.

"A sword?" he said, advancing on her slowly. "This should be interesting."

In her peripheral vision, Carey saw Kat step up beside her, unsheathing her sai and giving them a twirl.

"Together?" she whispered to Carey, her eyes trained on Saar.

Carey had been ready to take on Saar by herself, but the moment Kat had stepped to her side, it seemed ridiculous to have thought she would have to. This was all their fight – hers, and Kat's, and Ji's. She nodded.

"Always."

Saar struck.

Carey blocked the curse with her sword. She and Kat split, each taking a side. Kat attacked first, a curse, following it with a strike with her weapons. Saar blocked her easily and Kat stumbled backwards. Carey took this moment to pull at the magic around her, drawing it into her. As Saar rounded on her, magic flying, Carey swung her sword, magic crackling bright blue down the blade before lancing through the air and striking Saar on the shoulder. He spun from the contact, turning to face Kat just as she lunged again, a violent strike of red magic hitting him in the chest. His shoulder blackened from Carey's hit, Saar dropped to his knees with a pained grunt, his dark hair falling about his face. With his back to her, Carey ran at him, sword raised, but his hand shot out, fire whipping from his hand and curling around her ankle. Saar pulled it back into himself and Carey fell onto her back.

"Carey!"

Kat screamed in fury, magic burning at her fingertips as she threw it at Saar, murderous intent etched all over her face. Saar blocked it with a wave of his hand and pulled himself to his feet in one swift movement. Kat sliced with her sai, magic following. Saar backed away, dodging each of her attacks with impossibly fast moves for someone who'd just been hit twice, before managing to land a hit of his own. The force of his spell threw Kat from her feet and she tumbled over and over until she came to a stop against a tree, a cry of pain spilling from her.

Saar raised his hand to strike again, but Carey had pulled herself to one knee. She wove threads of magic around Saar, then wrenched him backwards, his curse flying wild as he fell. She was on her feet before he'd come to rest and she strode towards him, gathering the magic around her as she went. She felt it tighten, its protection coalescing with her intent, and it sparked within her. Saar was hauling himself to his feet, his face wild with unchecked fury, his teeth bared. He charged at her, both hands up over his head as he summoned his magic. Carey felt the magic building around him, the power within her matching it, and as Saar brought his hands down to retaliate, she spun away from him.

His eyes went wide as his curse flew past her.

His mouth opened in surprise as she brought her sword back around to meet him.

And he stopped completely as she slammed it into his body.

The brightest blue flashed through him, and Carey drove the sword and her magic further into him. Saar dropped to his knees, weakly grasping for the hilt of her weapon. Blood bubbled at his lips. Magic flickered and died at his fingertips, Carey having driven it all from his body. Keeping her sword where it was, Carey leant into him, her pulse thundering in her ears.

"Now, it's your turn," she said, before wrenching the sword free from between his ribs.

Saar collapsed at her feet, silver eyes staring at her. No words escaped his lips – none would ever do so again.

With one last shuddering breath, he stilled.

~Chapter Thirty-Nine~

The End

Carey stared blankly down at the man who'd caused her so much pain and wondered why she felt nothing at his passing. She'd expected relief, satisfaction even, but as she watched his blood stain the ground beneath him, all she felt was… empty.

"What an interesting display."

Malevolence's voice rang through the stillness and Carey tore her gaze from Saar to look into the cold eyes of the Empress. The indifferent expression on her face showed just how much she truly cared for her fallen general.

Carey squared her shoulders and faced Malevolence. Out of the corner of her eye, she saw Rupert scoop up Kat, who looked confused but otherwise unhurt. Carey let that knowledge buoy her heart as she gave the Empress her full attention.

"You don't seem concerned by the fact that I just killed the man who made you."

Malevolence's lip lifted into a sneer. "Made me?" she said slowly. "Even a rabid cur can be of use if manipulated the right way. Let him think he was important when, truly, he was nothing more than a mongrel all along."

Her words were calm, almost bored, but Carey could feel the malice rolling off her as she spoke. The darkness was gathering around Malevolence, the pull within Carey's chest growing stronger. A light wind whipped up around them. Carey clenched and unclenched her free hand, the tingle of her own magic still humming through her body. Keeping her gaze locked on Malevolence's, Carey slowly bent to one knee and placed her sword by her feet. As she returned to standing, Malevolence's eyes narrowed.

"Laying down your weapon?"

Carey set her jaw. "I have others."

This seemed to amuse Malevolence. "Such tenacity. I would ask you to join me if I didn't already know the answer. Two halves of one whole. And more than that – we're blood. That is stronger than any magical bond."

The reminder of their familial ties brought a sour taste to Carey's mouth but she swallowed it back.

"You ceased that connection the night you killed your father," she retorted as the rush of magic thrummed in her chest and sparked beneath her skin.

"He was a fool," Malevolence said, and the winds surrounding them increased.

Carey sensed the shift of power surging within her enemy.

It was dark, and evil, and all the malice of the realms churned and whipped about her, but Carey held onto that immeasurable brightness she was connected to, and it gave her strength.

Courage.

"He failed to see the potential of that which he guarded so fervently," Malevolence said. "And our kingdom had grown weak. I sought to remedy that."

Carey took a deep breath, all the while keeping Malevolence's gaze. The swell of magic was coming faster now, and it was impatient to be free.

"You're the fool," Carey breathed, heat sparking behind her eyes. "You split that magic thinking you could rid yourself of that weakness you so despised and look where that got you."

Malevolence's eyes flared and Carey steeled herself. The winds were gale force now, whipping up snow and leaves. Shadows encased them, blocking out the moonlight and the stars. Carey pushed back against it, her own magic infusing light, illuminating the two of them where they stood. She could no longer see the others – she was completely cut off.

Perfect.

"Indeed," the Empress answered, her voice vibrating with the magic surrounding them. "Not to worry. I plan to rectify that too. Right. Now."

With a sudden sweeping motion, Malevolence pulled at the shadows surrounding them and enveloped Carey.

Jody and Laurel stepped out from behind the trees, hands outstretched to show they meant no harm. Several of the Essedarian leapt to their feet at the sight of the two girls and within moments, the pair were on their knees at the centre of the camp, surrounded. A tall woman stepped from behind the guard keeping them in place and lowered her hood. She had short- cropped hair the colour of steel and eyes of ice blue. She wore the same cloth as the Essedarian, but there was something about her that set her apart. Carey watched from the edge of the camp, her gaze darting between this woman and her sisters.

"Jody and Laurel Lee, if I'm not mistaken. Children of the rebel filth," she spat.

None of the Essedarian moved, watching their leader with apparent anticipation.

Jody spoke up, her voice soft but steady.

"We come offering our services," she said, her eyes lowered. "We want to join the Empress."

A short, stunned silence followed, and Carey looked at Anthriel, who merely watched with ill-disguised boredom.

"And why would you do that?" the woman asked them.

Laurel said, "Because, we see the futility of our parents' fight. The Order is doomed, we know that now. The only way forwards is with the Empire."

The shadows pressed in on Carey, suffocating her. The wind howled and for a moment she was blinded. A light sparked within her, setting her aflame, and Carey didn't hesitate.

She let if free.

A blinding explosion erupted around her, banishing the shadows. Carey drew the light into her, protecting herself as she found Malevolence once more. She was still standing opposite her, and her arms were raised at her sides as she commanded the storm. Her face was set with murderous intent, her eyes black and her hair whipping about her in a wild flurry.

"Your command of your magic is commendable." Malevolence's voice surrounded Carey, rushing past with the wind. "But you cannot kill me. It will only end as before. And there will always be others willing to do what is needed to ensure I return."

She drew her arms up higher and a bolt of lightning crackled overhead.

"This is our destiny, Carey Lee."

"We offer ourselves as spies for the Empire." Jody lifted her head, looking up at her captor. "We are willing to pass information from within the Order to the Empress herself."

"We are here to destroy the Order," the leader of the Essedarian said. "How did you find us?"

"Rumours, whispers," Laurel said, her expression confident. "We've been looking for a way out of the Order for a while now."

"But if you kill our families tonight," said Jody, kneeling a little straighter, "the chance to get more information will be lost. We are not the only ones fighting for the Order. If our families are killed, there are others who will take their place. We can help bring them all down."

There was a pause; Carey's heart beat a wild tattoo against her chest as she watched. Then, the woman standing before them jerked her head at the Essedarian guarding Jody and Laurel. They hauled the two girls to their feet and the woman drew in close to them.

"The Empire accepts your offer," she sneered. "But know this – go back on your word and the Empress will show no mercy."

Carey's body was thrumming with magic now. As Malevolence's winds thrashed about them and lightning split the sky, she let it fill her, pulling at every thread and weaving it together. It was no longer just a tingle; it burnt red hot, the intensity almost driving the breath from Carey's body, but she held it back, waiting. *At the exact same moment.*Malevolence raised her hands higher until they were stretched out over her head. A bolt of lightning struck at her fingertips and Carey squinted against the blinding light.

Through the roar of the wind and the crackle of the lightning, Carey heard her name.

"They sacrificed themselves."

Carey and Anthriel stood upon the mountainside once more. Her heart was pounding and she felt light-headed.

"Yes."

That single word fell from Anthriel's lips as a tear rolled down Carey's cheek. Everyone thought Jody and Laurel had betrayed them when really, they'd given their lives to save them all. Worse still, they'd lived the rest of their lives in the service of an empress who, once she was done with them, had them executed, tossed aside as though they meant nothing to her.

"Did Malevolence know what they really were?" Carey asked Anthriel, tears continuing to fall down her face.

Anthriel turned his cool gaze upon Carey. "Yes. She knew from the very beginning."

"Then why did she let them live?"

"Because Jody and Laurel were, in fact, able to give her information on the Order. She also gained a perverse kind of pleasure from having them carry out her will, knowing that if they refused, they would show their hand."

Carey closed her eyes, holding back a wave of nausea. "But she killed them in the end anyway."

"Yes. Because they were beginning to waver. Their attack on you and Katrina Lawrence at your family home was meant to be deadly. They failed."

Clutching at her chest, Carey gulped back a sob. For so long... Everything they'd done, everything they'd sacrificed, they'd done to save their families.

An absolute sense of clarity swept through Carey at this revelation.

All they had sacrificed...

"There is no other way," she said, looking up at the sky once more. A shooting star streaked across the blackness, bright, brilliant, fleeting.

"No."

Carey nodded slowly, the memory of Jody and Laurel's determined expressions filling her mind. They'd given everything on the mere chance that the Essedarian might listen. She had so much more.

Perhaps it was time to accept her destiny.

Ji's voice came to her through the storm.

"Carey..."

A whisper that cut through the chaos. It curled around her ear and warmed her heart.

"Courage."

Lightning crashed and the storm descended on them completely. Snow and earth, leaves and debris swirled violently. Malevolence curled her fists above her head, bringing into herself the power of the night. She screamed over the noise and the wind, her face no longer serene or beautiful, but hollowed by the darkness she possessed.

"It is time you met your destiny, child," she howled at Carey. "Tonight, you will die!"

Carey lifted her hands, feeling the magic swelling to a crescendo. There was so much of it. Almost too much for her to wield. But it needed to be done. She wanted it to burn through her.

"I know. And so will you."

And she let go.

All the light of the realms cascaded from Carey, burning as it went. She saw it hit her enemy just as Malevolence's attack struck Carey in return. They were engulfed in a storm of brilliant white light and deep, endless darkness. The worlds beyond were insignificant, inconsequential. There was nothing but magic, pure and intense and chaotic.

But Carey's strike had landed true. She focused everything she had on the empress, reaching out and taking hold of that which mirrored her own. She pulled hard.

And Malevolence reciprocated in kind.

There was a painful lurch and Carey's body convulsed. Then fire. Her magic, all of it, was being torn from her body. She screamed in agony as it was dragged from her, the darkness consuming her as the light devoured Malevolence.

It was just as she had planned.

To die at the exact same moment – those had been Anthriel's words. And that moment had finally come.

She could see Malevolence trying to fight back, trying to stop Carey, but it was useless. The magic she'd once wielded was beyond her control now, just as it was for the Seeker. It surged again, stripping Carey of every last vestige of magic, and Malevolence released a guttural scream along with her. It was everywhere at once, unimaginable pain tearing at Carey from the inside out. She forced her eyes open as it overwhelmed her and she begged for it to end.

Ji stood before her, a smile lighting his lips.

The fire within flickered and died, the light and the dark and the strain upon her soul ebbing away as she stared back at him. He held out his hand, gave her a slight nod. Carey reached for him.

Her hand fell into his.

He grinned.

Malevolence's screams stopped, and the empress collapsed, limp and lifeless.

The storm of light and dark dissipated, debris dropping to the ground, the clearing suddenly, eerily still.

Kat screamed, lurching forwards as Carey fell to her knees.

"Carey!"

Kat caught her and lowered her to the ground.

"Carey? Carey?"

Kat shook Carey's shoulders gently, cradling her head in her lap. Rupert ran over to them and laid a hand on Carey's chest. His frantic whispers were all that filled the silence surrounding them.

"Rupert?" Kat's eyes were wide. "Rupert? Please."

Rupert stared down at Carey, squeezing his eyes shut before reluctantly shaking his head.

"I'm sorry, Kat."

"No." Kat began to rock back and forth, pulling her friend close as tears began splashing down her face. "No…"

There was nothing more to be said. Nothing more to be done. Malevolence and Saar lay forgotten, the tyranny of their lives now at an end.

And overhead, the stars shone brighter than they had in a long time.

Epilogue

Snow was falling softly, brilliant white flakes drifting on the late-afternoon wind. Kat stood on her balcony overlooking the courtyard. The memorial statue at its centre was lined with red roses, two new names carved on its surface, and the courtyard was empty, all mourners having returned to the warmth of the castle. She tightened her grip around the necklaces in her hand as she stared out, not quite seeing.

A tall figure stood behind her, his wings carefully folded at his side, long white hair framing his elegant features. He watched Kat with his usual calm expression as he spoke.

"She wanted you to know," he said in low, soothing tones, "that this was her decision."

Kat nodded. Anthriel gave her a slight bow and then he was gone. Kat closed her eyes, letting out a long breath into the cold air.

A soft knock came at her door.

"Come in," she called wearily, and Rupert entered. He rested his forearms on the balustrade beside her.

His hair was a light blue today, more subdued than normal, but then, it was to be expected.

"The Council's askin' after you," Rupert said, looking out over the city. "Ilvisar and his lot will be leavin' soon and he wants an audience."

"I'll go down soon. I just…" She grimaced. "How's Seramina?"

"Better. She's still a way ter go, now she has regular magic like the rest of us," Rupert answered with a small smile. "But she'll recover. Kyna is watchin' over her." He paused. "Carey did good."

The sound of her name brought tears to Kat's eyes, as it so often had recently, and as one rolled down her cheek, Rupert gently wiped it away.

Fixing her gaze on the statue below, Kat took a deep, steadying breath. "Anthriel was just here."

Rupert stilled beside her, waiting for her to continue.

"He told me why Carey did what she did." Kat's voice cracked but she forced herself to keep talking. "He told me why she… died." Slowly, Kat recounted the Ancient's testimony. When she was done, she lifted her gaze to Rupert's. "Why didn't she tell us? I knew something was different, remember? The day before Anoueshka's camp was attacked? That's when she'd decided to…" She let her sentence die, unwilling to put voice to the rest.

"I think," Rupert began, his voice gentle, "that she didn't tell us because she knew we'd try ter stop her. I know you would've."

Scrunching her face up against the overwhelming urge to scream that *of course* she would have, Kat straightened, looking up at the red-tinged sky. It had been a week to the day. A week since their armies had defeated Malevolence's. A week since word had spread of the final downfall of the Empire. And each day had felt like a millennium. She looked down at the pendants in her hand.

"I miss them," she whispered, her voice breaking and tears falling anew. "I miss them *so much*, Rupert."

Rupert wrapped her hand in his, Carey and Ji's necklaces enclosed within.

"I know. So do I. But do yer see all that?" He gestured to the city beyond the castle walls. The sun was setting and Kat could hear the distant sounds of laughter and chatter as the world was enveloped in a soft orange glow. "That's what they gave us."

Kat looked back at him with a frown, and Rupert smiled in return.

"Freedom."

Translations and Pronunciations

The language of Ethellen spoken by Ilvisar and other citizens of Suvheil in this book was created using a Japanese-inspired grammatical structure and sounds based on Japanese, Arabic and Hindi. Below are the words and sentences used, their pronunciations, and translations.

Gabeh (Gah-beh)
  Get up

Mek gabeh (Mek gah-beh)
  Get up, now

Kasek! Moragenau. Toka bin Zakindeh (Kah-sek! Mor-ah-gen-ow. Tok-ah bin Zah-kin-deh)
  Filth! You are not forgotten. You will die with them.

Bikha dun, jakin kech bekrani (Bi-kah doon, jah-kin ketch bek-rah-nee)
  I swear to you, I will see you in hell.

Kasek (Kah-sek)
  Filth

La'in eweh (Lah in ei-weh)
  Your Highness

Bahsh (Bah-sh)
  Stand

Safeh, Suvheil fa'hi (Sah-feh, Soo-veil fah-hee)
  Go, for Suvheil

Shadun (Shah-doon)
  Come/come on

Author's Note

Even though Carey's world is largely fictitious, this final foray into her adventures dipped a little into the historical.

The city of Petrovsk-Port, where Carey, Kat, Rupert, and Kyna find themselves on their arrival in the Common Realm, was the name of the city now known as Makhachkala in the Republic of Dagestan, Russia, between 1857 and 1921. This book was set in the later part of the year 1900 so ensuring the accuracy of this city's name was imperative given the many times its name has changed throughout history. Although it's difficult to know the exact dialect of the people who lived in Petrovsk-Port at the time, considering that it was, and still is, part of southwestern Russia, for the purposes of this novel I have assumed that people within that region would have had at least some knowledge of standard Russian. Considering its interconnection with other parts of Russia and Europe via the railway at the time, this would be a fair assumption to make. The clothing and descriptions of the city were based on photographic research that I managed to unearth, although with anything of this nature, probably still hold inaccuracies.

The Exposition Universelle that Carey and the crew found themselves amidst was an actual event that occurred from the 14th of April to the 12th of November 1900 in Paris, France. The building Carey and the others see on their arrival at the event was the Grand Palais des Champs-Élysées, which sits at the end of the Pont Alexandre III bridge and is still there today. The building that Carey sees as they run down to the banks of the Seine pursued by vampires is the Ville de Paris, which was one of the many pavilions built for the event. There is much that's been documented with regards to the exhibitions provided during the Exposition, yet for all the research I conducted, I was unable to find any mention of night-time events for it. However, given the sheer size and lengthy time period for which it was held, I took some creative liberties in imagining that it would've drawn a sizeable crowd had it accommodated night-time revelry. Besides, vampires during the day just aren't as fun to write.

Acknowledgements

So, wow – writing this series has been one epic adventure all on its own. Considering it's taken an inordinate amount of time to finally finish it, I'm both excited and terrified that it's finally come to an end. There have been so many who have helped and inspired me during this journey, and I am eternally grateful to the following wonderful people:

My street team, who have been absolutely amazing and invaluable in spreading the news about *The Innocent*. You truly made marketing my baby so much easier and heaps of fun, and reading your reactions to the ARC made it all worthwhile.

Maf and Caitlyn, for being the most amazing artists. You brought my characters to life with your incredible skills – they still make me giddy every time I look at them.

My beta readers over the years – Amanda, Kate, Katrina, Jemma, and Star. Thanks for making sure it all made sense – without you guys I wouldn't have put out my best work.

Jason and Chloe, my awesome editors. You've helped make my work as shiny and polished as possible and I'm forever indebted to your magic wordsmith skills.

All my fabulous Instagram friends and followers. You've made it possible for people who might never have heard of my books to find them and join in the fun.

My teachers, all the way back in high school. Whether you knew it or not, you made it possible for me to write my very first manuscript, hidden away in a giant Winnie-the-Pooh folder on tattered pages of foolscap. Sorry if it made me look like I was busy doing Maths, or English or whatever I was actually supposed to be doing – at least I feel safe in owning up to this twenty years later…

My husband, Mubin, for putting up with the long nights of writing and editing and all the support along the way. You're the enabler to my madness and I love you for it.

My kids, Sophie and Elijah, for making me feel like the coolest parent ever and spruiking my books all over school.

My family, for telling everyone about my books and making me feel more famous than I actually am.

My friends, who from the very beginning inspired me and have given me an endless supply of encouragement and character traits to use.

My bestie, Kat, for putting the idea in my head to start with. Without you, I'd have never even thought to actually put pen to paper in the first place. Ergo, I blame you for all the sleepless nights. Love you lots.

And finally, my readers. This final instalment wouldn't have been half as fun to write if it had been just for me. I'd have had just a bunch of words on a page and no one to make cry. I know you hate me for it, but I love you more than anything.

About the Author

Alysha King is a Young Adult fiction author who lives in Canberra, Australia with her husband, two young children, a very large dog, and a sneaky white cat. She began writing the Rose Chronicles in high school after being inspired by such writers as Eoin Colfer and Isobelle Carmody. She revels in fantasy and sci-fi and has a soft spot for Enid Blyton, citing her works as some of her all-time favourites and of which she has quite a large collection in her home library. Alysha also enjoys historical fiction and is currently researching for a number of future novels. When she is not writing or collecting vintage copies of works by famous English writers, Alysha can be found indulging in any number of her other hobbies which include cosplay costuming with her son and daughter and baking overly sweet treats. Alysha can be found on social media and via her website www.alyshaking.com.

www.ingramcontent.com/pod-product-compliance
Lightning Source LLC
Chambersburg PA
CBHW020011120726
47903CB00004B/1234